Praise for *Havana World Series:*

"A wonderful piece of social history and a stylized tableau full of major crime figures and colorful small-time hoods who glide across the landscape of Havana's nightlife . . . The plot is intricate. . . . Small human dramas are imbedded within the larger flow of the story. . . . The characters are fascinating, the story compelling. . . . You couldn't ask for more."
—Richard Crepeau, *The Orlando Sentinel*

"The complications Latour throws in are priceless. . . . Much of the appeal of *Havana World Series* lies in the likable assortment of upwardly mobile thieves who just want to come away with enough cash to establish a foothold in the Cuban lower middle class." —Richard Lipez, *The Washington Post*

"Cuba's slickest thieves have been hired by Lansky's enemies to make a bold and lasting statement about criminal monopolies. . . . Latour has written an evocative and compelling tale about a special place and time."
—Peter Mergendahl, *Rocky Mountain News*

"Latour draws wonderful, believable portraits of Lansky, the erudite but ruthless Jewish gangster, and the lackeys around him. He brings to vivid life the milieu of that Cuban gambling heyday." —Robert Mayer, *The Santa Fe New Mexican*

"Latour has written a first-rate crime novel, and with a graphic description of 1950s Havana—with all its warts."
—John A. Broussard, *I Love a Mystery*

"Latour writes beautifully in prose that's lean and lucid and never overwhelmed by noir 'style.' An additional bonus is his perceptive depiction to the late-fifties Cuba."
—*Kirkus Reviews* (starred review)

"A lively, entertaining read . . . [*Havana World Series*] pits Cuban crooks against an American crime boss in bustling, pre-Communist Havana."   —*Publishers Weekly*

"In a documentary-like narrative that combines the gritty fatalism of *Bob Le Flambeur* and the meticulous detail of *Ocean's Eleven* . . . The portraits of Lansky, Bonanno, and other gangsters are full-bodied, but it's the fictional blue-collar crooks, led by mastermind Ox Contreras, who give the novel its appeal and afford the vest of view of Cuban life."
—Bill Ott, *Booklist*

"José Latour has written a rich and nuanced story of the mob-infested Havana of the fifties and its colorful and violent finale. The combination of la Cosa Nostra, Major League Baseball and the last days of the Batista regime is just about irresistible."
—Scott Phillips

HAVANA
WORLD SERIES

HAVANA

WORLD SERIES

José Latour

Grove Press
New York

Published simultaneously in Canada
Printed in the United States of America

FIRST GROVE PRESS PAPERBACK EDITION

Library of Congress Cataloging-in-Publication Data

Latour, José, 1940-
Havana World Series / José Latour.
p. cm.
ISBN 0-8021-4186-2 (pbk.)
1. World Series (Baseball)—Fiction.   2. Gambling—Fiction.
3. Cuba—Fiction.   I. Title.
PR9240.9.L38H38 2004
813'.54—dc22   2003060716

Grove Press
an imprint of Grove/Atlantic, Inc.
841 Broadway
New York, NY 10003

05   06   07   08   09   10 9 8 7 6 5 4 3 2 1

This novel is for Jordan, my grandson.

PART ONE

One

The last day that Angelo Dick spent in Havana, Cuba—October 1, 1958—began in a most auspicious way around 2 A.M., in the ascending elevator cage of the plush, twenty-two-story apartment building where he lived. Angelo appreciatively eyed the smiling, pretty brunette holding a blue plastic ring a yard in diameter. He was wont to flirt with regal dames from the Havana nightlife, but this hustler was a sight for sore eyes. Five foot six in three-inch heels, mid-twenties, green eyes, coal-black hair that tumbled down her back, full lips, creamy skin, and a tawdry but perfectly fitted dress which insinuated a great body.

"What's that for?" he had just asked on the ground floor, pointing to the weird contraption, as they waited for the elevator.

"You'll see," had been her enigmatic answer.

Angelo had spotted her for the first time that same evening, a little after 10 P.M., when she'd set foot in Casino de Capri on the arm of a middle-aged Norwegian salesman. As the couple traversed the gambling hall, headed for the nightclub, Angelo and several patrons had peered at the object. Why did the babe bring *that* to a casino and nightclub? What purpose did it serve? The damn thing was eclipsing a flesh-and-blood goddess, the gaming executive had thought. Suddenly he had realized it was a fabulous sales gimmick.

Three hours later he had seen her again, calmly sashaying among casino tables, hoping to be picked up. But as Angelo very well knew, compulsive gamblers won't leave a table for a dame, not even for an Ava Gardner look-alike carrying an intriguing plastic ring. The Norwegian was nowhere to be seen.

Nick Di Constanzo, Casino de Capri's general manager, had repeatedly warned all those under him never to mix business with pleasure. *You want to have a drink, sweet-talk a broad, engage in conversation with a friend, you do it after hours.* But Angelo was only human. Tired of call girls, he felt like a ring girl. So, he had approached the young woman with a jaunty step and his most engaging smile, accompanied her to the bar, ordered the bartender to serve the lady whatever she pleased, and said he would be free in less than an hour.

During the short walk from Casino de Capri to the building where he had rented apartment 15-A almost a year earlier, a mere three blocks, Angelo had learned that her name was Gloria, "glory" in Spanish. He had felt sure it was going to be a glorious night indeed. The only thing that Angelo didn't approve of in this particular broad was her perfume: Chanel No. 5. Ever since Marilyn Monroe went public on what she wore to bed, he hadn't found a high-priced chippie who smelled different.

And finally, sitting on his living room couch, sipping his first drink of the night, Angelo discovered what purpose the ring served. Gloria took a moment to change the position of a floor lamp and the coffee table, placed the sound track of *The Eddie Duchin Story* on the record player, and stripped as she danced. Once buck naked, she started rotating the hula hoop with such a slow, sensual swaying of her hips that it looked as though gravity had been conquered.

As a man of the world, Angelo had seen a lot. He knew that certain moments in life merit special appreciation, and on this particular night, for some reason he couldn't define, he suspected that he was watching a unique performance he'd never see again. Angelo wanted to prolong this very private show as long as possible, memorize everything, including its concomitants: the music, the soft lighting, the flavor of the Black Label highball. But Gloria slithered languorously across the room, getting nearer every few seconds. After three minutes, Angelo succumbed to the erotic flexibility radiating from her superb body. They rolled over the carpet kissing and touching in blind sexual frenzy as he pulled his clothes off.

Angelo Dick kissed Gloria good-bye next to the front door at 6:30 A.M., when the rising sun was purifying the greenish tint of his living room's picture window and the charcoal gray of the nearby sea. *Amazing what twenty bucks buys in this town,* Casino de Capri's hall supervisor concluded five minutes later as he flopped onto his bed. He signed off smelling Gloria's perfume on his pillow.

Nearly five and a half hours later, the ringing phone on the bedside table awoke him. The Breitling strapped to Angelo's left wrist read 11:58. *Who can it be at this hour, for Chrissake?* Angelo registered the discomfort of a full bladder and a slight hangover as he propped himself on his elbow and picked up the receiver.

"Hello."

"Hold the line, Angelo," a baritone voice said.

A few seconds went by as a handset changed hands somewhere. The hall supervisor frowned in confusion.

"Angelo?"

"Yeah."

"Did I wake you?"

Angelo swiftly swung his legs out and sat up as soon as he identified the voice on the other end. "No, sir."

"Good. Your place is in a high building by the sea, right?"

"Sure."

"Is your antenna on the roof?"

Angelo didn't get it. There had to be an agreed-upon code he had forgotten. He massaged his forehead in exasperation, trying to remember. "Excuse me, Mr. Lansky. My antenna?"

"Your TV antenna, Angelo," Lansky repeated in a patient tone, as though talking to a kid. Angelo's embarrassment grew.

"My TV antenna," the hall supervisor said, groping for understanding.

"You sure I didn't wake you up?" Lansky asked, sounding suspicious.

"Oh, no. Sure."

"Well?"

"I . . . uh . . . believe it's a multiple antenna for all residents. You plug it into a socket. And, yeah, I believe it's on the roof."

"Channel 6 will broadcast the first game," Lansky said following what sounded to Angelo's ear like a repressed chuckle. "But a friend told me the picture ain't too sharp, 'cause the signal comes from a plane flying over the Keys that fields it from Miami, then relays it. People in high buildings close to the coast will get a clearer picture. That's why I wonder if I could watch the game at your place."

"Of course you can, Mr. Lansky, it'll be a real pleasure to have you."

"Okay. Thanks. I'll be there around two. See you."

"Bye, sir."

Angelo Dick hung up and mulled over the conversation. He knew that Meyer Lansky lived at a rented two-story mansion in Miramar, but he also had a suite for his exclusive use at the Riviera and the new hotel was . . . well, not as high as his own building, but high enough. Angelo never had heard that Number One was such a devoted baseball fan and suspected that something else was brewing. What could it be? Discussing last-quarter results? Estimates for the coming winter season? Angelo got up and shuffled in his slippers to the bathroom. A fat lifesaver vibrated over the elastic band of his boxer shorts.

Angelo Dick was a swarthy, thirty-three-year-old man so sure of himself that he considered his performance as gambling-hall supervisor at Casino de Capri impeccable. Income forecasts were consistently surpassed and the expansion into sports bets was registering amazing results. Would shacking at the Someillán bestow on him the privilege of entertaining the boss? Angelo shook his head in disbelief and flushed the toilet. Probably Lansky would have lunch before coming, he reasoned next, but if Number One felt like having a snack during the game or once it was over, he should be able to oblige.

Returning to his bedroom extension, Angelo dialed the Capri's switchboard and ordered from the cafeteria two pounds of sliced ham, one of cheese, twelve bottles of Miller beer, a small flask of pickled cucumbers, two quarts of milk, and two packs of Pall Mall. He hung up, remembered the prevailing disorder, sighed, and went back to the bathroom. Within fifteen minutes Angelo had taken a shower, shaved, and brushed his teeth. Back in the bedroom, he donned fresh underwear, tan slacks, a short-sleeved black shirt, brown moccasins. Next he picked up and rinsed glasses and plates, returned the floor lamp, the coffee table, and two cushions to their proper places, emptied ashtrays, checked his liquor reserves. By the time the two humming air conditioners and an air freshener had cooled and purified the living room, a busboy arrived with the order. Angelo watched as the man placed in the refrigerator two plates covered with aluminum foil, the milk, and the beer; the cigarettes and the flask of cucumbers were left on the auxiliary kitchen table. The hall supervisor signed the check, walked the attendant to the service elevator, and tipped him a dollar.

Angelo made himself two sandwiches, poured a glass of milk, and had brunch standing up while recalling what little he knew about his visitor. The man had conceived and carried through the Cuban expansion. He had brought in Santos Trafficante, Nick Di Constanzo, Wilbur Clark, Fat Butch, and several other lesser-known wise guys. Even though he'd personally secured the fourteen million of Las Vegas dough required to build the Havana Riviera casino and hotel, now Lansky had the nerve to turn up on the payroll as kitchen manager. In fact, he was the Commission's ambassador to Cuba and a close friend of President Batista.

According to underworld rumble, he had always been cunning, crafty, mysterious; a repository of cool and wisdom.

Having cut the mustard for over thirty years in a very tough environment, Meyer Lansky had become one of the living legends hatched by the American press after being pronounced by all—including J. Edgar Hoover—the best criminal mind in the U.S. Allegedly he had convinced mobsters that crime was just business. He also made them realize that businessmen don't resolve their differences shooting each other because . . . it's bad for business. Angelo Dick reflected on the paradox that the guy who shunned applause, shared victories even with his enemies, and hid from notoriety had emerged as the brightest, most capable of them all.

Angelo Dick had climbed the gaming ladder quickly, for several reasons. Although he was intelligent, hardworking, and ambitious, what really made him stand out in Vegas, his most highly regarded trait, was his amazing numerical memory. While munching the second sandwich, Dick mentally reviewed Casino de Capri's latest results. Income from roulette, craps, baccarat, blackjack, one-armed bandits, and the last quarter's grand total. He was also in charge of supervising the external collection network spread across private companies, government offices, stores, and any other place of work or student body where bookies could operate, so he racked his brains on net profits from bets laid on baseball games, boxing, horse and dog races. Angelo also checked expenditures, bribes, commissions paid, and his preliminary forecast for October, November, and December. He simultaneously finished picking his brain and the milk at 1:40 P.M., five minutes before the doorbell rang.

Meyer Lansky and Jacob Shaifer nodded, removed their hats, and took in the place. *Two Jews together, the gentile gets fucked,* thought Angelo, but he smiled politely, accepted the

9

hats, and led them to the living room. Decor, furniture, and temperature gave the room a nice ambience. The callers eased themselves down onto the couch, facing a 21-inch TV set. The host turned it on, then apologized for his hesitation on the phone; he thought "antenna" was a code. His visitors exchanged a swift glance and smiled—slightly forced smiles, Angelo fancied as the screen came alive with a flow of commercials.

Five foot seven inches, 160 pounds, and sixty-two years old, Lansky looked like millions of other well-groomed elderly men all over the Western world. Gray hair, sober clothing, thirty-eight-inch waist, manicured nails, the unhurried movements of retired people. His brown eyes made all the difference: They possessed the vitality inherent in the very bright, sparkled with reflections of full mental faculties. Shaifer—bodyguard, confidant, driver, and Lansky's personal friend for twenty-five years—had just moved into his fifties with relative grace. His dull, gray irises looked across glasses in black plastic frames that leaned on a beaked nose. Few hairs survived at the top of his head and he was as talkative as a turtle. Both men wore sport jackets made of lightweight material over open-necked white dress shirts and slacks.

"What are the odds for the Series, Angelo?" Lansky asked as he took off his jacket, folded it, and let it rest on the low coffee table.

"Thirteen to ten for the Yanks."

"And for this game?" the boss asked while crossing his ankles.

"Eleven to ten. Whitey Ford is starting and . . . you know, he's near forty."

"Who's throwing for Milwaukee?" Lansky wanted to know as he lit a cigarette.

"Haney said Warren Spahn."

The exchange dried up. Angelo was mixing a whiskey and soda for Lansky when the first takes of County Stadium appeared on the screen. Cuco Conde, a Cuban sports commentator, told viewers that *Gillette's Sports Cavalcade* had the pleasure of presenting, live from Milwaukee and making use of CMQ's "Over the Horizon" technology, the first game of the 1958 World Series between the teams that had won the American and National League pennants, the New York Yankees and the Milwaukee Braves.

"Damn, they're speaking Spanish!" Shaifer fumed. He also had taken off his jacket, and Angelo guessed that the automatic in his shoulder holster was a .45 Colt Commando.

"What did you expect?" Lansky asked.

Having handed Lansky his drink, Angelo poured two beers in tall glasses for Shaifer and himself. They watched and listened in silence, only partially understanding the confirmation of the designated pitchers, that the weather was cooler than expected, and that 46,377 mad fans huzzahed the local players as they took the field. During the first two innings, Lansky and Angelo pooled their scant knowledge of Spanish and managed to understand most of Conde's comments. At the top of the third, Lansky asked what the Capri man had been waiting for:

"How much did we collect for the outcome of the Series, Angelo?"

Dick unfastened his gaze from the screen, placed his half-full glass on the table at a safe distance from Lansky's jacket, and cleared his throat. His guests kept watching the game.

"In round numbers, 223,000 for the Yanks and 63,000 for the Braves."

"How do we stand?"

"Thirteen-to-ten odds mean a net loss of around 100 thousand if the Yankees win and a net profit of 125 thousand if they lose."

"Bets for this game?"

"Three sixteen for the Yanks and ninety-two for the Braves."

Shaifer whistled low and cut a sideways look at Angelo Dick, who anticipated the next question.

"We'd lose around 195 if the Mules win. If Milwaukee takes the lead, we'd make roughly 215."

Lansky seemed to be following the plays as he sipped his highball, but his mind juggled figures and explored opportunities. Only the set's audio and the humming air conditioners could be heard. At the bottom of the third inning, following ten minutes of silence, he made an observation.

"On the first game these people bet, only with us, almost four hundred eight thousand bucks, over forty cents for each man, woman, and child in the city."

Angelo Dick nodded reflectively before speaking. "You consider bets controlled by natives and those among buddies, maybe the total is over a dollar per person. Just like in New York or Chicago."

"There's something to learn from this," Lansky said, turning to Shaifer. "We have to redirect the Cubans' devotion to gambling. Take them to the wheel, the bones, the bandits, anything gives us better percentages. We ought to figure out some sort of small, low-overhead joints in Havana's downtown and middle-class districts to take in natives who will never gamble at the Riviera, Capri, or Deauville. We gotta rise to the occasion, increase the profit potential of all that sports dough from fifty to eighty, eighty-five, or ninety per cent. Now, Jacob, the biggest amusement park here has a cheap gambling parlor operated by a Cuban. I've been told the guy's making a killing. Give it a look-see, willya? Talk to the guy, tell him we'd like to do business with him."

"I'll see to it," Shaifer said.

In the top of the fourth, Bill Skowron, the Yankees' first baseman, hit a home run and opened the scoring, but in the bottom the Braves scored two runs. With Hank Aaron on third base, Del Crandall singled to left field; another hit by Andy Pafko moved Crandall to second; then a sharp liner to center field by Warren Spahn allowed Crandall to score. Angelo Dick refreshed drinks, lit a Pall Mall, and reclined on his armchair for the fifth. With one out, Whitey Ford walked and Hank Bauer, the New Yorkers' right fielder, homered into the left field bleachers to give his team a 3–2 lead.

The three men watched with the poise typical of professional gamblers. For the financial reward involved, a vague inner satisfaction settled in just after the Braves took the lead, even though none needed to be reminded that the next day's score could offset a first-game profit. Lansky smoked placidly, sipped his drink, or drummed his fingers on the arm of the couch. Shaifer, shirt cuffs folded up under the elbows, had the inscrutability of a Siamese cat. Angelo Dick methodically reviewed figures in his mind, waiting for a new round of questions. Through the huge picture window, under a brilliant sun, the sea and the sky merged blues on the horizon.

At the start of the lucky seventh, Lansky turned a little in his seat and stared at Casino de Capri's gambling-hall supervisor.

"How's the other business, Angelo?"

"It's okay, Mr. Lansky. I still haven't got the final figures for September—you know, the accountant is working on it now, month ended yesterday—but we are hoping for a 160-grand net profit, not bad for the dead month. Nick is very pleased, especially with roulette results. We made 83,000 in it, 33,000 in baccarat, 28,000 in—"

"Not the Capri, Angelo," interrupted Lansky.

"Sir?"

"I mean your other business."

"My other business?"

"This angel factory you've opened up."

Angelo Dick's only visible reaction was a touch of paleness. To elude Lansky's stare, he looked at the TV screen. *Wiretapped* was the first thing that came to his mind.

"Tell me, how're you doing in the baby business?" Lansky insisted.

Angelo kept watching the game. "It's no big deal, Mr. Lansky."

"Is that right?"

"Yes, sir," he said, starting to look befuddled.

Lansky kept his eyes fastened on Angelo Dick. "Really? Four hundred twenty-three abortions in six months, your cut is a hundred for each little thing, and it's no big deal? At the casino you make forty-eight grand a year; the bonus pushes you up to what, fifty-five? Sixty? At the rate you're shipping angels to heaven you'll make almost ninety grand a year. No big deal? Give me a break."

"In fact—," Dick began, taking a stab at mollifying Lansky, eyes still on the screen.

"Look at me, you sonafabitch!"

The old man read fear in Angelo's eyes. Lansky was glad that it was out in the open at last. Life had burned out his self-control; twenty years earlier he had been capable of dancing around a punk like Angelo for months, work and party with him as if nothing had happened, and never feel anger boiling inside him. He rose from the couch and walked over to the huge picture window, hands in his pockets. Jacob Shaifer hadn't moved an inch, but he wore a different expression now: that of a predator ready to leap over an unsuspecting antelope. The hall supervisor felt his bladder in need of relief and admitted to himself it was part beer, part panic. He now knew why the boss had invited himself to his apartment.

Lansky stared out through the window. His gaze plummeted a hundred feet down, across the wide avenue to the dog's tooth rock beyond the seawall. Tame waves caressed it lovingly, white foam cooled it off, salt flavored it, seaweed adorned it. Lansky took a deep breath. Angelo's greed had opened him to ridicule, and he needed to relieve his frustration with the jerk responsible for it. His cardiologist had advised him to at his last appointment. *Seething is bad for you. Let the steam off; don't repress your feelings all the time. Kick the furniture, yell at incompetent bastards—that's the best therapy.* Besides, it was part of the act, one of those rare occasions in life when what must be done perfectly matches up with what you feel like doing. He turned around and faced Angelo.

"Didn't you know New York is trying to force its way in?" he hissed.

Angelo Dick nodded energetically.

"Didn't you know Anastasia wanted to retire Frank?"

Second lively acceptance.

Lansky was fuming now. "Didn't you know I had to call a meeting here with the Commission and the dons of the Five Families and tell them all that whoever wanted to invade the fucking Cuban territory would be sleeping in a wooden pajama one day after getting off the plane?"

Third mute approval.

"Talk to me, scumbag. Did you or didn't you know all that?"

"I did, yessir."

"And knowing it, you go and line up with a Joe Bananas *sottocapo* to perform abortions here on every New York slut gets pregnant."

Angelo looked at the floor, weathering the storm.

"You almost had to charter a fucking plane! A hundred twenty-six broads flew over in August! Three gynecologists at three different clinics, for Chrissake! This keeps growing, you'll have to rent office space and a coupla secretaries, goddammit!"

During a fifteen-second pause, Lansky got his breath back. Jacob Shaifer was enjoying the performance enormously.

"I know everything, Angelo, everything," Lansky went on at last. "The dame pays four hundred. Two cover medical attention. You and Joe Notaro split the other two."

"Excuse me for interrupting, Mr. Lansky," moaned the culprit, "but I'm not making a hundred per patient. I gotta pay the interpreter that picks them up at the airport, taxi fare, tips—"

"You *are* stupid. I'm discussing principles here, not nickels and dimes. Can't you see, asshole, they've used you as the foot in the door?"

"Just a second, sir," Angelo said, holding up his hands innocently, minding his choice of words. "This is a misunderstanding. Notaro has never said a word about gambling, never mentioned that Bonanno wants to open shop here. Fact is right now there's a lot of heat against illegal abortions in New York and prices have shot up to a thou, even twelve hundred. And since it's legit here, including airfare each patient saves between four and six hundred dollars. I give you my word, Mr. Lansky, it was just a business opportunity. Nobody asked me how are we doing or suggested I change sides."

Lansky moved his eyes to the screen for a few seconds to process the new information. Probably. Joe Bananas, Mr. Nice Guy, didn't have the balls to go ahead on his own. Maybe Bananas' closest ally, Joe Profaci, whose daughter married Mr. Nice Guy's son, wasn't sure yet. The hypocrite bastards.

"They don't feel sure yet," Lansky said as if muttering to himself. "They know I'm pretty powerful here." And again addressing Angelo: "For twenty-one years I've done business in Cuba, you hear? Twenty-one years."

"I'll explain everything . . ."

"You sure will."

". . . but I gotta pee."

"You already peed outta the piss pot. Keep an eye on the schmuck."

Lansky motioned his last remark to Shaifer by jerking his head and remained alone in the living room as both men marched to the bathroom. Bottom of the eighth. The Braves' Eddie Mathews walked; Hank Aaron lined a double into right field, sending Mathews to third. Casey Stengel emerged from the dugout and sportively trotted his sixty-eight years to the pitching mound for a talk with Whitey Ford. Fans knew that Ford and Stengel didn't get along, but talking in front of the cameras they looked like father and son. Stengel rested his right hand on the pitcher's shoulder and signaled for Ryne Duren. The game proceeded and Adcock fanned for the first out before Wes Covington flied out deep to center field, and Mantle's throw couldn't beat Mathews to home plate. Tied, 3–3.

Angelo and Shaifer returned to their seats and watched the action. The hall supervisor awaited sentencing smoking nervously and trying to sort out his predicament. He suspected that Lansky had ordered Shaifer to monitor him in the bathroom to prevent him from flushing some compromising papers—that had to be it. Treason entailed death, but that was out of the question; he hadn't betrayed. He'd be reprimanded and that would be all. Nonetheless, the flustered Angelo envisioned his future in Havana as uncertain as the outcome of a baseball game tied at the start of the ninth.

Shaifer rose and ambled over to the pantry, opened the refrigerator, rolled up and gobbled two slices of ham and one of cheese in three bites. He came back into the living room wiping his fingers clean on his handkerchief, then arranged himself on the sofa.

"You fucked up, Angelo," a calm Lansky said once he had concluded that the egregious blunder deserved the punishment agreed on beforehand. "You fucked up when they offered you the deal and didn't mention it to Nick or to myself; fucked up again when operations started; and perhaps you also fucked up with something more serious nobody knows about, like blowing the gaff."

"No. I give you my word," Angelo averred.

"Let's hope so. Nick and I agreed you'll take a plane to Tampa, report to the Colonial Inn, and mop floors or wash dishes till I remember you again."

"Yessir."

"You sound like a fucking Marine," Lansky quipped with a grin.

Angelo thought that joking entailed forgiveness and, relieved, smiled broadly. Shaifer shook his head in admiration. His boss was one of the greatest actors on earth.

Minutes wore on and not another word was spoken. In the bottom of the tenth Hank Aaron was called out on strikes, Adcock singled to center, and Wes Covington flied out. Then Adcock took second on Del Crandall's single and Bill Bruton came to bat. Benched at the start of the game with knee trouble and because left-handed Whitey Ford was pitching, he took Andy Pafko's place in center field after Duren relieved Ford. On the third pitch Bruton stroked a line drive to right field and Adcock scored the winning run for the Milwaukee Braves.

Meyer Lansky rose from the couch, turned off the set, slowly slipped into his jacket and put his hat on. Shaifer did the same after unfolding his shirt cuffs and followed his boss to the front door. Angelo Dick, right behind them, heard the lock clicking open, and believed himself home free. It was the proper moment to say good-bye with humble elegance in a diffident tone.

"Thanks for your understanding, Mr. Lansky."

"You're coming with us, Angelo. Get your jacket," was Meyer Lansky's soft-spoken indication.

. . .

Brought along by a weak cold front, drizzle fell that night. At dawn it was cloudy; before ten it started pouring all over Havana. Heavy drops plopping on a wooden louvered window awoke the man sleeping in one of two cabins at a private sanatorium for mental patients.

Mariano Contreras did a big stretch, got up, shuffled into a tiny bathroom, and urinated. At the sink, he coughed and spat prior to brushing yellowish teeth. The medicine cabinet mirror reflected a deeply wrinkled forehead, loose gray hair, green-gray eyes, white stubbles on his cheeks and chin, a bushy salt-and-pepper mustache, and a skeptical expression on cardboard-thin lips.

After inserting a new blade in the safety razor, Contreras returned to the bedroom, lit a La Corona cigarette from a pack on the night table, and went back into the bathroom. The shaving brush worked a rich lather and he shaved cautiously, pausing to smoke, thinking that he would have to trim his mustache soon. When he was done, he dropped the stub into the toilet bowl and flushed it, stepped out of his shorts, pulled his undershirt over his head, then took a warm shower. His lean body was almost totally covered with hair—brownish on his legs, the pubis, the flat stomach, and his back, white on his chest. Once dried, Contreras rubbed alcohol on his face, sprinkled talcum on his feet, sprayed deodorant under his armpits, and combed back his hair. He dropped the soiled underwear into a basket and returned to the bedroom.

Putting on nylon socks, Contreras recalled his first visit to this sequestered place six days before. He had admitted to the shrink that he felt insecure, anxious, frightened. A friend of his, treated here for similar symptoms, had highly recommended a few months of peace and quiet at the same cabin in which he had regained his balance. The doctor's instant diagnosis had been psychasthenia. His prescription: indefinite rest at the institution. A balanced diet would be provided and the patient could come and go whenever and wherever he wished. The full treatment cost 400 pesos a month. Contreras had haggled the man down to 350 just to mask his enthusiasm.

The health resort was an eight-acre country estate with royal palms and numerous tropical fruit trees, located at the intersection of Barrera and Alday, in the Los Pinos district, part of the imprecise belt dividing Havana's urban and rural areas. Four years earlier, two practicing psychiatrists had converted its nineteenth-century sandstone mansion into a female ward, built a separate ward for males, and a thatched-roof outdoor lounge, a kitchen, and a dining hall. Rather optimistically, two cabins for married patients and their sane mates had been also constructed. They had hoped to attract and treat patients suffering from phobias, neuroses, manias, and similar mental conditions who could afford private care.

However, not everything came out as the owners had hoped. Fourteen competitors, some of them having many years of practice and prestige, had as good or better institutions in similar bucolic surroundings nearby, and charged equivalent fees. So the Hippocratic oath had been somewhat circumvented. Individuals as sound of mind as anyone, in need of monastic solitude at the tree-sheltered cabins for reasons of their own, were accepted as patients. The staff had been instructed to allow full freedom of movement to these people, including visitors at any time, orders for drinks and cigarettes, and permission to leave the premises whenever they felt like it. On the infrequent occasions when both cabins were rented, the sex life of truly sick married patients was deferred.

Contreras dressed unhurriedly, donning underwear, a white dress shirt, a dark blue tie, an off-the-rack gabardine gray suit, and black cordovan lace-up shoes. Into his pockets he dropped wallet, key ring, coins, handkerchief, cheap ballpoint, cigarettes, and matches. Finally, his head covered by a three-day-old copy of the newspaper *Excelsior* and relishing the smell of wet earth and foliage, he followed a sinuous footwalk, left the cabin key at the reception desk, and reached a small parking space, where he climbed into a black '47 Chevrolet Fleetline.

At a quarter past eleven Contreras pulled in behind an old Studebaker, twenty feet from the corner of Rastro and Belascoaín Streets, not too far from downtown Havana. The tires of cruising vehicles squelched on the asphalt; multicolored stripes of diluted motor oil crawled and disappeared into sewers, although it wasn't raining at the moment. He got out and in less than a minute covered the two blocks to La Segunda Estrella de Oro, a Chinese restaurant at 808 Monte Street.

The place, five times longer than it was wide, exuded the amalgamated smell of mixed fried rice and the subtler aromas of shrimp, red porgy, lobster, and pork. All the revolving stools along the fifty-foot-long counter were occupied; from behind it, five slant-eyed waiters dripping with sweat brought in trays with steaming hot bowls of *guy meing ton* soup, the ever-present *chen chow fon,* and fried, meat-filled wontons. As patrons poured in, the frantic attendants cleared used tableware and empty bottles, mopped the Formica top and set out paper doilies and clean cutlery. There was a continuous flow of regulars: the traders, roustabouts, and truck drivers from the neighboring Mercado Único. Wearing muddy undershirts, frayed jeans, shoes, baseball caps or five-gallon hats, and big knives in leather sheaths tucked into the waistbands of their pants, they talked shop in their jargon. Facing the counter, sitting in comfortable booths, better-dressed families or groups of friends who were in no hurry feasted on chop suey, chow mein, and other delicacies.

From a booth at the back, Contreras ordered *shong ton* soup, mixed fried rice, fried shrimp-filled wontons, and a bottle of Hatuey beer. Twenty-five minutes later, as he sipped espresso from a demitasse, a short, green-eyed, pink-skinned man approached him with the faintest trace of a smile on his full lips. Drops of rain dampened his clothes—a maroon, mass-produced suit over a white dress shirt a size too small for his neck, plus a beige tie—and sparkled on the vamp and the toecap of his nut-colored, well-polished shoes. His pro-truding belly and bald, close-cropped scalp smacked of old age, but the unlined face of a man in his early thirties made Fermín Rodríguez look around forty.

"Havana just had lunch," the newly arrived one remarked.

"Be my guest," Contreras said, indicating the booth's opposing seat.

"Nah, I beat you to it."

"Let's get rolling then," the gray-haired man said as he scooted from the booth and dropped two one-peso bills on the table. On the way out he lit up.

Buckets of rain forced them to take the street's arcades, seething with shoppers and staff on their lunch hour while waiting for the downpour to stop. Two pickpockets working the block spotted the pair as they left the restaurant; the older shook his head to the younger and turned to look for tame prey. Lottery ticket vendors, pitchmen, and shoeshine boys hawked their wares. A few despondent beggars dressed in rags extended their hands; one of them, to resemble Saint Lazarus, showed the pustules on his legs and kept three mangy dogs by his side. Fermín Rodríguez gave a wink to a pimp of his acquaintance. Contreras ignored the respectful nod of a con man whose main scheme was selling hand-operated machines that transmuted one-peso bills into twenties to gullible farmers visiting the Cuban capital.

They jostled and shoved until reaching the corner of Cuatro Caminos, where they took a left and darted down Belascoaín to the Chevy. In the passenger seat, Fermín wiped his head dry with a handkerchief as Contreras started the engine.

"What are the odds today, Gallego?" the leaner man asked.

"Eleven to ten the Series for Milwaukee; thirteen to ten the game."

"Spread's too wide for the game."

"No, it's right. Lew Burdette against Bob Turley. The Yankees' pitching staff stinks. Listen, Ox, the two best pitchers in the Series . . ."

Fermín made a man-by-man evaluation so as to prove his point. Contreras listened as he drove along Monte Street and the handed-down Calzada del Cerro, rolled around the corner at Lombillo, then took a right turn onto Ayestarán. The Chevy came to a stop by a two-storied apartment building at 527 La Rosa Street. Contreras cut the engine. His passenger opened the door and with four quick hops gained the porch. The driver braved the rain under the soaked newspaper as he unhurriedly locked the car. Then they took the staircase to apartment 4; Contreras opened the front door and switched on the light of his living-cum-dining room.

"Boys will be late," Fermín predicted as he mopped his scalp once again.

"Probably. Would you like a drink?"

"To fight this cold I have."

"Help yourself. I'm gonna dry my hair; need something stronger than a handkerchief."

Contreras left Fermín guffawing and entered the bedroom as the short man headed to the kitchen. The tenant took off his jacket, shirt, and tie, toweled his hair dry, combed it, then returned to the living room in his undershirt. Fermín had poured Tres Ceros brandy in two plain-glass tumblers and now sat on a rocker, facing a 17-inch black-and-white television set. Contreras took his place at the left side of a well-worn wooden sofa for three with wickerwork back and seats, then emptied his tumbler in two gulps. Fermín's face was a shade over his natural tone; sweat and grease sparkled on his forehead and chin.

"Want to take off your jacket?" Contreras asked.

"No, I'm fine."

"Why don't you turn it on?"

"It's early."

"We'll pass the time."

A political analyst contended that the overwhelming majority of the Cuban people supported President Batista. The viewers exchanged amused glances. Contreras was refreshing his drink when the doorbell rang twice; he went to open. A handsome, light-skinned Negro stood in the doorway. A shade under six feet, he had deep brown eyes and a well-kept thin mustache. He wore a soaked white guayabera, light blue slacks drenched below the knees, and dripping brown shoes. He looked undecided about leaving the wrapping paper he had used as raincoat in the hall.

"Come on in, *mulato*," the tenant said.

"I'll wet the floor. Hi, Gallego."

"Hello. How are you doing, man?" Fermín said from his seat.

"Fine. Fucking rain cooled my ass."

"Strip in the john and hang up your rags," Contreras suggested. "I'll lend you a pair of pants and a shirt."

At 1:31 the three men came together in the living room. The black man, in borrowed slippers, sat to the right of Contreras and warmed himself with a slug of brandy. "This is nice, *compadre*," he said, raising his tumbler.

"Why didn't you come yesterday?" Contreras asked, his calm voice discounting significance to the absence. Fermín shot swift glances at his two buddies.

"Greatest thing on earth, pal," Melchor Loredo said exultantly. "Was on my way here, bus breaks down at 70 and 21 and, well, like everybody else I got out to take the next one. Then this kid—he was just a kid, you know, under twenty—gets out a '58 Buick Limited that looked like a million bucks, leaves the engine idling, keys in the ignition . . ."

"I crap on you, Wheel," Contreras deadpanned in such a soft tone that Fermín grabbed the arms of the rocker, getting ready to stand between them.

"Let's have some respect, Ox," said Loredo, carefully choosing his words.

"Respect? You asking for respect? You showing respect for our job?" Contreras croaked, his face screwed up.

"It was a gift, Ox," Loredo pleaded.

"I don't care if it was," imperiously now. "I said you couldn't get into anything. And I meant it, 'cause we can't lose the driver at this point. No sooner you turn your back, you steal a hearse."

"I forgot everything, guys. It was like . . . a reflex, you know? As if the kid had made me a present . . . ," he said to provide a justification, looking at the floor.

"You were this close to getting busted," Contreras insisted.

"Well, nothing happened," Loredo said.

"Don't talk shit, Wheel," Fermín barged in, trying to patch things up. "At noon, in front of two dozen people. A prowl car turns around the corner, you'd be in the tank now, you chump."

"I level with you guys, you throw the horses at me?" said Loredo reproachfully.

Contreras clicked his tongue in exasperation. "Don't get an attitude," he said testily.

"Okay, I bungled it. Sorry. Just don't rub it in."

They watched the screen in silent anger for several more minutes. Then Fermín suggested espresso and got up to make it. Contreras left his seat to take a leak, Loredo lit a cigarette, tension abated. Distracted as they were by Gillette commercials, lineups, and weather forecasts, the black man's latest theft slowly faded out.

The home club won in the very first inning. In the top, Hank Bauer singled over second, then Eddie Mathews fielded

McDougald's high hopper but threw widely, permitting Bauer to reach third and McDougald second. Mickey Mantle was intentionally walked, filling the bases, and Howard bounced to Schoendienst, whose throw to Logan forced Mantle at second as Bauer scored. Berra grounded into a double play.

The Braves responded in kind. Bruton walloped a home run into the right field bleachers, Schoendienst lined a double to the wall in right, Mathews was called out on strikes. Aaron walked, then Covington singled sharply into right center, scoring Schoendienst and sending Aaron to third. Duke Maas replaced Turley on the mound. Torre flied to Howard in short left; Aaron scored, and Covington took second on the throw to home plate. Then Lew Burdette hit a homer, the first by a pitcher in a World Series since Bucky Walters sent it to the left field bleachers on October 7, 1940. Elston Howard crashed into the fence in a vain effort to catch Burdette's drive, injured his side, and was replaced by Norm Siebern.

"Gentlemen, Milwaukee has it in the bag," Fermín said.

Contreras and Loredo nodded in solemn silence, watching the screen as their minds checked angles. Loredo examined the initial, easy part of his job. Get as near as possible and fasten his eyes on the main exit. He would probably leave the engine idling to keep it warm and lubricated. As soon as he saw the flame, he would place the small taxi signs on the car's partially rolled up back windows, pull off the curb to meet them, offer the ride, open the left rear door from the inside. An almost embarrassingly simple piece of cake.

Then he would become the team's most valuable player for the next fifteen minutes. He hoped for the best. He would try to keep to the planned route of escape, skirting speed limits and hoping no police cruiser ordered him to pull over. But if for some reason they were chased, he'd have to unleash the engine's full power, estimate slopes and possible skids, and spin a path of hell-bent flight in the web of city streets without taking dead ends or hitting potholes, to safely carry his load of men and money to the hideout. His expertise had earned him the sobriquet "Wheel"; he was the best driver and car thief in Havana, with only one prison sentence after 7 holdups and 188 car thefts in ten years.

In the bottom of the third inning the phone on a small round chestnut table near an empty rocker started ringing. Contreras rose to his feet, lowered the set's volume, and picked up the receiver.

"Yeah."

"Can't make it. It's a deluge."

"No problem. But the meeting the day after tomorrow goes, even under a blowing hurricane."

"Okay. Bye now."

"Bye."

Contreras hung up and said "Abo" to Fermín and Loredo. He turned up the volume, recovered his tumbler, and swallowed the dregs of liquor.

"Can't he make it?" Wheel asked, dripping with sarcasm.

"Says the rain doesn't let him."

"The blonde, I'd say," Fermín chuckled.

Only a clairvoyant could have been closer to the truth. A mile away, in an apartment rented by the hour, twenty-eight-year-old Arturo Heller, dubbed "Abo"—for *abogado,* "lawyer" in Spanish, having gotten as far as the second year of the University of Havana's law school in the early fifties—hadn't interrupted his lovemaking as he dialed, nor during the brief exchange. On top of him, on her knees and leaning on his shoulders, a smiling young woman found herself reliving her childhood years, when she had ridden the carousel's rising and falling painted horses. Instead of tooting pipes and felt-covered mallets pounding out a tune, songs by Nat King Cole came from a radio on the bedside table. Every minute or so, with Heller's eager compliance, she buried his penis deep inside of her, then rubbed her clitoris against his groin, knowing that with the deliberate friction she would come. Fermín had only been wrong about the woman's complexion: She was a genuine brunette, with small breasts, a nice behind, rounded thighs, slanted eyes, and full lips. To prolong the pleasure she occasionally paused and sighed and waved back strands of long black hair and made ego-boosting remarks to her partner. Being so active, she preferred passive men, and Abo was an ideal partner: a commanding, proud macho in public, a complacent and governable lover in bed.

With her eyes closed, relishing every second of it, she demanded Heller's ejaculation in mid-orgasm. He let himself go. Afterward, they gradually overcame their panting and she slid back on the mattress. A few minutes later, Heller tuned the radio to Circuito Nacional Cubano to learn the score. The ceiling mirror reflected the superb body of the Pennsylvania Club dancer, and he ogled it admiringly. It was the first time in two weeks that his main consideration had not been the amount of money inside a certain safe. One minute after he fell asleep, Mickey Mantle hit his first home run of the Series.

At his place, Contreras figured that the five runs scored by the Braves in the seventh and eighth innings had decided the game and engaged in some mental calculations before mentioning an amount to his guests. Fermín nodded reflexively, as though his own estimate had been confirmed.

"We would be set up for life," Loredo said with low-key enthusiasm.

To prolong their agony, the Easterners scored three runs in the top of the ninth before losing, 13–5. Contreras turned off the set. Fermín stretched out. Loredo headed on back to the bathroom to don his still wet clothes and shoes.

"C'mon, I'll drop you guys where you like," Contreras volunteered when Wheel returned to the living room. "Damn rain," he added, then rose to his feet and marched to the bedroom to put on a shirt and jacket.

A mile away, following a raunchy exchange and a shared shower, and only half-listening to the soft music that Radio Codazos specialized in, Heller rubbed his nose on the dancer's curled pubic hair and playfully started a downward kissing plunge.

...

For the general public, Casino de Capri was an offshoot of the Capri Hotel. Those in the know maintained that the corporate relationship between the adjoining structures, on the corner of Twenty-first and N Streets in Vedado, was exactly the opposite.

In 1956 Casino Parisién had opened at the Hotel Nacional under Lefty Clark's expert management. This trial balloon proved to those in gaming that prosperity hinged on lodging as many wealthy patrons as possible in nearby rooms. Having replicated the Las Vegas experience in a different environment, Meyer Lansky and his associates decided to build the Riviera, Capri, and Deauville casinos and hotels. The owners of the Tropicana, Montmartre, and Sans Souci, as well as those of other, second-rate Cuban nightclubs with gambling halls, had felt threatened with extinction.

Casino de Capri's blueprint depicted a 72-yard-long, 24-yard-wide, 25-foot-high one-story concrete structure that had the gaming area in front, the nightclub at the back. The swinging, padded, and buttoned double door in green facing Twenty-first Street opened into a huge lounge in whose center four roulette wheels and four blackjack tables formed a circle. In the middle of it, behind a counter stacked with brand-new decks of cards and sets of dice, the chief inspector sat. Long, red velvet lampshades hung over each table. Drapes of the same material covered the walls.

To the left of the casino entrance were the cashier's glassed-in cubicle, a second double door to the hotel's lobby, and a hidden, glass-encased elevated hallway from which senior management and the security chief kept an eye on the place. By the wall to the right, a curved mahogany bar with ten stools and four tables offered a different recreation. At the rear, in the right corner, was a baccarat table close to the men's washroom; in the left corner were a craps table and the ladies' rest room. Between them, a third double door opened into the nightclub. One-armed bandits all over the place left little space free.

Naive visitors were seduced by a façade of overwhelming opulence that was the result of four perceptions. Their feet absorbed the change from the sidewalk and black marble steps to thick wall-to-wall carpeting. Murmurs, Muzak, and the clicking of plastic chips replaced street noises in their ears.

Their eyes registered the elegant decor and the stylish apparel of most of the gamblers and all of the staff. The smell of several expensive perfumes could be discerned too. In addition, there was the extrasensory expectancy of money on the move. Wilberto Pires, formerly employed as a collector of cork bark in his native Portugal, then a snapshot camera mechanic in Barcelona and later a male prostitute in Monte Carlo, dubbed Willy Pi by the rest of the staff, watched out of the corner of his eye as Marvin Grouse approached his table. Promoted to the post of gambling-hall supervisor, Grouse was in his second night on the job. The extremely good-looking Portuguese dealer adjusted his black bow tie as he waited for a last bet. Three customers sat at his varnished cedar table, but the woman still hadn't decided where to place her chips. Willy Pi would be calling the bilingual "*no va más;* the betting is closed" between four and six seconds before the ivory ball jumped from its perfect circle to the spinning wheel.

Grouse watched the bouncing ball indifferently, heard Willy pronounce the winning number and color, observed as the rake quickly drew in losers' chips, and winners were paid off. The dealers were trained experts, so Grouse never subjected the bet to close scrutiny. Instead, he kept his eyes peeled for sweat on their foreheads, a dirty spot on the cuffs, underpolished shoes. The new hall supervisor also looked for overflowing ashtrays, drinks not replenished by waiters, and lack of courtesy shown to players.

During his seven years as assistant gambling-hall supervisor in Vegas, and now in Havana, Grouse couldn't recall ever completing what he termed a "look-see" without finding some kind of trouble, such as at Willy's table in this precise moment, where the smoke from a cigar a client was puffing on irritated the Canadian lady to his right. Grouse leaned over the ear of the plump fiftyish woman and whispered something for half a minute. The satisfied matron smiled, picked up her chips, and, accompanied by Grouse, moved to another roulette where two men, nonsmokers apparently, were playing.

Barry Caldwell, the inspector overseeing Willy's table, took mental note and reflected on variations. Had the lady refused to move, Grouse would have induced the smoker to change tables by offering him anything—twenty-five pesos in chips or a free meal at the nightclub—to achieve gaming's supreme goal: clients picked clean but pleased about it.

Followed by the eyes of one of the players at Willy's roulette, Grouse ambled over to the craps game. "Make your bets, gentlemen," the Portuguese dealer suggested as he spun the ball on the bowl's track with a flick of the wrist. Green Chips bet five pesos on black, five on odd, five on the third column, and five on the first dozen. As White Chips and Blue Chips made their bets, Willy Pi briefly glanced at the breed of player who displeases casino operators the world over.

In his early thirties, Green Chips was somewhat fleshy for his medium height. He had light brown eyes, dark blond hair combed back, deep acne scars on his cheeks. The man knew how to make his money grow; Willy recalled having seen him once or twice before, always around midnight. The ball came to rest on 17. Green Chips won ten pesos for odd and black and lost ten because the number didn't belong to the third column or the first dozen. White and Blue Chips, less gifted at combining probabilities with pure chance, lost fifteen and twenty-five pesos, respectively.

"Make your bets, gentlemen."

Looking very sure of himself, Green Chips bet five on red, five on pair, five on the first column, and five on the third dozen before lighting a Partagás Superfino cigarette and spying Marvin Grouse by the dice table. Tilting his head backward, he blew smoke toward the ceiling, then stole glances at the cashier, the lobby door—guarded by a man in a brown suit—and the dial of his Ardath watch: 12:22 A.M. The lucky number was 28. Green Chips lost ten pesos for its being a black, even number, and won twenty because it belonged to the first column and the third dozen.

Barry Caldwell recalled that the guy had started with sixty pesos and had ninety-odd a half hour later. Peanuts, of course, but he knew he should point him out to Grouse. That sort of customer had to be watched. If Green Chips limited himself to a monthly visit he would find the welcome mat out, for the moderate winner provides a glimmer of hope to systematic losers, but in the event he fancied making thirty or forty bucks on a daily basis, some beefy security man would coolly send him packing.

At 12:30 Orestes Ordaz and Henry Bernstein replaced Willy Pi and Caldwell. Prior to taking his break, Caldwell whispered something in Grouse's ear as the new supervisor watched baccarat. The man turned around, located the offender, nodded to Caldwell, and returned his attention to the card table. Following the dealer turnover, White Chips called it quits; the other customer kept at it. Green Chips blew frequent kisses to the beautiful girl with honey-colored skin, boyishly cut hair, and dark eyes escorting a Texan, far gone in bourbon and money, at the nearest roulette. Every few minutes Green Chips sipped beer from a tall cup close to his left hand, his gaze scanning the place, as though he was undecided between the wheel, a broad, or another form of entertainment.

Three dealer turnovers later, Green Chips had a pile worth 135 pesos stacked in front of him. Like most of the other customers, Blue Chips had left after reducing his net worth by three hundred pesos. At 1:45 the casino was nearly empty. Closing time was postponed only if a high roller wanted to keep playing, but this particular night no table seemed to have a Croesus on a spending spree. Leaning on the girl, the drunk Texan had left at 1:15.

Green Chips turned in his chair, snapped his fingers to a waiter, and ordered a fresh beer. The ball fell on the zero's canoe; he was spared what he had bet on color, even, and high. Again he glanced at the cashier's cubicle, where two men were going through a shop-closing routine. Suddenly, the gambler registered that the ball wasn't spinning on the track; his eyes searched the dealer's. The man stared over his head. Green Chips whirled around, looking up.

"Good evening, sir," Jimmy Brun, the chief inspector, said in passable Spanish. Clad in a tuxedo, the tall, red-haired American smiled at the gambler with the warmth of an Arctic Ocean walrus.

"Good evening," Green Chips replied, a touch of caution in his eyes.

"I regret to tell you that we'll close in fifteen minutes."

"It's okay. I was leaving after this beer anyway," Green Chips said as he reached for the full cup from the tray presented by the waiter.

"I hope you'll visit us again. It's always a pleasure to see someone who knows how to."

"Not before November," Green Chips said, and swallowed a mouthful.

From the observation post, behind gray-tinted plate glass, Nick Di Constanzo and Marvin Grouse peered at the client as he calmly finished his beer and dropped the chips into the right pocket of his sports jacket.

"He takes his time," Di Constanzo commented.

A close business associate of Frank Costello's for thirty-five years, Di Constanzo had been in charge of Casino de Capri since it opened. Somewhere during his early forties he had started carefully cultivating what a girlfriend with literary ambitions had referred to as a "patrician countenance." Since then, Di Constanzo had made enough money to wear Savile Row suits, handmade English shoes, and the most exclusive silk ties. Only the best barber in town took care of his wavy, thick, silvery hair. He observed how well-bred people behaved in public in order to copy and even improve upon their aloof and polished manners. Intellectually speaking, Di Constanzo was the opposite of the punctilious Grouse. He had no eye for detail, but his perception of relevant facts made him formidable on strategic issues. Meyer Lansky respected him for his wit, common sense, business experience, friendship with Costello, and the indisputable merit of having reached his sixtieth birthday with his skin intact.

"Small fry. Takes seventy or eighty bucks from a table that grossed twelve hundred today," Grouse said.

They heard steps on the short staircase, turned around, and saw the chief inspector approaching. Brun lit a Camel, dragged at it, and for a second observed the departing gambler. "Says he's coming back next month," he reported.

"See, Nick? Guy knows his trade; we won't have to chase him off," Grouse said.

"I suppose so," said Di Constanzo, but he kept pondering the fact that an expert who visited the twelve city casinos once a month and stuck to roulette, betting small amounts, not touching cards or dice, could average four or five hundred a month. He would have good and bad days, weeks of winning six hundred, months of losing a thousand, but he'd earn his bread and butter.

"Anyway, I don't like this kinda guy," Di Constanzo said. "I hope he finds another way of making a living and quits giving free lessons to others."

Below, the man under discussion was the last to cash in. He pocketed 130 pesos before pushing through the door that opened into the hotel lobby. There he chose an easy chair facing the casino exit and lit a fresh cigarette.

The delicate lighting matched the late hour and softened contrasts between furniture, curtains, carpets, and paintings, wrapping in shadows the few guests passing time. Sitting on a couch to the gambler's right, two chorus girls from the nightclub waited for someone, their makeup bags resting on skintight jeans, a dash of frivolity in their hushed youthful giggling. The attendants of the two elevators, like the doorman and bellboy and both desk clerks, talked in whispers to lubricate the slow course of the small hours.

From the inside breast pocket of his jacket the player extracted the evening's copy of *Alerta*. He unfolded the newspaper and simulated reading it, elbows on the arms of the chair, while spying on the casino's aluminum-and-glass swinging door through a small hole he'd punched in the page. At 2:16 the cashier and his assistant pushed it open; each carried a briefcase. Two men with identical brown suits escorted them. All four stepped into an elevator that ninety seconds later returned the guards to the ground floor. At 2:23 Nick Di Constanzo and Marvin Grouse came through the same door and boarded the elevator. Only then did Green Chips fold the newspaper, blow kisses at the chorus girls, wish the doorman a good night, and leave the building.

Two

S aturday morning was overcast too. A gale blew, huge waves smashed against the city's seawall, and thirty-foot-high sheets of water came down on the few cars cruising by the new stretch of Malecón, between G Street and the tunnel under the Almendares River. Both the avenue and the tunnel had been part of the government's public works, at the request of a few influential property developers, of whom Meyer Lansky was one. No road prolongation, no Havana Riviera.

Shortly before noon, the parking valets, doormen, reception-desk clerks, and other attendants at the resplendent casino and hotel began speculating on the possibility that American gaming investors in Cuba would hold a meeting.

Wilbur "Lefty" Clark and his second-in-command, Tom Magenty, from Casino Parisién, drove down Paseo Avenue in a majestic '59 Cadillac De Ville at 11:29. They were followed ten minutes later by the Deauville's Santos Trafficante and his partner, Joe Bischoff, riding in a sumptuous Chrysler Imperial with sixty-three miles on its odometer. At 11:57 Nick Di Constanzo and Marvin Grouse showed up in a brand-new Lincoln Continental.

On the Riviera's top floor, Meyer Lansky and Eddie Galuzzo—the second-generation American who managed the casino—bid them welcome at the sumptuous suite permanently reserved for visiting dignitaries. Though slightly distorted by the seawater mist on the glass, the coastline and the foam-speckled Florida Straits could be watched through the living room's picture window, but neither hosts nor guests seemed predisposed to get lost in contemplation. Having exchanged greetings with the aplomb characteristic of leaders in all fields, the well-groomed lot reclined on soft seats, made jokes, munched shrimp fried in batter, and sipped fine liquors. The best hotel waiters, chosen to handle the cream of the crop, served them. Three TV sets, two in the living room and one in the dining room, were tuned to the third game of the World Series.

After a few minutes, in conformity with the power structure, two groups formed. By the studio bar, Lansky and Trafficante perched on stools, Clark and Di Constanzo standing, the bigwigs conversed in low tones. Despite the apparently untroubled atmosphere and the irrelevancy of the topics, the deference bestowed on Number One was evident to all. A slightly looser mark of respect was shown to Trafficante, Havana's second-in-command. Magenty, Bischoff, Grouse, and Galuzzo sat close by and chatted amiably, their ears flapping to overhear their bosses and keep up with trends, variations, and moods to make sure they would give the right answer if they were asked anything.

At 1:02 P.M., from the dining room doorway, a maître d' gave a respectful nod to Lansky and the boss waved his guests to lunch. They followed the baseball game on a 21-inch RCA set while, interspersed among the comments that good plays induced, appreciative remarks were made on the consommé, the lobster Thermidor with ground almonds, the sauté meuniere red porgy basted in melted butter, and the 1949 Mersault. Bischoff gobbled down his food and slurped three glasses of wine; Lansky nibbled a few bites and didn't touch the white. The rest ate and drank reasonably.

Hank Bauer hit a single with bases loaded in the bottom of the fifth, scoring Siebern and McDougald. In the top of the seventh, the Braves lost an opportunity when Schoendienst was called out trying to score. In the same inning, Bauer slugged a 400-foot homer into the left field stands for two more runs, and Don Larsen's good pitching kept the Braves' hands tied in the eighth and ninth.

After coffee the group returned to the living room and each man took a seat. Having settled himself onto a club chair with wings, Lansky shot a glance at Galuzzo, then shifted his gaze to the TV sets. Both were turned off. The guests realized that the meeting was about to begin. The agenda was unknown to all except Lansky, and the others were burning with curiosity. Conversation died out. Number One waited for Galuzzo to reach his armchair before making the introduction.

"Okay, guys. I need to discuss something. You all know that last Saturday I took a plane to New York and had a talk with Frank," Lansky began. "We discussed results here; they are excellent, more than anybody had hoped for. But we couldn't reach a decision on expansion. The architects and engineers completed their calculations and are ready to begin the project you all know about—filling in the seabed down there to build eight casinos and hotels in a first stage."

Lansky paused and looked at the carpet, considering how to word his ideas.

"It figures. Business logic says you invest in good times, fall back in hard times, so, if we look at the numbers, we should grow. But Frank says that last August he had a talk with Nick, who's worried about this revolution in the eastern part of the island, the chances of survival of the present administration, and the outcome for us if this government falls."

When Lansky crossed his legs or emphasized something by waving a hand, he looked tired out. Having nodded a couple of times, Nick Di Constanzo now stared at Number One and remained unfazed. With one exception, the rest were getting ready to watch a very peculiar confrontation. The exception was Marvin Grouse. As a Di Constanzo protégé, he dreaded the possibility of being considered a party to such a serious disagreement, and furtively glanced at his boss.

"Frank suggests," Lansky went on, "we hear out Nick and sort this out. Now, I want to thank Nick for watching over our interests so closely. It's always useful to hear a second opinion. Maybe I've overlooked something."

All caught the left-handed nature of the compliment. Galuzzo thought it wise to sneer at this and squinched up his face in a contemptuous look, directed squarely at Di Constanzo. He was peeved to discover that Lansky hadn't observed his groveling.

"I invited you here today so we could have lunch, listen to what Nick has to say, then learn what the rest of you guys think, one by one. So, if you please, Nick . . ."

"Thank you, Meyer," Di Constanzo said, then leaned forward, rubbed his hands, and gazed around the room. "I . . . uh, flew to New York in late August to check out a deal my former hall supervisor, Angelo Dick, had cut with Joe Notaro, a capo in the Bonanno family some of you may know personally. . . ."

The abortion-racket story took five minutes. Di Constanzo wanted to make very clear that it was the owner who first spotted the dog's flea, not his next-door neighbor.

"Before flying back I had dinner with Frank. I told him about Angelo, then we talked business here. Frank was optimistic, I was cautious; he wanted to know why and . . . Well, it's a thirty-five-year friendship, guys. I didn't realize I was unloading on him things I'd kept to myself. So, first of all I want to apologize to Meyer, and to the rest of you gentlemen, for going over your heads."

Voices overlapped in full understanding. Hands were waved, legs crossed and uncrossed, cigarettes lit.

"For us, the present government is a blessing," Di Constanzo continued; the others piped down. "This law allowing a casino in any new hotel that costs over a million bucks to build is great, Cuban unions finance part of the deal, the twenty-five thousand down payment for an operation permit and the two thousand monthly fee are pretty cheap, labor regulations make us legit here, police are cooperative, hundreds of thousands of tourists flood in, and the result of it all is: We're making a bundle. It's too good to be true, or to last. We move from our places to the casinos, pick up a broad, see a show, then go back to our places. We never leave a small section of the city, except to take a plane at the airport. But whoever cares to ask finds out that a rebellion is in full swing, that people on both sides are getting killed, and that the government is losing the fight. And I don't base my opinion only on personal observation."

Di Constanzo paused to light a cigarette, dragged on it, then leaned back. As he resumed speaking, puffs of smoke came out with the first words.

"Pan American Protective Service, besides transporting money and securities, runs a private investigations branch with agents all over the country. It has good contacts with the CIA, the FBI, the Cuban government, police brass. Maybe it has some people with the rebels as well, I don't know for sure. Well, once I got back from New York, I ordered a survey of the political situation here from them. A month later one of their guys dropped in with a sixty-two-page report and a two-gee bill."

"Sixty-two pages?" an amazed Wilbur Clark asked.

"Sixty-two, Lefty."

"How about that," Clark quipped. "For me Cuban politics couldn't fill three pages."

Everyone shared a laugh.

"If I had known we were going to debate this, I would've brought it with me," Di Constanzo said, making it clearer that he had been hit below the belt. "But everything is considered, and it adds up like this: The government controls the western provinces and one named Cam . . . something."

"Camagüey," Lansky volunteered with a condescending smile.

"Right. In Las Villas, rebel actions are increasing; in Oriente the government's no longer in charge. Ninety percent of Oriente is either in rebel hands or a free-fire zone; guerrillas collect taxes from sugar factories and big landowners, name provisional mayors, open up schools in the mountains, you name it. Batista controls cities and big towns where bombs go off at night, there're blackouts, shoot-outs, corpses line the streets. What the government still holds is by force. Except for his cronies, almost everybody is against Batista: businessmen, lawyers, priests, Rotarians, Lions, Freemasons, students, doctors, terrified mothers, journalists, every-fucking-body. This coming election—November 3, right?—won't change a thing; even snotty kids know it'll be a comedy."

"And?" Trafficante made it sound patient.

"And . . . in six months, a year maybe," Di Constanzo pressed on, "a change seems inevitable. Either the Army over-throws the new president or the rebels win the war, but an anti-Batista administration will be in power. Can anyone be sure that our concessions will last? Suppose they do—will we keep operating tax-free? Get fresh financing from Cuban unions if new labor leaders are elected? I don't have definite, clear-cut answers to these questions, and that's why I think it would be best to wait, see how the next rulers react to our line of work. And those are my worries, in a nutshell."

"Thank you, Nick," Lansky said as he pressed a button close to his right hand. The maître d' showed up and the boss asked for two Alka-Seltzers in half a glass of mineral water. The man scrawled orders for coffee, cordials, cigarettes, then departed. In the ensuing pause, some discussed weather and sports. Not Nick Di Constanzo, though, who stared at the ceiling as if it were the Sistine Chapel's. Santos Trafficante also remained silent, and examined the toecap of his shoes through the thick glasses that corrected his advanced myopia. The maître d' came back, followed by a waiter pushing a wheeled table. Having served everything, both employees left.

"You believe Batista's finished?" Lansky asked Di Constanzo after swallowing most of his antacid and belching.

"Yes, Meyer. I'm sorry—I know he's a lifelong friend of yours, and that thanks to him we're in business here, but all that mustn't make us close our eyes to reality."

Lansky turned to Grouse. "Marvin, you share Nick's opinion?"

Grouse had his noncommittal response ready. "I never get to first base in politics, Mr. Lansky. Maybe Nick is right, I don't know."

"What's your view, Santos?"

Trafficante raised his eyes, crossed his legs, then brushed a lock of straight hair from his forehead with an unconscious movement. His father had bequeathed him the leadership of Tampa's organized crime after having taught him how to restrain ambitions, make deals, share influences, and escape legal nets like an eel. He would have been the valedictorian of his class, had a class existed, and his brains had propelled him to the national hierarchy as the Florida representative. Following Anastasia's murder on October 28, 1957, he had asked for the floor at the Appalachin crime convention and speculated that maybe those interested in wresting casino gambling in Cuba from the hands of Lansky and Costello might share the fortune of the executed executioner. Frank Hogan, district attorney in the Anastasia murder trial, sub-poenaed Trafficante. Under oath, the head of Casino Deauville expressed his dismay over the assassination and his total ignorance of motives.

"I wrote off Batista last March, when American arms sales stopped," Trafficante said. "But I believe that whoever comes after him will respect our interests. Army brass takes over, everything will stay just like it is; rebels win, same thing. Tourism is the second industry here; no government or union will fuck with investors that build modern hotels, create jobs for the natives, and bring in thousands of tourists who leave their dough here. We ought to expand now."

"I see. Joe?"

"I share Santos's view, Mr. Lansky," was Bischoff's succinct reply.

Lansky sipped the remaining digestive, placed the glass on a coffee table, and carried on with his survey.

"Lefty?"

The Las Vegas veteran sighed, then shook his head as if reluctant to express what he was about to say. "Jesus, Meyer, this is paradise! Money rolls in by the truckloads. I still can't believe my place recovered installation costs, seventy-five grand, in the first two nights! Climate is nice, dames are gorgeous—I wouldn't like to leave, ever. But suppose the next government gets messy, huh? A fifty or sixty percent tax on profits would affect us, 'cause capital recovery is based on present profit levels. Even if we keep double sets of books we'd have to bribe a lot of people, which hurts profits too. I mean, what do we lose if we wait one more year? See what happens before committing such a bundle?"

"Okay. Tom?" Lansky said.

"I think Nick may be right," Magenty began. "Nothing seems to stop the rebels, but the fact that our government cut off military supplies in March clinched it for me. Chances are Dulles advised Ike to sever ties with Batista to win points with the opposition. I've been told Cuban Army buyers are roaming the world purchasing Sea Fury planes from the British, rifles from Trujillo, Uzis from the Israelis. . . ."

"So?" Lansky pressed on. He didn't want the weapons issue aired. Nobody in the room knew that he had arranged the contacts with Tel Aviv arms dealers and was getting commissions from them.

"Perhaps we should wait a while, Mr. Lansky," Magenty concluded.

"Yeah, well, let's take a count," Lansky said. "Nick, Lefty, and Tom don't think this is the right time; Santos wants to go ahead, an opinion shared by Joe and Eddie. Isn't that so, Eddie?"

Galuzzo nodded gravely when all eyes focused on him.

"Marvin hasn't got an opinion. So, it's three against, three for, one undecided," Lansky summarized. Then he lit a cigarette, blew out smoke, and, while looking at the gray sky, devoted a few seconds to remembering that one of the prerequisites of leadership was to inure oneself to criticism. So once again he coolly pondered the issue from every possible angle as, moving somehow among his neurons, business considerations beat down the anger of having had his authority challenged. Those present knew from experience he'd give his reasons before taking sides.

"I have faith in this country," he began. "Cuba will become the U.S. playground because of its beaches, casinos, hookers, music, and national spirit. I understand Nick, but I side with Santos, Joe, and Eddie. Who wins is irrelevant in these little wars, because all the winners want is to become millionaires as quickly as they can. And to get there they can do many things, except one: upset Uncle Sam. Cuban politicians have got to respect, protect, and attract American capital. But ours is in casinos and hotels. Under a different government the damn moralists, or those who pretend to be so, will preach that gambling corrupts people, and they'll stand in our way. I don't buy that, but even if it's true, the Cubans already were pretty corrupted when we got here."

Lansky dragged on the cigarette. He forced twin streams of smoke out through his nostrils as he snuffed the butt in the ashtray.

"When we opened the Parisién, the four Cuban-owned casinos were always crammed. Besides, there was the weekly state lottery, plus four numbers rackets with daily draws in Havana. Now these same four *boliteros* draw three times a day—can you believe it? There were horses, dogs, cockfights, and jai alai. Bets on baseball games and prizefights were anybody's guess. Newspapers raffled homes and cars, soap manufacturers hid prizes in the damn bars, Havana was choking on pinball machines, and if two Cubans had a drink in a bar, they rolled dice to decide who would pick up the check. At home, people played every conceivable game, from dominoes and bingo to poker. Street punks bet on nearly everything: the last number on the plates of the next car to cruise by, a cop's badge number, you name it. The whole fucking country gambled, for Chrissake! Right now, here in Havana, you know my estimate for the World Series winner? A dollar per person, believe it or not. And they bet another dollar on each new game. Did we corrupt them in a couple of years? Don't make me laugh."

But Lansky smiled and shook his head so facetiously to affect disbelief that the others chuckled.

"However, we should look far ahead. The next political bosses might label us the Mafiosi, the gangsters. Maybe they want to score with Hoover and deport some of us, repeat what they did to Lucky in '49, on trumped-up charges, of course. In fact, word is the arms embargo is our fault. The old faggot is mad because he can no longer get at us, so he asked Ike to sever ties with the present government. Batista refuses to budge, but if he finds himself in a very tight spot, has to negotiate, he'd give us time to readjust, name figureheads."

Marvin Grouse saw the scale tilt and started nodding in agreement every few seconds. By showing that he was going along with Lansky's view, he hoped to hide from everybody the fact that ten minutes earlier his boss's defiance had terrified him. Nick Di Constanzo groaned inwardly; the about-face of his newly appointed hall supervisor badly dented the respect he felt for the guy.

"So, maybe it's not such a bad idea to wait six more months before making a decision on expansion," Lansky concluded. "The winter season will be over, the next president will have ruled for a few months, or, if Nick's predictions come true, either the military or the rebels will be in power. In the meantime, we ought to bring in some new faces, people with a clean sheet who front for us. If a crusade against the bad guys were organized, they'd be in the clear. Whaddaya think?"

During the brief silence that followed, all eyes focused on Trafficante.

"Okay," the Deauville boss said. Joe Bischoff said he was in agreement. Eddie Galuzzo nodded for the second time.

Approving comments by Di Constanzo closed the subject. Stress dissolved into small talk. Then Lansky announced his intention of taking a nap. The rest got up to leave.

. . .

The debriefing session was taking place at a bar which was a rather extended enticement to liquor ingestion. Ninety feet long—seventy-five in a straight line parallel to Ánimas Street, the rest at right angles on both ends—it offered rotating ebony stools, a polished brass rail, and spittoons to its carefree clientele. For years the mahogany top had been saturated with spills of all kinds of distilled products, plus overflows of soda pops, water, and beer, that barmen had wiped clean a million times, unwittingly giving it a delicate gloss. Behind the bar were six stainless-steel sinks, ice chests, space for empty bottles, and shelves for cigars, cigarettes, matches, and condoms.

Moving on wooden platforms laid between the sinks and an enormous eighteen-door refrigerator on whose top stood over a thousand bottles, the bartenders revealed a sense of space comparable to that possessed by blind people. Among the multitude of possible choices, their hands would immediately close on the particular liquor ordered, no small feat considering that only three or four bottles of each brand were kept over the backbar. Among connoisseurs, Sloppy Joe's was rated the best-stocked bar in Cuba, and should an argument demand immediate elucidation, the antagonists would visit the place and ask for a bottle of Tres Raposos brandy or Glommen's aquavit. These were rare items, so the barman would snoop around for a few seconds, then flex his arm suddenly and settle the dispute.

At the corner farthest from the Zulueta entrance, Green Chips made his report in a normal tone, forearms resting on the counter, a Tres Ceros-and-soda highball in front of him. To his left, Arturo Heller and Melchor Loredo, wearing lousy suits, held *Cuba libres*. To his right, the smoke spiraling from a La Corona cigarette added another gray tone to Mariano Contreras's hair. Fermín Rodríguez had his eyes on the Bauzá cigar that he spun between thumb and forefinger. They all seemed deeply engrossed in what was being recounted, and their glasses remained almost full.

". . . the guards, like always. One by the front door, another by the lobby door, the third by the nightclub door, the fourth moving around. They never leave their posts except to take a leak, and then the guy making the rounds stands in the empty spot. Oh, I forgot, there was a new hall supervisor; maybe the other guy is on vacation or sick, I don't know. Around one-fifteen both cashiers start their shop-closing routine and right then the front-door guard moves a little to his left. . . ."

Valentín Rancaño—Meringue in Havana gaming circles—was recounting his fourth reconnaissance of the Casino de Capri in three months. The one-hundred-by-forty-foot rectangle behind those at the bar was packed with customers gabbing loudly to make themselves heard. The square-shaped central columns and the walls were covered with photographs of visiting celebrities, most of them in black and white, the ones of screen stars colored in with brush strokes. Wooden-bladed ceiling fans circulated the fresh air flowing in through gratings that faced the sidewalks, thus cooling off patrons, waiters, and discreet peddlers of maracas, porno photos, lottery tickets, hand-woven palm leaf hats, and little Cuban flags.

Although tourism was Sloppy Joe's main source of income, enough locals had made it their favorite watering hole to provide a vernacular atmosphere. Wearing starched white drill trousers and linen guayaberas, as they downed rum or ice-cold beer, munched olives, roasted peanuts, or slices of cheese, most Cuban male customers swapped jokes and made wild boasts about their sexual prowess in a Spanish sprinkled with slang.

A wide diversity of professions, cultures, personal beliefs, and political ideas spawned affinities among lawyers and judges, wooing couples, politicians exchanging sophisms, hardened whores counseling their nubile replacements, tourist guides talking shop. Contrasts also stood out: a classical composer playing castanets, a 105-pound jockey sitting by a retired 240-pound heavyweight prizefighter, an eight-year-old boy guiding a blind elderly beggar, a bookie chatting to a priest in lay clothes, poets rhapsodizing over the raw expressiveness of an illiterate marijuana pusher, a court clerk playing dice with a professional pickpocket. The passage of time and liquor consumption made some initial attractions evolve into rejections, just as certain early repulsions became friendships in the long run. All this, plus the unmistakable smell of burning Cuban cigars and cigarettes, and the taste of *Cuba libres, mojitos,* and daiquiris, created a tangible, authentic Cuban environment which attracted inquisitive foreigners looking for the true thing.

". . . then this American looks like a carrot came over and said they were closing in a few minutes and that he liked my system—"

"Damn it, Meringue!" Contreras said through clenched teeth, holding back fury.

"What's the matter, Ox? Damn who?" the scout retorted.

"I told you not to attract attention, buddy."

"Yeah, and you gave me sixty pesos. How the hell you think I can stretch sixty pesos for nearly three hours if I don't play it right? Give me some leeway, for God's sake."

There was a moment of silence among the group. Contreras clicked his tongue, shook his head resignedly, then sipped from his glass.

"What else did the guy say?" Heller asked.

"Nothing else," Meringue continued. "I picked up my chips and went to cash them in. The safe was closed, both briefcases ready. I guess they keep a small fund there and the rest of the mazuma goes up. The money ride after closing time was the same as always."

"We don't know what goes on when a high roller plays after hours," the bald man said.

"Can't find out everything, Gallego," Contreras butted in. "Besides, the supervisor can write a check if the sucker hits the jackpot and there's not enough cash on hand."

A fresh pause developed. The conspirators looked the place over as they drank and smoked. There were bursts of laughter, bear hugs, and backslaps among a nearby group. The frantic rattling of dice inside leather dice cups could be heard. Heated arguments went on about the fourth World Series game, which had taken place that Sunday, October 5, in New York.

"Stupid," a miffed Heller muttered.

"Who?" Loredo asked.

Heller tilted his head to the side, to a Milwaukee fan basking in his team's victory. The others decided to take a break.

"Milwaukee didn't win the game, the Yankees lost it. Siebern lost it, not the Yankees," Heller fumed.

"Yeah, the poor guy had a bad day," Loredo said as he returned his empty glass to the bar.

"'Poor guy'? 'Bad day'? C'mon, Wheel, you know better than that. Right now the motherfucker is counting the dough the fixer gave him. Any eight-year-old kid on my block would've fielded Schoendienst's fly in the sixth; not Siebern—

he 'got confused' and turned it into a triple. Same thing with Spahn's fly in the seventh: another hit. In the eighth he lost Logan's liner and it went for a double. Anybody can bungle it, but three straight errors by a Major League left fielder in the same game? Fuck off, man."

"Nah, it's too much, Abo," Meringue said. "Player who sells out drops one ball, not three. They'd kill him."

"Hey, buddy, those three errors gave Milwaukee three runs," a scowling Heller said. "I guess tonight he'll bunk with New York's police chief to stay alive. Can you imagine how much dough changed hands on account of Siebern's 'bad day'?"

Sipping their drinks, Contreras and Fermín kept aloof from the discussion.

"How's Liberata?" the gray-haired man asked.

Fermín smiled before replying. "I came straight from her place. Had lunch with her today. She's fine."

Contreras nodded, sighed, then addressed the whole group. "Okay, gentlemen, let's get back to business. Tonight I'll introduce myself at the casino; tomorrow we go in. The day the Series is over we make our move. The least you go out, the better; cops are edgy with so many bombs and get nasty when they see two or three men together in the streets."

He drained his glass and placed it on the bartop, then inspected the other four jailbirds in a huge mirror over the refrigerator. Did those guys possess the right mix of experience, skill, courage, and ambition to pull off the job? He wasn't sure, but they were the best he knew.

"Abo, call me at eight tomorrow morning."

"Sharp," acquiesced the youngest with a smile.

"Okay, fellows, see you."

It was 5:32 P.M.

...

Four and a half hours later, Contreras was pacing around Casino de Capri, looking hesitant. He wore a three-piece, ten-year-old brown suit custom-made for someone else from excellent cashmere. In his left hand he held a Borsalino trilby manufactured in 1935; in his right, a superb Cinco Vegas cigar burned evenly.

Interested observation was nothing out of the ordinary in the casino. Frequently people went in, looked around, then left without betting a penny. Well aware that curiosity is the first encouraging sign, casino managers restricted onlookers only on packed evenings. For the past months, though, there hadn't been many night crawlers in Havana.

Grouse, Jimmy Brun, and the guards had noticed the quaint-looking Contreras. The man's obvious lack of sophistication, old-fashioned clothing, and wince of mild repugnance intrigued them. They suspected him of being a square snooping around before pulling his cash out.

After brief stops at the baccarat, craps, and blackjack tables, Contreras spent almost half an hour keenly observing the four roulettes. Suddenly, as if he had just made a decision, he lifted his head and gazed about, searching for someone or something, then approached the cashier's glassed-in box. A man too young to look after so much money smiled at him.

"May I be of assistance to you, sir?" the cashier said in Spanish, his accent barely noticeable.

"Yeah, I'd like to talk to the owner of this joint."

The cashier called a guard, who led Contreras to Marvin Grouse. The hall supervisor summoned José Guzmán, a Cuban inspector who dropped out of George Washington University's law school in 1952, spoke good English, and served as unofficial interpreter when necessary.

"My name is Romualdo Peraza, at your service," said Contreras as he shook hands with both men.

"It's a pleasure to make your acquaintance, señor," Grouse said. "I'm Marvin Grouse. What can I do for you?"

"My son wants to gamble here."

"Is that so?"

"We live in Pinar del Río. I own a thirty-hectare tobacco plantation in Hoyo de Monterrey. My son is an invalid—polio."

A hound sniffing a raw sirloin steak wouldn't have drooled more than Guzmán. He had enough economic awareness to infer that thirty hectares of top-quality Cuban tobacco yielded several hundred thousand pesos per year. After interpreting he added, in a low tone and in English, "Roughneck's loaded."

"Sorry about your son, señor," Grouse said with just a little bit of interest. "How old is he?"

"Twenty-nine."

"I ask because we can't allow minors on the premises. But go on, please, go on."

Contreras scratched the tip of his nose, looked around, and with his left arm took in the whole casino. "You are the only winner here, Señor Grouse. In the short run, somebody may take a few thousand from you; in the long run, you always make a profit. But I never deny my son something he enjoys. All he's got is his mother, me, a wheelchair, and the misfortune of being a born gambler—poker, bridge, dominoes, dice, gin rummy, you name it. At this time of the year I always bring him to Havana for his roulette tour and he throws away a few thousand. He was down on his luck at the Tropicana last year. Now he wants to give it a try here and stay at the next-door hotel. But I have him at my sister's because I need to strike a deal with you first."

"A deal, señor?"

"That's right. I'll give him five hundred pesos every evening, for as long as we're here. Perhaps he'll have a hundred left from the previous evening, or he might have won five hundred and have a thousand on him, but I'll give him another five hundred just the same; that's our agreement. But there're evenings when he loses everything half an hour after starting to play and then he . . . gets nasty. Asks the house for a loan, wants to cash a check or pawn his watch or diamond ring, and I can't do a thing 'cause he suffers spasmodic seizures if I interfere, can't breathe. So, my request is, if he runs out of money, you don't loan him any or accept one of his checks or his jewels as a deposit. When the house firmly turns him down, he waits for the next day under a cloud, but in good health. That's the deal I need to make, to have peace and quiet when I bring my son here."

Marvin Grouse hadn't interrupted out of politeness. Throughout his adult life he had heard similar requests dozens of times, always due to the invalidism, dipsomania, hysteria, mental retardation, arteriosclerosis, or just plain stupidity of rich people. Every professional knew how to treat these appeals: with acceptance, if the individual's bearing did not impose a deplorable sight on the clientele. If it did, then the approach was to suggest sending a dealer and an inspector equipped with what was necessary to the individual's home.

Categorical refusal occurred only when earnings wouldn't cover the cost of the second option. For Grouse, a young and lucid polio victim who might lose up to five hundred daily for ten or fifteen days was an adorable client, accepting his father's conditions a pleasant duty. And looking ahead, Grouse surmised that someday square pop would meet his Creator and his son would become a rich man with a taste for roulette. Grouse had the inescapable duty of doing everything within his reach to gain the invalid's confidence.

"This house is honored by your choice, señor," he said. "Your terms are within our code of ethics, so we agree to your request."

Guzmán interpreted.

"Well, I'm glad to hear that."

"You have our full understanding. Your son will gamble at his ease here. Since Señor Guzmán interpreted for us, I'll entrust him with welcoming you on your first evening and escorting you to the table of your choice. I shall personally instruct dealers on how to behave with your son."

"I'll appreciate that. You know, he's superstitious and never sits at the table before ten, but we'll arrive on the dot."

"Wonderful. Did you say you wanted to stay at the Capri?"

"That's exactly what I want, to spare ourselves the inconvenience of daily taxi rides."

"Have you made a reservation?"

"No."

"Give this card to the desk clerk when you arrive."

"Thank you, Mr. Grouse."

With a conciliatory smile, the tobacco grower reached for Grouse's card, the casino's monogram embossed on it. He slipped it inside his jacket's breast pocket, nailed the cigar with his left-side incisors, shook hands with both men, and left.

Contreras took a taxi and asked the driver to drop him at Twenty-third and Twelfth; he twice checked that he wasn't being followed during the ride. The streets were deserted; their numerous blinking neon signs seemed a waste of money. Few cars cruised by and there were no straphangers on the buses. Unbelievable for a Sunday evening, Contreras concluded.

Where he got out of the car, an old man in a cheap muslin suit and a straw hat was shouting a monotonous "Hot" time and time again, by which he meant renowned spicy tamales, which he was keeping warm in a can by his feet. Contreras ordered two, dropped the cigar stub, and entered the Veintitrés y Doce bar and restaurant. He pulled a chair out from under a square wooden table covered with a red checkered tablecloth, asked for a plate, a fork, and a beer, then dined, deep in thought. Twenty minutes later, after leaving the place, he lit up and strolled down Twelfth toward the sea. With his jacket unbuttoned, the cigarette dangling from his lips, hands thrust deep into the pockets of his trousers, and a sad look on his face, Contreras occasionally stopped at shop windows to watch the tenuous reflections in the glass and make sure no one was following him.

At Seventeenth Street he stepped on the butt and turned right. His old Chevy was parked by the curb, mid-block. He unlocked the driver door and slipped behind the wheel. One more time he peered at both sidewalks, then turned off his worried-man mask. A faraway explosion was heard. He ran his tongue over his lips, started the engine, and released the emergency brake. Then Contreras breathed a long sigh of relief, shifted from neutral to first, and drove to Los Pinos with the kind of self-confidence found in prophets who believe themselves infallible.

...

The small hurricane that had traversed central Cuba the day before made the sky over Havana exceptionally blue on October 6, a Monday.

At a quarter past eleven, Mariano Contreras and Arturo Heller arrived at the Capri Hotel in a '54 Packard cab. The driver helped the older man unfold a huge chrome-and-leather wheelchair and ease the invalid onto it. The doorman and the bellboy lifted the vehicle up the steps to the main entrance, propelled it into the lobby, and positioned it by a column. The disabled man kept smiling broadly all the time. *He's over it,* the bellboy thought as he went out again to haul in three old, genuine-leather suitcases, which he placed on a cart. Contreras paid the cabbie, tipped the doorman, and went in. Then he grabbed the wheelchair's handlebars and ambled to the desk.

With the palms of his hands on the marble countertop, the reception-desk clerk smarmily asked whether he could be of assistance. Contreras handed him Grouse's card and requested a room on the fourth floor. Frowning, the clerk checked a clipboard. By pulling and pushing the nickel-plated rings protruding from both wheels, Heller turned to inspect the high columns, the decor, and the few scattered guests waiting for someone or just passing time in comfortable armchairs. When the clerk raised his eyes from the clipboard, he looked befuddled. Contreras guessed something was wrong.

"Perhaps the gentlemen would rather stay in an upper floor. We have rooms with a breathtaking ocean view."

"Nothing available on the fourth?" Contreras wanted to know.

"Oh, yes, excellent suites," the embarrassed clerk said. "But all have two levels, living room down and bedroom up. There are ten or twelve steps in the staircase, and one turn."

"I see. You hear that, Tony?"

Heller had paid attention to the brief exchange. "It has to be on the fourth floor," he insisted with a surly look.

Contreras, trying to sound reasonable: "Son, you're too heavy for me to carry you up."

"You know four is my lucky number."

Clenching his jaws, the irritated father faced the attendant. "It's, uh . . . gambler's superstition. How could we . . . ?"

"Are there couches in the living room?" the son butted in.

"Yes, sir. Two in each suite," the clerk eagerly said. "And several armchairs."

"No problem then. I'll sleep on a couch."

"But, son, the toilet . . ."

"There's a small bathroom in the living room," the attendant explained. "For visitors, you know."

"Perfect. Fill in the cards, Dad."

With the laborious, slow handwriting of a poorly educated person, Contreras filled in two cards with the names Romualdo Peraza and Antonio Peraza, residents of Mantua, Pinar del Río. The clerk asked the approximate duration of their stay, summoned the bellboy, and handed him a key.

The elevator's soft dings, clicks, and hisses could be heard on the way up. The bellhop opened the front door of suite 406, tripped a switch, then rolled the baggage cart in. The guests entered a well-furnished living room that showed how impersonal interior decorators can get when compelled to please all kinds of tastes. There were two couches—one in black, the other in red—two marble-topped coffee tables, four armchairs, a writing desk, and side tables supporting lamps, ashtrays, and a phone. An ebony female statuette stood on a white marble pedestal. An expensive unit combining television, radio, and record player faced the red couch and two of the armchairs. Two Monet prints adorned opposing walls.

Contreras ambled to the drapes opposite the front door, parted them, gazed down at a section of N Street through an aluminum-encased glass window. Across the street, four- and five-story apartment buildings, cars by the curb, people on the sidewalk. A few strides to his left he found a door that opened into a fully equipped small bathroom, minus bathtub.

Following the bellboy upstairs, he came upon twin beds separated by a nightstand with a telephone extension, a second radio, an ashtray, and night lamps. There were a three-drawer dresser, two armchairs, a sliding-door closet, and a huge bathroom. The whole suite had wall-to-wall carpeting.

Back in the living room, under the paralytic's impatient stare, the attendant hauled the baggage up, instructed the hillbillies on how the safety latch worked, handed over the key, and closed the door behind him after pocketing a one-peso bill stripped from a fat roll.

The guests locked eyes and smiled. Heller stood up, faked the heel tapping of an Andalusian dance, and roared with laughter. Contreras demanded silence by frantically shushing on his forefinger.

"C'mon, pop, give me a break. Polio victims do laugh."

"Shit, Abo, everything is a joke to you."

"Okay, okay, the jig is up. Just kidding," he said, holding up his hands innocently.

"You shouldn't have pushed so hard for the fourth floor. Clerk might wonder."

"You said we should try to get a room on this floor."

"Yeah, but I didn't know there were fucking stairs in all the suites. A man in a wheelchair shouldn't stay here."

"It's done. Forget about it," Abo said, staring at the contraption. "By the way, does this thing have to be so big? This is for a four-hundred-pound fatso."

"Abo, stop talking shit. You know why."

Heller sighed, took off his white guayabera, dropped it carelessly on a coffee table, and keeled over onto the red couch. Contreras loosened the knot of his tie before removing his jacket and draping it over the back of an armchair.

"Hey, Ox, let's take the blanket to the casino," Heller said. "It's really hard not to move my legs."

"Okay," Contreras said vaguely, easing himself onto the other end of the red couch. Heller rose to his feet and turned on the TV. In full concentration, his partner watched as the screen filled with three white diagonal lines on a gray background. Suddenly Contreras jerked to his feet, hurried to the phone, and asked the operator for the desk.

"Desk."

"I'm in room 406. Are you the young man we talked to a few minutes ago?"

"Yes . . . Señor . . ."

Contreras could picture the desk clerk picking up the blue cards.

". . . Peraza," the man said finally. "What can I do for you?"

"Would you be so kind as to send up some sort of small chair or stool my son can shower on?"

"Oh, sure, Señor Peraza. No problem. I'll explain the situation to the housekeeper. It might take a few minutes, but you'll have it in a little while."

"Thanks."

Contreras hung up and faced his smiling partner.

"Brainy guy," the younger man said.

"A jerk's what I am. How could this escape all of us? Even in a bathtub, an invalid has to sit. Missing this kind of detail makes you a loser."

"Yeah. Well, now it's fixed. The game starts in a few minutes and I'm hungry. How about you?"

"I had an early breakfast."

"Okay, let's order."

As the first views of Yankee Stadium were shown, Heller called room service. At 12:30, a table with collapsible sides was wheeled in. While watching the game the guests had rice, well-done beefsteaks, French fries, tomato salad, white bread, beers, caramel custard, and espresso, all off gold-rimmed china.

In the bottom of the third, Gil McDougald hit the third pitch into the screen alongside the left field foul pole for a home run to put the Yankees in front. The top of the fourth was starting when a young, attractive cleaning lady brought a small revolving metal stool with four rubber-tipped legs. After placing it in the shower stall, she came out, smiling sheepishly. Her attempt to control her curiosity about the young paralytic failed, and she stole a look. The woman took her tip pondering the irony that such a sexy-looking hunk should be confined to a wheelchair.

Contreras rolled the table out and they watched the rest of the game from the red couch, their legs outstretched. In the top of the sixth, the Braves threatened when Bruton singled over Kubek's head, but Elston Howard made a spectacular tumbling catch of Schoendienst's fly to short left center and doubled up Bruton, who had rounded second.

The New Yorkers retaliated in the bottom of the same inning. Bauer singled between third and shortstop, Jerry Lumpe fouled out, and Mantle hit a Texas leaguer, moving Bauer to third. Berra doubled into right field, scoring Bauer and sending Mantle to third. Howard was intentionally passed, and with bases full Skowron singled to right and Mantle scored.

Manager Fred Haney marched to the mound, probably told Burdette that it wasn't his day, then replaced him with Juan Pizarro. McDougald was given a ground-rule double when Covington lost his fly in the sun and the ball landed in the visiting team's bullpen in deep left field, scoring Berra and Howard as Skowron stopped at third. Kubek struck out, but Bob Turley contributed with a single to left, scoring Skowron and McDougald.

"Seems to me we'll sleep here tonight," Heller said.

Contreras nodded soberly. If the Manhattan Mules won, they would have nothing to do on Tuesday while the teams traveled back to Milwaukee to decide the Series in the sixth or seventh game. The date of the robbery moved according to each game's outcome, as a prolonged Series fueled more bets. Contreras reckoned that a tie after six games might pile up $500,000 in the main collecting office, located sixty yards and nine steps away, on the mezzanine between the Capri's fourth and fifth floors.

Restraint was his responsibility. The rest of the team wanted to highball it, arguing every conceivable reason except the most pressing: to get their hides off the line. He stole a glance at Heller. The man was living the foolish years most males go through. Overconfident, irresponsible, hoping to screw the brains out of every beautiful broad who crossed his path. Contreras had forced him to plan ahead on what to do after the hit. In his youth he had behaved pretty much like Heller; maybe it was why he felt some kind of parental obligation to the gang's youngest. These days Contreras found himself tired of masking his insecurity beneath a veneer of tough-guy bluntness. Looking forward to his retirement, he admitted to himself having replaced raw courage with common sense, to having honed his precision to allow for slower reflexes. But the most important thing he had learned in his life was that you never trust anyone.

Heller, looking at the screen with the boredom brought on by an insurmountable lead, reflected on his part. He was a bundle of contradictions: the experienced gambler whose intelligence was sporadically nullified by passion, an expert on probabilities with a psychic streak. He closed his eyelids, and the sharply delineated layout of a roulette table popped into his mind.

After a minute he spied the older man out of the corner of his eye. It saddened him to watch Contreras writing anything, like at the reception desk. Ignorant people shamed Heller, but those among them who were extremely clever saddened him. He wondered how Contreras had learned to read and write. Taboo subject, the kind of thing you never asked. The team's leader could read fast enough, but when it came to writing . . . Well, reading was the truly essential thing, and the man had a mind like a steel trap. Once he had read something truly significant to him, it would stay in his mind forever. Heller felt a little drowsy and yawned prodigiously.

"I'm gonna take a nap, Ox. You want me to turn it off?"

"No. I'll watch it to the end."

Heller was sound asleep on the black couch, his clothes hanging untidily on the wheelchair, by the time Contreras turned the set off and went upstairs. He divided the contents of two suitcases between the closet and the dresser. Except for new underwear, everything else came from pawnshops. The third suitcase was stored unopened in the closet. Back in the lower level, he transferred the "Do Not Disturb" sign on the doorknob to the outside, turned the safety latch, and climbed the stairs again.

Contreras undressed, hung his clothes, took a shower, then lay in bed. For a little over an hour he reviewed the months of planning in search of a loose end, any unseen omission like the bathing stool. He even indulged in a measure of self-criticism and acknowledged that he was losing his cool, taking it out on others, like the day before yesterday with Wheel, yesterday with Meringue. Contreras had learned from experience that the touchstones for leading men were to never lose your temper, and to cajole, not browbeat. He'd have to shoulder the blame for undetected blunders and miscalculations. He'd been hired to do the job, and the casino's internal organization and routines had been painstakingly enumerated to him. Hatching the scheme and finding the right guys were his responsibility. Now it was on, and all his men were firmly committed; there were no major snags, no reason for turning back. His brain started unplugging sections of itself and sleep came only when a feeble sunlight was glowing under the bedroom's drapes.

Heller showered in the living room bath and shortly before 8 P.M. took the stairs and awoke Contreras. They got dressed, ordered and had supper, then watched TV until 9:45, at which time the older man pulled the knot of his tie up and slipped into the jacket of the suit he had worn the previous evening. Heller was in a light gray suit. A pin crowned with a pearl fastened a tie with diagonal stripes in different shades of green to the front of his white, long-sleeved dress shirt. Strapped to his left wrist was a beautiful, solid-gold watch. On his left ring finger an impressive diamond set in gold sparkled.

While Contreras fought off a smile, Heller squatted and jumped several times, made rapid dance steps for half a minute, then marched into the toilet to urinate. Contreras went upstairs and returned with a coffee-colored blanket. Heller came back to the living room and eased himself onto the wheelchair, cursing the odd things he had to put up with to make a living. He spread the blanket over his thighs and legs.

"Ready?" Contreras asked.

"Ready."

José Guzmán saw both men coming in through the lobby door at 10:02 P.M. and approached them with his best smile. He shook hands with Contreras, then introduced himself to the disabled man and invited him to choose a table. Several clients noticed the offbeat newcomers, and even those lost in the whims of chance briefly watched the silent progression of the smiling, eager paralytic and his lugubrious companion. Heller opted for the same roulette table at which Valentín Rancaño had conducted his reconnaissance, and with terse greetings acknowledged the bald insurance agent and the aged landlord playing at it. Guzmán whispered something to the dealer. Contreras bought five hundred pesos of blue chips, Heller stacked them in front of himself, adjusted his distance by maneuvering the wheelchair, and, assisted by Contreras in what escaped his reach, placed his first bet.

By 12:45 A.M. all Heller had left were fifty pesos. A mortician from Vermont and a Mexican fiddler had replaced the insurance man and the landlord. Six different dealers had turned the wheel and Contreras's cigar, though now a smelly butt, still survived between the fingers of his left hand. Disappointed with his poor results and annoyed at the forced immobility, Heller felt the pressure of his full bladder cutting the night short. He positioned the remaining chips on number 20, turned a little, looked up at Contreras, and spoke as if on the fringe of collapse, a drop of hysteria in his voice.

"Dad, I need some fresh air."

He faked a light gasping, felt stared at. Contreras frowned and leaned over Heller's right shoulder as he waited for the end of the play. The ivory ball lost speed, fell into the revolving wheel, jumped between canoes, and came to rest in one of them.

"*Veinte negro;* twenty black," the dealer said.

Heller lost control and almost jerked to his feet, but Contreras gripped his shoulder and brought him back to his role. The younger man's panting was as genuine as his smile.

"Congratulations, son," the father said unemotionally, as the rake placed in front of the amazed gambler chips worth 1,750 pesos.

Three

At first sight, Elias Naguib brought to mind a huge, expensively wrapped parcel. Excellent suits in quiet tones softened the impression made by 206 pounds unevenly squeezed into a five-foot-five-inch frame with fifty-three years of wear and tear. Above his deeply lined forehead, close-cropped curly hair evolved from ash-gray in front to white on the back of his neck. Bushy black eyebrows and permanent dark bags framed hazel eyes that never tired of calmly gazing around, taking in people and objects. Dating from the time he had started using a dental prosthesis, Naguib had developed the tic of pressing together his thin lips every minute or so.

Colonel Orlando Grava, general inspector of the Cuban police and chief of the Bureau of Investigations, had the demeanor of a politician campaigning for reelection. His flashing dark eyes, smooth white skin, wavy and combed-back dark hair, and frequent smiles made up for his plump physique. His jacket's long narrow lapels moderated the contrast between his youthful-looking forty-five and his paunch. Police pundits affirmed that, five years earlier, Grava hadn't been able to afford a fake stone for his wife's engagement ring. At present, he reminded people of the church mouse that had found the crown's treasure. A bracelet set with several small brilliants girdled his right wrist, a costly watch was strapped to his left, and the two gold rings on his fingers—an amethyst set in one, an emerald in the other—looked quite expensive. When he wore open-necked shirts, the heavy chain and medal in eighteen-karat gold hanging from his neck made people gawk.

Both men stood by the rectangular mid-room bar of the Havana Biltmore Yacht and Country Club, a huge plush building on the shoreline west of Havana, half a mile from the small coastal town of Santa Fe. The bar was stylishly furnished with precious woods and genuine leather, large seascapes in oil, and two huge eighteenth-century mirrors. Bohemian glassware and a cool temperature were also provided.

The club's select membership included many of the oldest and richest Cuban families. As in all clannish associations, personal wealth and the right sponsors were issues very seriously pondered when making decisions on new acceptances. Grava's application had been turned down a year earlier, and the colonel hoped that Naguib, a member since 1952, would be one of his new sponsors this time. In April his host had started frequently inviting him to the clubhouse for drinks and meals.

The Lebanese sipped mature Cuban rum diluted with bottled spring water; the snobbish cop's favorite tipple was whiskey and soda. No other patrons were present, the discreet bartender had retired as far away as he could, and the two men were talking things over at midday on Tuesday, October 7. Naguib was clinching his first calculated move after a quarter hour of apparently idle chatter.

". . . the sonofabitch's doing bad," he concluded with a self-taught Spanish pronunciation in which the emphatic, guttural accent of his native tongue survived, "so he's trying to make some money by importing cocaine."

"Really?" a surprised Grava exclaimed.

"Now, I don't want you to get me wrong. I've done my share of shady deals and have nothing against smuggling something, or cooking the books to pay less tax. But drugs are different. Marijuana, it's not too bad. But cocaine?"

"I couldn't agree more."

"Right now he has no less than eighty thousand dollars' worth of coke stashed away in his jewelry store's safe."

It looked as though Grava couldn't believe his ears. "Are you sure?" he asked suspiciously.

"Absolutely."

"Something must be done," Grava said, straightening up and looking official. "Thanks for coming forward, Mr. Naguib. You're a responsible citizen."

"I certainly try to be one. Do what you think best. And . . . changing the subject: How are you getting along with the revolutionaries?"

It was his second move. Grava raised his left eyebrow, put the glass to his lips, finished its contents, then signaled for another round. By the time the barman mixed the drinks, refilled the bowl of salted peanuts, and returned to his distant corner, the colonel had his reply ready.

"Here in Havana, the revolutionaries are finished. In Oriente, they still resist the Army's offensive."

Naguib tilted his head, as though in deep thought. Then, after a couple of seconds: "Don't you think . . . I mean, I don't want to pry into other people's affairs, but wouldn't it be prudent for certain folks to make sure they know where the fire escape is?"

"Folks like you?" the Cuban asked with a grin.

For an instant Naguib lifted his eyes to the ceiling and forced a smile as he shook his head. Then he stared at the colonel. "No, not for me, no. I'm a foreigner, I don't hold a position in this administration—I'm fairly certain the rebels don't even know I exist. But I have a friend, a top government official, up to here in this mess"—Naguib's right-hand fingers touched his chin—"who's looking for a small yacht and a passport; you know, his photograph with a different name. He's desperate for a quick way out."

Grava's silence was full of information. Naguib pressed his lips against his dentures and let his gaze slide over the rows of glassware and bottles. He kept talking, a man revealing his innermost thoughts. "The wise man never nails a door shut, because he doesn't knows if he'll have to open it one day. My friend could be wrong, but being cautious won't hurt him. He'll have his yacht to sell whenever he wishes. He can burn the passport if he feels he won't need it . . . but for the moment he keeps his options open. You own a boat?"

"No," replied Grava, letting Naguib carry him along.

"What a shame—the Bureau is so close to the river. Deep-sea fishing is extremely soothing. Ask club members."

Third move.

The colonel sipped from his glass, considering something. "Fishing in the Gulf Stream must be quite an experience," he said at last. "Since I read Hemingway's *The Old Man and the Sea* I've been considering buying a pleasure boat."

"Well, I could try and find out if there's a good one on the market."

"You sell everything?" asked Grava with a fresh smile.

"From microscopes to coffins. The client orders, Elias serves. Reasonable prices, guaranteed quality."

They chuckled before sipping from their glasses. The Lebanese lit a Lucky Strike with a Zippo lighter. Grava popped a few peanuts into his mouth as he pondered the pros and cons of trusting the Lebanese. Naguib closely watched the colonel's facial expressions and determined he had pinpointed the main reason for concern.

"Maybe, if you can afford it, I could buy it in my name, then lease it to you on paper," he said.

Grava nodded reflectively, then said, "Good alternative. What would a medium-sized cruiser cost?"

Naguib pulled down the corners of his mouth, tilted his head, fixed his eyes on the wall behind Grava. "I really don't know. I suppose it depends on when it was built, its length, breadth, type of engine, and the owner's rush." Then, locking eyes with Grava, he made his fourth move. "But keep in mind this cocaine I just told you about. Maybe some American or Mexican would pay sixty for what's worth eighty."

The colonel bit his lower lip and evaded the probing eyes. He never felt comfortable with this man who constantly outfoxed him. The guy was incredible! Recent acquaintances didn't cut deals this way. This wasn't the right manner to address the chief of the Bureau of Investigations, for Chrissake! It was galling! But he begrudgingly admitted that the Moor was right: These were hectic times; the island was in the throes of insurrection. He needed a way out, just in case things took a turn for the worst, so this was one of those moments in which swallowing one's pride was the right thing to do. And he could sell the yacht abroad if, God forbid, the fucking fanatics opposing President Batista forced him to leave Cuba for a few months, until things got back to normal.

"You could be right, you know?" Grava said at last. "The thought would've never occurred to me. I usually have drugs burned."

"Tell you what," Naguib whispered. "You seize the cocaine. I'll try to find a buyer for it. If I manage to sell it, you give me the money and I'll buy you a cabin cruiser in my name. Then we sign a sales contract for you to keep, and a fake lease contract, just in case anyone asks about this new boat of yours."

Grava raised his left eyebrow again. "I don't know, Mr. Naguib. I have to think it over. But if we manage to do what you suggest, my gratitude shall be eternal."

Checkmate, Naguib thought, then waved away the compliment. "I'll consider the score even. I owed you one for the list of consultants."

"That was nothing," the colonel said, smiling distractedly, still immersed in the possibilities opened by this amazing exchange.

"Contreras is good," Naguib commented.

"So, you chose him."

"Sure. He made an impression."

Grava knitted his brow and shook his glass; the ice rattled. "I've been told he's rounding up hoodlums who served time with him. My Robbery Department recommends a full investigation."

"That's not necessary. He's working for me now," Naguib said, perhaps a trifle abruptly.

"Is he? I thought you were done with him. It's been nearly four months since you asked."

"I'd appreciate it if you leave him alone."

Grava felt a dismissive dryness in Naguib's tone. "And I'd appreciate it if he doesn't give me any trouble," the colonel said.

"Let us hope he doesn't."

Grava declined Naguib's invitation to lunch, adducing urgent police matters, and the Lebanese walked him to the club's colonnaded entry. In the parking lot, five bodyguards had locked themselves in Grava's two 1958 black Cadillac sedans, air conditioners blasting. Both vehicles glided to the portico when the colonel stopped at the doorway to shake hands with his host.

After seeing Grava off, Elias Naguib instructed his driver to have lunch in the servants' cafeteria, then sauntered over to the restaurant. Blas Chacón, Naguib's driver since 1940, felt certain his boss would enjoy a leisurely meal, so he took his time polishing off the white rice, black bean potage, ground beef, and fried plantains that he ordered. Naguib would leave the club around two o'clock and ask to be taken to the offices of Luis Mendoza y Compañía, traders in sugar futures, Blas figured.

The afternoon had turned splendid by the time Naguib lit a Lucky and nestled in the backseat of his 1957 De Soto to enjoy the drive. The eleven-mile-long, tree-lined Fifth Avenue was reputedly Havana's most beautiful boulevard. It had a ten-yard-wide median divider with a cemented central footwalk, along which manicured flowerbeds, ornamental trees, and lawn thrived. Some magnificent residences could also be admired. The tunnel under the Almendares River marked the beginning of a six-lane freeway flanked by a seawall known as Malecón to all city residents. Naguib took a

deep breath of sea breeze. His gaze swept over the water sparkling under the blinding sunlight and came to rest on the
Morro Castle's lighthouse. It had been the first thing Cuban
he'd seen from the boat on his initial, exploratory trip many
years earlier.

Once the vehicle entered Old Havana, the hub of Cuban
finance, Naguib shifted mental gears and started thinking
sugar. He got off at 305 Obispo Street, went down a stairway to the traders' basement, and studied the evolution of
prices in New York on Monday and Tuesday morning. Next
he bought fifty lots of raw sugar for next March, discussed
probable margins for the October closing position, then exchanged views with his agent about the impact of the rebels'
economic sabotage on the upcoming sugar harvest. The Lebanese considered the sweetener a national barometer which
foretold effects on most segments of the Cuban economy,
unceasingly absorbed information about it, and speculated
following sober cause-and-effect analysis.

At 3:16 P.M. Naguib returned to his wholesale jewelry
business at 418 Muralla Street. He inspected a shipment of
Brazilian emeralds, approved two new ring designs, tele-
phoned three retailers, and skimmed over the September 30
profit-and-loss statement. As over the years the Lebanese
launched new business ventures, this shop had diminished its
share in his total net profits to less than 10 percent, but it
remained his toy and only haven of sentimentality.

Naguib had become acquainted with precious stones in
1926, when a New York–based uncle—an expert on two fancy
cuts: heart and pear shapes—lured him from Beirut. The man
tried to teach his nephew lapidary art, with poor results. Elias
had lacked the indispensable combination of eagle eyes and

steady hands required to become a faceter, so he was relegated to sawing off diamonds with a rotating phosphor-bronze disk. Laid off when the American economy went into a tailspin in 1929, Naguib became a homeless, hungry wanderer who begged coins and dreamed with a diamond's white fire.

At half past four the Lebanese arrived at 523 Vives Street, home to Motor Auto Company Limited. His latest acquisition was a retail spare parts front for cars stolen in the U.S. and shipped to Cuba from Key West by ferryboat. He inspected ten Willys jeeps legally bought as Army surplus in Miami, then checked invoices, signed checks, and, accompanied by a building contractor, toured the site approving repairs.

At 5:50 P.M. the De Soto climbed a ramp to the indoor parking space of Centro Comercial La Rampa, on Twenty-third and P Streets, Vedado. Blas Chacón cut the ignition, left the keys in it, got out of the car, and went home, pleased to quit early, feeling certain that his boss had a new love affair. The Lebanese remained in the backseat. The poor lighting provided by a few incandescent bulbs wrapped him in shadows, causing him to blend in with the walnut-colored upholstery. Getting ready for his next interview, he engaged in the complex mental interweaving of refined schemers.

Shortly before 6 P.M., Contreras leisurely came up the ramp, peering at parked cars to his right and left. He spotted the De Soto, casually looked over his shoulder, approached the left rear door, pulled the handle, and got in.

"Good evening, Mr. Naguib."

Faithful to his role of a rich, antiquated tobacco grower, Contreras had on a well-worn, navy-blue gabardine suit over a starched white dress shirt, and a red tie. The arabesques on the toecap and vamp of his black-and-white thousand-eye shoes were filled with a chalky paste. A lock of hair fell onto his forehead when he removed his hat.

"Good evening, Contreras. How's it going?"

"As planned. We're in suite 406. The maid cleans when we're in. We only go out at night, and only to the casino." Contreras made a short pause. "My man won around thirteen hundred last night."

Naguib chortled before lighting a cigarette. Contreras accepted the Zippo's flame and lit a La Corona, blew smoke out, then rolled down the window a few inches.

"Your . . . man, as you say—is he good at this polio act?"

"He's doing fine so far."

"How about the rest of the team?"

"They're ready. I talked to them all over the phone a while ago."

Naguib nodded his approval. "Did your scout notice anything unusual last Saturday?"

Contreras immediately shook his head, looking at the back of the front seat, then raised his left hand to ask for a few moments. "Yes, he did. There's a new hall supervisor. I talked to him Sunday night; name's Grouse. I suppose first string is on vacation or something."

"Probably. Need any money?"

"No. I was falling behind a little, but that piece of blind luck last night solved the problem."

"Is there anything on your mind?"

Contreras thought it wise to seize the opportunity. Naguib had promised to do the unthinkable.

"You talked to Grava?"

"I did. He'll keep things quiet."

The ex-con hoped for something more explicit. "Look at it my way," he began. "Even if the papers don't print a word, even if Lansky instructs Di Constanzo not to call the police, somehow this will leak out, 'cause it's too big a hit and Grava has stooges all over town. He'll get descriptions from casino and hotel staff, maybe have them take a look at a few mug shots, and being the kind of sonafabitch he is, he's gonna come after us no matter what to grab as much silver for himself as possible."

"And you've taken precautions according to this scenario."

"You bet."

"Well done," the Lebanese said, then took a final drag from his cigarette and crushed the butt on the ashtray in the back of the front seat. "But listen: After you do the job, a couple of days later, I'll talk to Grava again. I'll tell him why it was done and make clear that you and your men worked for a percentage. When he learns who ordered it, he'll take it easy. This guy knows what's best for him. If to this you add your own precautions, I believe you can feel pretty safe."

"Amen," Contreras said, sounding convinced, though he wasn't.

"We'll meet again on the ninth if the Series ends tomorrow, the tenth if it goes to Thursday."

The Cuban nodded. "At the Château, ten P.M."

"Be careful during the getaway. No traffic violations. A casual clash with a police cruiser is the only real danger I can foresee."

"Right. Anything else?"

"No."

Contreras dragged on his cigarette and threw the butt out. "Good evening, then."

"Good evening, Ox. And good luck."

Contreras released the door handle and turned to look at Naguib. "First time you call me that."

The Lebanese nodded, with something resembling curiosity seeping from his eyes. "We've been together in this for three months now. We could become friends. So . . . why Ox?"

"First thing I stole. See you soon."

. . .

The two-story wooden country house looked like a frustrated project in progressive decay. Behind the padlocked Cyclonefence gateway entrance to the four-thousand-square-yard lot, the driveway opened into a small parking area. Four steps led to the front door and a verandah that went around the left side of the residence. The ground floor consisted of a small foyer, a spacious living room, a dining room, a guest room with a small bathroom, the kitchen, and four closets. A narrow, creaky staircase led from the foyer to the top floor's three bedrooms and bigger bathroom. Thirty yards behind the house, a smaller wooden structure served as garage at ground level, servants' quarters above. Fruit trees were scattered throughout a neglected garden choking on dead leaves and dry twigs.

Crawling between the plain wood strip flooring and the supporting boards, amongst coffers, beams, moldings, and paneling, the house lodged colonies of mice, cockroaches, scorpions, spiders, and ants, all mutant survivors of ineffectual fumigation. In the last five years this fauna had resoundingly defeated the three different families that had leased the place looking for a retreat in the outskirts, yet close enough to Havana via the two-lane Calabazar Highway.

The sequestered chalet needed two coats of paint outside and one inside, its roof leaked in places, and the rent was too high, but when Fermín Rodríguez signed the lease, he had other considerations on his mind. The nearest neighbor was roughly a block away. The bindweed-covered wire fence offered partial protection from peeping strangers. A closed exit at the back of the lot could become an escape route to wasteland. As the owner showed him around the place, Fermín fed him a load of bullshit. The house would become the shop, the garage the warehouse, for the publicity products made by his company, a burgeoning new firm that had outgrown the room it presently rented in the capital. It would manufacture decals and print leaflets for the moment, then progress to billboards, neon signs, and TV spots in a few months.

Valentín Rancaño, scout and gambling expert, and Melchor Loredo, getaway driver, replayed their Monday and Tuesday act on Wednesday, October 8. They arrived by bus dressed in blue mechanics' coveralls, sipped espresso at a small cafeteria three blocks away, and, jabbering on about the World Series, headed for the house a little before 8 A.M. At 8:14 Fermín showed up in a dilapidated 1950 Ford pickup, opened the padlock, removed the chain. He left the vehicle in the parking area and went inside, followed by his assumed hired hands. They opened the sash windows, turned on the lights, a radio, and the water pump. Next all three busied themselves unloading mostly empty cardboard boxes from the pickup, shouting orders, dumping garbage, and banging on loose

boards, but to kill time until 4 P.M. it became almost impera-
tive to sit on the floor with a deck of cards and reminisce about
their younger years or daydream about what the future had
in store for each of them.

"If I come out with ten or fifteen thousand, I'd build a
house in Párraga or Mantilla and open a three-cent espresso
stand," Loredo said, introducing the subject.

"And if you come out with thirty or forty thou?" Fermín
wanted to know.

"Don't talk shit, Gallego. That's just Ox's pep talk."

"Just for the heck of it, suppose you come out with that
much," the bald man insisted.

Loredo's stare eloped through an open window and
came to rest on the lilac and green of a camellia shrub. He
had been hoping for a turnaround since childhood. Born
thirty-two years earlier in Caimanera, Oriente, the son of a
mulatto prostitute and an unknown American sailor, he had
been raised by his black grandmother in Santiago de Cuba
on the monthly remittance his mother regularly sent until she
was killed by a drunken Marine who accidentally shot her in
the head. Loredo's education ended in fifth grade. At twelve
he peddled candies on the streets. At fifteen he found himself seduced by a white high-society lady while employed as
her houseboy. At seventeen he went to prison on a rape charge
after the husband caught them in the act.

Loredo moved to Havana in 1947, learned to drive while
washing and parking cars in a garage, and a year later stole
his first heap, a '34 Chevy sold to a fence for twenty pesos.
From 1952 to 1954 he served a second prison term at the Isla
de Pinos penitentiary on account of a new security device that
locked the steering wheel of '48 Lincolns. In 1955 he found

love with a strikingly beautiful, affectionate, good-natured black woman. Now Loredo longed to raise his two sons in a somewhat different way.

"*Compadre,* if I got that much, I'd build a four-unit apartment building and open a bar and grill."

"I'd open a gambling joint," Rancaño said unasked. "I've spotted a vacant loft above a bar on Avenida del Puerto that's out of this world. Around there people play craps in the street, poker games in their homes. This retired hooker has bingo in the dining room of a tiny apartment and she's making thirty, forty bucks a day. With a couple of thousand I'll buy a second-hand wheel, furniture . . ."

Rancaño presented a well-argued case for opening a cheap gambling joint in 1958 Havana. He was born in Rodas in the province of Las Villas, where his father had felt relieved of further paternal duties after securing him a job as clerk in the town's general store. He lived a rebellious childhood, disregarding both his mother's emotional pleas and the punishments meted out by his old man. Valentín finally drained the sweet woman's kindness when, at puberty, he tried to find daily relief for his insatiable sexual voracity among her sows and hens.

During his first year in the store, Rancaño kept himself busy learning the trade: its inexhaustible diversity of things and gadgets, assortments and prices, orders and shipments. But at fifteen, a card-playing barber introduced him to games of chance and the teenager found his reason to live. The hormonal imbalance that covered his cheeks with a severe acne made him retreat into himself and jerk off madly. Terrified by the lack of opportunities in the rural backwaters, in 1946 Rancaño stole twenty-five pesos from the general store's cash register and fled to Havana. His father refunded the owner; no charges were pressed.

In the Cuban capital he had brief stints as a poolroom attendant, numbers collector, and apprentice mechanic of vending machines before becoming a seven-and-a-half dealer at a clandestine gambling hall in the town of Bauta. One evening police raided the place and he was busted, booked, and eventually incarcerated for illicit gambling. A very experienced gambler serving a life term for strangling his wife taught him a whole bag of tricks, but after his release his criminal record prevented him from getting a job at a casino and he took to cleaning suckers out in flying joints set up on a park bench or in the back room of a bodega. A dice specialist, Rancaño owned eleven loaded pairs, seven which had been shaved down, six with duplicated faces and countless good ones, perfect and imperfect, made from cellulose or other plastic, transparent or opaque, with red or black flush spots. Rancaño mastered thirteen dice games, from the plebeian craps to the *barbooth* played in the Middle East.

"I'll keep the police off my back with twenty or thirty pesos each day. I'll start with three dealers and a guard. In two or three years I'll be 'Señor Rancaño' in Havana, trading in my Cadillac each September, with broads and white drill suits by the dozen. How's that for starters?"

"Sounds all right," Loredo said diplomatically. His poor results on bets made him loathe all sorts of wagers.

"That's a good area," said Fermín, plucking the cigar out of his mouth. "Stevedores, truck drivers, and Customs people make good money. Sailors come ashore loaded too. Your joint might come off okay. Hey, I'm hungry, how about you two?"

At noon on Monday, a lousy chicken with rice at a distant greasy spoon had prompted Fermín to suggest buying some kitchenware and provisions. It would make them look more on the up-and-up, he had argued—and lunch decently as well. The idea seemed amusing to Loredo. On Tuesday, Rancaño had spoiled the rice, and that Wednesday he was sentenced, two votes against one, to do the dishes and scour the saucepans. Lunch consisted of the ever-present rice cooked by Loredo, two cans of red beans heated bain-marie in a pan of water by Fermín, one pork sausage each, crackers, and coffee. Afterward they turned off the radio and lay back on the floor to take a nap over old newspapers, folded cardboard boxes serving as pillows. By 12:25 P.M., Fermín's soft snoring became the only sound in the dining room.

Loredo awoke at 1:15, lit a cigarette, and smoked distractedly for a couple of minutes. Then he turned on the radio and tuned in to Circuito Nacional Cubano. To his surprise, over heavy static a voice was emotionally describing plays of the sixth World Series game from County Stadium, Milwaukee. He glanced sharply at his watch.

"Hey, guys, wake up, the game's on," he bellowed, turning up the volume.

Fermín supported himself on his right elbow and glanced at his watch. "It can't be," he mumbled.

Nearly a minute elapsed before the commentator explained that the game had started at 12:30 due to a threat of rain that might still force a cancellation. It was drizzling in Milwaukee, the humidity was 95 percent, and wind speed had reached fifteen miles an hour. A quick recap of the action let them know that the Braves led 2–1 in the top of the fourth. Hank Bauer had slugged a home run in the first inning, his fourth in the Series, tying a record held jointly by Babe Ruth, Lou Gehrig, and Duke Snider. In the bottom of the first the Braves had scored on a Hank Aaron single to left field with Schoendienst on second. In the second inning, Warren Spahn had hit a single to center that brought Covington home.

Fermín asked for an act and they went out pretending to be busy. Back inside, Loredo brewed fresh espresso as the others used the toilet. Finally, all three sat on the dining room floor to follow the rest of the game.

His attention frequently wandering to the unkempt garden or the peeling paint on the walls, Fermín realized that his once fervent rooting for the Yankees had faded into nonchalance. He wondered whether in the future, living a new life that would have been so influenced by baseball, he would ever feel his old passion for the game. The bald man lit a fresh cigar and listened as his team tied the game in the top of the sixth, when Mantle singled over Logan's outstretched glove, Howard lined a hit to center, Bruton fumbled the ball for an error and Mantle took third. Berra flied to Bruton in deep center, scoring the runner on the sacrifice fly.

The bald man was making plans too, both overt and covert. Number one among the former was setting up an elegant, disease-free, respectable brothel where drugs, 8mm porno films, and multiple sex would be taboo, for of late he had become a man of archaic immorality. Prominent among the latter was ordering ten pairs of special Italian shoes, at fifty dollars each, to add a couple of inches to his height.

Shortness was his Achilles' heel. It made him feel lessened as a human being, and in his childhood any observation regarding his stature had started fierce fistfights that had to be broken up by adults. Son of a housemaid from Murcia,

Spain, and a Majorcan dry cleaner from Ibiza who died of TB in 1924, Fermín had got an education on a scholarship granted by the Brothers of the Virgin Mary and graduated as a bookkeeper in 1934. Firmly inserted by his widowed mother in the lower echelons of Havana's Spanish colony, he had landed a job as collector of monthly fees at the Centro Asturiano social club and got to know the city like the back of his hand. Introverted and analytic, Fermín had realized that hard work meant nothing better than a meager livelihood for most club members. For years he had considered business opportunities, none of which materialized because of his lack of capital. By his mid-twenties, the short man had left behind the set of values and traditions his mother and the priests had carefully planted.

At twenty-four, strongly influenced by the wave of defeated Spanish Republicans arriving in Cuba in search of a future, Fermín had embraced, with equal passion, anarchism and a tall, slim whore. The young woman, who worked the Colón district, fell for the burning desire, rosy skin, and green eyes of her most devoted client. The four-inch height gap had aroused local glee, but Fermín fought his corner well and reached the position of Gloria Street's most respected amateur pimp. He kept his job at the Centro Asturiano, though, for the five years it took him to master the prostitution business.

By the time World War II was about to end, Fermín had two too-tall women working for him and had befriended other prostitutes, who had heard he didn't beat his ladies, took care of everything they needed, and let them keep a fair percentage of the fruits of their labor. He had been giving serious consideration to opening a brothel of his own when one night he had to stab a husky boxer in the liver. The fighter had been kicking the living shit out of him and calling him names: "Crap Dwarf" had made Fermín climb the wall with anger. Two months later he was sentenced to eight years for manslaughter.

In prison he lost his hair and found in Contreras the close friend he had never had. Both men took Heller under their wings when the young and inexperienced former law student arrived in the Presidio Modelo to serve two years for complicity in a payroll holdup. With the know-how of the hardened criminal, plus his wit and cynicism, Contreras became the indisputable leader of the threesome. Fermín had raw courage, imagination, and a fanatic's determination; Heller possessed the smoothness of good mediators, an above-average education, and a wealth of joy that made his two friends laugh with a frequency that was amazing, given the circumstances. Freed years apart, they reassembled in Havana and pulled off small swindles, burglaries and holdups as they waited for The Job—which was now within their reach.

The baseball game remained tied during the seventh, eighth, and ninth innings. Fermín read in the newspaper about Pius XII's brain clot, the shellings of Quemoy and Matsu, the opening of a Spanish film by Sarita Montiel, and Elvis Presley's arrival in Germany for his obligatory Army stint.

The game recaptured everyone's attention in the top of the tenth, when Gil McDougald, the New Yorkers' second baseman, banged Spahn's second pitch over the left field fence for a home run. Hank Bauer flied deep to Bruton and Mathews threw out Mantle, but then Elston Howard and Yogi Berra singled to right. With runners on first and third, Fred Haney replaced Spahn with Don McMahon and

Skowron singled to right, scoring Howard. After Ryne Duren struck out, Loredo sighed and cut a sideways look at Fermín.

"Series is tied. We won't do it tonight, either."

In the Braves' last chance, McDougald fumbled Schoendienst's grounder but recovered in time to throw him out. Logan walked on a full count, but then Mathews swallowed his eleventh strikeout of the Series. With two outs and a lonely runner on first, the outcome of the game seemed nearly a foregone conclusion when Logan stole second unmolested as Duren wound up. Then Hank Aaron singled to left, scoring Logan.

The phony admen were mesmerized. Rancaño bit his nails; Loredo had his eyes stapled to the floor; Fermín chewed on his cigar.

Bob Turley replaced Ryne Duren and was disrespectfully greeted by Adcock with a single to center, Aaron taking third. With Felix Mantilla running for Adcock, Frank Torre, batting for Crandall, sent a soft liner to the edge of the outfield grass that McDougald grabbed to end the game with a Yankee victory.

"Waiting is over," Fermín said, and heaved a sigh of relief. "Tomorrow we'll be rich."

...

Angelo Dick's corpse turned up in Queens, New York, at 6:16 A.M. on Thursday, October 9, 1958. It lay prone on the gravel footpath leading from the sidewalk to the porch of his abortion-racket partner, Joe Notaro. Once he recovered, the Bonanno *sottocapo* dialed a number in Hempstead and ordered a servant to wake up the boss.

"I've got trouble at home, Mr. Bonanno," the racketeer said when the fifty-three-year-old don of one of the five New York Mafia families came to the phone.

"What is it?"

"Frankie found a stiff in the garden. Guy I used to know: Angelo Dick."

"Never heard of him," the boss said too fast. Bonanno assumed his phone was wiretapped on a permanent basis.

"He used to work at a Havana casino. Hadn't seen him for months."

"You called the cops?"

"Not yet."

"I think you ought to. Right now."

"Sure. I just wanted you to know I'll be late."

"All right, Joe."

"Bye."

"See you."

Bonanno hung up and smiled. He had the guileless looks of a church minister, a scientific genius, or any other man who only learned about organized crime on the screens of his TV set or local theater. Well aware of this, he was given to examining his reflection in the bathroom mirror to ponder how, by his shifting from smile to laughter, his brown eyes became more candid. Or how much kindness flowed following the relaxation of his frown, or the measure of astonishment in his lips when they rounded into an "Oh" brimming with admiration. But even in its normal state, his face displayed a childish innocence that perfectly masked a mind in permanent unscrupulous activity.

Sitting on the swivel chair behind his desk, he reflected on the news. Unbelievable precision. The date lacked significance since he just needed to project weakness before launching the offensive. But this sacrifice of the pawn twenty-four hours prior to the first raid was a Naguib masterstroke. His agent had aged the way good wines do—superbly.

He remembered when, unemployed, starving, and in ragged clothes, Elias Naguib had begged him for work one night in 1930. Naguib was an immigrant like himself, approximately his age. He had felt something close to commiseration for the poor bastard, so he took him for granted, slipped him a fin, and sent him to Frank Labruzzo, figuring the Lebanese would sweep floors at one of his warehouses. But after six months of taking on increasingly complex jobs, Naguib had become rookie of the year, doing everything and doing it well. By 1935, though, the now husky and well-clothed Elias became sick and tired of being constantly bypassed for promotion because he hadn't been born in Sicily. And even though Bonanno had understood the unfairness of that code and how it harmed business, as the youngest of the original capos he had to wait ten more years to bend it. Naguib had the good taste to keep the true reason to himself during the interview at which he asked permission to invest his savings in his own Cuban venture.

Bonanno knew the country. In fact, it had been the first stop he had made after leaving Marseilles aboard a freighter in 1923. Not a bad place. Good living standards if compared with those of other banana republics, graced with a pleasant climate and some pretty nice pieces of ass in the streets, what with the racial mixture. He had spent a few weeks in Havana before Sicilian friends smuggled him into Florida.

His former subordinate had moved to Havana in 1936, floated a small company to import precious stones, gold, and silver, and became a wholesaler. He visited New York often for transactions, paid his respects, and took Labruzzo to dinner at fine but inexpensive trattorias in Brooklyn. In 1948, embarrassed as if demanding an undeserved honor, Naguib had invited Bonanno to the 21 Club. The don had realized that the favorable winds of prosperity were blowing over Cuba, or at least over that part of the island where the Lebanese had his business.

Naguib was never ostentatious, never bragged or asked for favors, yet three years later, on November 15, 1951, at Bonanno's twentieth wedding anniversary, the Lebanese presented Fay Bonanno with a quite expensive diamond necklace. This prompted the don to take the self-effacing Lebanese seriously; he ordered an in-depth investigation.

The grateful Elias was found to have excellent governmental, judicial, and police connections on the island, a little over $500,000 deposited in a savings account at the Metropolitan Avenue branch of Chase Manhattan, a new $85,000 residence in Havana's choicest suburb, and was setting up a huge operation: shipping stolen cars from Key West to Havana to sell them all over Cuba. The man would become a multimillionaire in a short time. As was true everywhere else in the world, knowing the right people was the touchstone for success in Cuba, Bonanno had concluded at the time.

Then a military coup and the ensuing replacement of hundreds of government officials had utterly pulverized the influence network woven by the Lebanese. The reconstruction was complete by 1955, when Meyer Lansky and Frank Costello had made their big push in Havana.

Bonanno knitted his brow. It was only fair to acknowledge Meyer's contribution to the Cuban expansion, his

long-term observation and frequent visits, how he had preserved old relationships and nurtured new ones, the way he had
oiled gears with favors and money. Bonanno had done the same
in Montreal, but hadn't declared it off limits to friends. He
wasn't reluctant to share alcohol—during or after Prohibi-
tion—gambling, loan-sharking, or protection. But now Lansky
and Costello refused to share Havana and were closed to reason—despite the fact that in the Commission calm deliberation had always prevailed.

In 1957 Anastasia had clumsily tried to force his way in
by organizing the hit on Costello, and now he lay six feet
underground. Lansky had grown better entrenched than ever
in Cuba, so Bonanno had devised and presented to Joseph
Profaci—father-in-law of his son Salvatore and don of another
Mafia family—a common strategy to bolster their position
in the Commission and persuade Lansky and Costello to
change their minds. Remembering Naguib had been unavoid-
able: What the Man on the Spot did best was map out perfect schemes that he then had others execute while he pulled
the strings like a consummate puppeteer.

Bonanno glanced at the wall clock, looked for a personal
phone directory in the middle drawer of his desk, dialed a very
special phone company number, and asked for an immediate person-to-person call to Havana. He carefully returned
the receiver to its place and recalled the Cuban survey he'd
ordered last Christmas. Millions in gambling, large-scale
smuggling, additional profits in the hotel trade, the probability of marijuana farming. His grateful former subordinate
would secure for himself a good bite in future Cuban profits
if he could discredit Lansky, force him to admit his arrogance
and excess confidence, make him realize that those he had

excluded from the Cuban turf had long arms. And when simultaneously overwhelmed by hits within the stronghold, emphysema, gastritis, and hypertension, Lansky would allow the Bonannos, the Profacis, perhaps even the Colombos, to dance the rumba.

The phone rang.

"Hello."

"Your Havana party is on the line, sir."

"Thank you. Elias?"

"Morning, Joe," Naguib said.

"Morning, Grumpy, how are you?"

"Fine, and you?"

"I'm not complaining."

"How's everybody?" the Lebanese asked.

"All right. Listen. Joe pulled me out of bed fifteen minutes ago. Found a stiff in his garden. Dick something. No, wait, Dick's the last name. Name is . . . Oh, hell, I can't remember. Joe says the guy used to work down there; he could use your help. You knew this Dick?"

"No," Naguib said.

"Maybe you could find out. Just in case cops want to pin anything on Joe."

There was a silence. Both men were smiling broadly. "Listen, my friend, this is a big town," was Naguib's guarded response. "You happen to know what this guy did for a living?"

"Joe said something about a casino."

"Not my line, but I'll keep my ears open and let you know if I learn anything."

"Fine. Hey, Elias, just out of curiosity, when did that business rumble you told me about surface?"

Naguib pondered the question for a few seconds. Probably it referred to the date when Di Constanzo had been tipped off about the abortion racket. "You mean the airline company rumble?" he asked tentatively.

"Yeah."

"By the end of August, around the twenty-fourth, maybe the twenty-fifth."

"I thought so. Okay, I guess that's all. Will you watch the game today?"

"Wouldn't miss it for anything in the world," Naguib said. In fact he couldn't care less.

"I hope we win. Well, take care, Grumpy. Bye now."

"Bye-bye."

Bonanno made some mental calculations after hanging up. A week to verify the source, two for investigations, and two for consultations. Then a couple of days to question and calm down the lamb, one for travel, one more to finish him off and plant the body where Profaci and himself would learn of their failure. Lansky had swallowed line, hook, and sinker. By noon tomorrow he'd learn how the Jew took the first solid punch. Bonanno was hoping for a brain hemorrhage resulting from uncontrollable high blood pressure.

Four

On G day—the G standing for graduation, according to Heller—Mariano Contreras awoke remarkably calm. He had anticipated the same stress he'd experienced in the past when something long awaited or carefully mapped out had been about to take place, like the day he had been released from the penitentiary, or that on which he had perpetrated his first really profitable, well-planned heist. Instead, he lay relaxed by seven hours of deep sleep, satisfied with what they had accomplished so far, confident of a favorable outcome.

Contreras believed self-satisfaction dangerous and never devoted more than two or three minutes to it. He jumped out of bed and went into the bathroom. Fifteen minutes later he came out, donned his clothes, ordered breakfast, then trotted down the steps and woke Heller out of a bad dream. From the smaller bathroom, his partner hummed a song that had been in fashion for a while. He was still at it when he returned to the living room rubbing shaving lotion on his face, naked to the waist.

"You happy?" an intrigued Contreras asked.

"Just whistling in the dark."

Contreras smiled. Abo had never bungled a job, but like all ex-cons he hated holing up; Contreras knew he could use a change of air. "How about going up to the pool after breakfast?" suggested the man in charge.

"Hell, yes! Let's get out of this mousetrap."

A half hour later, wearing jackets over open-necked dress shirts, both men sat by the swimming pool on the roof. Several guests on deck chairs tanned their limbs under a benignly warm sun. Four teenagers gave up their clownish pirouettes on the diving board after realizing that Heller was watching them. Suspecting that they didn't want to make him feel bad, the fake paralytic maneuvered his wheelchair to face the vast gray sea; Contreras also turned his reclining chair around. They sipped espresso and smoked in silence, taking in the cityscape and the sea, the breeze playing with their hair.

"I've never broken anyone," Heller suddenly said.

Contreras turned a little to look at his buddy. He had the resigned expression of first-time blood donors lying on stretchers, facing an initiation that couldn't be postponed.

"You may not have to."

"But you never know, right?"

"Let me put it this way," Contreras said, and made a reflective pause. "You take nothing for granted. If tonight one of those bastards thinks you're afraid, sees you hesitate, he'll try to knock you over, and then you'll have to break him. So, he should know you mean it. You tell him 'Don't move' and he moves, you beat him with the stock—once, hard. Best way to operate is by talking and acting tough. I believe they'll go along okay, 'cause some guys are willing to risk their lives for their dough, but for other people's dough . . ."

He didn't complete the sentence; instead Contreras laboriously lit a cigarette against the wind. Heller pretended to rearrange the blanket covering his legs in order to scratch his right kneecap unnoticed.

"Yeah, but our actions should be commensurate with their reactions. If they—"

"'Commensurate.' A lawyer's fancy word. You know what our actions should 'be commensurate with'? With our goal, Abo. And our goal is to clean the fucking place, no matter what."

Heller nodded thoughtfully, and for almost a minute pondered whether he should voice his last reservation. Contreras treated him like a son; he trusted the man and knew how to calm him down if he blew a fuse. So, he risked his wrath.

"Ox, we've been frank to each other all the time . . . ," he began, in a soothing tone of voice.

"Hail Blessed Virgin Mary! Abo, please, don't make one of those cheap lawyer's introductions of yours. What the fuck is on your mind?"

"You sure about the alarm? I mean, it's unbelievable that with so much mazuma in there . . . ," said Heller, eyeing Contreras warily.

"I'll be damned!" Pretending to be angry, Contreras rolled his eyes and clapped his hands once. "To the others that was a pleasant surprise; nobody mentioned it again. You've been mulling it over for God knows how long. There's no alarm, *compadre;* that's a fact. For three reasons: First, the keister is embedded in concrete and the only door to the office is barred; second, they take security precautions; and third, they believe nobody here has the guts or the brains to go after them."

Heller took the demitasse to his lips, sipped the espresso, and let his gaze rest on the monument to the victims of the *Maine*. "Perhaps tomorrow they'll reconsider," he said.

...

At 11:15 A.M., Nick Di Constanzo ascended the two steps to the porch of Lansky's leased house, rang the bell, then lit a cigarette. The two-story, sixteen-room sandstone residence at the corner of Fifth Avenue and Thirty-second Street, Miramar, had marble floors, a swimming pool, and a four-car garage. The front and back doors and the windows, built of precious wood, were protected with ornate security grilles.

Casino de Capri's top executive wore a dark green sport jacket over a white Van Heusen polo shirt, light gray slacks, and black loafers. He splurged on clothing and devoted no less than ten minutes every day to choosing what to wear. He also experienced the delight of art collectors when he found a tailor capable of making a garment that fit him well.

Jacob Shaifer opened the front door, nodded curtly, uttered "Hi," and then led Di Constanzo around a costly and excessively furnished living room to the poolside terrace, where his boss was taking the sun and having breakfast.

"Morning, Meyer."

"Hi, Nick. Take a seat; let me finish with this."

As Shaifer left, Di Constanzo sat on a yellow iron love seat with thick plastic-covered cushions and gazed around the well-kept garden, enjoying the cool breeze and the rustling leaves of a tall mango tree. Lansky wore a mustard-colored silk bathrobe over his pajamas and appeared to be rested, at peace with himself. Between sips from his third cup of coffee, Number One lit a cigarette.

"Okay, shoot," Lansky said.

"They found him this morning."

"Says who?"

"Pete."

Lansky arched an eyebrow, cocked his head, looked at a second-floor window. "Chapter closed. I suppose we won't eat bananas for a while," he halfheartedly said at last, then smiled at the overused play on words.

Even though Meyer Lansky didn't like Bonanno, he perfectly understood his keen interest in new places. But since meeting him in the Roaring Twenties as a Maranzano subordinate, he had scorned the Italian's nice-guy looks and prosperous-banker demeanor. The man was as unscrupulous as anybody, something that Lansky would have sincerely admired had the Italian cast his façade only toward the public. But as the years went by and Bonanno further developed his sanctimonious front, he had come to love his act so much he even performed it during Commission meetings. His lines always included high-sounding platitudes, in which words like "brotherhood," "friendship," "respect," "understanding," "sharing," and "peace" abounded. The kind of crap politicians feed to fools, Lansky had long ago concluded. Well, he had called the Italian's bluff.

Di Constanzo stubbed out his butt in an ashtray atop a glass-topped iron coffee table. He had misgivings—he couldn't get rid of a measure of respect for Angelo's work, and considered him naive, but not a traitor. Even after being pistol-whipped, the hall supervisor had not only rejected any direct or indirect Bonanno representation in Havana, but had denied that Notaro had tried to lure him into changing sides. Angelo's eyes had reflected the sincerity that only a superb actor could have faked in such critical moments.

"I believe Notaro manipulated him," the Capri man said.

"Maybe. You let people manipulate you, you're an asshole," Lansky opined, wanting to stave off any additional questioning of his judgment. "Now we've reasserted that this is our turf and we're ready to stand up for it. The whole problem boils down to lack of initiative. Bananas and Profaci have the whole Caribbean open to them. Mexico, the Bahamas, Jamaica—there're a hundred places where they can set up shop. But no, they want to cash in on my turf, benefit from the years I've spent here building from scratch. They envy my patience paying off. Fuck them. Cuba is ours."

Di Constanzo resented having the gospel foisted upon him. He knew it by heart. However, he kept a respectful silence, eyes on a flowerbed, sidestepping a confrontation.

"Our people will hear about it," Lansky elaborated. "And if someone was considering working for the competition, he'll reconsider. Believe me, Nick, these things have their bright side, too. They strengthen the organization, reassert people. I hate losing a good man, and he was pretty good, but if we'd let him walk, in less than a year Bonanno would've opened his first Havana casino."

"Meyer, I also need to consult with you on the Series," Di Constanzo said, to cut the crap.

"What are the odds today?"

"Even."

"Who's pitching?"

"Burdette and Larsen."

"How much would a Yankee win set us back?"

"Almost half a million," the man from Capri said. "One hundred and ninety-two grand for the Series and nearly three hundred grand for the game. So, I suggest unloading in Miami. We've got two and a half hours."

"Okay. Call from here. Jacob! Hey, Jacob! Show Nick to the phone, will you?"

...

At the forlorn wooden house, inside an old wood-and-tin-plate icebox beneath fifteen pounds of ice bought early in the morning, lay ten juicy sirloin steaks. The kitchen cupboards stored four bottles of red Rioja wine and one of Tres Cepas brandy. But out of superstition, Fermín Rodríguez, Valentín Rancaño, and Melchor Loredo refused to celebrate in advance. Lunch consisted of rice and slices of a six-egg omelet with ham, sausage, fried potatoes, and onions thrown in. Wheel and Meringue agreed they should tune in at twelve as a precaution against an early start, but Gallego had the nerve to take a nap by the babbling radio.

"This guy's unbelievably cool," said Loredo, eyeing the snoozing man.

"And doesn't look it," Rancaño agreed with a nod. "You see this egg-bald, potbellied short guy walking down the streets, you figure him wrong. But brother, he's got banging balls."

Loredo clucked with what sprang to his mind. "Once we went to steal this truck loaded with GE fans," he gleefully recalled. "We were broke, man, didn't have a penny in our pockets, no irons, nothing, and Gallego says to me, 'You'll see, we're gonna make a thousand sticks each with this job.'"

Rancaño shook his head and grinned. "Always calls the dough 'sticks.'"

"It was a six-wheel, '52 Chevy closed truck. Each time the driver loaded at the Ward Line pier, he used to go fuck a hooker in San Isidro. Can you believe it? He could go earlier, when the truck was empty, but no, the guy always went for pussy after leaving the pier. Big bastard, you know, but Gallego had him well cased and knew he used to stay inside the brothel no less than thirty minutes. Gallego knows everybody in the neighborhood, on account of Liberata having lived there so many years."

"Piece of cake."

"That's what *we* thought. I brought the tools and Gallego had a fourteen-inch-long iron pipe in a rolled-up newspaper. The jerk pulls over, rolls up the window, locks the door, gets into the whorehouse. I worked the door and we got into the cab. I'm doing the wires when the jerk hits the bricks after a couple of minutes. To this day I don't know if the hooker was sick or out, but he sees us, can't believe his eyes at first, then screams, 'You won't steal my truck, *cabrones*,' and pulls out a knife this long."

"*Coño.*"

"Then Gallego says: 'Get this started; I'll take care of him.' He jumps out, hits the guy on the wrist with the pipe, picks up the knife from the sidewalk, orders him to back off. The guy's howling in pain, feeling his busted arm with the other hand. Then Gallego goes behind him, stands on the top front step of the whorehouse—there were two, you know, and he had to stand on the second to reach the guy's neck and put on a stranglehold. The truck wouldn't start. I must've flooded the carburetor—fucking nerves. A crowd had gath-

ered by then. It was eleven in the morning, for God's sake!
Gallego, cool as a penguin, is *talking* to the truck driver,
compadre. I'm seeing his lips move and I ask myself, *What the
fuck's Gallego saying to that beast?* Then, as if by magic, the
engine caught and we took off."

Rancaño found himself smiling in amusement. "You ask
him what he said to the guy?"

"You bet. We were celebrating that same evening—
made fifteen hundred each—and I asked him, 'Gallego, what
the fuck were you saying to the sonofabitch?' Says he told him
not to be an asshole, that Casa Giralt was covered by insurance but that no surgeon would be able to sew his head back
in place if he moved. And the guy froze like a fucking statue."

"He's a bunch of balls."

"Listen. Game's on. Wake him up."

...

Lew Burdette's first pitch whooshed over home plate at
1:54 P.M. The strike was cheered by 46,367 County Stadium
spectators, watched or listened to with anticipation by countless millions all over the world. Except for the second game,
each of the previous six had kept people alert to the very end,
raising expectations about this final clash to decide baseball's
World Championship.

The Manhattan Mules had had a thorn in their side
since the previous season, when the Braves had won baseball's supreme prize, leaning, above all, on a staff headed by
Warren Spahn, one of the best left-handed pitchers in the
sport's history, and Lew Burdette, spitball and screwball
specialist.

Now, a year later almost to the day, New York fans hoped that Mickey Mantle and Yogi Berra, both hitting .325 in the first six games, would take matters into their hands. But the fans hadn't checked all the statistics: The two star players had produced only four of the twenty-five runs scored by their team.

At least seven men watching the game or listening to the play-by-play description of radio commentators didn't really care. There were also millions of mothers and fathers and uncles and aunts, millions of wives and perhaps even a few thousand husbands, who would merely put up with the cheers and hullabaloo. But the seven men had a very special reason for their indifference.

Elias Naguib didn't begin to understand sport as a social activity. His childhood and adolescence had been so focused on survival, he hadn't had the time to kick balls or play games. Naguib found boxing and wrestling sensible, given the number of punches and shoves he had landed and accepted in his youth. But it seemed to him that when grown-up men could make a pretty nice living by throwing, hitting, or kicking balls, running after them, and passing them as millions of spectators applauded or booed them, something was very wrong in the Western world. One of the many reasons democracy appeared to be losing the struggle against Communism, the Lebanese concluded. So when in the bottom of the first Schoendienst singled to left, Bruton walked, Torre sacrificed, Aaron walked, and Covington grounded to Skowron, who beat the runner to first as Schoendienst scored and the others advanced, the Lebanese let loose the first of a long series of yawns.

Contreras displayed his indifference in the top of the second. Berra walked and Howard bunted, but Frank Torre threw wild to Burdette, covering first base, and Berra reached third. "Yesterday it looked as though they'd be snowed out and today, look, the geeks are wearing T-shirts!" said Contreras.

"The commentator said it was sunny and warm," Heller explained.

"Did he?"

"You were taking a leak."

"Oh."

Torre scooped up Jerry Lumpe's bouncer and again made a poor throw to Burdette covering first. In his usual state of mind, Heller would have unwrapped one of his sarcasms, like "This guy's Milwaukee's Norm Siebern," but he remained silent. With bases full, Skowron grounded to Logan, whose throw to Schoendienst forced Lumpe at second as Berra scored and Howard took third. Then Kubek lined to Covington, Howard scoring after the catch. The game was 2–1 for his favorite team when the former law student opened the newspaper to scan the dog track results.

Joseph Bonanno amusedly studied his son Salvatore— "Bill" to the rest of the family—as he exulted over the lead. The aspiring don and his wife Rosalie had arrived from Phoenix on the seventh, exhausted by a long Indian summer, to snoop around New York. Eighteen years earlier, Bonanno had bought a mansion in Tucson while looking for the right place to heal Salvatore's permanent ear suppuration. As a college boy the young man had moved to Phoenix, and he remained there after his marriage to Rosalie Profaci. Cynics had considered the union a calculated, medieval parental arrangement.

The family had gathered on the back porch of the Hempstead house, facing a 21-inch color TV set. Bonanno sat at center, Fay on his left, and Bill on his right, as Rosalie flipped through the current issue of *Life.* The heir was over-joyed when the Braves lost an opportunity in the third in-ning: Del Crandall grounded out to McDougald with bases full and two outs. The don listened to his son opine on Bob Turley's relieving Don Larsen, nodded with a smile, and for some reason the next thing that popped into his mind was the pregnancy and imminent delivery of his favorite Holstein—Lady Florence—at his Middletown farm. Like Naguib, his attention was focused eleven hours ahead, reducing his lack-luster interest in sports to virtually nonexistent.

Up to the moment that Del Crandall smashed a home run over the left field fence to tie the game in the bottom of the sixth, Fermín Rodríguez, Melchor Loredo, and Valentín Rancaño had engaged in telling stories, making jokes, smok-ing, gobbling up a can of peaches, and turning the pages of a *Carteles* magazine. But the tie rekindled a passion born in boyhood, when most destitute Cuban kids swung discarded broomsticks against balls made from rags, and for the last three innings they were hooked.

In the top of the eighth, Burdette dominated Gil McDougald, who flied to Aaron; then Mickey Mantle was called out on strikes. But Berra doubled off the right field wall and Howard singled to center, scoring the Yankees' catcher. Andy Carey singled off Mathews's glove and Howard stopped at second. Burdette was tired after eight innings of pitching, but he also remembered the beating he'd taken during the sixth inning of the fifth game, and that kept him going.

Bill Skowron brought his .192 batting average to the plate. The first pitch was a called strike, and then came a low curveball. Burdette decided his third pitch ought to be a high fastball. Skowron saw it coming, swung with all he had, and hit a 363-foot home run.

A thick coat of stunned silence spread over County Stadium and the whole city of Milwaukee. Colossal rejoicing gripped New York. The Yankees held a four-run lead, and the Braves had only two more innings to overcome it.

Those who cared, from Casey Stengel and Fred Haney to radio listeners in Asia, were seized by a feeling of consummation. To have hoped for a turnaround would have set a new record for wishful thinking, and the Braves deflated.

In the bottom of the last two innings, Bob Turley faced men going through all the motions expected of confident players arriving in the batter's box: The hand-rubbing athletes measured their distance from home plate with the bat, then swung it viciously against the air, vainly threatening to hit hard, unreachable liners. But it was just cheap acting. They all knew Milwaukee wouldn't win the 1958 World Championship, and the whole team anxiously waited for the end to get out of the damn place, take a shower, and guzzle a six-pack.

Commentators were describing the joy that overwhelmed the New York players after the last out when Fermín Rodríguez turned off the set, stood up, and dusted off the seat of his pants.

"It's over, fellows. No rainout, no brawls, nothing. Tonight we'll light the fire under the can. Be at Las Delicias de Medina by eleven. Now, let's close the windows."

Bonanno glowered over Bill's euphoria. His son looked childish celebrating so expansively—shouting, jumping around the porch, kissing his mother and his wife before going to get the bottle of champagne that had been waiting in the refrigerator. At moments like these, it seemed absurd to consider him as his replacement. Salvatore was microscopic in experience and maturity compared with John Morale, Frank Labruzzo, even Joe Notaro. Bill filled his father's glass, stepped back, lifted his own, then proposed a toast.

"To victory, Dad."

"To victory," the don concurred, wondering about a possible victory elsewhere and if he should allow himself to celebrate it in advance.

In Havana, Contreras and Heller watched the screen in silence way past commercials and the station's farewell.

"Turn it off, Ox," said Heller in a begging tone.

"I'm waiting to see if you've really become disabled after a few days of playing the part."

"C'mon, be a good buddy, will you?"

"Okay," Contreras said, and got up. "But let's start getting ready."

"So soon?"

"The waiting is over, Abo. Let's get moving."

And Elias Naguib, happy to get back to his usual routine, briskly crossed the hall of his Alturas del Country mansion to order his car brought out.

. . .

The guests of suite 406 went up to the bedroom fifteen minutes after the final curtain descended on the World Series. Contreras retrieved the third suitcase, which had remained unopened in the closet, and let it rest on the bed he hadn't slept on. He checked the hair under a tiny strip of Scotch tape on the left side, just where both halves joined, before unlocking the suitcase with a small key and unbuckling the straps. He laid several bundles wrapped in old clothes on the bed.

Each man assembled one sawed-off, double-barreled 12-gauge Remington shotgun. Having repeatedly checked their lock and percussion mechanisms, Contreras unwrapped a bayonet, positioned its handgrip under and between the barrels of his shotgun, and, with Heller holding it in place, spent two yards of electrical tape to firmly bind it to the shotgun. A second bayonet was attached to Heller's weapon. Whispering something about their contribution to the design of modern firearms, Heller handed over four cartridges to Contreras. The gray-haired man examined their brass bases, then inserted them in the chambers, locked the guns, and placed both under his bed's mattress.

Next, two .38 Colt Cobras were freed from rags. Six shells were slid into each cylinder before stuffing the pieces in leather holsters and putting both alongside the shotguns. Then Heller reached for a spool of fishing line—sixty-two threads of braided 3mm-thick linen with a 200-pound resistance—cut twenty 40-inch-long sections with a penknife, and made a running knot at one end of every section. While he was at it, Contreras unfolded two white-and-blue-striped pillow linings. Each had a zipper at one end, and he tested their run several times. Satisfied, he extracted two white pillowcases from the suitcase, which joined the linings inside a night table drawer.

"The strongest man in the world is Charles Atlas, ain't he, Ox?"

"How the hell should I know?"

"Well, I tie up Mr. Atlas with this and give him a week to break loose. If he does, I'll let him hang me by the balls with this same line."

Contreras chuckled and waited as Heller divided the pieces of cord into five sets of four sections each, folded each set while taking care not to tangle up the strings, then tucked them into different pockets of his jacket. Contreras reached out for two pairs of white cotton gloves, tossed one to Heller, and began putting on the other.

"Okay," the older man said. "Let's do it."

They devoted an hour and a half to cleaning their fingerprints off everything. Downstairs, Heller conscientiously rubbed a cloth over the furniture, doors, moldings, light switches, and assorted gadgets as Contreras determinedly did the same upstairs. They plopped down on armchairs and lit cigarettes just after half past five.

"Gloved cats don't catch mice," said Heller, looking at his hands.

"We're the mice here, so keep them on. I have the feeling we've overlooked something."

Not one word was spoken for almost three minutes as they went over details in their minds.

"If all goes well, the shotguns stay here, right?" Heller asked.

"Sure."

"Let's wipe them clean."

"My fault," Contreras said, standing up.

Later, the gloves were stripped off for showers and a change of clothes; then again at 7:50 P.M., to admit a busboy who brought supper. As soon as the man left they put them on again and dined on soup, salmon steaks, mashed potatoes, glazed carrots, beer, bread, and espresso. Contreras lit a cigar, Heller a cigarette. Pretending to be unconcerned, they watched *Jueves de Partagás* on Channel 6. Heller didn't even smile at the jokes of a comedian doing a marvelous "affectionate drunk," didn't object to the flow of commercials, didn't praise the beautiful chorus girls. His ashtray had accumulated three butts in three hours, unusual for a six-a-day smoker. Contreras's mind kept moving from the suite to the casino to the country house. From Heller to Fermín to Loredo to Rancaño to Naguib. Back to the shotguns, the tape. Did fingerprints remain on the sticky side of tape? Maybe, but when it was pulled off they disappeared—or didn't they? And the pieces of cord . . .

"Abo?"

"What?"

"Where's the cord?"

"Here, in my . . ." Heller stopped mid-sentence as he felt the pockets of the jacket he was wearing. "Damn!"

"You left them in the other jacket. Go get them."

At 10:11, Heller rolled up to the side of the roulette table, looking confident and unconcerned in a chocolate-colored poplin suit, a white dress shirt, and a beige tie. Several women tried to picture him physically fit. Pushing the wheelchair's handlebars, Contreras re-created the sadness of a self-sacrificing father who finds himself taking his son to the last place on earth he'd want him to be. The short lapels of his outdated suit hardly allowed a glimpse of the pale green tie he wore. The spurious paralytic placed his chips on the green felt, enthusiastically rubbed his hands, then nodded politely to the Philadelphia physician who seconds earlier had been the only player at the table.

"Señor Peraza and his scion," a smiling José Guzmán said. "Welcome. Make your bet, Señor Tony. And good luck."

. . .

Las Delicias de Medina was an old-fashioned bar-restaurant on the brink of collapse. For many years the old Reina Mercedes Hospital had provided 90 percent of its clientele. Patients and their relatives abounded, but so did doctors and nurses, paramedics, ambulance drivers, lab technicians, and funeral-home staff. Las Delicias was the closest eatery to their place of work. During its golden years—the forties—two shifts of cooks, waiters, barmen, and lunch-counter attendants were kept busy eighteen hours a day, seven days a week. But in 1955 the medical institution had moved to a new building a mile away and the old building had been razed. The choice open lot—two and a half acres flanked by Twenty-third, Twenty-first, L, and K Streets, in the heart of what was rapidly becoming the new downtown Havana—waited for investors ready to fork out several million dollars. Complicating matters further, half a block away a recently inaugurated self-service cafeteria sucked in most people in the vicinity with tasty, low-priced dishes.

The dismayed owner of Las Delicias, a Spaniard from Valencia, tried to cope by extending service hours, pampering the dwindling numbers of loyal patrons, and praying to Our Lady of Montesa for her kind intercession. Unable to see the transformation taking place all around him, he hadn't grasped that with checkered tablecloths on square cedar tables, areca palms in concrete jardinières, antiquated ceiling fans, and traditional Spanish cooking, the place was condemned.

By 11:12 P.M., Valentín Rancaño joined Fermín Rodríguez and Melchor Loredo at one of the tables on the cool terrace overlooking L Street. From there they could keep an eye on a '56 blue-and-white Ford Victoria parked by the curb on Twenty-first Street. On the wall, a pay phone discreetly served time. Four poorly laid out fluorescent tubes provided lighting.

Contreras had earlier tried to convince them that it made sense to be there three hours ahead of hit time. They'd all gaped at him. "For God's sake, Ox. Three hours doing nothing in that place?" had been the mildest comment, made by Fermín. But the team leader had decreed they had to be there at eleven. Fermín ordered paella, a dish that required at least one hour to prepare. Meanwhile they would nibble canned salted anchovies and sip beer. As soon as the waiter who served them the fish rolls and filled their glasses with Cristal retired, Fermín warned his companions:

"Easy on the blonde, guys. Let's nurse this one till the paella is served and then we'll order another. No more."

By 11:17, Heller had only 235 pesos in chips left. Restless and worried, he dried the palms of his hands on his trousers. He felt like standing up and getting the hell out. As he bet five pesos on red, ten on the second dozen, five on pair, and five on the 31-32-34-35 block, he wondered how people would react if the polio victim suddenly rose from his wheelchair, nodded to those nearby, and with his best smile and long, graceful strides walked out of the casino. To cleanse his mind of impure thoughts, he watched as the ivory ball slid along the groove.

Contreras's gaze roved about the hall with a lack of interest bordering on contempt. He saw Jimmy Brun whispering to several attendants, who nodded, said something to the players, and resumed their work as the customers exchanged a few words. Contreras knitted his brow. The chief inspector finally reached his and Heller's table and for ten or fifteen seconds murmured to Barry Caldwell and Willy Pi, then left.

The dealer addressed the physician first, in English, before turning to Abo and Contreras.

"Gentlemen, in mourning for His Holiness, Pope Pius the Twelfth, the house shall close at midnight," he said in a passable Spanish in which a Portuguese cadence could be felt.

Heller's lower jaw fell in amazement, his hands knocked down his chips, and nobody noticed the jerky movements of his legs only because they were under the table. "What did you say?" he roared. Contreras's right hand gripped the muscles on Heller's collarbone.

"The Pope passed away, sir," Willy Pi replied patiently, as if talking to a mentally retarded person. "All over the city public places are closing in mourning, and the casino will do the same."

"It can't be!" Heller exclaimed. Contreras's thumb and forefinger dug into him unmercifully. The ball fell on 17.

"Easy, son, take it easy," the tobacco grower advised. "Breathe deeply. He's . . . a devout Catholic. Get him a glass of water, quick. Breathe deeply, son, deeply."

The physician had a puzzled expression. The inspector snapped his fingers at a waiter and mouthed the word "water." Willy Pi recovered and raked the casino earnings in. Heller managed to control himself and began gasping. Willy Pi raked the winnings out. The waiter presented a glass of water to the invalid. With shaking hands Heller gulped down a mouthful, before lifting his eyes to Contreras.

"I guess we should leave, Dad. Don't you think?"

"Yeah. We'll go call your doctor," Contreras said as he pulled back the wheelchair.

"Your chips, sir," said Willy Pi.

The distressed father's indecision lasted one second. "Leave them at the desk. The clerks know our room number," he said, and then resumed pushing the wheelchair toward the door opening into the hotel lobby.

The three men at Las Delicias de Medina had made desultory attempts at conversation, but had no real interest in talk. They were nibbling at the anchovies and sipping beer when at 11:26 the pay phone rang. Fermín Rodríguez glanced at his watch, got up from his chair fully convinced the call had nothing to do with them, and answered. From a distance, the waiter stared at him.

"Hello," he said.

"Gallego?"

"Ox?"

"Everything moves forward two hours, everything. Get your ass here right now."

"Whaddaya mean 'right now'?"

"I mean the Pope died on us and the place is closing at midnight. In mourning. We have to move it forward two hours."

"*Cojones.*"

"The others there?"

"Sure."

"Get going, Gallego."

Contreras hung up, closed his eyes, sighed deeply, then opened the folding door of one of the two phone booths in the lobby.

"Doctor's on his way," he told Heller before propelling the wheelchair to the main entrance with an unhurried stride. He stopped five yards away. By flexing two fingers and nodding, he beckoned the man in the absurd uniform to come closer. Staring at the gasping paralytic, the doorman complied. Contreras handed him a five-peso bill.

"My son's not feeling well. I just asked his doctor to come over. He's a short bald man. He'll be here in ten or fifteen minutes. Please, show him to the elevator and remind him we're in suite 406."

"Suite 406," the attendant repeated as he pocketed the bill. "Get well, sir," he said to Heller.

Loredo and Rancaño were left speechless and gaped at each other. The handsome light-skinned Negro felt something in his chest. The white man with the acne scars judged what had happened a bad omen.

"What a coincidence," Rancaño mumbled.

"This new schedule . . . ," Loredo said, doubtingly.

Fermín barged in. "'This new schedule' nothing. It's the same plan. Let's not futz around. Look on the bright side: We'll finish earlier. Waiter—hey, waiter!"

Fermín paid the bill and tipped the waiter, muttering something about an accident. Rancaño and Loredo were still stunned as they left. All three boarded the vehicle and Loredo eased it out from the curb.

"Tune in to Radio Reloj," said Fermín from the backseat.

Rancaño turned on the radio and spun the dial in haste. The station had a unique pattern: Two newscasters broadcast news and commercials 24/7 over a clock's monotonous tick-tock. Loredo took a right onto M Street, crossed Twenty-third, and drove into the parking lot of a funeral home. He killed the lights first, then cut the engine as Fermín stripped off his jacket, tie, and shirt. From a shopping bag, the bald man extracted a white short-sleeved smock, worked himself into it, slipped the jacket back on.

"Okay. Open up the trunk, Wheel," he said, pulling the left-door handle.

Keys in hand, Loredo stepped out and did as told. Fermín recovered a black leather doctor's bag from the compartment. Holding it with his left hand, he closed the trunk lid and, followed by Loredo, approached Rancaño's passenger window.

"Give me ten mi—"

"Shh. Listen!"

"*. . . the Sovereign Pontiff suffered a severe hiccup attack on October fourth at the papal residence of Castel Gandolfo, then sustained a brain hemorrhage on the fifth and fell in coma. We repeat: Around ten o'clock tonight, His Holiness Pope Pius the Twelfth—*"

"Turn it off," Fermín snapped.

Rancaño complied. "What a coincidence," he commented, still bewildered.

"It's not a trap," Fermín said. "Give me ten minutes. Meringue . . . Well, you know your part. How do I look?"

"Like a broke chiropractor," Rancaño quipped with the trace of a smile.

"Chiropractor I'm not; broke I am. Let's see if I can improve my financial situation soon. See you."

In the suite, once Contreras closed the door, Heller bolted from the wheelchair as if he had been sitting on nails, then started vigorously rubbing and slapping his legs. He was abashed.

"Sorry, Ox," he said.

"Put your gloves on."

"I . . . lost control; it was like after we had just blown out the candles somebody was taking the cake away."

"It's over. Put your gloves on. Let's wipe the wheelchair clean."

While they were at it, Contreras said he felt certain the money would go up, as always, between ten and twenty minutes after closing time.

"What's this mourning act? These people don't give a damn," Heller said. They were sliding a rag over the main door.

"It's public relations. Others close, especially musical shows, and they run a nightclub."

"If you hadn't asked the boys to . . . Hey, man, are you clairvoyant or something?"

"Fuck clairvoyants. I learned from my own failures that on big jobs everybody, and I mean everybody, has to be in his place three hours before the hit. That way you slip into your role gradually and if a factor changes you have time to react."

"Anyway, it's pretty spooky."

"Yeah, supernatural. I'll cast out the spirit—boooo. Let's get ready, for Chrissake."

The gear was moved downstairs, the shotguns placed on the red couch, the holsters slipped on belts. Heller moved the sheaves of strings to the pockets of his pants; the pillowcases went into the inner breast pockets of his jacket. Contreras did the same with the pillow linings.

"Gotta take a leak," the older man said, and marched to the living room bathroom. Once Contreras came out, Heller relieved himself. He was reentering the living room zipping up his fly when someone knocked on the door.

"Who is it?" Contreras asked.

"It's Doctor Benítez, Señor Peraza."

Contreras and Fermín shared a smile. Heller embraced the short man, kissed his bald head, called him brother. Gallego looked the place over, said something about the good life, then described the shock of the team members waiting at Las Delicias. Heller recounted his own confusion so vividly that Fermín guffawed over the palm of his hand.

"Gentlemen, it's eleven forty-four," Contreras admonished.

Fermín wiped his tearful eyes dry with a handkerchief, placed the bag on the seat of an armchair, and, still smiling, opened it. He slipped on gloves first, then drew out a stethoscope, a sphygmomanometer, and a thick, cotton-plugged test tube containing a five-cc syringe and several hypodermic needles.

"Tell me, Gallego, in all confidence, is this your secret, lifelong ambition? As a kid, did you dream of becoming a doctor?" Heller asked.

From under a white napkin where all the medical paraphernalia had rested, Fermín removed three identical Frankenstein rubber masks, which he dropped on another armchair. Then he unbuckled his belt, tucked the smock's flaps under the waist of his pants, and buckled up. A Luger Parabellum from the bag went to his waistband. The medical supplies returned to where they'd been.

"I'm ready," he said.

At 11:46, Valentín Rancaño entered the Capri's lobby holding a rolled-up copy of *Prensa Libre* in his right hand, approached the desk, and asked for a room. Ten minutes later he had registered as Eduardo Blanco and paid fifteen pesos; the key to room 1211 and a receipt were in his pocket. Having confided to the desk clerk that he was waiting for a lady, he approached the same armchair he had occupied five nights earlier, unfolded the newspaper, and began spying on the casino door.

The same two men with briefcases came through it at 12:03 and swaggered to the bank of elevators, followed by two security guards. All four shared the cheerful expression of staff members who'd just received an unexpected, paid reduction in their working hours. Two and a half minutes later the guards reentered the casino. Rancaño let thirty more seconds slip by, then approached a phone booth, dialed the hotel's switchboard, and asked for suite 406.

"Hello," answered Heller.

"Sorry, wrong room," Rancaño said, and broke the connection.

Heller returned the receiver to the cradle, looked at his buddies, nodded. Contreras reached for a shotgun, opened his jacket, placed the butt under his sweaty armpit, and held the weapon by both barrels. He buttoned the jacket with his left hand; only the tip of the bayonet was visible. Heller did the same. Fermín handed them the masks, which were quickly pocketed. The three men approached the suite's main door. Contreras turned the lights off.

Heller operated the handle. Fermín checked the deserted hall, then nodded. They went past the elevator doors and pushed a swinging door to the service staircase. Fermín ascended a few steps to the fifth-floor landing. Contreras and Heller trotted down to the third-floor landing. Heller guessed the sphygmomanometer would read 300 if he strapped it to his arm.

. . .

Every night, Di Constanzo's last routine was visiting the office to read and approve the casino and nightclub gross-intake reports, oversee the net results of the sport bets, then close both the safe and the office. Once in a while, when he felt like it, Di Constanzo requested a cash up from the four subordinates, who had everything ready by the time he got there. Since his stand-in had to be well acquainted with the procedure if for some reason he wasn't available, the hall supervisor always accompanied him to the safest place in the building.

The two men entered the lobby from the casino at 12:14 and ambled over to the elevators, keeping their eyes on the floor scale. Di Constanzo wore a tuxedo over a dazzlingly white shirt. The smoke billowing from his cigarette coiled around him, giving a bluish tint to his aristocratic appearance. At his side, Grouse brought to mind a bad rent-a-suit ad.

From his armchair, Rancaño sighed to release tension. An elevator door dinged and slid open; the two men entered the cage. The attendant pressed a button, turned the lever, and the brightly illuminated metal box went up to the fourth floor.

Di Constanzo and Grouse stepped out, turned left, and went through the swinging door. They took a second left before reaching the service stairway, ascended nine steps to the mezzanine, then turned right into a carpeted hallway, at the end of which a security grille safeguarded a closed wooden door.

Grouse thought he heard something—carpet-muffled steps, the rustling of cloth—so he turned his head, and registered a human form out of the corner of his eye. Without breaking stride, he turned a little to his left to confirm that it was a hotel employee. There were only offices in the mezzanine; it would have been unusual to find a guest in it. Grouse stopped dead on his tracks when he saw the three men behind him.

"Nick," he called.

Di Constanzo slowed down, swung around to look behind him, froze. The shortest of the masked marauders swiftly faced the casino boss, stuck the muzzle of a Parabellum in his chest, and in understandable English said:

"The keys."

The tallest of the three men pushed Grouse against the wall and positioned the tip of a bayonet under his double chin. The hall supervisor felt the cold tickle of the metal, gaped at the mask that was less than fifteen inches away from him, and felt fear worming out of its hideout at the back of his mind.

Di Constanzo was not a coward. He had fought ferociously in Nantes during World War I and had risked his life for the Commission many times. Three punks wearing ridiculous masks did not intimidate him.

"The keys," the short man insisted, poking Di Constanzo with the muzzle.

"No, peewee, I ain't giving you no fucking keys," Di Constanzo deadpanned as he shook his head.

Grouse's Frankenstein didn't know a word of English, but having heard "No" twice, he made a sudden upward thrust. The bayonet went through skin, tongue, and the palatine and cranial cavities as if piercing a loaf of white bread. The left parietal bone finally stopped it. The hall supervisor hopped, his eyeballs bulged out, broken nerve connections lost control, sphincters yielded. Urine and excrement gushed freely, the body jerked convulsively, and life fled away in a whirlwind of contradictory impulses. The executioner pulled the shotgun free and a ludicrously small stain of blood, saliva, and cephalic fluid flowed over the victim's shirt as his body collapsed to the floor.

"The keys," the short raider snapped.

Shocked by the brutality of the murder, Di Constanzo realized these guys were playing very hard ball and had to be taken seriously. It suddenly dawned on him that he didn't want to die. Not yet. And not for this reason. His hand went into his left trouser pocket and produced a key ring.

"Which?" Peewee Frankenstein asked. Di Constanzo sorted out two from five keys.

The third man, a spectator so far, shifted the shotgun to his left hand and reached for the keys. After squinting at their trademarks, he stepped up to the security grille and read the bas-relieved name on the lock cylinder: Corbin. He chose the same-brand key and nodded. The hostage was pushed to face the entrance and the man with the keys slipped in the first of them, turned the lock, slid open the gate. Then he inserted the second key into the door's lock and turned it.

The Frankensteins with shotguns barged in, covering the room with sweeping motions. Four nonplussed men lifted their eyes to the unexpected.

"Nobody moves. Lewis, translate," Grouse's executioner said in Spanish. After a two-second hesitation, a perplexed young man sitting in front of a desk complied.

It was a windowless, shipshape, thirty-by-fifteen-foot office. On the wall, to the left of the door, a gaping Mosler safe showed two cubic feet of neatly stacked U.S. and Cuban bills. A wheeled table with empty plates and glasses stood alongside three gray, four-drawer filing cabinets. In the center, atop two light green metal desks, were phones, three calculating machines, two ashtrays, and assorted office supplies.

"Hands on desktops," was the subsequent instruction that Leroy Lewis, born twenty-seven years earlier in Eau Claire, Wisconsin, dutifully translated. Formerly a Spanish teacher at a Youngstown high school, now he was Casino de Capri's assistant cashier. Obviously having been adding figures on a Victor calculating machine an instant earlier, his arm rested on several strips of paper. Behind the desk sat Melvin Zemach, a twenty-five-year-old assistant accountant who in 1955 gave up a business administration scholarship to Wharton, tempted by a Las Vegas job opportunity.

Nick Di Constanzo entered the room, prodded by the Parabellum's muzzle, now resting on his spine, and was forced to sit in a chair near the door. Behind the desk he faced sat Richard Falwell—formerly with the National City Bank, now the casino's cashier—and Lee Nelsen Sullivan, a fifty-two-year-old CPA who graduated from Tufts in 1930. Di Constanzo glanced at the two reports he was supposed to check and sign on the desktop. The short Frankenstein, panting and puffing, dragged Grouse's body inside, then closed the security grille and the door. The stench of excrement invaded the office.

"We had to take care of Grouse 'cause this guy here thinks he's pretty tough," the Frankenstein in charge said. "Lewis?" he asked after a pause. The assistant cashier stammered the translation.

"Anybody else feel like giving us a hard time?"

The number crunchers, terrified, kept their eyes on the floor.

"I thought so. Di Constanzo, get on your feet," the man ordered. Pale but composed, the boss stood once Lewis interpreted.

"Lie down on the floor."

The marauder who had turned both locks began tying up Di Constanzo. The Frankenstein-in-chief approached the safe, leaned his shotgun against the wall, and pulled out two pillow linings. As the casino's top executive was being immobilized, the short man cradled his buddy's shotgun in his left arm, his own Parabellum firmly gripped with his right, aimed at the not-yet-tied hostages. But it wasn't necessary. The paper shufflers, well removed from heroics by their beliefs and outlooks, followed the example set by their boss with admirable acquiescence. The third invader, meanwhile, was stuffing stacks of bills into the pillow linings.

In six minutes he filled both to the brim. His two companions, having nothing to do once the staff had been immobilized, watched him without a word. He zipped the linings up, asked for the pillowcases, slipped the loot into them. Then the intruders filled their pockets with wads of the highest denominations that remained in the safe.

"Pull out the phone cords," Frankenstein One said.

The short man stuck the Parabellum under his belt before rendering the phones useless. The other two gathered near the door, covering the shotguns with what looked like huge pillows. The short man operated the locks and peeked into the hall.

"Clear," he said.

They came out, closed the door and the security grille. Fermín pulled his mask off and did the same for Contreras and Heller, who had their hands full. With ruffled hair, they darted down the hallway and took the steps to the fourth floor. While he covered their backs, Fermín's hands squeezed the rubber masks, which he hadn't been able to slip into his overstuffed pockets. They paused by the swinging hallway door, made sure nobody was waiting for the elevators, and returned to the suite unseen. Contreras turned on the lights and, running his hands through his hair in a poor attempt at rearranging it, snapped the final orders.

"Shotguns on the couch. This pillowcase on the wheelchair seat. Yours on the back. Sit. C'mon, c'mon, sit. Now the chair's the right size, ain't it? Abo, you're paper-white!"

"Really?" the younger man asked, panting, in bug-eyed surprise.

"Very convenient, ain't it so, Doc?"

"Perfect," Fermín approved.

"Open the bag, Gallego," Contreras went on. "The dough in our pockets. Here. Take some more. Pass yours, Abo. Here, Gallego. C'mon, c'mon. Jesus, this is the biggest heist in Cuban history! Hurry up. Your rod goes in too, Gallego. Pull out the flaps of your smock. What's missing?"

"The masks," Heller said.

"First thing I dropped in the bag," Fermín said.

"Abo, loosen your tie, undo your shirt, mess up your hair a little more. Okay. Off with the gloves and into the bag."

They frantically tugged at their cotton gloves; a few moments later the medical bag was closed.

"Let's get the hell out," Contreras said.

Fermín turned the handle and they went into the hall. The fake doctor pulled the door close, then pocketed his handkerchief. Contreras, deep lines of worry on his forehead, clutched the handles and pushed the wheelchair in which Heller passably mimicked an acute respiratory crisis with moans and wheezes. The elevator on the left was coming down from the eleventh floor; in less than twenty seconds the door slid open. The attendant and two Venezuelan oil executives on their way to the airport moved aside to make room for the distressed threesome.

"Lobby—hurry up," Contreras ordered.

Staring at the pale face of Abo, who kept his eyelids closed as if seeking relief in blindness, the amazed employee pulled the lever. Embarrassed, the South Americans shied away from the patient and his escorts.

At the hotel entrance, Rancaño kept scanning around as though his date was late. An unlit cigarette hanging from his lips, he kept shifting his weight uneasily from one foot to the other and clicking the lid of a windproof Ronson lighter open and shut. The doorman and the bellboy on duty eyed him curiously and shared an intrigued glance.

From where Rancaño stood, the elevators' floor scales weren't clearly visible, but from the horizontal, right-to-left blinking of the small bulbs, the gambler guessed a cage was coming down. The second he saw the wheelchair he turned to the attendants and said, "Hey, what's going on?" tilting his head to the lobby. The doorman and the bellboy gaped at the sick man in the wheelchair. Rancaño spun around, worked the lighter, placed the flame several inches away from his face, and a second later brought it slowly to the cigarette.

Seventy yards up Twenty-first Street, Melchor Loredo clearly saw the flame. From the passenger seat he snatched two six-by-three-inch metal sheets folded in half, the word "Taxi" in blue over a white background, and inserted them on the top edges of both half-rolled-up rear windows. He turned the ignition; the engine came alive with a purr. Loredo pressed the clutch, shifted into first, and drove away from the curb as he turned on the lights. At the intersection with N Street, he tapped the brakes. Heller and the wheelchair were in the arms of two attendants, Contreras leaned over the invalid and Fermín looked his way to signal for a quick pickup. A driver from the hotel cabstand was briskly approaching his black '56 Cadillac, parked on the other side of the street. Loredo made sure no other vehicle was coming uphill on N, lightly stepped on the gas pedal, let the clutch out, and reached Contreras.

"Taxi, sir?"

"Yes, taxi, open your back door!"

"Hold this for me," Fermín said as he handed the medical bag to Rancaño, posing as Good Samaritan.

Loredo, still in his seat, leaned backward and opened the left rear door. Contreras lifted Heller by the armpits, Fermín took his legs, and with much pushing and shoving they managed to sit the choking invalid in the middle, his father by the other door. The doorman and the bellboy watched in commiseration. Fermín handed the pillowcases to Contreras, folded the wheelchair, and positioned it in the empty space by Heller, between the car's backseat and floor.

The taxi-stand cabbie watched in relief. It was a fare he didn't want, and probably the Venezuelans needed a taxi too. Fermín scurried around the car, followed by Rancaño, who surprised the hotel doorman by concisely declaring, "I'm coming with you." Both slid over the front seat, and Rancaño closed the door. Loredo released the brake, gunned the engine, and the car glided along Twenty-first before taking a right onto O Street. It was 12:36 A.M. on Friday, October 10, 1958.

PART TWO

Five

Shortly after 1:30 A.M., the parking attendant on duty persuaded his latest girlfriend to make love on the backseat of a brand-new '59 Edsel. Late models turned him on. No different from the rest of the species, he abhorred interruptions when screwing a broad and decided to approach the doorman first and find out what was keeping the few remaining casino staff from going home. Didn't those damn Yanks know the proper thing to do was to go into mourning for the Pope? Fucking Protestants!

Thirty-seven minutes later, the desk clerk phoned Bertier Pérez, the hotel's general manager. He reported that Mr. Di Constanzo and Mr. Grouse had been last seen heading to the casino's mezzanine office a few minutes after midnight. No one had left the place since; nobody was answering the phone, either. Pérez was inured to the unpredictable working hours of hoteliers and ignored his wife's protestations and her repeated slaps of her pillow as she tried in vain to return to sleep. He got dressed in a hurry, then bolted to the mezzanine. Nick Di Constanzo had had nearly two hours to chart a course of action, for it was 2:19 A.M. when Pérez, staring at the stain on the carpet and frowning at the smell of excrement, knocked on the wooden door. A chorus of anxious voices came from inside the office. Pérez identified Di Constanzo's when it ordered the others to shut the fuck up.

"Who's there?" the casino boss asked.

"Bertier Pérez, the hotel manager, Mr. Di Constanzo."

"Okay. You listen good, Pérez. Phone 2-4500, ask for Mr. Lansky, tell him to come at once. If he's not there, try the Riviera—find him somehow, and give him my message. You got the number?"

"Yes, sir: 2-4500."

"Fine. Next you call a locksmith. He's to pack his tools and get his ass here as fast as he can. When Mr. Lansky arrives, the locksmith opens the gate and the door. Don't let him open before Meyer—I mean Mr. Lansky—arrives. Am I getting through to you?"

"Perfectly."

"Good. Get one of those laundry handcarts, drop five or six clean sheets and towels in it, and bring it here."

"At your service, Mr. Di Constanzo. Anything else?"

"Yeah. Once the gate and the door are unlocked, only Mr. Lansky and those he names can come in. You and the locksmith go back to bed. And, Pérez . . ."

"Yes?"

"Bag your lips."

"Sir?"

"No comments, to anyone."

"Understood. I'm leaving now."

"Hurry up, Pérez."

Bertier Pérez was born in Littleton, North Carolina, of a Paraguayan father and an American mother. Fluent in both languages, he had joined the hotel trade in 1931. At present,

Pérez was a forty-nine-year-old monogamous Catholic who occasionally washed blood from his hands when, on vacation at home, he sliced an expensive cut of beef for a barbecue. But the experienced executive was pragmatic enough to reconcile his respect for the laws of God and men with the realities of managing hotels owned by mobsters. Most of the time he doubted that such nice, smiling, magnanimous men would engage in a diversity of criminal acts capable of exhausting the provisions of the thickest penal code, but something always happened—from a sudden scowl to the unexplained disappearance of someone—that planted new seeds in his cautious mind. So, the Capri's general manager followed instructions to the letter and, on his own initiative, made known to the switchboard operator and the desk clerk that Mr. Di Constanzo and other casino staff were working late and mustn't be disturbed. And he gave room service a standby order for ham-and-cheese sandwiches and a half-gallon thermos bottle of freshly brewed coffee, just in case.

From 3:36 to 3:38 A.M., Meyer Lansky and Jacob Shaifer watched as Ricardo Benavides unlocked the gate and the door and put away his skeleton keys in a metal box. The general manager handed a fifty-peso bill to the locksmith, took hold of his elbow, and steered him from the mezzanine, thanking him most kindly. Once they were out of sight, Lansky pulled out a .38 Smith & Wesson revolver and Shaifer drew a .45 automatic Colt Commando.

"I'm coming in, Nick," Lansky said.

"Okay, Meyer."

Shaifer crossed the doorway, looked around, and nodded to Lansky before shoving the gun back into his shoulder holster. His boss first gazed at the open and virtually empty safe to confirm what only an idiot wouldn't have suspected, then scanned the room, where five impatient men, lying on their stomachs, stretched their necks up like hungry turtles. A sixth remained as uninterested as only corpses can be. The stench of excrement was overpowering inside the office.

"Got a blade, Jacob?"

"Sure," Shaifer said, fishing into the left pocket of his trousers.

"Cut them loose," Lansky ordered, pocketing his gun.

By the time Di Constanzo finished rubbing his wrists and ankles, the other four had been freed too and a cash up was ordered. The younger men began counting what was left in the safe; Falwell and Sullivan consulted records. Lansky and Di Constanzo retired to the filing cabinets, where the man from the Capri told Lansky what had happened. After recounting Grouse's murder, he presented his carefully considered reason for giving in.

". . . The keys were in my pocket. They could've bumped me off and taken them anyway. It would've gained us nothing, so I gave it to them."

When Di Constanzo finished, Lansky closed his eyes. He was mildly surprised at not feeling the symptoms: the buzzing in his ears, the heat on his face. Next he fixed his gaze on the apple-green carpet. In twelve hours, a day at most, all Commission members and gang bosses in the U.S. would learn that Meyer Lansky had been taken for . . .

"Ask them the fucking figure," loud enough for all the others to hear.

"Lee?" Di Constanzo asked.

"Six hundred twenty-seven thousand," Sullivan reported.

Di Constanzo shot a glance at Lansky. The man was

perceptibly shaken by this egregious loss of prestige. Bonanno's probable reaction sprang to Lansky's mind, and his brain paused to consider that probability. The quiet humming that usually preceded the buzzing started in his inner ear.

"Bonanno?" he asked, lifting his eyes to Di Constanzo.

The man from Capri mulled it over for about ten seconds. "I don't think so, Meyer. This must've taken weeks, even months of planning."

"Precisely."

"He ain't got anyone here."

Lansky kept to himself the "who knows?" that came to his mind. "Who's your man fluent in Spanish?"

"Hey, Leroy, get over here."

Still affected by the recent ordeal and impressed by Lansky's presence, Lewis traversed the room. Even though nobody had said a word about internal complicity, the five men from Casino de Capri felt certain an insider had supplied vital information to the raiders. Leroy Lewis feared that, having been ordered to interpret, he might be considered a likely suspect. His own knowledge of his total innocence wasn't a great comfort.

"Mr. Lansky wants to have a word with you," Di Constanzo said to the assistant cashier.

"At your service. It's a pleasure to meet you, sir," Lewis muttered.

"Thanks, kid. These bastards knew you by name; they used you as interpreter."

"Well . . . yes."

"Did their voices sound familiar to you? Identify anyone?"

"No, sir."

"Was their Spanish genuine? I mean, did you notice an accent?"

Lewis could have given an instant reply, but he took his time, eyes on the floor, to give the impression he was recalling every word. He shook his head one last time.

"Genuine Spanish is only spoken in Spain, Mr. Lansky, in Castile specifically. They talked Cuban Spanish, but genuinely Cuban, no foreign accent. Besides . . ."

"Go on."

Lewis smiled, shook his head some more. "This may sound strange to you, sir, but they smelled Cuban. Over here people shower on a daily basis, use deodorants and perfumes. The one who tied me up smelled Cuban."

"Anything else?"

"No."

"Okay. Thanks."

The assistant cashier rejoined the other office workers. Meyer Lansky studied the group for a moment. They didn't know whether to volunteer for anything, sit down, talk among themselves, or ask permission to leave. Melvin Zemach frequently raised his eyebrows and glanced at the ceiling, both hands stuck in his pockets. Slouching, Richard Falwell held his hands at his back, looked at the carpet, and every minute or so pursed his lips in disapproval. With one leg thrown over the corner of his desk, Sullivan was chewing his nails to the quick. Lansky felt certain the traitor was not one of them: All four seemed to belong to the mass of gutless folks whose mantra was "I have ultimate respect for the law." Like most men of action, the Hebrew had a very low opinion of paper pushers.

Lansky sighed. "Gentlemen, we've been had," he said. "Tomorrow at ten A.M. I want you to hand Nick a list of all your close Cuban friends, with their home addresses. If some guy was curious about how the casino operates, asked a lot of questions, place a check mark next to the name. Whoever asks what happened here tonight is told you were working late, the door lock broke, and you couldn't get out. Not one word more. Sleep well, if you can."

"Gimme your keys, Lee," Di Constanzo said to the accountant.

The four men slipped into their jackets and left. For a while Lansky, Di Constanzo, and Shaifer discussed their next moves. Next the bodyguard lightened Grouse of his wallet, keys, watch, and rings before rolling the handcart requested by Di Constanzo into the office. Assisted by the Capri man, Shaifer lifted the body and placed it prone on the handcart, chest over folded knees, towels under the wound to absorb any flow there might be. Once the corpse was covered with clean sheets, they hurried to Bertier Pérez's office to make several phone calls.

Lansky's counterattack began at 4:53 A.M., just after the handcart moved from the Capri's freight platform to a '57 GMC panel truck. The driver, Fat Butch, helped Shaifer dump the body at a vacant lot on Twenty-seventh Street. In the Havana Riviera they tore the cart apart, threw away the wheels, then burned the sheets, towels, and canvas in the incinerator. Butch took Shaifer back to the Capri, then drove through the tunnel under Havana Bay to get rid of the cart's wooden parts along the deserted coastline, near the town of Cojímar.

Joe Silesi from Casino de Capri and Dino Cellini from the Havana Riviera Casino dashed along the passenger terminal of Havana's international airport at 5:23 A.M. They were under orders to hop a plane bound for New York, report to Costello, and fly back ASAP. Fifteen minutes later, Charles White and Eddie Galuzzo hurried into the same terminal to collect in Miami and bring to Havana the half-million dollars won with the covering bet on the seventh game's result.

But Lansky didn't want to welsh on what he owed to those who bet on the Yankees; rumors would be spreading all over town if they didn't get their money in the course of the day. So, at 5:40 A.M. he phoned Roberto Suárez—Cuban senator, legal consultant of the Havana Riviera Corporation and close friend for twenty-one years—to ask for a cash loan of five hundred thousand pesos to be paid back three days later at a flat 1 percent interest rate. Half an hour later a half-awake Martín Balbuena, vice president of Banco de los Colonos, learned of Lansky's request. Since the money had to be available by 9:00 A.M., Balbuena made fourteen phone calls from his home before getting back to Suárez at 7:55 to report that the cash would be available at a 1.5 percent interest rate.

Bertier Pérez was ordered to sound out desk, lobby, and elevator attendants for anything unusual that had happened between midnight and 1:00 A.M. When the general manager reported the acute respiratory crisis endured by an invalid staying in suite 406, Lansky smiled faintly, glanced at Di Constanzo, and suggested a look-over. At 6:02 both men stared at the shotguns on the red couch.

The sun was rising when a servant in the residence of Santiago Tey—former secretary of the interior in the Batista cabinet, senator, and lawyer—took the message that Mr. Meyer Lansky requested an interview at Mr. Tey's earliest convenience. Mr Lansky suggested 9:00 A.M. at the senator's home at 552 Twenty-first Street.

Tey was a compulsive gambler who fifteen months earlier had persuaded Lansky to install a roulette wheel in his home and to send attendants whenever he felt like playing. Back then, Tey used to spend more time at casinos than at his ministerial post, frequently losing thirty or forty grand in a couple of hours. The adverse publicity had caught up with him, and Havana gossip claimed it was one of the minor reasons he had been sacked. The major reason, according to what were euphemistically called "reliable sources," was that Tey had been shaving the president's cut of the graft money he made by selling influence, pardons, and driver's licenses, collecting bribes from suppliers, and inflating the payroll with nonexistent employees. Over the course of time, the civilian who had been in charge of the Cuban police force became one of Lansky's best customers.

By 9:06 A.M., with José Guzmán interpreting, the unflappable Lansky worded one of the weirdest requests the Cuban senator had yet heard. According to the Hebrew, a Cuban with a record of armed robbery had seduced the daughter of an American industrial tycoon who manufactured world-renowned candies and cookies. The father—one of Lansky's very close friends—didn't want the press to learn that his beloved daughter had eloped with an ex-con, and he had hired private investigators to unearth information that could reveal the whereabouts of the seducer and his innocent victim. Lansky hoped that Tey would exert his considerable influence with police brass and have them move their files and mug shots to the Riviera, where the multimillionaire's PIs would examine them.

Batista's crony stared at Lansky. The Hebrew looked back self-assuredly. Tey appreciated the courtesy of Lansky's having devoted five or six minutes to concoct a story that would allow him to keep up appearances. On the other hand, he wanted Lansky to owe him.

"I can't do it, Meyer. I can't ask the Bureau of Investigations to take their armed-robbers files to the Riviera and leave them there for a day or two. It's . . . too much. But maybe I can ask Colonel Grava to bring them here tonight and pick them up tomorrow night. He might say yes or he might say no; we'll see. But if, as a very big personal favor to me, he agrees, these . . . private eyes could drop by my library and take a peek at them."

"That'll be fine, Santiago. Tomorrow at nine A.M.?"

"We'll see."

"There's no less than ten dicks hunting this dude, so it's better if they come in three groups, at nine and eleven in the morning and at one or two in the afternoon. No problem with that?"

"I'll talk to Grava and call you later, okay?"

"I'd really appreciate it if you lend me a hand with this, Santiago."

"It'll take a lot of persuasion, Meyer. But we'll see."

. . .

In the master bedroom of the sequestered house, the booty lay on an oilcloth spread on the floor. Silence presided as the five criminals stared at the bundle of money. None of them had ever seen $627,000 before. The count had been completed a few moments earlier and even Melchor Loredo, the least proficient in arithmetic, realized he'd get over sixty thousand pesos. Each man lost himself in his daydream; time slipped by unnoticed.

The open windows revealed a thin layer of clouds sifting the glow of the sun. The distant whining of an industrial siren and the roar of an approaching bus marred the sound of whispering foliage and the chirping of birds.

The celebration had taken hours. While waiting for Loredo, who had to ditch the Ford on the other side of the port and make his way back behind the wheel of Contreras's Chevy, some light drinking and solid cooking had taken place. After Loredo's safe return, well-done steaks and French fries were washed down with red wine. Sipping brandy before dawn, in a swirling fog of cigar and cigarette smoke, a buoyant Heller had described the highlights of the days spent at the hotel to Fermín, Rancaño, and Loredo, occasionally asking for confirmation from Contreras, who just smiled and nodded. In a more sober tone, Fermín recounted to the driver and the scout what had taken place in the mezzanine. The news of Grouse's assassination had made Rancaño and Loredo frown. The Pope's death was discussed in amazement, and when Contreras was unanimously complimented on his foresight, the others realized that the organizer had hardly said a word and the conversation fizzled out.

"You had to do this guy, Ox?" Loredo asked unexpectedly, sort of wet-blanketing the celebration.

Contreras raised his eyebrows before presenting his case. "Suppose I didn't. We'd have had to start an argument—in the hallway, in the middle of the night, three armed and masked men arguing with two casino execs. What would've happened if somebody came along, if one of them hollered for help? Suppose we finally got in without capping anyone and found the safe closed. We'd have to beg them to open it up. Di Constanzo would've known we didn't want to go all the way. I'm sorry for the poor bastard, but . . ."

Loredo's forehead furrowed in resignation, and Rancaño didn't like it either. Heller and Fermín, pretending to be unconcerned, kept up their tough-macho act as they glanced at the booty. In light of which Contreras said:

"I suppose we ought to see how much's in there." Then he stood, dusted off the seat of his pants, and lifted the pillowcases. From a closet, Fermín extracted an old beige oilcloth a former tenant had left behind. The floor was littered with empty plates and bottles, cigarette butts, old newspapers. "Let's go upstairs," Heller suggested.

It took them almost thirty minutes, because Contreras insisted on making sure every stack had one hundred bills. Fermín was asked to jot down numbers on a piece of paper and add them up at the end. When the total was announced, they all kept quiet for so long the mice and ants and cockroaches and spiders may very well have paused and wondered.

Heller was the first to snap out of it. He had regained his color and typical sense of humor after the steak and half a bottle of wine. "Well, gentlemen, here's a pen," he said, pulling a ballpoint from the pocket of his dress shirt. On a corner of the oilcloth, he wrote the total. "Let's see, six-twenty-seven divided by two . . . hm . . . yeah, one left, I bring down the zero . . . Mr. X gets 313,500 pesos, half of it. And each of us gets . . ." After nearly thirty seconds spent dividing by five he joyously hooted, "62,700 coconuts!"

"Holy Mother of God!" Loredo whispered from the floor, where he sat with arms locked over crossed legs.

"I wanna say something," Fermín, hunkering down, announced. "We agreed to cut it five ways, but Ox was in charge. He rounded us up, figured out how to ace in and beat the joint. Had to finish a guy off, too. I propose each of us hand him the twenty-seven hundred pesos and keep a clean sixty thousand, so he can come out with a little over seventy thousand."

Contreras weakly tried to oppose a motion he in fact considered fair, but Heller and Loredo gave their immediate and enthusiastic approval, compelling Rancaño to halfheartedly agree. The money was divided into six piles: an impressive 50 percent that belonged to Naguib, four with 60,000 pesos each, one with 73,500.

With the intense concentration of a man who's actually manipulating his future, Loredo placed his cut in a brown paper bag, then conscientiously folded the top over. Rancaño put his share in a cardboard cake box, then tied it up with a thin cord. Fermín stuffed his money in his adman briefcase. Heller crammed his cut into a paper bag he'd found on the ground floor that had originally contained the two towels and the bar of soap that Fermín had bought five days earlier for the country house. Contreras went downstairs and came back with a half-full can of crackers, which he emptied on the bedroom floor. He placed his money at the bottom, then covered it with crackers.

"Bring the suitcase, Gallego," he said while pressing the lid on the can.

All five were helping pack the Lebanese's money into a medium-sized suitcase when Rancaño verbalized what Loredo and Heller were only thinking.

"How can this bird find out if we take him for fifty grand?"

Kneeling on the floor, Contreras looked up, noticed four pairs of eyes locked on his own, then smiled with the bitterness of those who see a nasty prediction fulfilled.

"He's got an inside man, that's for sure," Contreras said, trying to sound patient, "and he'll learn exactly how much silver we made off with. This dude has been around: If we fuck him he either sends a goon to get me or crosses me off his nice-fellows list and when he figures out a new angle gives the job to someone else. He doesn't know who you guys are, just like you don't know who he is. I'm the one who has to hand this to him—wait till he counts it, case you didn't know. So it's no, we don't take him for nothing."

"It was just an idea," Rancaño mumbled in a mollifying tone.

They resumed storing away Naguib's cut. When all was in the suitcase, the lid was lowered and the spring locks snapped. All rose. Contreras picked up the suitcase and his can of crackers, turned to go downstairs, took two steps, then turned around. He heaved a deep sigh. For a moment it appeared as though he wanted to say something to the others and was wondering whether he should. He had been so quiet all morning that everybody was curious.

"What is it, Ox?" Heller asked.

Contreras squinted. "Listen, I'll be seeing Gallego once again, but I won't see the rest of you for a long time. I wanna thank you for the cut you took to give me some more silver. I really appreciate that." His eyes went to the floor for a second. "You've all got good knockers, did a good job; I have no complaints. But before leaving I wanna tell you guys about my plans, 'cause I'm pretty sure in less than a week this Mafia mob will find out about Abo and myself, maybe about

Gallego, too, and they're gonna come after us. And I mean fucking *come*. If they find me they won't take me to the nearest police station and I might go wrong, so I don't wanna know where any of you guys are holing up."

Contreras made eye contact with each man for an instant before going on. "I'm gonna elope. México? Panamá? Cacocum? Aguada de Pasajeros? All of them are fair bets." He paused briefly and smiled. "Havana won't see this kisser for six months; bet your lives on it. Now, giving unsolicited advice is a waste of time and I won't do that, but I hope you guys figure out what's best for you. What I'll do is lock up my silver"—he shook the can, and the crackers rattled—"and keep some, two or three thousand, so I can spend a year like a toad under a stone. No parties, few drinks, and when I approach a dame it's to screw her, not to tell her the story of my life. Whoever starts throwing away his mazuma slips his head into the hangman's noose. Well . . ."

Contreras deposited the suitcase and the can on the floor, shook hands all around, recovered the money, and went down the creaky stairs, followed by the others. In the foyer, he waited until Loredo opened the front door for him, then crossed the verandah, descended four steps, approached his Chevy, and stored the suitcase and the can in the trunk as Fermín opened the padlock, removed the chain, and pulled open the Cyclone-fence gate. The car started, backed out. From the two-lane road Contreras waved at the group, then sped away.

Rancaño kept his eyes on the Chevy until it disappeared. Then he did a big stretch, yawned hugely, and said: "If he thinks I'm gonna wait six months to open my gambling joint . . ."

Smacks of carelessness, Fermín thought. What he said was: "Let's vacate the shack."

They went back inside. The dirty kitchenware and the glasses and cutlery were wrapped in old newspapers and stored in cardboard boxes, which were then hoisted to the pickup's bed. The radio and an unopened bottle of wine were placed on the front seat. Two raw steaks, five sausages, the surplus eggs, sugar, rice, potatoes, onions, coffee, and salt ended up in the garbage can. Fermín showed how attentive to detail he was by disconnecting the electric meter as the others closed windows and doors.

Loredo and Rancaño headed for the bus stop, and the short bald man, watching them from the gate, confirmed the reason cops could spot wrongdoers so easily. The driver and the scout kept glancing around, and they held the brown paper bag and the cake box the way shipwrecked sailors hold lifelines. Fermín slipped behind the wheel of the pickup. Loredo and Rancaño boarded a bus at the same moment Heller was fastening the padlock to the gate's chain. When his pal got in and closed the passenger door, Fermín sped away.

Ten minutes later, as the pickup approached the intersection of Diez de Octubre and Acosta, Heller asked, "Where did Wheel leave the Ford?"

"In Regla. Then he boarded the public launch and drove Ox's Chevy to the house."

Heller grinned. "He probably threw copper pennies to the Virgin. *This* is what *I* have faith in," he said, patting the shopping bag.

"Don't run wild, Abo."

"I won't, don't worry. I'm not stupid. But I'll revel all night long; get the stiff outta my mind, if you catch my meaning."

"Keep the wine."

"Such a spender."

"Fuck you."

"Just kidding. Thanks for the ride, Gallego. Slow down. I'm getting off right there, at the taxi stand."

Fermín jettisoned the leftovers into a garbage can off Lawton, abandoned the pickup on Luyanó Avenue, then took a cab to the corner of Monte and Someruelos. A two-story mansion that at the turn of the century had been the lavish residence of a very rich man, had over the years been down-graded to a tenement house whose thirty-eight residents shared four bathrooms and two kitchens. Fermín entered the place, went up to his room, stored away the briefcase in his oak wardrobe, and sat for a while on his bed, mulling things over. Then he undressed, set the alarm of his old Westclox for 1:30, and a few minutes later was sound asleep.

After the nap he put on a green bathrobe, dropped every-thing he needed into pockets, wrapped a towel around his neck, and marched to one of the communal bathrooms. He showered, shaved, brushed his teeth, then went back to his room. At 2:10 P.M., carrying his briefcase with what he hoped seemed confident detachment, he went into the Monte Street branch office of Banco Agrícola e Industrial. He rented a safe-deposit box under an assumed name, emptied the briefcase into it, counted out three thousand pesos, slipped them into the inner breast pocket of his peach-colored sports jacket, and left the bank at five minutes to three.

A half hour later, Valentín Rancaño finished stowing fifty-five thousand pesos between the picture tube and other parts of an old Emerson TV set. TeleHogar was a radio-and-TV repair shop on the corner of Zanja and Belascoaín where the scout, who couldn't tell apart a condenser from a resistor, had been driving a panel truck and sweeping floors for fifty pesos a month since last April.

As he screwed on the set's back cover, Rancaño gloated over his acting job of four weeks earlier, when he had sweet-talked the shop owner into selling him the piece of junk for sixty pesos, to be paid for in a five-peso installment plan, deductible from his monthly wage. The boss had warned his jack-of-all-trades that he could take the set home only after it had been fully paid for, which was precisely what the scout had expected. Rancaño tittered anticipating the surprise his resignation would cause in exactly twenty-one days, on the pretext of a job at a new, nameless casino. He'd suggest to the owner settling the balance with his monthly salary, and he'd take the antique set home that same day.

Arturo Heller put on his best smile and rang the bell at precisely 4:02 P.M. Most tenants in the three-story apartment building at 501 Estrada Palma Street were low-income clerical workers pretending they didn't mind being losers. Heller's fiancée, Esther Sosa de Quesada, was the only child of a married couple in their fifties.

Even though the chaste, twenty-year-old blonde Pentecostal had a sunny disposition, what led people of all ages and races to stare at her had nothing to do with her outgoing personality and Christian values. In his rather vast experience, Heller had seen great bodies and beautiful faces, but not before Esther had he found a woman with an unbelievable body who was in addition graced with adorable, perfect features. The student teacher with the peachy skin and the long-lashed turquoise-blue eyes also had high cheekbones, a slightly upturned nose, and well-formed lips that gave away a radiant smile to nearly everyone.

For eight months, posing as a hardworking salesman who spent most of his time on the road, the onetime law student had stalked Esther as a jackal follows a wounded gazelle. At present, formally engaged to Esther, he only visited her home on Sunday evenings, as was the custom. The fact that her parents behaved like security guards hadn't reduced his yearning for the luscious blonde. From Monday to Friday, as though she were seven, Señor Sosa punctually picked Esther up at the Normal School. When Heller came by, her mother would read the Bible on a living room rocking chair, six feet away from the sweethearts. Were he to take Esther to the movies, both papa and mama would tag along. But Heller was not one to despair. He felt certain of overcoming all obstacles. At the right moment and place—what a day!—Esther would surrender her virginity to him.

The young woman's surprised mother—it was a Saturday—opened the front door and let Heller in. He gave her a peck on the cheek and ascribed his sudden return from Cienfuegos to brisk sales. But Papa and Esther were at choir rehearsal and wouldn't get home earlier than six, the lady made known. Heller explained that the motive for his untimely visit was the lovely stool he held. Two hours earlier he had admired it in Orbay y Cerrato and decided he wanted to present it to his future wife, for her dressing table. Wasn't it fit for a queen?

The pleased mother reached for and tactfully eyed the round, four-legged piece with the vinyl-covered seat. All the goodwill in the world wouldn't make it grace the bedroom of a ruined baroness, but she accepted it and assured Heller that as soon as her daughter arrived she'd give her his present. Beaming, he again kissed the matron's cheek and left, telling her that tomorrow evening he would arrive at eight sharp. The good soul couldn't even dream that from that day on her daughter would be resting her perfect behind on fifty-seven thousand pesos hidden between the stool's stuffing and the frame.

Certain that the Virgin had performed a miracle on him, Melchor Loredo prayed for directions to the proper hiding place and during his after-lunch nap dreamed of a well-drilling rig at work. When his wife woke him, he sipped his usual cup of espresso distractedly, figuring things out. Forty-five minutes later, at a home-appliances store on Sixtieth and Twenty-third Avenue, in Marianao, Loredo bought two Presto pressure cookers. Back at his small apartment, he locked himself in the bathroom, packed fifty-eight thousand pesos into them, adjusted the lids, and put the gadgets into a multilayered paper bag. Then he took a cab to the small town of El Calvario.

His parents-in-law dwelled in a thatched hut built from royal palm wood on the town's southeast border, alongside a dirt road that petered out at the dairy farm where his wife's father made a living. Loredo accepted an unbelievably good espresso, handed out cigarettes, made small talk until dusk, then borrowed a pick. He wandered off into a pasture ground, and near a luxuriant mango tree waited for a half hour to make sure he hadn't been followed. Then, in full darkness, Loredo dug a three-foot-deep hole, buried the pressure cookers, and, as he shoveled the remaining earth into the paper bag, sadly wondered what would happen to the money were he to die suddenly, or be sentenced to prison. He slowly retraced his steps, pondering whether he should tell his wife where the treasure lay. Tormented by feelings of guilt for distrusting the woman he loved, he handed a crisp, fifty-peso bill to his be-wildered father-in-law.

The Security Packers and Storage Company stored fur-niture, works of art, tapestries, rugs, and other property of people who spent long periods abroad. The warehouse was at Tenth between A and B in Lawton; working hours were from eight to twelve and from two to six. That same after-noon, the attendant on duty glanced at his watch when an old black Chevy parked by the curb. The dial said 5:40 P.M. *Fucking latecomer,* the clerk thought. The gray-haired guy who opened the trunk and pulled a suitcase from it sauntered in and asked for six months of storage. A courteously superficial inspection ensued—for without offending clients, the atten-dant had to make sure no practical joker left a dead dog—money changed hands, a receipt was extended, and the customer shuffled out.

Contreras headed straight for the psychiatric institution, feeling beat. The quiet suburb came to his mind. Modern homes peopled by middle-class families with kids, dogs, ser-vants, and cars, all pretending to be unconcerned by the prox-imity of a madhouse. He anticipated the orderlies' discreet welcome. Wondering about tips, they would say it was great to have him back. Yes, Contreras thought, he had found the ideal hideout where in a few hours he'd fall back, like a snail into its shell, for a long season.

...

Rumbling waves—endlessly coming in and breaking on the dog-toothed rock, then falling back to get ready for the next thrust—echoed along the dark coastline. Sixty yards inland, the Chevy pulled over next to the corner of First Avenue and Sixtieth. Fermín switched off the headlights and cut the ignition. A waning last-quarter moon played hide-and-seek with thick clouds; down the street, weak cones of streetlights on power poles cast a few bright spots into the darkness.

Contreras had asked Fermín to drive when he picked him up at the corner of Infanta and San Miguel Streets. The short man had sat behind the wheel, grunted, moved the seat all the way forward. He wore the same sports jacket over a tan poplin shirt, brown slacks, and his favorite nut-colored shoes. In the passenger seat, leaning on the door, Contreras didn't look like a man who had stayed awake all night. After a warm shower, a shave, and a hot meal, he had got into a navy-blue gabardine suit.

Now, their eyes were fastened on an L-shaped building that sparkled against the pitch-black background of underbrush and rocks one block away. The Château Miramar had five floors, of which the upper four had rows of balconies whose white French windows contrasted with the chocolate-colored exterior. The tenants of the exclusive aparthotel were mostly wealthy tourists, plus several rich eccentrics in love with the place and a few refined mistresses of corrupt politicians. On any given evening the Château could simultaneously host a high-society wedding reception, a respectable family gathering, and a private party where sodomy, marijuana, and whiskey went hand in hand with flagellation, heroin, and champagne. The management succeeded in making certain that such diversity coexisted harmoniously and offered first-class service at its fashionable restaurant and bar.

"Arriving there in this heap is like going to the Pope's funeral in shorts and tennis shoes," Fermín quipped as he watched the main entrance, where a doorman and a parking valet looked after people going in or out.

Contreras smiled and glanced at his watch—9:50 P.M. "They'll take us for upscale messengers; heap instead of bikes."

"Messengers delivering a nice package," Fermín said, patting the huge, brand-new rawhide travel bag on the front seat.

"I'm supposed to go to apartment 35," Contreras revealed. "The man will probably count it; then we'll wait for a guy who's supposed to come in at eleven. I guess he's the singer from Capri. The man doesn't trust him—he asked me to flatten out and keep an eye on him."

"Why should you flatten out?" Fermín objected. "It's better if the hot wire sees the man has some backup."

"The singer insists on not being known by any of us, according to the man, so I'll have to do a crouch."

"And see him anyway."

"You bet. If I'm not here by eleven-thirty leave the keys in the ignition and take a powder, just in case."

Fermín nodded, still looking ahead. He was partly flattered by having been chosen, partly reluctant to face new—and unpaid—risks. "Well, should we go in?" he asked.

"Go ahead."

The block was covered in a few seconds. At 9:52, Contreras forced a smile in the direction of the grinning doorman, who pulled the plate-glass door open for him. Fermín drove away to park at the same place, light a cigar, and wait for his buddy.

"I have an appointment in 35," Contreras informed the desk clerk. The man glanced at a notepad, picked up an extension, asked for Señor Naguib's apartment, and respectfully told someone that a visitor had arrived. He listened for an instant before raising his eyes to Contreras.

"Is your last name Toro, Señor?"

Contreras suppressed a smile. "Yes," he said. *Toro,* Spanish for bull—an authentic though unusual surname. The bull was intact, the ox castrated.

The clerk said yes, it was Mr. Toro, then listened some more while staring at the newcomer. "Yes," he confirmed. Finally he said "Immediately" and hung up.

"Those are the elevators, señor. Third floor, right turn."

Contreras took in the lobby as he crossed it. Main staircase to his left, a second plate-glass door to the restaurant, two closed wooden doors. A black man brandishing a skimming spoon picked cigar and cigarette stubs from tall, sand-filled metal ashtrays. In typical fugitive fashion, Contreras had tuned his senses to essentials: He registered the crystal chandelier hanging from the ceiling, but missed its beautiful arabesque ornaments; noticed the furniture, but not its daringly modern design. He was not listening to the Muzak coming from hidden speakers, didn't register the smell of the regularly atomized deodorizer.

Contreras left the cage on the third floor, turned right, took the corridor until reaching a mahogany door to which a 3 and a 5 in silver and copper had been nailed. He pressed the buzzer; a beaming Naguib opened. The Lebanese wore a white dress shirt, its collar open, the knot of his pale blue tie resting on his sternum. His trousers were charcoal-gray, his black shoes of the lace-up kind. He pumped Contreras's right arm the way captains compliment fine platoon leaders, then waved him in.

The guest chose a chair from the French Regency–style living-room suite, watched as Naguib deposited the travel bag on a coffee table, then accepted a crystal goblet with a neat slug of Antiquary brandy. The host selected an armchair upholstered in a costly thin brocade with a pattern of golden branches and leaves on a white background. Then he opened the travel bag, pulled out the stacks of bills, and started to count. His fingers slipped over the corners of the notes with a teller's ease. Soon Contreras gave up his original idea of following the count with his eyes and instead inspected the living room.

The sophisticated decor showed that this wasn't a place rented for occasional meetings; no one who could afford such a plush apartment would debase it with a lease. The majesty of furniture and mirrors, drapes and lamps, paintings and ornaments went beyond the borders of the love nest to become a small temple. Due to his poor origins and cultural insufficiency, Contreras couldn't guess that the small nymph in marble on the Louis XV console table was a piece by Canova, or that the blonde girl smiling from the canvas hung on the opposite wall was a genuine Boucher, but ignorance couldn't impede admiration. His anxiety momentarily dissolved.

After his second sip of brandy, Contreras lit a cigarette and wondered if his being there was proof of trust or extreme distrust. He pictured men in hiding watching him. No, it didn't figure. No motive, no benefit. He smoked placidly, then crushed the butt. He had to wait another eleven minutes for Naguib to finish.

"Is it all right?" he asked once the Lebanese put aside the last wad.

"My source said you'd taken six fifty; I expected three twenty-five."

"Your source is wrong," Contreras snapped. "We got six twenty-seven. There's half of it there."

"Must be a mistake," Naguib said soothingly.

"We left behind a lot of five- and one-peso stacks 'cause our bags were full," the Cuban explained. "Maybe they had six fifty in the keister and we left behind twenty-three."

"Okay. Nevertheless, I'll give my inside man half of three twenty-five, not to disappoint him," Naguib said.

The opaque indifference in Contreras's gaze indicated that the Lebanese could do as he pleased with his cut. Naguib raised his glass, arranged himself on the seat, leaned back. Priding himself on sizing up men accurately, he stared at Contreras with satisfaction. There was an otherness in the Cuban that intrigued him. Kind of guy who makes a great team leader, lousy team player. The intention was to discredit Lansky, not steal the money, and he would've given odds of 7 to 3 that the gang would vanish into thin air. With this in mind, that afternoon he had brought a fourth of the figure reported that same morning by his Judas to the apartment and hoarded it in the chest of drawers. But Contreras's chivalrous behavior, which he'd considered a remote possibility at the beginning of the Bonanno-inspired plot, opened up new and vast opportunities.

"Give me the details, from the moment you entered the casino last night."

Naguib lit a Lucky. It took Contreras sixteen minutes to make a comprehensive account of the heist, up to the minute when they left in the getaway car. "The only snags were the Pope's death—that was a total surprise—and the guy I had to bump. The rest went as planned, no trouble at all."

"Good work, Contreras," Naguib said, as he filed away the fact that the guy was good at improvisation, adjusted rapidly to changing conditions. He lit a fresh cigarette, then added: "A pleasure to do business with you."

"Same here," Contreras obliged. "I won't be available for a spell, but after I get back to Havana I'll give you a ring."

"Fine."

"Could you tell me anything about this source of yours? I'll see him anyway, and it'd be best if I have an idea as to what we can expect from him."

"We can expect anything," Naguib said. "He's not a pro. I talked him into it and he has . . . sort of changed in the last two months. Not a bad guy, but he's too emotional, unpredictable, so when he gets here you just slip into the bedroom and be ready to come out if I ask you to."

Contreras nodded and started pulling a cigarette out of the pack. Naguib rushed to offer him a Lucky; the Cuban shook his head.

"You shouldn't light that one, then," the Lebanese warned. "He knows I smoke Luckies, and the different smell could give you away. It's ten twenty-six already."

Contreras returned the pack to his right jacket pocket. In a couple of minutes Naguib separated stacks adding up to 162,500 pesos that he left on the coffee table, dropped the remainder in the bag, then got up to wash Contreras's glass and dispose of the butts in the ashtray. He came back to his armchair, glanced at his watch.

"Twenty-three more minutes. How old are you?"

"Fifty-three."

"You from Havana?"

Contreras shook his head. He didn't like to be questioned. Suddenly he remembered he was facing the man who had made him prosperous and could eventually make him rich.

"I was born in Morón. That's in the province of Camagüey. And you?"

"I'm from Al Mansouriyé, a village near Beirut, Lebanon. Know the country?"

"Who wouldn't, with a war going on."

A minute of uncomfortable silence passed away.

"Your parents—they immigrated from Spain?" Naguib probed.

"No. My four grandparents did, though."

"Are your parents alive?"

"Mr. Naguib, I'm gonna make an exception with you, 'cause I admire your style. But I don't like to be questioned on family matters, personal matters, any matters. In fact, I don't like answering questions at all."

"Then don't. I just wanted to pass the time."

"Let's pass it. My father joined the rebels in the last war against Spain. He was fifteen—can you believe it? At that age everybody is a sucker, and he swallowed the pill. You know, all that baloney about the 'solitary star,' 'Run to combat, *bayameses,*' and 'Dying for the Motherland is living forever.' Two years later he came back to his hometown with three scars from bullet wounds and landed a job laying out railroad tracks at new sugar mills being erected in Camagüey. He hung himself in 1915. A sledgehammer blow had busted his right hand and he couldn't feed his wife and three sons on his veteran's pension. He was thirty-four. My mother worked like a beast of burden but we never had enough, so at fifteen I stole an ox. I got salted. You know what 'getting salted' means in Cuba?"

"Yeah, I know."

"I served a year in the Camagüey penitentiary. Then I roamed over half of Cuba, became a bad boy. Rustler, petty thief, pickpocket, smuggler, loan shark, counterfeiter, pimp, you name it—but I never nailed a track for anyone. In '32 I came to Havana. Being my father's son and under a dictatorship, I swallowed my own pill: 'The Motherland is an altar, not a stepping-stone.'"

"An altar?"

"Yeah. Like in church."

"Oh."

"It means that the Motherland is an altar to be worshiped, not a ladder to climb up. José Martí said that."

"I see."

"So, I became a revolutionary. I planted bombs, shot cops, and was a stupid jerk till I learned, around . . . '35 that it's neither shrine nor stepping-stone—there's no Motherland anywhere. There are wise guys and suckers, hawks and doves, lambs and wolves. I held up several numbers cash spots and did two banks. Then the war began and I had three easy years with the black market. Tires, gas, lard, the works, but all good things come to an end. When I tried to hit the third bank, I got busted. Did a jolt from '45 to '54 at the Presidio Modelo. I came out four years ago and said to myself—"

From the round table near the right end of the sofa, the phone rang softly. Both men glanced at their watches.

"Twelve minutes early; anxious to collect," the Lebanese said, lifting his eyebrows. Then he rose and answered.

"Yes."

"   "
. . .

"Ask him if his name is Señor Vila Real."

"   "
. . .

"Is he a good-looking guy, around thirty, dark hair, five foot nine or ten?"

"   "
. . .

"Okay, send him up."

Naguib returned the receiver to the cradle, made a "Follow me" sweeping arm motion, grabbed the bag, and with Contreras on his heels went into the master bedroom. It was long and wide, with walls upon which oil paintings, pastel drawings, and two rectangular mirrors hung. A dark green velvet drape framed the only window. An enormous Italian bed stunningly displayed Baroque at its height. The oak headboard had an elaborate, tiny, ascending carving that seemed cocoa froth immobilized by a supernatural action. On both sides of the bed, on the wall, two kneeling angels carved in cedar kept vigil with distressed expressions. From the bed's legs grew spires that stood one yard above the mattress, as if hoping to recover a canopy. Naguib dropped the bag on the Nile-green bedspread.

"I'll leave the door ajar, so you can hear and see through the slot," the Lebanese said.

"The guy could try to pull off something without warning. How will I know?"

"I'll holler for you real loud," Naguib replied, smiling broadly. Then he turned off the lights and returned to the living room. Two minutes went by. Contreras tried to adjust the door so the slot offered maximum visibility, but where he and Naguib had sat remained out of sight. He was reflecting on how convenient it would be if the new arrival chose the left side of the sofa when the buzzer rang. The Lebanese approached the front door and opened it.

...

Wilberto Pires—former collector of cork bark in his native Portugal, snapshot camera mechanic in Barcelona, and male prostitute in Monte Carlo, Willy Pi to the rest of Casino de Capri's staff—stood in the doorway.

The handsome man wore a beige sport jacket over a brown polo shirt, coffee-colored slacks, and loafers of the same shade. He was carrying a plastic KLM handbag. With his charming smile, he brought to mind a young movie actor headed toward worldwide recognition.

"Come in, come in," the host said.

Naguib had chosen him from among thirty-odd candidates for several reasons, in particular the mixture of frustration and ambition which occasionally gleamed in his eyes. For the last ten of his twenty-six years, Pires had gathered enough personal experiences to write a treatise on the misfortunes of good-looking insolvent males. Most men thought he might tempt their girlfriends, wives, sisters, or daughters into sinful fornication. The well-off women he had successfully approached in Monte Carlo developed expectations impossible to fulfill; all wanted to transform him into either an ornament, a stallion, or a slave—and sometimes into all of three things at once.

Five months after landing in Cuba, he'd met Naguib at Johnny's Dream Bar in what he considered fortuitous circumstances. After making certain that his latest friend was rich, heterosexual, and single, the dealer had accepted invitations to Le Vêndome, the Saigon, Havana's Lebanese Club, and the Turf. In the course of three weeks, Pires admitted to Naguib his unfulfilled ambitions, repressed longings, and considerable nostalgia for his beloved Portugal, for Vila Real and Serra do Marao, for the Douro and Peso de Régua. Many opportunities had been denied him, Pires affirmed plaintively. His host, rather than commiserating over the injustice of so many frustrations, had underlined the dealer's right to move ahead, especially considering that a big new opportunity was up for grabs. "What do you mean?" a puzzled Willy had asked. And Naguib had the nerve to make the incredible proposal during lunch at the 21 Club last July, across the street from Casino de Capri.

Astonished beyond words, Pires had limited his reaction to getting to his feet and leaving the place. But that night after work, as he lay awake in bed, he had started ruminating about the plan. What he'd considered the beginning of a friendship had in fact been the cool scheming of a mobster. But who the hell was he working for? What were the ethical standards of his employers? How did they start their careers? Where did all the dough the suckers bet go?

Naguib had already registered a misjudgment when Willy called to say he wanted to discuss the deal. The Lebanese accused him of going with the story to Di Constanzo, threatened him with all kinds of horrible deaths, but when he was reasonably sure that greed had turned the dealer to his side, Naguib explained that all Pires had to do was watch and report. Only Naguib would know of his involvement, and Pires's cut— 25 percent of an estimated four hundred thousand dollars— was more than enough to get him back to Portugal, where he could buy a farm and live like a prince for the rest of his life.

Between secret meetings, as he measured distances, drew sketches, and gathered information, Willy Pi had developed strange ideas. In the beginning, he had just considered himself an indispensable member of the team. By August, he'd felt he was the crucial element. In September, he came to believe he was the brain directing operations. Naguib had read in his eyes and heard in his voice the transformation from baby goat to jungle creature and took precautions, one of which was having a true wild beast guarding his back a few steps away.

"Is everything okay, Elias?"

"Everything's perfect."

"Will they suspect me?"

"Of course not. You're clean as a whistle. Take a seat."

"They ordered all of us to go tomorrow morning to some place and take a look at mug shots. Is it true the job was pulled by an invalid and his father?"

"Of course not. An invalid indeed!"

"Well, that's the rumble. I dealt for these two guys and I don't think—"

"There's your cut," Naguib interrupted, pointing to the money on the coffee table.

"All that?" a flabbergasted Pires asked.

"Sure. Wanna count it?"

"I . . . think I will."

"Go ahead. White Horse and soda?"

"Okay."

During the brief exchange, both men crossed the door slot and Contreras recognized the dealer. Mild surprise made him smile. But Willy's comment pointed to police intervention, quicker than he'd expected; he would speak to Naguib about it later on. Unable to see them now, he strained his ears while gazing at the dark window. For another six or seven minutes all that could be overheard were impersonal noises: ice clicking in a glass; a Zippo lighter being opened, worked, and closed.

"It's a fortune," the dealer said at last.

"All yours, Willy."

"All *ours*, Elias. Your cut must be somewhere around."

"True."

"I hope this bag can hold it all."

All ears, Contreras registered a zipper running. There was a brief interval, followed by two sharp reports, the way corks popping from bottles of champagne sound, then a liquid discharge, as if a spout of fluid had shot out of a pipe. In the ensuing silence the Cuban's mind twirled, went back to normal, twirled again. With his right had he drew the Colt and turned swiftly to look through the slot. After a few seconds, Willy Pi stepped backward into his field of vision, pale as Abo had been the previous night, gripping a gun with a silencer attached, eyes glued to where Naguib probably was. Contreras's reasoning powers were blocked. Then he saw the dealer approaching the bedroom, and self-preservation washed away his remaining traces of prudence. The second Willy Pi gained entrance, he lifted the revolver, aimed it point-blank at the dealer's temple, and pulled the trigger.

The explosion deafened him. A tiny fragment of the victim's right temporal bone scratched his forehead. Pires died instantly, collapsing onto the floor and remaining motionless there. Contreras stared at him, gradually recovering his reflective ability. He stepped over the corpse, left the bedroom, and reached Naguib, now slumped on his seat. The Lebanese's death was almost accidental. One bullet had run through muscles above his right collarbone and left without doing much apparent damage. The second slug wouldn't have been fatal either, if it hadn't pierced the right carotid, freeing a powerful jet of blood that landed a yard away, then gradually weakened until soaking into the armchair's brocade and the man's clothes.

Contreras took a deep breath. Staring at Naguib's half-closed eyes, he saw the tight spot he'd been wedged into, from which he had no idea how to extricate himself. He pondered his next moves for almost a minute. Upon making his decision, he reholstered the gun, returned to the bedroom, and reached for the bag on the bed. Back in the living room, he packed into it all the stacks on the coffee table, approached the front door, and closed his eyes to concentrate on hallway noise. Voices in close proximity were hypothesizing on the probable cause of the explosion. Contreras unlatched the door, went out, and spied two middle-aged men in pajamas giving him the eye, as if he could explain things. He turned to face the door, waved good-bye to Naguib's corpse, and wished him good night loud enough for the tenants to overhear. Then he pulled the mahogany door shut. As he approached an overweight man who was obviously getting ready to question him, he seized the initiative. "That noise we heard—was it around here?"

"No sir," answered the tenant. "Wasn't it in 35?"

"No. We thought it came from over here. Oh, well. Must've been kids playing with firecrackers. Good evening."

Repressing his urge to flee, Contreras took the stairs. Other residents might not be placated so easily, and he wasn't sure whether Naguib's front door, when closed from the outside, bolted itself. He traversed the lobby and stopped by the reception desk.

"Señor Naguib asked me to report that his extension is dead and to please send the repairman in the morning."

"Thank you, señor," the clerk replied. "Did you hear anything strange?"

"Yes—a bang, sort of. Señor Naguib thinks it was a fire-cracker."

"Several tenants reported it."

"I see. Well . . . good evening."

"Good evening, Señor Toro."

As he left the building, Contreras felt certain that the desk clerk wouldn't give his description to the cops. No, he'd give them a color snapshot, including the tufts of hair sticking out of his nostrils. Twenty yards away he heard the Chevy start up, and hope bloomed. He refrained from dashing for the heap and, after what seemed like an eternity, finally reached it. He hopped in, placed the travel bag on the seat, and pulled the door closed.

"Get going, Gallego."

"Everything okay?"

"Everything's not okay. The shit hit the fan."

"Whaddaya mean?"

"Gallego, for your mother's sake, get going. There're two stiffs in apartment 35, three-hundred-odd thousand in this bag, and I got myself into the biggest mess of my whole life."

When nobody answered his insistent buzzing and knocking, the aparthotel manager put two and two together. There had been an explosion of unknown origin, tenants were alarmed, the visitor who walked away had reported a malfunctioning phone. Dialing 2-1195 was justified. Thirty minutes later Corporal Francisco Polo, of the Fifteenth Police Station, called the officer on duty from the manager's office and reported his findings. Second Lieutenant Tomás Hernández, well aware that a double murder went beyond his station's capabilities, notified the Bureau of Investigations. At 5:10 a.m., experts from the National Identification Cabinet and the Legal Chemistry Laboratory concluded their forensic, anthropological, ballistic, fingerprinting, and photographic preliminary routines, collected their gear, then had a hearty and free breakfast at the Château's still unopened cafeteria.

Six

Colors gradually reemerged at the break of dawn. Clean air scented with the fragrance of flowers and the volatile aroma of dew permeated the country house. Chirping birds, clucking hens, and barking dogs supplanted the meowing cats and screeching mice and bats that roamed the place before sunup.

On the living room floor, Mariano Contreras and Fermín Rodríguez slept soundly. They had dumped the Chevy on the third floor of a modern parking service on the corner of Concordia and San Nicolás Streets. From there a cab had taken them to Zanja and Belascoaín, where at the O.K. Bar they gobbled two huge Cuban sandwiches each, washed down with Mackeson's black ale. A second taxi had dropped them in La Palma, where they took a Route 1 bus and got off at its last stop: the Quinta Canaria. A mile and a half on foot along the shoulder of the highway and they reached the place that a few hours earlier both had thought they would never go back to. At 2 A.M., exhausted beyond words, they had relieved themselves, taken off their jackets, rolled them into makeshift pillows, removed their footwear, and lain back down.

Four and a half hours later, Contreras was dreaming of having sex with a woman he hadn't seen in fifteen years. They were naked in bed, she was ready, he was ready. In the dream, his calves were tangled up in the bed linen; with one foot he tried to free himself. In reality, eleven red ants curiously exploring the unprotected skin between his sock's elastic band and the hem of his trouser felt attacked. This compelled them to bite and transfuse formic acid. Torn between his desire to ejaculate and the burning sensation in his leg, Contreras tried to hang on to the dream. Several seconds elapsed before he lifted his eyelids and glanced at the strange living room in confusion. Then he slapped at his invaded calf and insulted the insects with his worst prison vocabulary.

The rapid-fire succession of slaps and the flow of invective woke Fermín. He learned of the ants, inspected his own calves, then grinned. He marched to the toilet at 6:36 A.M. Contreras ambled over to the kitchen, found out that there were no groceries around, washed his face in the sink, and then wiped it dry with his handkerchief. He urinated as soon as the bald man left the bathroom, and a few moments later they reunited in the living room. Having run out of cigars, Fermín accepted the La Corona offered by his pal. For a while they smoked in silence, looking at the trees and plants. A fluttering bee hummingbird, its long thin beak inside a daffodil, provided a few moments of total obliviousness to their imbroglio.

"It never crossed my mind we might come back to this place. Otherwise, I would've left some coffee and sugar in the cupboard," Fermín said, breaking the spell.

"Yeah, and what happened last night never crossed mine," Contreras said dourly. "Otherwise we wouldn't have pulled the job."

Fermín squinted, turned his head to stare at Contreras. "Why, *compadre*? Now we're rich."

Contreras sighed and decided that Fermín deserved to know. "Chances were Lansky wouldn't report it to the police. Naguib had said to me: 'It's considered dishonorable to go to the police. He'd be the laughingstock of the U.S. underworld.' It sounded right to me; made sense. After all, that's our code too. He'd come after us with his own people. But if he did go to the police, the case would be assigned to the Bureau, and the Moor had Grava on his side. Don't ask what he had on the sonofabitch, I don't know, but Grava would just *pretend* to be chasing us."

"*Coño,*" Fermín snapped.

"What?"

"You didn't tell us a fucking word about *that.*"

"I didn't want you guys to become cocksure and give yourselves away. Look what happened. It's a different ball game now."

Fermín mulled this over. "Why should it be different? Maybe Lansky won't report it."

"Police will dig it out anyway. They'll try to find out what the Moor and this Capri dealer were up to, how come they were together, who's the gray-haired schmuck who got away."

"And they'll pay a visit to the casino."

"Go back, you mean. They must've been there yesterday to pick up Grouse's body."

"True. I wonder what Di Constanzo told them about Grouse."

Contreras curved his lip and lifted an eyebrow in speculation. "It depends. If they want to keep the heist under wraps, he'll feed them crap. A desperate loser went after him and then got away, a jealous husband, anything. But now, after this dealer, coppers will wonder what the fuck is the matter with casino staff. Ask a lot of questions."

"You sure you didn't leave your calling card at the apartment?"

"I'm sure. The Moor washed my glass; I heard the splashes in the sink. And I didn't touch anything else, except my gun. I lit cigarettes with this matchbox, my chair had no arms, I didn't . . ."

A recollection flickered on his mental screen. He paused in mid-sentence.

"The door handle? As you were coming out?" Fermín guessed.

Contreras nodded slowly, eyes nailed to the floor, recalling his mother's favorite saying: "The worst damages are self-inflicted."

Fermín's expression was grave. "What are you gonna do?" he asked after taking a drag on his cigarette and blowing out smoke.

"We'll split the money and get lost. Return the keys of this dump to the landlord and stash yourself away. Everybody knows you, Abo and I are pretty close; cops are gonna come after you, too."

A second split occurred, this time 313,500 two ways, and greed eased anxiety. Fermín left to buy what he'd need for stashing his cut; Contreras planned ahead. He forced a contraction of his rectum to feel the stainless-steel, bullet-shaped, made-to-order hollow receptacle where, tightly folded, lay the receipt for the double-bottomed suitcase stored at the warehouse.

His mind searched for a second hiding place. There was this mausoleum built by a rich and now extinct Spanish family at Cementerio de Colón, whose last burial took place in 1921. The vault had an ornamental amphora where in 1944 he'd concealed six handguns and eleven sticks of dynamite in a well-preserved package. Ten years later, after his pardon, he'd found everything in perfect condition. But nowadays it was pretty risky to visit the cemetery: Police used it as a secret dumping ground for murdered revolutionaries.

Contreras decided he ought to search for a spot as close as possible to the mental clinic—maybe the abandoned old residence two hundred yards away. It probably had nooks and crannies he could check over as often as he wanted to; one or two containers could be buried there. He also had to buy a secondhand car. Change his appearance, too—dye his hair, shave his mustache off. Teresa came to his mind. Being a beautician by profession, she could help him; a three-year steady relationship made him trust her.

Anxious to get going, he impatiently paced up and down the ground floor for a half hour and smoked two cigarettes. Fermín came back at 8:25 A.M. He carried a bulging leather portfolio holding four roast beef sandwiches wrapped in wax paper, a five-cent cellophane package of ground coffee, and a small paper bag full of sugar; they had breakfast in a hurry. Later, standing by the front door ready to face the risks of broad daylight, Fermín searched Contreras's eyes before voicing his thoughts.

"Listen, you know there's no spoon for us up there," he said, alluding to their shared intention of never going back to the Havana prison on top of a hill, overlooking the Cuban capital.

"I know."

"We should stay in touch; agree on some sort of meeting."

Contreras didn't like it, and remained silent.

"Now, don't get me wrong. I don't mean we ought to bunch together," Fermín pressed on. "It's just to . . . find out if one of us learned anything the other doesn't know, if someone needs help."

The gray-haired man wanted to make a categorical refusal without insulting his partner and didn't know how. His gaze roved from one place to another with something approaching patience. Fermín realized what his pal was thinking.

"Okay, Ox. Anyway, just in case, the new National Library opened a few weeks back at the Civic Plaza—it's nearly empty most of the time."

"You sound like a damn bookworm."

"Cut the crap. I'll be there on Fridays, between five and six P.M., for the next two months. Ground-floor reading room, left wing."

"I don't think you'll see me there."

"It's up to you. Let's blow now. Good luck."

"Same to you, Gallego. Say hello to Liberata for me when you see her, okay?"

"Sure."

...

At 8:51 A.M. that same morning, once he'd finished a steamy cup of espresso, Colonel Orlando Grava nodded his assent solemnly. The aide considered this authorization to report on the minor matters handled by subordinates while their boss had seized $100,000 worth of cocaine from a jewelry store on Prado Promenade; the morning papers called it "a stunning blow to drug trafficking." Grava lit a Rey del Mundo cigar as the second lieutenant in regulation blue began reading from a clipboard. Twenty seconds later he had Grava's full attention.

". . . finding two cadavers that, according to the NIC fingerprint archives, belong to (1) Wilberto Pires, Caucasian, twenty-six years of age, of Portuguese citizenship, admitted to Cuba on January 11, 1958, holder of a specialist certificate issued by the Ministry of Labor, employee of Casino de Capri, S.A., whose other vital statistics remain at the moment unknown, and (2) Elias Naguib, Caucasian, fifty-th—"

"WHO?" Grava bellowed.

The aide, like most aides a coward, backed up a step. Fearing the wrath of his lord, he lowered his eyes to the name typed on the page.

"It says here 'Elias Naguib,' Colonel, sir."

By 11:04, goaded by numerous phone calls from the terrified aide, experts completed a three-page summary which, due to haste, reached Grava with numerous typing errors. The pathologist cited as cause of death for Deceased Number One an encephalorraghia caused by a spent bullet, fired at short range, to judge by the powder traces. Number Two had bled to death, the consequence of a punctured right carotid artery resulting also from a spent bullet, presumably identical to the one dislodged from the cadaver's right shoulder, in what could be termed a nonlethal wound.

Ballistics stated that the .38-caliber slug extracted from the bedroom's eastern wall was so deformed it had been im-

possible to determine the firing weapon's model and manu-
facturer. The two .32 slugs recovered from (1) the right shoulder of Deceased Number Two and (2) the living room's south
wall had been fired by the Llama pistol with attached silencer
found at the premises. The paraffin test done on Deceased
Number One was positive. Measured distances and angles
followed.

Dactyloscopy reported that the .32-caliber Llama automatic with attached silencer found in the bedroom had the
fingerprints of Deceased Number One. It also reported that,
among other fingerprints, on the front door handle and on
the bedroom door impressions had been lifted pertaining to
former convict Mariano Contreras, aka Ox, Bureau of Investigations record number 1720.

"Son of a whore," Grava mumbled.

Attached to the report were thirty-two 8-by-10 glossy
photographs and a provisional hypothesis suggesting that
Deceased Number One, while sitting on chair B, had fired
against Deceased Number Two, sitting in armchair A. Then
Deceased Number One went into the bedroom, where a third
unknown person had shot him point-blank.

"'Unknown' my ass," Grava murmured.

The dry, matter-of-fact police prose couldn't hide a
measure of surprise when it hypothesized that the third person who walked away probably didn't know about the
162,500 pesos in cash found in the chest of drawers.

Grava finished reading the report and scanning the
photos shortly before noon. He was alone in his office, a 25-
by-20-foot room with two air conditioners in full blast and a
set of old-fashioned Mexican office furniture made from carved
hardwood and embossed cowhide. Besides the desk and two

huge armchairs, a tall glass-fronted bookcase stood behind Grava. There were also two filing cabinets, three aluminum-and-vinyl chairs, and a glass-topped table where a thermos bottle and six clean and upturned demitasses could always be found. A large blotter and an inkstand, two direct lines, an extension, and an intercom were on the cop's desktop.

Grava stared at the door facing him. Obviously Naguib and Contreras had pulled off something big, and he didn't have the faintest idea what it was. Ballistics exonerated the ex-con from responsibility in Naguib's death, but what if Pires shot the Moor on orders from the man who a minute later murdered him? And what about the money? Obviously, Ox hadn't known about it. Why did Naguib have such a huge amount there? And nobody could touch a cent! Several witnesses, including the Château's general manager, signed the draft of the minutes taken. Somebody knocked on the door.

"Come in."

"With your permission, Colonel," the aide said before coming in.

"What the fuck's the matter, Lieutenant?"

The bootlicker found the courage to enter and closed the door behind him. "The body of a white male was found at a vacant lot on Twenty-seventh Street this morning. Blade wound in the head."

"In the head?"

"Yes sir. Somebody rammed a knife under his chin and it went all the way to the brain."

Grava chuckled. "That breaks the mold. Has he been IDed?"

"His prints are in NIC. An American named Marvin

Grouse. He's registered as deputy hall supervisor at Casino de Capri."

Grava stared at the aide for half a minute, his eyes reflecting a mind frantically processing information. Out of the effort, a sequence creeped out: Naguib killed by a Casino de Capri dealer, a mid-level executive of the same casino murdered, the mug shots loaned the day before to a compulsive gambler and former minister of Interior. He had acceded to this as part of the usual favor-swapping among *batistianos*.

"Listen, Lieutenant. Call Tourism and tell them I wanna know whether last week anything unusual happened at the Capri, the Riviera, and other big casinos. Order them to milk their goats and send me the bucket at noon tomorrow. Got it?"

"Yes, Colonel."

"Call Ureña and tell him he's to conduct the Château Miramar investigation. Put Garrido and Castillo under him."

"Very well."

"Phone Dr. Tey's residence and tell his secretary, or whoever the fuck is taking messages, that we'll pick up our records at three P.M. sharp."

"Very well."

"Will you ever say 'Very bad' to one of my orders, Lieutenant?"

"No, sir."

"Good boy. Now blow."

...

In the master bedroom of the Fifth Avenue residence, Nick Di Constanzo fell silent. Jacob Shaifer presented a hypotensive pill to his boss, who was wearing red silk pajamas and had his back against the headboard of his queen-sized bed. Lansky swallowed the pill with a sip of water. He left the glass on the bedside table and reached for a pack of Pall Malls and a Ronson lighter. The Commission's ambassador to Cuba tapped a cigarette on his thumbnail as he pondered his next move. He'd just learned that selected casino staff and hotel attendants had unanimously picked two Cuban criminals out from among 111 mug shots as the faking bastards of suite 406.

Lansky lit the cigarette and returned the pack and the lighter to the bedside table. Knowing that he needed a clear mind to figure out the counteroffensive that could vindicate him, he'd slept placidly. Di Constanzo sat in a chair upholstered in sky-blue moiré. Shaifer, standing, rested his flexed right arm on a long-legged cedar wardrobe that reached the level of his armpit.

"We gotta find the canary before he dusts out," Lansky said. "And we gotta do it fast, Nick, so we'll take it easy. I wanna personally check with you every single person with access to the office, from the Cuban waiters who serve food and drinks to Marvin himself."

"Whaddaya mean Marvin?" an amazed Di Constanzo asked.

"He could've been double-crossed by these three creeps at the last moment, to cut him out of his share."

"Jesus, Meyer, the man was with us for seventeen years."

"Nobody's excluded, Nick."

"So, I'm included."

"And myself. The Commission will sit in judgment of us unless we recover the money," Lansky coolly stated. Then, after a short pause, he added: "But for me, personally, this isn't so much about the money as who's behind it." His lips twisted in a way Shaifer and Di Constanzo had seen many times. It signaled his wish to change the subject. The boss dragged on the cigarette, then stubbed out the butt as he forced twin smoke streams through his nostrils. "Anything else?" he asked.

"Before I came over," Di Constanzo said, in the tone of a man readying himself to present the worst of bad news, "the aide to the chief of the Bureau of Investigations called. He left the message that . . ."

Di Constanzo glanced at a piece of paper he'd just extracted from a pocket of his sports jacket.

". . . Colonel Orlando Grava wants to have a word with me and would I please call 3-9951? My guess is they found out something. How should I handle it?"

Lansky, observing the white sheet that the nails of his left hand were scratching, remained silent for a longer time than Di Constanzo expected. Up to a point it was possible to deflect Cuban police. Beyond it, their collaboration or indifference had to be bought, the boss had long ago concluded.

"Deny what's deniable," he instructed. "The man asks if something happened at the office, tell him the lock jammed or snapped or did whatever broken locks do. If they learned about the heist, laugh it off, say it's an outright lie, unless by some miracle they recovered the money. If they found Marvin's body, pretend to be surprised, ask when, why, how. We may change course tomorrow, but let's do that for the moment, till we know what Grava knows and what he wants. And watch your step, Nick: This guy's no fool."

Di Constanzo drove back to the Capri and sent for Bonifacio García, the casino's lawyer and official interpreter.

From his office, Di Constanzo asked García to phone Grava, who informed the lawyer that the body of Marvin Grouse had been found in a vacant lot. The Capri's top man agreed to visit Bureau headquarters at four o'clock to learn the details.

He marched into the gray building at the corner of Twenty-third and Thirty-second Streets seventeen minutes late, what he considered the right delay when summoned by a banana republic cop. Sitting in one of the two squeaking Mexican armchairs, he displayed the frigid courtesy of superior people forced to deal with the lower classes and intimated that his cooperation was a tribute to the memory of a trusted subordinate. He said he'd seen Grouse last on the tenth, after the casino closed in mourning for the Pope, and peremptorily demanded to know what had happened.

Grava belonged to that ilk of men who base their behavior toward others on social hierarchy. Toward his superiors and for the rich and influential, he was all kindness, friendship, and smiles; his equals he treated matter-of-factly; the rest of mankind he crushed under his heels. Given his present position, most of the time he abused and affronted pliant subordinates. However, he restrained the impulse to bully Di Constanzo a little, for even though the old fop clearly wasn't a superior, he seemed a bit oversized for the "equals" slot.

In this mood, Grava explained the Bureau's findings in the Grouse case and suggested robbery as a possible motive. Then the colonel announced that he would question casino employees during the ongoing investigation. A next meeting with Bonifacio García was scheduled, to agree on who would claim the body and whether it would be buried in Cuba or the U.S. It looked as though all essentials had been dealt with when Grava exacted his revenge with certain finesse.

"Have you experienced any other inconvenience where I can be of assistance, Mr. Di Constanzo?"

"None whatsoever, Colonel," Di Constanzo replied through García.

"Bear in mind that it's my duty to serve you."

"I know that, thanks."

Di Constanzo rose to his feet, getting ready to leave. Bonifacio García imitated his client.

"May I ask a small favor from you?" Grava asked as he also stood.

"Of course."

"Could you instruct one of your dealers to drop by at seven this evening to make a statement?"

Immediately Di Constanzo realized that something was wrong, but he forced a smile before tossing up his own question.

"Sure. What's his name?"

"Wilberto Pires."

"Why him?"

"A trifling, a small matter he may clear up for us."

"Very well, I'll pass on your summons. Thank you and good-bye."

"My pleasure, Mr. Di Constanzo."

Grava had given careful consideration to which corpse he should momentarily conceal before selecting the dealer's. He pondered his lower rank in the gaming organization, the man's inexplicable link to Naguib, and his own need to unearth additional information. The deciding factor, however, had been time. Grouse's autopsy showed that the man had died at least a day before Pires; possibly Di Constanzo didn't know he had to cross out a second name on the payroll.

Grava hit the nail on the head. At 5:20 P.M., Jimmy Brun told Di Constanzo that Willy hadn't shown up, adding that the dealer missed that morning's mug-shot session and was apparently sick, since last night he'd left at ten with a splitting headache. Di Constanzo was not easily annoyed, but now he was peeved. With Brun in tow, he drove to the 8 y 19 Hotel, where Pires rented a furnished room by the month. Nobody had seen the dealer since the previous afternoon; his '53 Pontiac was missing from its usual parking space. The Capri's top man ordered Brun back to the casino and steered his Lincoln toward Fifth Avenue.

Lansky was about to get in the backseat of his car for the short ride to the Havana Riviera when Di Constanzo parked in the driveway and asked for a five-minute conference. The Commission's ambassador to Havana, his bodyguard, and Eddie Galuzzo reentered the mansion, and Lansky eased himself into a nineteenth-century French armchair in the living room. Shaifer and Galuzzo remained standing. By 6:19 Di Constanzo, sitting on a sofa, had finished recounting in plain, concise terms what he'd learned in the last two hours.

"Bring me ten gees, Jacob," Lansky ordered the instant Di Constanzo concluded.

And at seven sharp, having reconsidered his perception of proper delay when summoned by a banana republic cop, Di Constanzo laid on Grava's desk a sheaf of hundred-dollar bills bound with two rubber bands.

"Mr. Di Constanzo wants to anonymously donate ten thousand dollars to the Retirement and Pensions Commission of the Cuban National Police," Bonifacio García said with a knowing smile. "He'll consider it an honor if a superior officer as upright and honest as yourself would serve as intermediary."

"I express my profound admiration for such a noble gesture," an immutable Grava declared.

"If our recollection is precise," the lawyer went on, "this afternoon you made an offer of assistance to my client."

"Your recollection is perfect. I'm here to serve you."

García turned to Di Constanzo, nodded slightly, and half-closed his eyelids.

"Where's the sonofabitch?" Capri's top man asked.

"Do you, by any chance, happen to know Mr. Wilfredo Pires's whereabouts?" García translated.

"As a matter of fact I do. He's presently at the morgue, Mr. Di Constanzo," a beaming Grava said.

...

Utterly exhausted, Mariano Contreras turned off the headlights of a light green '56 Buick Special, killed the engine, rolled the windows up, stepped out, and locked the door. It was 7:12 P.M.

The attendant on duty gaped at the cabin dweller before handing him the key. Having shaved his mustache off and with his hair dyed, the patient looked ten years younger. As he took the footwalk, Contreras surmised that the man must have interpreted this as further confirmation that he was fucking nuts. His steps resounded on the hard surface, and the crickets interrupted their chirping. Contreras paused and glanced at a deserted round pergola built over wooden beams and thatched with palm leaves. On its cement floor, rustic high-backed armchairs welcomed him to a serene listening experience. Cutting across the lawn, he gained access and eased himself into one of the seats.

After a few moments, the insects' symphony peaked again and Contreras dived to the bottom of his vast sea of memories. The family hut his father had built, with walls that came from the fibrous tissue found at the top of royal palm trees, a roof of palm leaves, and packed earth for floor, came to mind. He could almost sniff the smoke from burning firewood under an iron pot in which sweet potatoes boiled; see the blue-black sky, tinted to the west with the receding glow of sunset, sprinkled above with flickering stars. Untamed nature—one of the few pleasant recollections of his childhood.

And right then, like a lightning bolt, his own mortality struck him for the first time ever. It occurred to Contreras that, way past middle age, he'd achieved nothing aside from a moderately successful criminal career. No family, no business, no education, no hobby, few friends. What he could really call his own was a permanent distrust of the human race. His virility was slipping away too. That afternoon, after more than a month of sexual inactivity, he'd known he shouldn't take a shot at a second round of lovemaking with Teresa. Those great years when he believed himself to be stallion to the world were just a dim memory.

And now, with over 200,000 safely salted away, more than enough to retire on and live like a king, he had to hide for God knew how long—in a madhouse, of all places. To his mind came the phlegm he spat after clearing his throat in the mornings. Did something lurk in his lungs? What would he die of? Bullet? Cancer? Cardiac arrest? Wasn't it time to get out of the fast lane?

Teresa was the sweetest woman he'd ever met. Somehow she managed to pump all his cynicism out and fill him with peace and gentleness. And the present physical condition of the forty-six-year-old divorced beautician clearly indicated she must have had a fabulous youth he'd missed. He toyed with the idea of choosing her for a long-term relationship. Her hopes dovetailed with his own. She never asked questions, had followed today's crazy demand as though she'd been thinking along the same lines. "Yeah, great, let's dye your hair; I recommend chestnut—Roux's the best." His right hand moved to his chest and felt the gold chain and Saint Barbara medal. She'd taken it off and slipped it over his head when he was about to leave, begged him to wear it until their next meeting.

The realization that life was depriving him of boldness and hormones in an indivisible, irreversible process led him to shake his head in wonder and smile. The promise of a normal life had never been closer. He told himself he shouldn't get involved in new schemes, nor throw away his money the way he used to. Now he felt, could virtually touch, the promise of a nice quiet future, if he had enough brains to be cautious and discreet. The notion of having reached a turning point in his life fully dawned on him. From now on he'd be a different man—not better or worse, just different. Overwhelming fatigue seized him. He closed his eyes, and big waves of sleepiness engulfed him. Grabbing the arms of the seat, Contreras pulled himself up and trudged toward the cabin, imposing a new fearful pause on the crickets.

...

At 3 A.M. sharp on October 12, a Sunday, at a Hotel Comodoro suite mutually agreed upon as neutral ground, Meyer Lansky and Orlando Grava conferred.

The six-year-old, six-story building was located at First Avenue and Eighty-fourth Street, very close to the shoreline. Lansky had arrived fifty minutes early, accompanied by Bonifacio García, Jacob Shaifer, and Eddie Galuzzo. The bodyguard, assisted by Galuzzo, had checked thoroughly for hidden microphones before declaring the place clean. The suite's spacious living area was decently furnished and acceptably decorated, but it looked like a fleabag to men accustomed to the best.

Grava came in at 2:50, escorted by two plainclothesmen from his security detail. One of the gorillas knocked on the door; Bonifacio García let them in. Introductions were unnecessary; the men had met at a political banquet held in the Havana Riviera nine months earlier. After a shaking of hands, the colonel gave a quick nod to his subordinates, Lansky waved Shaifer and Galuzzo away, and the four guardian angels ambled over to the hallway.

The Hebrew chose the right side of a sofa upholstered in magenta vinyl, signaled Grava to his left, lit a cigarette. The colonel unbuttoned his jacket before sitting down. Then he turned slightly to better watch Lansky and crossed his legs. The interpreter sat in one of the two armchairs facing the sofa.

A year earlier, Grava had spent three hours at the U.S. Naval Mission reading a dossier on Lansky, originally prepared for Interpol by the FBI, with an appendix devoted to the gangster's past and present Cuban operations. It was said that J. Edgar Hoover, incensed by the fact that Batista had provided a safe haven to the Mafia, was doing everything he could to punish the Cuban dictator and expel Lansky. Stanley Walburn, the FBI's liaison officer with the Bureau of Investigations, operating from a small office at the Naval Mission, had shown the dossier to the Cuban police colonel.

Few secrets escaped Grava. He knew that Washington and Havana strongly disagreed on how to deal with Lansky. For the Cuban regime, stimulating capital investment in Cuba was the top priority. For the U.S., the fact that some of America's most renowned gangsters were living abroad precluded the FBI from pursuing the day-to-day surveillance it wanted to keep them under. It also hindered efforts to send them to jail on income-tax evasion, the charges Hoover favored.

But Grava also realized that Fulgencio Batista and Meyer Lansky were mutually satisfied businessmen and friends, that the president signed the appointment to the post of chief of the National Police, and that he ought to cleverly reconcile all these conflicting factors to his own benefit. For this overriding reason, that evening, after having agreed to meet with Lansky, he had phoned Walburn, the FBI agent, and asked him for an interview the next day.

The colonel had fairly well inferred what had happened. Last June, Naguib had chosen Contreras from among three experienced Cuban criminals he'd been asked to recommend. After his last conversation with the Lebanese, Grava had concluded Contreras was involved in some sort of soft crime, like the car-smuggling operation informants reported Naguib had been fine-tuning. When to this he added the fact that the Moor had been murdered by a Capri dealer, then snuffed by Contreras, plus Grouse's corpse and a request to access Bureau files by a notorious Lansky client, the whole mess smelled rotten. To top it off, Tourism Police reported that in the small hours of October 10, Lansky had paid a surprise visit to the Capri, where a locksmith had to open some malfunctioning locks at an office where a lot of money was kept. The conclusion that Naguib had fed Lansky a spoonful of his own medicine was inescapable.

Grava felt betrayed and threatened. Everybody knew that the casinos were off limits because their owners contributed directly to the president's coffers, and Naguib had been a very well-informed man. Planning the heist, he must've reflected on the consequences, including the razzmatazz if anyone found that the chief of the Bureau of Investigations had actually recommended the man who pulled the job. Naguib had no right to do that to him, not even after presenting him with a hundred thou in cocaine, the colonel fumed.

Even though Lansky hadn't read any dossier on Grava, countless verbal reports had convinced him the man was his favorite kind of police official. Grava's corruption was legendary, his ambition unlimited. Lansky always tried to accurately catalog men and issues, for the right match was a prerequisite to success. He never assigned a third-category problem to a first-echelon man, or vice versa, and now he felt certain of entrusting a secondary issue—recovering the stolen money—to a second fiddle. A third-rater like Di Constanzo should clear up how and when he'd lost the loyalty of two subordinates. The fundamental quest was up to him—learn who had decreed his quick retirement and was acting on it.

Alternately shifting his gaze from Grava to the interpreter, Lansky gave a factual account of the robbery and told most of what he already knew in five minutes, except for the true cause of Grouse's death, for this would imply that he'd ordered the body removed. He named Contreras and Heller in giving details of the heist, then revealed that their identification had been based on Bureau files. Lansky also asserted that, obviously, Wilberto Pires had betrayed Di Constanzo and become the inside man. Then the Hebrew asked for three things: recovery of the money, arrest of the perpetrators, and the opportunity to interrogate them personally.

"Of course, Colonel," Lansky concluded, "you manage to get the money back, collar the sonsofbitches, and let me talk to them, you'll get twenty percent of the loot."

Grava assented and cleared his throat before asking his first question. "And this percentage could potentially reach . . . ?"

"Around a hundred twenty thousand pesos."

Grava lifted his left eyebrow. "You mean Ox made off with six hundred thousand?"

"More or less," Lansky confirmed aloud after he'd already nodded.

Grava furrowed his brow in admiration before changing the subject. "I understand you wish to keep this . . . incident under wraps."

"Right."

"I should warn you—that's impossible. Enforcing the Censorship Law can prevent publication, but this will be the talk of the town among police officers, journalists, the underworld. And of course, I can't hide anything from President Batista, or from the chief of the National Police, should they ask."

Lansky dismissed the comment with a shrug. "I don't believe that Fulgencio or Pilar will devote time to this nuisance," he said, to underscore that he was on a first-name basis with the president of Cuba and the country's chief of police.

"But if they want the details, give it to them. Say I dealt with you personally so as not to bother them with chicken feed."

Grava nodded to conceal his amazement—600,000: chicken feed. The old fart probably would just cluck his tongue and shake his head sadly if he were fleeced for a million.

"Maybe you should tell Walburn, too," Lansky added.

For a few moments Grava stared blankly. He knew he ought to say something, but all he could think of was that Lansky's informers knew their trade.

"Oh . . . really? You don't mind?" he finally uttered.

"Of course not—that's exactly the kind of thing the FBI wants to learn from you."

"Yeah, sure. Uh . . . I assume our . . . understanding can be restricted to this very close circle?" Grava said, staring at the interpreter.

"That's a fine assumption. Okay, Grava, cards on the table."

Colonel Grava ran the tip of his tongue over his lips and stared at the floor as he collected his thoughts. Lansky and García lit cigarettes.

"Wilberto Pires was found dead at a Château Miramar apartment. You know the place?"

"Yep."

"Close to his body was the corpse of the lessee, a Lebanese who settled in Cuba over twenty years ago. His name was Elias Naguib."

"Fags?" Lansky asked as García wrote down the name on a blank page of his pocket phone book.

"No, it doesn't seem so," Grava went on. "My people claim Pires shot Naguib and afterward a third party blew Pires's brains out."

"You know who?"

"Well, Contreras's fingerprints were lifted from doors. He's the older of the two guys your people identified as the perps. I bet my balls he did Pires."

Lansky scratched his right eyebrow. He did that only when something escaped his comprehension, but his companions didn't know him well enough to know that. Appearing relaxed, he dragged on the cigarette and then exhaled through his nostrils. "Tell me more about this Arab."

"Well, in fact it's too soon—the investigation is picking up speed now. From my files I've learned he was fifty-three, arrived from New York in 1936. Single, had no relatives, at least not in Cuba, was well-off. He imported gold and precious stones for his jewelry company, manufacturing and wholesale. He also dealt in the stock market and in used cars. His house in Alturas del Country is pretty huge—*too* huge for a loner, you ask me. In June of '54 he leased the apartment, to screw broads mostly, but from time to time some men visited the place, on business as it seems. That's all for the moment. We are working on it."

Lansky waited for García to finish jotting down essentials. "Okay, now tell me about Contreras."

Grava sighed disgustedly and rolled his eyes. "That man annoys me in spades. He's a pain in the ass. His file's this thick, Mr. Lansky; believe me, this thick."

The colonel raised his left hand and splayed its thumb and forefinger a couple of inches.

"He's been mean from the time he learned to walk. Specializes in armed robbery. He's even hit banks, at least four. Was caught red-handed in '45 when he went for a Bank of Nova Scotia branch on Galiano Street, and did nine of a fifteen-year stretch. He came out under an amnesty decreed by General Batista before the last election. Now he's back at it. Last year three men held up El Águila Imperial, an insurance company in downtown Havana, and fled with seventeen thousand. My people suspect Contreras was the brains behind it."

García didn't take notes on Contreras. Lansky asked whether some significant amount of money had been found in the apartment.

"It was one of the things that had me wondering—162,500 pesos were found in a chest of drawers, the kind of money nobody, and I mean nobody, keeps at home," Grava said. "Now I realize it came from the robbery."

Again Lansky scratched his right eyebrow. He stubbed out the butt and talked while crushing some tobacco threads that were still burning. "That's a funny percentage—twenty-seven point something. Doesn't look like somebody's share. Anything else, Grava?"

"Not at the moment. The whole thing happened twenty-eight hours ago and we're—"

"Okay, okay, now I'll tell you what I need you to do."

...

At 11 A.M. on Sunday, October 12, the Department of Communications of the Bureau of Investigations issued a request to the nineteen Havana police stations, the two independent squad-car divisions, the autonomous Secret, Judicial, Tourism, and Maritime police corps, and also to the Military, Regional, and Naval Intelligence Services. They were asked to hunt for and arrest Mariano Contreras and Arturo Heller, wanted for questioning on armed robbery and homicide charges. Twenty-six hundred front- and side-view mug shots were printed and allotted proportionally. Orlando Grava talked on the phone with thirty-two Army and police brass hats to hint that a nice surprise was in store for whoever collared the runaways. He also tapped the nationwide network of paid civilian informers.

Elsewhere, old-timers in police circles watched the vast dragnet unfold and concluded that Ox and Abo, unknowingly, had screwed someone closely related to Batista himself. By early evening, hundreds of men trawled bus terminals, hotels, railroad stations, travel agencies, airports, taxi stands, bars, and other promising places. Standing on corners, they showed the mug shots to drivers, conductors, cashiers, busboys, bellboys, attendants, bartenders, whores, pimps, and any other individual who might possibly have seen the fugitives.

Like a vibration perceptible only to a few varieties of the species, the chase escaped the attention of 99 percent of the population. In the small world of grade-A criminals, nobody tried to warn the runaways, figuring that by now the two perps were headed to the South Pole disguised as Argentine cowboys.

Around 6:30 P.M., Benigno Ureña, the very overweight police sergeant in charge of the investigation, recalled that Fermín Rodríguez was a close buddy of the two felons. Two hours later, the super of the old mansion at the corner of Monte and Someruelos Streets told Ureña that last Friday, Gallego had said he would spend a few weeks at some little country town where an unmarried aunt who owned eighty acres of sugarcane was dying without leaving a will. From there, the smiling sergeant headed straight for the Capri, where he asked the doorman whether he'd been on night duty last

Thursday. The man nodded; then the cop showed him the recent photo of Fermín that he'd removed from the criminal's rented room. Yes, that was the doctor who took care of the young invalid in suite 406. As he walked away, Ureña suspected that Gallego hadn't been identified at Tey's home because in that old mug shot he still had his hair, was twenty pounds thinner, and looked a lot younger. He was wrong; none of the casino staff who got to view the mug shots had seen Dr. Benítez.

As part of the search for leads, early Monday morning Marcelo Garrido and Gabriel Castillo, under instructions from Ureña, gave a look-see to the La Rosa Street apartment. Strands of hair identical to that found by the body of Wilberto Pires were collected. By pure chance, Garrido observed that page 918 of the Havana phone book was dog-eared. After scrutinizing the yellow page, the cops headed for Casa Fernández, on 617 Neptuno Street, where Everett & Jennings wheelchairs were sold and rented. A salesman identified Contreras the moment he glimpsed his picture, recalled renting a wheelchair to the gentleman, and, after checking records, told the detectives that on September 19 Señor Manuel Suárez had left the store with the biggest available chair. The guy also remembered that Señor Suárez had mentioned that his disabled uncle was a tall, very fat man.

The Secret Police scored when agents paid a visit to Compañía Importadora y Distribuidora de Autos de Uso, S.A., at the corner of Infanta and Manglar Streets. Over the years, Argimiro Mainieri had hawked dozens of cars to criminals and was considered a trustworthy middleman, but two weeks earlier, detectives had found three hot cars undergoing alterations in his shop. The head of the Robbery Section had been waiting for the opportunity to add Mainieri to his roll of informers, and after completing the paperwork he explained to the gloomy owner of the small company with the large name that future cooperation would determine whether his case reached court in less than a month, or if it would be mislaid in the wrong filing cabinet. So, when the cop showed him Contreras's mug shot and asked if he'd seen this man recently, Mainieri blew the whistle loud and clear.

Almost simultaneously, at 3:20 P.M., Jacob Shaifer notified his boss that Frank Costello was on the line. Meyer Lansky, who had just got up from his customary nap, hurried to the library. He hoped his close friend and business partner had something on Elias Naguib. Last Saturday morning, talking casually on the phone with Costello, Lansky had revealed that a casino dealer had shot dead a jeweler before killing himself. He'd mentioned Naguib's name, said he'd come from New York twenty-odd years earlier, and asked his partner in the Havana operation to see whether anybody in the Big Apple remembered who the guy had been. Lansky felt sure the shrewd Sicilian would realize Naguib was somehow involved in the Capri heist Silesi and Cellini had reported to him.

"Hello, Frank?"

"How're you doing, you damn Jewish bastard?"

"Can't complain. I'm sixty-two, my fucking heartburn keeps me awake at nights, hypertension is busting the veins in my face, and still a lot of gorgeous chicks try to hook me."

"You were always a handsome fellow."

"Yeah. Gotta lot of charm in the roll . . . of bills."

Costello laughed softly, and for a couple of minutes they performed a ritual conceived to drain off bile. They made jokes on themselves and indulged in a small measure of self-criticism not to be shared with subordinates. Then they became cautious, just in case.

". . . weaker with each passing day, Meyer," Costello said of his mother-in-law. "The tumor is malignant. She's getting the best therapy money can buy, including this radium, but I have no hopes, 'cause when you least expect it, the patient dies on you, like this guy we used to know, remember him? The one who loved banana splits? Died when he looked his best. So I say to the wife, 'Get used to the idea, any moment your mama . . .'"

Lansky immediately identified and decoded the message. If he wanted to learn the whole story, all he had to do was send a man to New York. But details were useless. Elias Naguib had been a Bonanno man. Joe Bananas and Joe Profaci had organized the heist. Realizing that Angelo Dick had been just a decoy made him blush like a schoolboy caught jerking off.

"Meyer?" Costello asked after a two-second pause.

"I'm sorry to hear that, Frank. Please, call me the minute it happens. I want to personally give my condolences to your wife. We attend more funerals with each passing day."

"Sad truth. We share so many friends that when I give condolences to someone I also do it in your name."

Lansky smiled. Frank would let Bonanno know his man had been snuffed; make it seem as though they had got to the guy one day after pulling off the heist. "Thanks, pal. Friends should know that even if I'm away I share their moments of grief."

"Give me a ring when you feel like it," Costello said.

"I'll drop around as soon as I fix a couple of things here."

"You're always welcome. Watch your blood pressure."

"I'll do that. Bye, Frank."

"See you, Meyer."

Frank Costello returned the receiver to the cradle and smiled in anticipation of his next call. Close to retirement, the Commission's first among equals wholeheartedly enjoyed every pleasant moment life presented him with. He poured a goblet of an exquisite Marsala wine, lifted the glass against the light to admire its dark amber color, and sampled the traces of burnt sugar suggested in its flavor. He lit a Marlboro and between sips and streams of smoke gazed at the not-too-fascinating Central Park view that could be seen from the window of his apartment on Fifth Avenue and Sixty-first Street, on Manhattan's East Side. When the wine and the cigarette were halfway gone, he dialed.

"Yeah?"

"Is Joe in?"

"Who's calling?"

"Frank."

"Oh . . . one moment, Mr. Costello."

The Sicilian dragged on his cigarette, then let it rest on an ashtray. No more than ten seconds went by.

"How are you, Frank?

"Fine, Joe. How's Fay and the kids?"

"Fine, thank you. I heard about your mother-in-law. How is she?"

"Not so well. I suppose in a couple of months she'll be gone."

"What a shame. Such a fine lady."

"Life is full of sad moments, Joe. I've got some bad news for you, too."

"Oh, really?"

"Yeah. Remember Elias Naguib?"

A short silence ensued as Bonanno tried to pull himself together. Three days earlier the Lebanese had called to report, with restrained satisfaction, the successful conclusion of their joint venture, and now . . . Beaming and waiting, Costello sipped some more wine.

"The name does ring a bell, but I don't recall the face," said Bonanno at last.

"A Lebanese used to work for you back in the thirties."

"Oh . . . yeah. I remember now. Smart kid, too. He moved to Mexico and was doing well last time I heard."

"Cuba," Costello butted in. "He moved to Cuba."

"That's right. Cuba. More or less the same thing. Lots of Indians, right? But I haven't heard from him since . . . Oh, I don't know, maybe '47, '48. What happened to him?"

"Somebody bumped him off, says Meyer. He asked me to give you his condolences."

Bonanno recovered fast, but not fast enough. "Thanks. You know if there's an address to send flowers or something?"

"No. Will you fly over?"

"Well . . . he was a good guy, but he went on his own a long time ago."

"Then, I apologize for the interruption."

"No, on the contrary. I'm very grateful, both to Meyer and yourself."

"Bye, Joe."

"Bye, Frank."

As a nonplussed Joseph Bonanno tried to figure out what had gone wrong and ascribed a high mark for efficiency to the Lansky-Costello organization that in this case it didn't merit, Colonel Orlando Grava was reading the dispatch that would be immediately radioed to all police cruisers, motorcycles, and unmarked cars. It instructed officers on duty to look for a '56 light green Buick Special, license plate 112 127. At the bottom of the sheet, Grava scrawled, "Do not detain. Inform position and probable route. Follow at maximum permissible range," then handed it back to his aide, who turned and left, closing the door behind him.

Grava had spent the morning poring over all sorts of written material impounded at Naguib's residence and apartment. He hadn't found incriminating evidence against himself, and now had a unique opportunity to rise in the estimation of both Lansky and the FBI's Walburn by feeding them photocopies of the Lebanese's business dealings. Naguib's phone book contained 162 numbers, of which 19 had obviously been scrambled. Under the G and O pages, the colonel closely inspected two coded numbers until he felt sure neither was one of his own. He had no way of knowing that Naguib had committed nine telephone numbers to memory, among them Grava's direct line. The voice of his aide crackled on the intercom.

"With your permission, Colonel."

"Speak up," Grava said, pressing and releasing a key.

"A suspect in the Château Miramar double murder has been taken into custody."

"Really? Who is he?"

"Fermín Rodríguez, aka Gallego."

...

According to parish records, on February 7, 1891, the priest of the town of Limonar, in the province of Matanzas, had christened the black baby "Liberata"—Liberated—based on the consideration that she was the only one of her mother's five children that was born free. The venerable old clergyman, secretly a Jacobin and an abolitionist, had wanted to partly compensate the child for the surname she would carry all her life—Milanés. It belonged to the rich sugar-mill owner on whose barracks the baby's father had been born forty-odd years earlier.

Liberata had grown up in horrifying misery. She had walked barefoot on red clay until she turned seventeen, had performed all kinds of household chores in the family hut since she was five, had reeked of firewood smoke up to the day when she fled Matanzas. Liberata never attended school and became a woman in one stroke when a neighbor six years her senior raped her in the cool shadows of a guava plantation. She was ten years old at the time.

Eight years later, after countless anorgasmic copulations and a bloody abortion that left her barren for life, Liberata Milanés had fallen in love with a handsome, light-skinned Negro violinist during the festivities held to honor the patron saint of Limonar. She eloped with him, but the four-day Havana honeymoon ended with her being dumped in a San Isidro brothel, where for twenty-three years she made a living turning tricks at rock-bottom rates with mostly underprivileged, generally foul-smelling clients. In 1932, while the Machado dictatorship and the Great Depression afflicted Cuba, Liberata had struck out for six consecutive days. The following afternoon, the madam in charge had stared at her for nearly a minute before decreeing that Liberata should make up her mind: Either she substituted for the appallingly bad homosexual cook, or she would have to find some other place to work and live.

And the illiterate, humble, gentle Negro woman had discovered her gift for cooking. When Liberata lightly fried onions, garlic, and red pepper in olive oil, the entire block salivated. Hustlers closed their eyes to better savor her bean *potajes.* Her rice was always loose, sparkling. Sliced fried plantains, if ripe, tasted like a delicate confection; if green and salted, crunched noisily when chewed. Ground beef, seasoned with olives, raisins, onions, and green pepper, left the chippies speechless.

The madam hadn't known what to do when her long-time customers started regularly sampling the full-blown dishes prepared by the former whore. At the outset, it had been just a spoonful of the milk-and-rice dessert sparkled with ground cinnamon; this progressed a month later to a cup of chicken broth or *mamey* ice cream; then her hot thick cocoa became a winter favorite. "This ain't a fucking boardinghouse, for Chrissake," the madam complained, but she operated on the principle that the customer is always right, and patrons assuaged her concerns with adulation. Then, on a certain Saturday evening, two of the boldest had brought five pounds of kidney beans, two of smoked pork, and five Spanish red-peppered sausages for a Sunday-noon *cocido* to be prepared by the woman who had come to be San Isidro's most famous cook.

Eventually the Sunday brunches became part of the neighborhood's folklore, and at one of them, in May 1942,

Liberata Milanés had met Fermín Rodríguez. On Fridays the whores and their cook performed a lottery, sort of. A dozen folded pieces of paper with the names of prospective guests, one for each woman, were deposited in an iron pot. Then Liberata drew next Sunday's two male table companions. Pimps, boyfriends, relatives, neighbors, and the owners of close-by businesses had been eligible, but they had to be aware of the special nature of the invitation and know that guests weren't allowed more than two beers and that hard liquor was banned.

When Fermín and Liberata met he was twenty-seven, she fifty-one. After so many misfortunes the woman reacted well to flattery, and the then-handsome short man had praised her dishes with the solemnity he usually reserved for political debates. He'd made her explain step by step how she prepared each course. Mutual feelings developed. One year later they were engaging in long conversations on a thousand different topics, swapping jokes, and discussing which lottery numbers to play on Saturday afternoons, based on the dreams they had had along the week. Liberata committed her first dishonest act ever on a Friday, when she had cheated at the raffle—hiding between her fingers a paper with Fermín's name on it—to make sure he would be one of the guests at brunch that Sunday.

Unaware of maternal or filial undertones, they became like mother and son. Liberata proudly introduced him to strangers as her godson; Fermín called her godmother. She cared for him when he caught colds; he took her to the town of Regla, across the bay, to worship the Virgin. If for some reason they hadn't seen each other for a few weeks, their next meeting was a sight to smiling onlookers. Some evenings, once she'd finished washing the dishes, they took leisurely strolls along Alameda de Paula. Those who had studied them realized they were not blood-related only by reason of the racial difference. In all other respects they behaved like a loving mother and her affectionate son. The well-known sexual preference of Spaniards and their descendants for beautiful *mulatas* had made some suspect that Liberata was the bald man's mother-in-law.

Their friendship had endured short- and long-term separations, including Fermín's prison stretch. A cigarette-induced emphysema weakened Liberata, and in 1956 Fermín had persuaded her to quit working and to live her remaining years in peace. For the second time in his life, the pimp had taken outstanding care of an old woman, just as he'd looked after his own mother before she passed away. Liberata and her protector had visited dozens of rooms before finding one she approved of and could afford at Estrella Street between Ángeles and Águila. From then on, every Wednesday evening and at noon on Sundays, Liberata had served Fermín his favorite dishes at her modest abode.

Two weeks before the heist, with cash advanced by Contreras, Fermín had started looking for a safe hideout. He rented a small apartment in a six-story building where three streets—Galiano, Dragones, and Zanja—formed a triangle. Nearby, a four-story general market spawned round-the-clock surging crowds, and tenants entering or leaving his building went unnoticed. Fermín also valued two other important advantages: The apartment had a phone and Liberata lived three blocks away. He'd bought a few pieces of old furniture and a mattress at a nearby flea market, plus kitchenware, groceries, a battery-operated radio, and some linen.

On October 5, a Sunday, the ex-con had lunch with Liberata, listened to the fourth World Series game on her radio, and before leaving for the Sloppy Joe's meeting told the old lady he would be away for a couple of months on important business. As he remorsefully left the building, wondering who would take care of Liberata should she fall seriously ill, one of her neighbors bumped into him. The middle-aged, communicative, blessed soul had happily said hello to Fermín. And then, on an impulse, he made a crass error of judgment. He fed her the same important-business fib and scribbled down his new phone number, saying it belonged to a friend of a friend, and that these buddies might be able to contact him should anything happen to Liberata.

After learning that Fermín was one of the Capri thieves, police routine collided with a stroke of luck. On Monday morning, the most senior and trusted San Isidro informer denied knowing where Gallego was, but suggested Liberata's place as a possible hideout. Sergeant Gabriel Castillo thought it highly improbable; he was experienced enough to know that most hardened criminals did all they could to never involve close relatives and guiltless friends in their doings. But he had no better lead to follow.

Fifty minutes later, with three plainclothesmen as backup, Castillo knocked on the old lady's front door at the end of a long, ground-floor hallway. From their own door-frames or windowsills, several housewives watched the tall, stylishly dressed Negro come in. They exchanged puzzled expressions, wondering what the man wanted from Liberata. Castillo presented himself as a close friend of Fermín's, declined a cup of fresh espresso, and sitting on her best rocking chair told the old woman that he'd just arrived from Costa Rica and was doing a twenty-four-hour Havana stopover on his way to the Dominican Republic. A Cuban lady residing in San José had sent Gallego $400. Did Liberata know where he could find her godson? Liberata shook her head and explained that Fermín would be out of town for two or three months, on business.

Castillo had to waste six more minutes of his time. How could a friend of her godson come to his godmother's and refuse a "little sip"? After sampling the espresso, he stared at Liberata. It was the best demitasse he'd had in a long time. The cop had bid farewell to Liberata and was about to leave the building when the middle-aged, communicative, blessed soul couldn't contain her curiosity any longer and courteously asked him who he was looking for.

Castillo knew his country and his people a lot better than Fermín Rodríguez did. He estimated that 95 percent of Cuba's decent and hardworking housewives loved gossip, that maybe 90 percent would go out of their way to help a stranger, that probably 80 percent would be willing to make a small sacrifice if assisting a stranger also meant helping an acquaintance. Accordingly, he repeated the story fed to Liberata. Then, absolutely convinced that she was doing Gallego a big favor, the woman ran back to her room and recovered the piece of paper with the phone number. Castillo jotted it down as she pointed out that maybe Fermín's friend could tell him where to send the money.

At 1:25 P.M., Gallego was awakened from his afternoon nap by the ringing phone. It was the first call he had got since moving to the apartment.

"Hello," he said guardedly.

"Is this 5-6639?" a strange, quavering woman's voice asked over background noise that included traffic.

"Yes."

"Oh, señor, look, the kerosene stove blew up and Fredesvinda wants you to tell Fermín that Liberata is badly burned and on her way to the hospital," the woman blubbered.

"What?"

"Liberata, the godmother of a man . . . Oh, señor, don't you know who Fermín is? Short guy, bald, middle-aged . . . ?"

"Yeah, yeah, but what happened?"

"Her stove blew up, or turned over, I'm not sure, and the poor old lady got burned all over. She's been taken to the Hospital de Emergencias."

"Okay, señorita, I'll . . . notify Fermín. Thanks. Bye."

Fermín hung up and stared vacantly at the wall for a few seconds, the time it took his feelings to overcome his prudence. Plainclothesmen busted him in the fourth-floor corridor and shunted him to the Bureau of Investigations. Sergeant Ureña ordered the handcuffed prisoner to sit down on a backless granite bench and went to see whether the Bureau's special interrogation room was in use. It wasn't. The obese sergeant steered Fermín to it, closed the door behind them.

"You know what goes on in here, Gallego?"

Fermín took the place in. It was painted gray, and in the center of it was a high-backed hardwood armchair with buckled leather straps for arms and legs. The indescribable smell of fear could be discerned. Two nightsticks and four three-foot-long pieces of rubber hose lay on a table close to the only door. To his right, a tape recorder on a small writing desk. A typewriter to his left, on a tiny four-wheeled typist's stand. Three wooden chairs, a three-legged piano stool, two huge buckets, a sink, a fan. A four-tube fluorescent lamp hung from the ceiling. In a far corner, on the floor, lay a heap of hand tools. The room deserved the top mark on the scale of luridness.

"Sergeant, I haven't done anything."

Ureña sighed patiently. "I don't approve of this. But ten minutes after I start interrogating you, they'll ask me if you spilled the beans. If you haven't—and I know you're thinking of sticking to this dumb 'I haven't done anything' line—they'll bring you here. I won't be part of it, but I can't prevent it, either. You understand what I'm saying? And in here, my friend, you'll tell all the secrets of your life. If some nasty old man buggered you when you were ten, if you can't get it up, if your mother was a whore or a saint—everything, Gallego. In here, people confess to crimes they haven't even dreamed of committing. And we know you were in on the Capri job, with Ox and Abo. So, what's it gonna be?"

"I don't know anything 'bout any job, Sergeant, I swear it on my mother's grave. Who was, by the way, a saint," he said in a pat, unconvincing response.

Ureña shook his head in commiseration, called it a day, and went home. By the time he was taking his shower, Fermín was getting the standard punch-and-kick treatment. While the sergeant was slurping his soup, the prisoner was being stripped naked and then strapped to the hardwood armchair. The fingers of his left hand were spread out and immobilized by the five tubes of an iron contraption specially designed and forged for interrogations. The palm of his hand rested on its base. The tubes left the fingernails exposed.

Corporal Talavera had broken new ground in the field of duress. He was a gray-eyed man of average height and build who smiled a lot. That evening he wore regulation blue, the cuffs of his long-sleeved shirt folded up to his elbows. Had he been treated for sadism, his medical records would have made it to a world congress on psychiatry. Sitting on the piano stool facing the prisoner, gripping a pair of pliers and smiling broadly, he asked once again:

"Who pulled off the Capri job, Gallego?"

"I don't know what you're talking about, Corporal."

The corporal plucked them off unhurriedly, like a manicurist intent on doing a fine job. The prisoner groaned and howled and screamed and sweated like never before. Under the chair, blood and urine formed a stinking pool. Having finished with the little finger, the corporal raised his eyes to those of the prisoner, which were closed. Fermín was gasping heavily.

"Who talked you into it, Gallego?"

"Nobody talked me into nothing."

The iron contraption was moved to the right hand, whose fingers underwent the same ordeal. Later, the corporal paused to wash his own blood-soaked hands in the sink. He also let water run over the pliers before dropping them in the corner, where two more pairs of pliers, one hammer, a clamp, and two screwdrivers rested. He looked the implements over carefully, scattering them a little with the toecap of his left shoe. A stainless-steel surgical knife flashed ominously under the fluorescent lighting. Sergeant Ureña was watching the evening news when Talavera picked up the knife and went back to the stool.

"I'm gonna cut off your balls, dwarf," he said with a toothy grin as he oscillated the shimmering scalpel in front of the prisoner's eyes.

Fermín knew this was no vain threat. It was common knowledge that in the outskirts of Havana had often been found the emasculated bodies of revolutionaries. Perhaps this same man with this same knife had been their gelder. For the first time, he became absolutely terrified. The excruciating pain suddenly abated. He blinked openmouthed several times as his scrotum speedily contracted.

"Corporal, you're gonna disgrace me for the rest of my life, and I'm innocent."

"Later, I'm gonna take one of those nightsticks over there—see them?—and shove it up your ass all the way. Maybe you'll like it. From pimp to fag in five minutes."

"Don't do this to me, Corporal, please," panting hard.

"I'll do it real quick," Talavera said as he deftly reached for Fermín's testicles with his left hand. Gallego made a superhuman effort to back off; the straps held him firmly. He watched in horrified fascination as the knife edged up to his lap, giving him time to realize what was about to happen; then he felt the blade graze his left testicle.

"NO, *CONO.*"

"Then spit it out, cocksucker."

"Ox talked me into it!"

"When?"

"Last July."

Talavera rose. His smile vanished; the fun was over. Fucking fatso's orders. He marched to the table and turned on the tape recorder. The mike had a long cord, and he took it back with him to the stool.

"Suspect Rodríguez, who talked you into the Capri robbery?"

Fermín stared at the door. The beaming corporal raised his right hand, and the scalpel glistened in front of the prisoner's eyes.

"Ox talked me into it," in a whisper now.

"And who is Ox?"

"Ox is Mariano Contreras, my buddy."

In the beginning, Fermín tried to reveal a bare minimum. He kept to himself the participation of Loredo and Rancaño; didn't say a word about the Naguib connection, the rented house, or the Château Miramar murders. But when Gabriel Castillo replaced Corporal Talavera, the suspect was expertly cornered.

"C'mon, Gallego, you want me to believe you didn't know who was driving the getaway car? You think I'm stupid or what?"

"Ox brought him in. Didn't say his name. I only met the guy a couple of hours before the heist."

"What's his name?"

"I . . . really don't recall. It was an alias."

"What did he look like?"

"He was a *mulato,* short and overweight."

"Short and overweight like you?"

"More or less."

"You leveling with me, Gallego? Witnesses say he's a *mulato* all right, but young, tall, and good-looking, like me."

"If they say so . . ."

"Tell you what. Talavera must have finished his supper by now. I'll leave you with him. I feel like screwing a broad I met yesterday. She's a dish, you know?"

"Sergeant, for the love of God, don't call that beast."

"Let's cut a deal then. You tell me the name and address of the driver, I'll send for a coupla cones of water. You must be pretty thirsty, ain't you?"

"Yeah."

"There's a cooler out there. Ice-cold water."

"Promise me you won't hurt him."

"Not if he cooperates."

"His name is Melchor Loredo, Wheel his aka, and he lives in Marianao."

Two paper cones of water.

After he fingered Rancaño and explained what he did, Fermín's arms were unbuckled and ethyl ether was sprayed on the tips of his fingers. His legs were untied when he concluded an overview of the planning and organizational stages. Delineating the roles of Ox and Abo during the robbery won him enough credit to get dressed. And finally, at 5:35 A.M. on October 14, a Tuesday, just as Sergeant Ureña was getting up after a restful night and the protracted questioning was drawing to a close, the crestfallen and totally demoralized Fermín Rodríguez moved from admitting the undeniable to blurting out unverifiable details.

"You don't know him, Sergeant. His right hand doesn't know what his left is doing. He wouldn't tell his hiding place to his own mother."

"You leave me no option. I'll send for Talavera."

"You can send for him; he can cut my nuts and throw them to the dogs, or I can start making up addresses to remain a man a little longer, but I don't know where Ox, Abo, or any of the others are hiding. Just like they didn't know where I was."

"But you told him you'd be at the National Library on Friday afternoons."

"Exactly. He said he wasn't gonna go."

"And you didn't go up to apartment 35 of the Château Miramar on the night of the murders?"

"I didn't."

Sergeant Gabriel Castillo pretended to do some hard thinking for half a minute. During the night, other officers had corroborated Fermín's story. Witnesses at the Château Miramar had denied the possibility that a third nonresident could have entered Naguib's apartment. Police cruisers had found the pickup and Contreras's Chevy where Fermín said they were. Di Constanzo, after consulting with Lansky, had admitted why and where Grouse had been murdered and that no, it wasn't the shortest of the Frankensteins who had done him.

"I'm gonna give you a break, Gallego," Castillo said. "But gut instinct tells me you're hiding something."

"Nothing, Sergeant, I swear it," the prisoner said, trying to sound convincing. He knew that if he mentioned the only thing he'd kept to himself—the Grava-Naguib connection—he was a dead man.

"Okay. I'm gonna send you to the infirmary for a cure. Then you'll have breakfast and at nine we'll go for a ride."

"Where to?"

"To the bank, Gallego. To pick up all that dough."

...

"Nah, that guy's older, and look at the uniform—he's a bus driver," the man sitting on the left of a '57 Dodge Kingsway's backseat said; then he coughed and spat out the window. The other three officers in the car remained silent.

Six minutes later a dark-skinned Negro emerged from the roofless hallway. A Glidden cap and paint stains on his shirt and trousers gave away his trade.

"Too black, too short," the driver said after a few moments.

The unmarked vehicle was parked on Sixty-sixth Street between Thirty-first and Thirty-third Avenues, a block with four long, two-story apartment buildings that provided modest homes to poor families. An experiment in low-cost housing was going on in that section of the city. The goal was to triple invested capital in twenty years, a 10 percent annual capital gain.

The cops on the stakeout were looking over early risers on their way to work.

"What's his apartment number—I forget," the man sitting in the passenger seat asked.

"Eleven. It's in the back," a hoarse voice directly behind him answered.

A cigarette was lit. The men in the front wore regulation-blue drill uniforms, corporal stripes on the left sleeves of their shirts. The pair in the backseat wore civvies. Around 6:17 A.M., the hoarse-voiced man spoke.

"C'mon, let's go."

After quietly closing the doors, they crossed the street. The plainclothesman in charge carried a Thompson .45-caliber submachine gun. His partner had a .30-caliber M-1 carbine. As they entered the hallway, the uniforms pulled .38-caliber regulation Colts from their hip holsters.

"Cover the other building, Rigoberto. If he's in, he

might try to hop over the backyard wall and take a powder," the man in charge whispered.

The civilian with the carbine did an about-face, turned left at the sidewalk, and entered the next building's roofless hallway. He sized up the wall to his left. Nothing impressive—maybe nine feet high, a single line of bricks with a flimsy sand-and-cement facing. Ten yards ahead of him a thin middle-aged man opened his front door, gaped at the weapon-toting stranger, fell back inside, shut himself in. The cop suppressed a smile.

In the adjoining hallway, the three police officers reached apartment 11, next to last on the ground floor. One corporal stood to the left of the front door, the other to the right. The plainclothesman knocked softly three times.

Melchor Loredo came out of his customarily light early-morning slumber and experienced foreboding an instant before realizing what was going on. It surprised him to feel just a little sad, almost melancholic. He'd never own an apartment building, never open a cafeteria. His gaze focused on the single bed where two small boys were sound asleep. Then Loredo rested the tips of his fingers on the full lips of the woman by his side and smiled at her as she awoke.

"Ask who it is," Loredo whispered. Silent as a cat, he got up and reached for his pants.

"Who is it?" the beautiful black woman shouted, an edge of alarm in her voice.

"Is Wheel in?" wanted to know a hoarse voice with a friendly inflection. She threw a questioning look at her husband. Loredo shook his head as he buttoned the waistband.

"No, he's not. Who wants him?" she said, loud enough for the man to hear, in a frightened tone.

"We've never met. I've got a message for him, from Gallego. I can leave it with you."

Her fearful gaze shifted back to Loredo, who was simultaneously putting on a shirt and slipping his feet into loafers. He nodded.

"Well . . . tell me," she said.

"Lady, I'm supposed to give this message to you or to your husband, not the whole block."

"Then you'll have to wait a minute. I'll get dressed."

"Okay. I'll wait."

From under the mattress, Loredo produced a .357-magnum Smith & Wesson. His wife wrapped her arms around his knees and whispered "No, no, no" over and over. Loredo inserted the gun in his waistband, freed himself, then hurried to the kitchenette, where, without a sound, he slid back the bolt of the narrow door to a tiny courtyard. Right behind him, the wide-eyed woman grabbed his arms, rested her left cheek between his shoulder blades, and whispered, "Give yourself up, honey, please, give yourself up." The black Venus had on light blue panties, nothing else. Loredo stepped into the courtyard, lifted his eyes to the rose-tinted sky, and sniffed the morning air like a wild dog.

"Señoraaaa . . . ," the voice said, closer now to the limit of its patience.

"Coming, señor, coming . . ."

Loredo quickly kissed his wife, reached for the top of the courtyard wall, and pulled himself up, feeling the gun scratch his crotch. When his eyes reached the top, he stole a look at the hallway of the neighboring building, then gave one more powerful upward jerk. For an instant he sat astride the wall, then he slipped down the other side.

"Don't move, Wheel," ordered a voice at his back.

The fugitive spun around as he pulled the gun free and fired, but his aim was terrible. A powerful impact on his chest threw him back; a flame caught his eye. Falling, he realized that the bang from his shot had been absorbed by a second, booming roar. Loredo couldn't figure out whether life was kissing him good-bye or if death was welcoming him to perpetual darkness, but he sure felt glad he'd told his wife where she should dig if something happened to him. Then he hit the ground with a nasty thud and lay still, gazing at the sky, as rivulets of his blood started zigzagging toward the closest of five drains.

...

Valentín Rancaño was living unforgettable hours. Everything had softer shades, sweeter fragrances, tastier flavors, richer sounds, more tender surfaces. He dipped the well-toasted triangle of bread into the milk-and-coffee combination Cubans favor, then studied the butter varnishing the surface with golden streaks. Life looked promising; with each passing minute he felt increasingly certain he wouldn't lie low until November. He raised the piece of soaked bread to his mouth and enjoyed its savor.

Having brushed aside Contreras's advice, and not given to de-emphasizing his sudden transit from rags to riches, Rancaño had splurged on expensive new clothes and shoes; he carried a fat roll of bills in his pocket too. The previous afternoon he'd rented the place for his gambling joint. From there he'd sauntered over to La Marina, a restaurant famous for its seafood on the corner of Amargura and Oficios. There he had lobster enchilada, rice, fried plantains, and two beers.

Feeling horny, he'd taken a cab to the Shanghai Theater, a porno movie house. Surrounded by tourists of both sexes, the women hiding under dark glasses and headgear, he'd watched three twenty-minute films before dim lights were turned on. A slide projector began showing ads on the screen: nearby clubs and fleabags, a venereal disease clinic, aphrodisiacs sold at drugstores, contraceptives. Later, musicians took their seats in the pit and the last show began. Tatiana fascinated Rancaño; the top star was a beautiful natural redhead with a wonderful body. When the final curtain fell, the gambler felt like doing something he had never done before, so he went out to wait by the artists' exit. Tatiana had come out accompanied by her tall, husky, handsome pimp. Smiling mischievously, Rancaño had cut into their path waving a fifty-peso bill. The pimp had seized the note, inspected it carefully, grinned, and transferred the woman to the acne-scarred client.

Around the corner, a flophouse advertised clean, air-conditioned rooms by the hour, and Rancaño took one. He found out that Tatiana was great onstage but lousy in bed; she didn't even pretend to be having a good time. So, after three ejaculations he'd told the woman to get dressed and get out. At 2:10 A.M. she forced a parting smile at the naked man sprawled on the mattress. He had flipped her a quarter.

"What's this for?" Tatiana had asked.

"Tip. You have the best body I've ever seen, but you fuck like a turtle—a frigid turtle at that."

He awoke at ten past six and ordered toothpaste, toothbrush, razor, razor blade, and a bottle of mineral water. Rancaño had shaved, showered, and brushed his teeth before drinking two glasses of water, getting dressed, and lighting a cigarette. He paid the bill, left, took Zanja Street. Feeling hungry, he had entered the nearest coffee shop to have breakfast.

Promising to himself perpetual sybaritism, he asked for a second helping. Yeah. From now on he would indulge his every whim, fuck as much as he wanted, dress like a movie actor, buy a Cadillac—LIVE, for God's sake! No more self-repression. No longer was he forced to figure out whether he could afford a second *café con leche.* The only limits he would accept would be those of reason.

Five minutes later, Rancaño left a one-peso bill on the marble tabletop, then stood. He delighted in the waiter's surprised stare at the liberal tip. Once again he strolled at a leisurely pace along Zanja's right sidewalk, anticipating the surprise his resignation would cause as he drew nearer to Tele Hogar, his place of work.

Four blocks away, all three plainclothesmen killing time inside a '58 Rambler stationed at the corner of Zanja and Lucena knew about the colonel's personal involvement in this case and didn't want to screw up. TeleHogar's hired hand for odd jobs should have arrived around seven, to wash and service the closed van before eight. But it was 7:17 and the mother-fucker hadn't showed up. The cops were frustrated and tired after a sleepless night stalking the perp's rooming house, at 619 Virtudes Street, where Rancaño shared a room with a clothing store clerk and a drugstore messenger. The vanish-ing trick made them nervous. Then suddenly, their patience paid off. Their man was approaching the TV shop.

The three cops left the car at the same time, and the nearly simultaneous sound of slamming doors made Rancaño look back. Nonplussed, he froze and watched as two men fanned out to the left and right and the one in the middle approached him in a straight line, eyes fastened on his, gun drawn. His huge Technicolor fantasy suddenly deflated. Despondency descended on him. He didn't even think about resisting arrest or trying to escape, as he was absolutely certain he couldn't endure physical punishment. So, he merely winced when handcuffs closed around his wrists and The Big Question was posed.

"In there. Stuffed in a set," was his answer.

The first thing that came to his mind was that were it not for the heist, he would've never given three brush daubs to Tatiana.

Seven

A t noon, Colonel Grava told his aide he was not to be disturbed, then bolted the office door and plopped down on the creaking swivel chair. From the right middle drawer of his desk he took a blank page, and for ten minutes he made calculations. Rancaño's deposition upheld Gallego's as to the total stolen and the split. The 213,750 pesos found in the safe-deposit box authenticated Gallego's version of what happened following the Château Miramar murders. It seemed increasingly possible that the 162,500 pesos found in Naguib's chest of drawers weren't part of the loot.

The Lebanese was nobody's fool, and only a fool would store money in excess of four or five thousand pesos in a piece of furniture sitting in his living room. After a few minutes, Grava gave in. He couldn't make sense of it. Upset and frustrated, he checked the figures once again. Could he get away with filching 155,000 pesos from Fermín's share? If he gave back the money found at the aparthotel to Lansky, plus what had been retrieved from Rancaño's TV set, and only 58,000 of Gallego's cut, the Hebrew would receive 275,000, nearly half the take. And he'd feather his nest with 210,000 pesos, coming from Lansky's 20 percent reward, plus the 155,000 spirited away from . . . from where? The safe-deposit box? Impossible. Bank officials demanded that the receipt had to be sworn to before a notary. But Lansky didn't have to know that Gallego had stored his cut in a fucking bank. He could concoct a different story—say the guy had stuffed his money in an old suitcase at his godmother's, for instance.

Grava wiped off his sweaty palms on the legs of his pants. He knew he was playing with fire. He had told Lansky about the money stashed at the Château Miramar because it had become public knowledge. The amount retrieved from the bank could be learned, and Lansky had the connections to do it, should he want to. But why would the old fart check where the money had been found? He wanted to recover his mazuma, not trace where it had been hoarded.

Besides, and most important of all, every government official with half a brain worried about the future of the regime, tried to figure out how to save his ass in case President Batista decided to do what President Machado had done twenty-five years earlier: go into exile to live comfortably for the rest of his life while the small fry took all the heat. Nobody was in the mood to squeal on friends who cut a few corners to weather the storm. And he had lots of friends. On an impulse, Grava spun around in the chair and pressed an intercom key.

"Lieutenant."

"Yessir."

"Call Mr. Lansky's residence and ask for an urgent meeting at three o'clock. Here, there, wherever he pleases."

Two hours and thirty-five minutes later, Colonel Grava ambled into the Fifth Avenue mansion clutching a briefcase;

Shaifer showed him into the library, where Lansky and his lawyer, Bonifacio García, waited. The drivers of his two black Cadillacs and one of the bodyguards remained inside the cars to luxuriate in the air-conditioned interior and keep an ear on the police radio; the two remaining bodyguards chose to swap what they had recently heard on the grapevine as they paced around the arched driveway connecting the porch with the street. Shaifer ordered a maid to serve snacks to the five policemen, then sat in a living room armchair, next to the library.

The colonel utterly failed in his effort to underplay what his men had achieved. He was breaking the news with a there-was-nothing-to-it tone in his voice. But his eyes sparkled and he kept fighting the smile that pulled at the corners of his mouth. It was a blatant attempt to win his respect, Lansky thought. He registered Grava's brand-new cobalt-blue gabardine suit and the pearl-gray tie before focusing on the colonel's gaze. In his opinion, a guy who didn't lock eyes with the person he addressed was hiding something. But he masked his reserve with encouraging nods and by discreetly arching an eyebrow during those parts of the story where Grava obviously expected some measure of controlled surprise. When the colonel began embellishing the story with nonessential information, Lansky admitted to himself that the man had worked fast, and that he could become a worthy ally eventually.

". . . Nobody seems to know where the driver's cut is. My men searched his place and found nothing. His wife suffered a nervous breakdown, his two snotty kids were bawling like hell, neighbors sided with the bitch, so we'll have to wait a couple of days before taking her in and see if she knows anything. But these bastards rarely involve relatives in their scams; she might not know the hiding place."

Lansky nodded. The colonel cleared his throat, searching for something more to say. "And . . . well . . . I guess that's all. The two guys we collared spent around seven thousand. Rancaño dished out eighteen hundred on a six-month lease of a spot where he planned to open a gambling joint."

Garcia translated, and Lansky guffawed for the first time in days. The lawyer and Grava acted confused for a few seconds, then grasped the irony of it and contributed their own embarrassed grins. Lansky wiped his eyes dry with a handkerchief. He was wondering about the missing five thousand dollars. Two punks couldn't throw away that kind of money in two or three days in a country where first-class whores charged ten bucks for a trick and a bottle of the best rum cost two or three pesos. Clearly, the upright arresting officers had skimmed the top.

"I'm not interested in their expense account. How much do you bring?"

"Two hundred seventy-five thousand."

"Twenty percent is . . ." Lansky did his mental calculation distractedly, while looking at a Delacroix original hanging on the opposite wall. ". . . fifty-five thousand. Garcia, give sixty thousand to the colonel."

The lawyer opened the briefcase, extracted twelve wads of five thousand pesos each in fifty-peso bills, then passed them on to Grava. While Lansky lit a cigarette, took a deep drag from it, then crushed it on a Murano glass ashtray, the colonel produced a folded, nine-by-twelve-inch Kraft-paper envelope, spread it out, placed the money in it, and closed its metal clasp.

"Give your men the extra five thousand in my name, and tell them I appreciate results, okay?" the Hebrew said.

"I will, sure. And I thank you in their name."

"Don't mention it. Up to now your work is very, very good. But incomplete. I need to know who's behind this job, and, with this Naguib dead, the only guy can shed some light on it is Contrary."

Garcia said "Contreras" when he translated.

"Okay, Contrary Contreras," Lansky went on, pleased that he could still set verbal traps for fools. "Perhaps I'll question him personally. So, you gotta catch him alive. What happened with the driver can't happen with him. Do I make myself clear?"

"I guarantee that," Grava said, as he started pondering how to make certain that Contreras was shot dead as soon as he revealed where he had his cut.

"Do you have any clue as to where he might be?"

"A few. But he's the smartest of them, and it'll be difficult to collar him. Don't worry, Mr. Lansky: In a week, two at most, the case will be closed."

...

The Orkin Man inhabited an unpretentious red-brick house on Fifth Street, in Guanabo. The place belonged to a Campo Florido cattleman whose family loved to spend the summers in this beach town fifteen miles to the east of Havana. To recover land and construction costs, the owner rented it from September to May at a modest thirty-peso monthly rate. The house consisted of living-cum-dining room, two bedrooms, a bathroom, a kitchen, and a cemented back patio with a shower to wash sand away from legs and feet. Inexpensively furnished to discourage thieves, it had only three electrical appliances: a 1935 General Electric fridge, a 17-inch Dumont TV set, and an ancient Motorola radio.

The present tenant's billfold included two identity cards, one from the Havana Center of Salesmen and Trade Representatives and another from the Cuban Trade Association, attesting that Ubaldo Barrios, occupation salesman, born in Havana in 1927, was a member of both institutions. But every morning Señor Barrios assumed the personality by which he wanted to be known to town residents: that of Otto, the Orkin Man.

The Orkin Exterminating Company, Inc. with main offices in Atlanta, Georgia, claimed the dubious honor of being the biggest pest control company in the world. It fumigated warehouses, factories, ships, trains, libraries, agricultural produce, furniture, homes, and every other place where a worm, rat, cockroach, termite, ant, or mosquito could thrive. Its Cuban representative, with offices at 1509 Twenty-third Street in Vedado, two blocks away from the Bureau of Investigations, had agreed with Señor Barrios that from September 25 on he would become the Orkin Man in Guanabo.

Nobody expected miracles, for in winter even mosquitoes beat a retreat, but if the energetic young man could hook ten or twelve grocery stores, the cinema, three or four yachts, and forty or fifty homes, it was worth the trouble to send an exterminator on a Cushman motor scooter once a month, collect three or four hundred pesos, and pay a 15 percent commission to Señor Barrios.

Acting under such a powerful incentive, in the mornings the Orkin Man would visit two or three businesses and five or six homes. He explained to potential customers that the exterminator would make free recommendations and provide a cost estimate. There was no obligation to fork out any money. The good-looking Orkin Man had persuasive powers and an engaging smile. By October 14 he had phoned in thirteen addresses to the Havana office.

The salesman ate his meals at a greasy spoon favored by low-income patrons, wore cheap clothes, had never been seen hitting the bottle, went to bed early, and didn't seem inclined to get intimate with any of the young servant girls who opened front doors at the most affluent-looking houses. But on Thursday afternoon the Orkin Man became nostalgic. He recalled the fortune hidden in a certain stool, by association his fiancée's coveted behind flashed in his mind, and in a few seconds he experienced an erection.

Señor Barrios shook his head and tried to concentrate on the sports pages. A few minutes later he learned that Sweet Flash, his favorite bitch, was in that evening's seventh race. Shit. He closed his eyes to project the brilliant oval in his mind, sniff the smell of wet clay, anticipate the race's suspense. Two blocks away from the Havana Greyhound Kennel Club, the Pennsylvania Club dancer would be wiggling her no-less-tempting rump. She was a better prospect than Esther, who, besides believing him to be in the city of Holguín on business, wouldn't satisfy his burning lust. Going to the city would be a stupid thing, the Orkin Man reasoned as he got up and marched to the bedroom to start getting dressed.

He rode a bus to Havana, flagged down a Piquera Gris cab on Egido Street, and asked the driver to take him to the dog track. For the next twenty minutes, the '57 Nash cruised the Malecón and Fifth Avenue. The Orkin Man avidly gazed out the backseat windows, taking in everything. Those five days he had been away felt like five months. This was his natural environment, the place he belonged. He wasn't listening to the exchanges between a dispatcher and other cab-drivers on the short-wave radio, nor was he aware of the searching glances the taxi driver shot at him through the rear-view mirror.

A rumor that had been circulating widely among city residents for over a year had never reached the ears of the Orkin Man. He didn't know that the largest, best-organized Cuban cab company was owned by the widow of a National Police chief shot to death by a revolutionary in 1957, and consequently hadn't learned that a considerable number of its drivers were ex-cops collecting a twenty-three-peso monthly government check for informing on passengers. Each and every snitch driving one of those cabs had seen the mug shot of the Orkin Man.

At the racetrack, the passenger got off, paid the fare, and approached the entrance. The cabbie kept him under observation until he went inside, then reached for the mike and pressed its send button.

"Seventeen," he said.

"Go ahead, seventeen."

"I'm at the dogs. I'm gonna take a leak and have an espresso."

"Gotcha."

The cabbie steered the car to a gas station fifty yards ahead, stepped out, and from a pay phone dialed a number.

"Command."

"This is agent 414."

"Puke it."

"A minute ago I dropped a guy looks like the youngest of the two men wanted by the Bureau—at the dog track."

There was silence at the other end of the line. "What is he wearing?" the voice asked.

"Light gray sport jacket, black slacks and shoes, dark green shirt, no tie."

The snitch would have sworn he could hear the frantic scratching of a pencil.

"Is he carrying?"

"I don't know. Maybe."

"Where are you now?"

"Gas station right in front, by my cab, number seventeen."

"Stay put until someone gets there. Keep an eye on the exits. You see him coming out, tail him."

"Listen, I—"

The noise of a receiver banging onto its cradle made the stoolie stare at the earpiece. He finally hung up and walked back to his car to get behind the wheel and do what he had been ordered to. Six minutes later, a dark green '58 Pontiac sedan noiselessly slid behind the taxi. Its driver stepped on the dimmer switch three times prior to turning off the lights and the ignition. The cabbie got out and approached the Pontiac's passenger door. He was greeted by a swarthy man in his early thirties whose bushy mustache was probably an attempted compensation for his high-pitched, effeminate voice.

"The guy still inside?" the cop asked.

"Affirmative."

"Okay, you can blow."

"You don't need me here?"

"Shit, no. Half the force is coming over."

"*Coño!*"

"I hope you didn't make a mistake, pardner."

"I didn't. He's the guy in the mug shot, only a few years older."

"Fine."

"See you."

"Sure."

At the Kennel Club bar, the Orkin Man was savoring an excellent lobster salad with Russian dressing washed down with Hatuey beer. After several days of ordinary meals he relished the delicacy, and before finishing the first helping he ordered a second. While waiting for it, as he poured a fresh beer into his glass, he thought he should find something out, just in case.

From a pay phone close to the bar's rest room, he called the Pennsylvania's dressing room and talked to the dancer. She sounded a little angry at first, and he fed her one of the business-trip stories he had improved to perfection over the years. Then he asked.

No, she couldn't; had a date with a customer. Wouldn't she drop the bastard for the man who loved her above everything else in life? Sure, the girl said; what she wouldn't drop were the fifty bucks the guy would give her for an hour of her time. Well . . . she knew he was broke—still owed her twenty pesos and had only two pesos in his billfold—but couldn't she reschedule the fellow anyhow? For old times' sake? There was a silence on the line, and then she said perhaps she could tell the sonofabitch she had her period. Would she loan him a couple of bucks to pay for the room? the Orkin

Man wanted to know. The woman cursed her stupidity, then asked how the hell he managed to get by, never having a frigging penny in his pocket. It was agreed that the Orkin Man would wait for her at the bar and pay for his drink, and that therefore he'd better nurse it. And if she caught him talking with, smiling at, or even looking toward where the cigarette girl stood, all bets were off. The Orkin Man returned to the stool with his left hand in the side pocket of his pants to mask his semierection.

He climbed the stands once the third race concluded, the evening's program in his hand. Having reached the top, he swept his glance across the sparse crowd; less than three hundred people rather than the usual weekend multitude. He also noticed that most of them were gawkers just passing time. The Orkin Man loved the ambience, from the superstitious bettors who made colored-chalk drawings on the cement floor to help their animals win to the unreachable mechanical rabbit. But figuring that prior results could have been influenced by stimulants, debilitating intercourse, or some other trick, he based his betting solely on the hound's bearing when it was paraded by the track's rail. From Robinson he had learned that dogs also laugh and cry; therefore, he believed that the animal's state of mind could be more important than its previous record, its sex, or its age. And during the walk, Sweet Flash was always playful and lively, swaying and flirtatious. She smiled merrily too.

The Orkin Man had been spared tender-age traumas. His middle-class parents were educated, progressive, intelligent people, and he had enjoyed a happy childhood. When as a kid he wanted something extra, he had to earn it by washing the family car or buying groceries. Good grades and daily collaboration in household chores were his permanent obligations. Allowing a dog into the family had been a major decision that involved moving from a fourth-floor apartment to a house in the suburbs with a big patio, so he was asked to be the best fifth-grader that school year and to promise he'd assume the responsibility for feeding, bathing, vaccinating, walking, and taking care of the animal in every other way.

Some of his happiest memories were linked to Robinson, one of the several thousand bulldogs named after Edward G., the movie actor. The Orkin Man was an only child, and Robinson came to be his favorite playmate from the age of ten to the day his father and mother perished in a car accident. The maternal aunt who was awarded custody of the fifteen-year-old loathed dogs and sent Robinson to the city kennels to be snuffed. It was the second big shock the teenager experienced and one of the reasons why he became a rebel with cause, and then a criminal.

Overjoyed at being back in this place he liked so much, filled with anticipation for the approaching sexual encounter, and digesting the lobster perfectly, the salesman didn't notice he was being watched. Notified at home of the find, Grava ordered the caller to wait for Contreras, suspecting a previously arranged meeting. The fifth race was about to start when the Orkin Man signaled an espresso vendor, one of the eleven agents in the dragnet. The smiling man poured from a thermos into a tiny paper cup as he boasted, "This is cream, my friend, pure coffee cream." The client gave him a five-cent coin before sipping the very strong, hot infusion.

After the sixth race, the Orkin Man went down to watch the walk. Sweet Flash looked like a winner in her lustrous beige hair; she jumped in front of the Negro trainer who held her leash as though delighted by the prospect of spilling her lungs out chasing a puppet. The Orkin Man ambled over to the betting windows and laid twenty-five pesos to win, at 4-to-1 odds. He couldn't imagine that the man right behind him was ready to collar him the minute the order was given.

Gate doors opened with a mechanical thud and seven fireballs bolted after the screeching prey. From the start, Sweet Flash was last. The irritated bettor swore under his breath, ripped the tickets, and left the dog track recalling the Spanish adage: "Bad luck in games of chance, lucky in love." As he watched the traffic for a chance to cross the street, two men grabbed him by the arms.

Next morning, the sports pages of *El Mundo* printed an exceptional seventh-race photo depicting Sweet Flash as, in her start-off leap forward, she crashed her head against the doghouse's top railing. The caption wondered how the bitch could finish only one second behind the winner after suffering such a severe blow. But Arturo Heller never learned that consoling piece of information.

...

For four consecutive days Contreras acted like a strongly sedated mental-asylum patient. He slept long hours at night, took mid-afternoon naps, digested placidly, and excreted abundantly. His brain coasted along in neutral. On the fourth day of seclusion he decided to take a peek at the world.

Squinting somewhat at the smallest type, he read practically every word of a forty-page *Información*. The Pope's wake was still ongoing; His Holiness's bedside doctor had been accused of leaking confidential information to the press; from all over the world cardinals were heading for Rome to vote on a successor. Quemoy and Matsu had been heavily shelled. A proposal to hold a Geneva nuclear disarmament conference had been tabled. Lebanon suffered under civil war.

In Cuba, a presidential campaign waged with constitutional rights suspended was in its closing stages, the winter baseball season had begun, there was a new ten-cent tax on every 250-pound sugar sack. A bus driver had been stabbed to death by the father of a teenager run over and killed a few days earlier by *another* bus driver who resembled the dead man. Two small merchant ships were being adapted to move Honduran bananas to Florida.

Contreras lifted his eyes from the paper and let it rest on the opposing wall. Ships, ports, Central America. What if he had to leave Cuba in a hurry? It was the first important question he had asked himself in ninety-six hours. He didn't know anyone at the airport or in the airline business, but had been chums with Silvio Molledo for over twenty years. Sharing the same cynical outlook on most issues, they had the kind of friendship that didn't need constant fertilizing. Each man knew the other was good in his trade, maybe the best, and that fostered a Top Man–to–Top Man respect, kind of. Money always changed hands when they did business, but more as an inescapable fact of life than as payment for services rendered.

Those who earned their keep at the Port of Havana knew that the manager of Vapores Luis Luis was sort of a master key that opened all waterfront padlocks. Born in 1896 in an eighteenth-century house at the corner of Oficios and

Lamparilla Streets, Molledo had held all sorts of jobs in the harbor without ever taking a day off. He knew everybody worth knowing at all the piers. In Flota Blanca, Arsenal, Vaccaro, Paula, Santa Clara, San Francisco, La Machina, and Regla, Molledo dealt on a first-name basis with a little over a thousand people, including Customs inspectors, brokers, captains, naval officers, pursers, boatswains, sailors, agents, clerks, smugglers, stevedores, cops, stoolies, drivers, beggars, and traders. He was decidedly the man to see if you needed to arrange something really tricky and had the dough to pay for it.

Contreras went back to the paper. The last thing he read nearly two hours later was on the final page of the rotogravure. The fad in men's fashion, dubbed "the boot," consisted of turning up a jacket's sleeves an inch or so. He ordered and had lunch, emptied the ashtray in the toilet, flushed it, then bunked down for a nap. Around four o'clock he showered, listened to the radio for a while, and took a stroll before heading for the car. He turned the ignition and, as he revved the engine, thought he should fire it up on a daily basis, just in case.

After supper, Contreras turned on the small Olympic TV set, didn't like what was being aired on any of the five channels, and marched to the pergola to delight in the smell of wet earth, the crickets' chirping, and the twinkling stars, until the wooden armchair made his back and buttocks suffer. By 10:45 he was in bed, sleeping like a woodcutter who had swung his ax for ten hours.

Next day—Thursday the sixteenth—he ordered *El Mundo* in addition to *Información,* napped for only half an hour, and in late afternoon walked away from the clinic pretending to be bored to death, a guy who just wanted to stretch his legs and kill some time. He zigzagged around the neighborhood, pausing to stare at whatever caught his eye: a beautiful house, a luxuriant tree, or the nice sorrel-colored horse grazing in a vacant lot. After twenty-five minutes of apparently aimless wandering, and before total darkness could reveal the light of a match, Contreras stepped into a neglected garden where thriving bougainvillea, croton, and bellflowers partly concealed an abandoned, half-demolished brick house behind their exuberant growth. Standing on the broken floor tiles of what had been a bedroom, he made sure that the two-gallon milk jug containing 150,000 pesos remained undisturbed two feet underground alongside the mildewed wall where he'd hidden it in his final—and certainly most tiring—task the previous Saturday.

On the seventeenth, sleep became elusive and he tossed and turned for nearly an hour.

Contreras devoted Saturday morning to a careful inspection of his lair. Both cabins stood on the farthest angle of the lot's irregular perimeter, beneath the shadow of two huge oaks. The cabin next to his admitted only medical staff—at odd hours, and one person at a time—apparently for after-duty rest.

Pacing off the walkways, wearing pajamas, shod in the same cheap sandals handed to other patients, Contreras smiled absentmindedly at doctors, nurses, attendants, and patients. He ambled along with hands clasped behind his back, convincingly acting the part of a slightly unbalanced person hoping for a quick recuperation. But his mind was filing away all that might be convenient to know in an emergency: entrances, exits, windows, padlocks, switches, fences, vehicles, and routines.

On Sunday, when the cleaning lady returned from the nearest grocery store, where she bought him cigarettes, razor blades, and toothpaste, Contreras again scouted around. Repressing an urge to split her sides, a nurse freed him from a menopausal nymphomaniac suffering an acute relapse. A little later he took a seat at a dominoes table and played with three other inmates, until his partner hurled the 9-9 piece at the shaven head of a silent schizoid because instead of saying "Go" when he couldn't match either end, the poor nut would stamp his feet on the ground.

Next morning Contreras began feeling affected by ennui. He was fed up with speculation and prophecies on who the next Pope would be; irritated by news dispatches concerning Nationalist China, the Near East, and the Algerian revolution; nauseated by official statements about the fairness of the coming elections in Cuba. He was bored by TV shows and radio broadcasts, sick and tired of checking the car daily, of walking around like a caged beast, of eating tasteless food. His early-morning erections were making him seriously consider sending for Teresa, who could also give him a fresh rinse.

Only visits to the hidden treasure and brief exchanges with Pedro, the night watchman, got him back to normal. He often wondered about the resignation with which he waited out his prison term. How come? Lack of alternative. The toughest challenges to willpower come from feeling free to make a choice, he concluded. On the twenty-third, a Thursday, Contreras decided he would remain holed up until February, shaving off two months from his original decision.

On Friday he sent for two beefsteaks and two beers and had supper in the cabin, then strolled leisurely to the pergola, smoking a cigarette. An overcast sky made the moon look unreal, adult bats flew around as their nestlings shrieked inside nearby cavities, and the call of an owl, perhaps in love, scared away the rodents she hoped to devour.

It occurred to Contreras that the lack of notoriety concerning what they had pulled off had induced part of his uneasiness. Neither newspapers nor radio and television stations had devoted a word or a second to it, and deep inside he believed they deserved some social recognition for having successfully hit the best pros in the world. All of a sudden, Gallego's idea seemed less absurd. Perhaps if he made a brief trip to the city he could tap his sources and visit Teresa. Maybe even get a pair of reading glasses, Contreras added to himself, sighing deeply: old age knocking on his door. He gave himself a week to think it over, and with a quick flexion of the forefinger flipped the butt. It fell on the lawn.

"Good evening, Señor Suárez," an approaching man said.

"Good evening, Don Pedro," Contreras replied, turning in his seat.

The night watchman, a sixty-two-year-old pensioner from the judiciary, had held the position of usher at six different Havana courts for thirty-six years. Pedro wore gray khaki pants, a dark blue, long-sleeved corduroy shirt, and black lace-up shoes. A black Spanish beret covered his bald head. From his shoulder hung a bulky clock, where a circular paper chart registered the punchings Pedro made every fifteen minutes using seven different keys scattered all over the place. In the mornings, the clinic's administrator retrieved the used chart, checked that Pedro hadn't snoozed, inserted a new one, and wound up the timing device for the next night. Pedro was a very busy night watchman who sincerely believed nobody could possibly suspect his astonishing propensity for quixotism.

"How are you tonight?" Pedro asked as he readjusted his belt. In a leather holster, the butt of a .32-caliber Colt topbreak revolver could be seen. The weapon had been fired twice since it was manufactured in 1883.

"Much better, thank you."

"Nights are a little chilly this time of the year."

"Yeah. I'm wrapping myself in the bedspread," Contreras commented as he offered his pack of La Corona.

Pedro pulled one out. "Thanks."

"You're welcome."

The night watchman lit up with a Japanese benzene lighter.

Contreras felt like keeping the ball rolling. "I see you carrying that gun and can't help thinking you don't need it."

Pedro cocked his head, an amused expression on his face, and blew smoke out. "And I see you unarmed and can't help thinking you ought to pack."

Contreras turned on his self-control and remained impassive. Then he rose from the armchair to face the night watchman, look into his eyes.

"What's that supposed to mean, amigo?"

Pedro arched his eyebrows. "It means that in this place patients are loonies but attendants are not fools, Señor Suárez."

Contreras didn't feel like a cigarette but lit one nevertheless to gain time. "You believe somebody might try to shoot me? Are there dangerous patients here?"

"No, sir, there're no dangerous patients in this clinic. What I and other people here believe is that you came down from the Sierra Maestra with a job to do."

Contreras had to call forth all of his acting capabilities to bury in his chest what probably would have been the biggest outburst of laughter in his life. His mind pondered alternatives at full speed.

"That's an outright lie that places me in a difficult position. Any *batistiano* working here might—"

"Everyone here is against Batista," Pedro interrupted.

Contreras massaged his forehead with his left-hand fingers before speaking. "Listen, man, I can't—"

"Of course, *compadre,* you can't talk about it," Pedro barged in. "Can't say why you're locked up here, dyed your hair, shaved your mustache, changed cars. But the word is you came to boycott the elections."

The night watchman thought Contreras's smile conspiratorial.

"Look, amigo, do me a favor, will you? Tell everybody to keep their mouths shut. They might compromise a harmless man and his no-less-innocent friends."

Don Pedro nodded gravely. "I'll pass on your message. And if you need assistance . . . let me know."

"Thanks."

"Liberty or death," Pedro said as he took his first step toward the next clock key.

"Liberty or death," Contreras felt prompted to mumble back.

He fell asleep around 2:30 A.M., once he had carefully considered the opportunities and dangers presented by the amazing conversation.

...

At 6:35 A.M., on October 17, a Friday, Señor Joaquín Sosa, eyes heavy with sleep, opened the front door of his apartment to two men in civilian clothes who flashed badges and asked him to let them in. They wanted to explain something to him and ask a few questions.

Ninety-nine point nine percent of Cubans faced with such a request in 1958 would have gulped, smiled sheepishly, and waved the visitors in. But Señor Sosa was not an ordinary Cuban. In fact, he belonged to that small percentage of good souls living on this planet who never tell a lie, commit a misdemeanor, or kill one of God's little creatures, except for cockroaches and mosquitoes. Señor Sosa didn't smoke and was a confirmed teetotaler. As a responsible employee, he had never been late in twenty-seven years of working for the Cuban Telephone Company; as a faithful husband, he had made love only to his wife; as a devout Pentecostal, he believed that the Lord was his shepherd and that not a living soul could bear any grudge against him. For all these reasons, Señor Sosa was a fearless man.

The sergeant and the corporal couldn't believe their ears when Joaquín Sosa adamantly said they would have to return in the evening, after 7 P.M. As the balding man explained that he was hard-pressed for time and proudly proclaimed he'd never been late for work in twenty-seven years, the cops exchanged a glance. Then the sergeant told Señor Sosa he had five seconds to make up his mind. They would go in peacefully or they would go in after kicking his big fat ass so many times he wouldn't be able to sit at his fucking office chair for the next six months. An openmouthed Señor Sosa realized that the Lord was caring for some other lamb in that precise moment, so he stepped back and let them in.

Señor Sosa had traces of dry shaving lather near both earlobes; his right cheek was clean, the left one showed white stubs. He wore an undershirt, pajama trousers, and leather slippers. The cops chose two rocking chairs and the sergeant told him the reason they were there. Señor Sosa was so absolutely astounded he didn't know what to think or do, not even when the cop finished the story and demanded the evidence they would otherwise requisition.

So, the head of the family asked to be excused, went to his bedroom, and found his wife behind the door, listening in, terrified to the bones. Some hurried whispering took place. Through the shared bathroom they entered their daughter's bedroom and shook her awake. Esther reacted like a tigress when her father explained. With her firm breasts hardly bobbing under the flimsy pajama top, statuesque bare legs visible beneath the hem of the shorts, and long auburn hair framing her lovely face, Esther stormed into the living room carrying the stool. She put it down on the floor, right in front the gaping cops, termed the charge a preposterous fabrication, defied them to rip the stool open right now, in her presence, and demanded that they then free her fiancé immediately.

Twenty-two minutes later, sitting in the police cruiser's front seat, the sergeant addressed the corporal before turning the ignition.

"That woman is the most beautiful piece of ass I've seen in my entire life. No makeup, no fancy dress, no hairdo, nothing. Just unadulterated plain beauty."

The corporal shook his head. "No wonder the guy hit a casino."

The sergeant stared ahead, still under the spell. Then he dipped two fingers into the handkerchief pocket of his jacket and extracted fifty twenty-peso bills folded at the middle. "Here," he said, peeling off five and handing them to the corporal.

"C'mon, sarge, be a buddy."

"Okay, here," and the sergeant detached five more bills from the wad.

...

Jacob Shaifer closed the door behind him, shot a glance at Lansky, then felt for the hypotensive pills in the right pocket of his jacket. His boss's face had the flushed tone well known to him; probably his ears hummed like a beehive as well, Shaifer thought. Lansky swallowed the drug and agreed to rest for a while at his private suite. He swayed as they waited for the elevator; Shaifer held him by the arm. At 10:36 P.M., while resting on his Havana Riviera bed, Lansky sent for his Cuban cardiologist.

His hypertension was totally unpredictable. It could go wild in the middle of a crisis or on the most placid occasion, like that particular day, when all had been propitious. In the afternoon, Lansky had welcomed the Dominican Republic's ambassador to Cuba at the Fifth Avenue mansion. General Trujillo's envoy expressed his government's interest in doing business with Mr. Lansky. He underscored that the terms his country was willing to offer would be as advantageous to all parties concerned as those agreed on with the Cuban government, maybe even better.

Before leaving for the Havana Riviera, Lansky had gotten a phone call from New Jersey breaking the news that a bunch of high rollers would arrive on the twenty-first. At the hotel he took a local call from Grava and learned that a fourth Capri creep had been canned and that the colonel would give fifty-six thousand pesos back to Mr. Lansky at Number One's earliest convenience. Trafficante had also phoned, to chitchat a little, and told Lansky that the previous evening a potato grower from the town of Güines lost forty-two thousand at the Deauville's wheels. Good news coming from every direction, but after the doctor measured Lansky's blood pressure, he gave the patient a shot in the arm. Alone with Shaifer at last, Lansky lit a Pall Mall as soon as the beehive in his ear subsided.

"You'll fly to Tampa in the morning," he said to the man he trusted most. "Nick has to be retired."

Shaifer assented reflectively. "Okay, but it'll create a problem with Mr. Costello."

Coming from Shaifer, the observation was disappointing, Lansky thought. Did his friend believe for a second he didn't know it would? Or was he just putting the most important outcome of his decision on the table for discussion? Possibly. Lansky knew that Shaifer was a lot brighter than he seemed.

"Let me put it this way. That problem will be less serious than that created by Nick, and we ought to be able to deal with it. He has managed to freeze a hundred-million-dollar expansion program by making Frank waver. A hundred fucking million bucks in cold storage because a guy *thinks* things *might* change. He doesn't approve of Angelo's retirement, believes I swallowed Bonanno's bait. Maybe he's making secret contributions to the rebels, building bridges to become the go-between if they seize power. He figures that my being Batista's pal would disqualify me to deal with a new government. But you're right—it'll bring trouble with Frank . . . unless you manage to make it look like an accident, or like somebody else did it. . . . Hey!!"

Suddenly looking delighted, Lansky slapped his forehead and paused to consider what had just popped into his mind. "Sure, let's make it seem Bonanno and Profaci ordered him retired on account of Angelo Dick. How could this not have occurred to me before? Of course! Let's work it out. I'll admit I was wrong at a meeting with Frank. Nick will be present, invited by me. I'll pretend there's no disagreement, no hard feelings. In the meantime you check out the torpedoes in the Profaci family, choose the most promising, pay him to take out the sonofabitch. When he fulfills his part of the deal, retire him, too, in the open, for going after one of our men. Meanwhile, you and Moshe organize a neat accident, in case the first plan backfires. Take your time—think, plan ahead. Money is not a consideration. I want two Christmas presents from you: Nick's retirement and a clean nose."

Shaifer nodded and smiled—a little sadly, perhaps. The man who had convinced everybody that wars between families were a waste of time and money was slipping badly in old age.

...

The Plaza Cívica was intended to become the new pulsing center of governmental power. On one square kilometer of choice real estate, brand-new public buildings encircled a huge square. Behind the monument to José Martí that served as focal point stood the Palace of Justice. Facing the statue were the General Accounting Office and the Ministry of Communications. To the right, the highest building of all would soon house Havana's municipal government. The National Theater and the headquarters of the National Lottery were still under construction. Including the wide new avenues, around one hundred thousand tons of steel had been embedded in half a million tons of concrete over three years.

On the eastern side of the Plaza stood the recently inaugurated National Library, a vast, four-floor cube with a central eleven-story tower that stored all forms of printed material. Compared with the just-vacated Old Havana building, it was an exercise in modern, sober functionalism. The limestone, glass, and aluminum exterior was in tune with a well-ventilated interior where marble, granite, and natural lighting reigned. The main entrance was on the first floor. In the basement were the children's and circulating sections. Visitors had to ascend a curved driveway, traverse a huge lobby, and stroll through a long, wide hallway before reaching the spacious, well-appointed reading room, with its new, made-to-order bookshelves, reading tables, writing desks, and chairs, all constructed of precious wood.

On October 17, a Friday, at 4:05 and 4:07 in the afternoon, Officers Garrido and Castillo marched into the library pretending they didn't know each other. Two female assistants patiently explained to each new reader how to fill out the forms. Garrido asked for a manual on automotive mechanics; Castillo chose a book on baseball. Sitting at different reading tables, neither seemed very keen on learning about car tinkering or how to throw curves.

"It looks like one of those days," Evelina Vergara said to Leticia Lesnik once she had finished with Castillo. In common with librarians the world over, the two women were used to dealing with a disproportionate quota of odd people acting strangely.

At 4:33 P.M., a short bald man puffing on a cigar arrived at the library. He approached a huge cabinet storing thousands of alphabetically arranged cards and slid a drawer out. The tips of his fingers were bandaged. Leticia glanced at Evelina and rolled her eyes. Did the guy bite his nails to the quick? Evelina whispered she thought she had seen him once before, but wasn't sure. Laboriously Fermín filled out a form for Alexander Braghine's *The Enigma of Atlantis* in an Argentinean edition. After the book arrived, he chose a table in the reading room, opened the volume, and began reading. At 4:46 an obese, middle-aged man shuffled in. Wearing a starched guayabera and dark green pants, Ureña asked for a book on confectionery, then took a seat at the end of the same reading room. Evelina and Leticia exchanged astonished glances. It definitely was one of those days.

As the time went by, the bald man's nervous glances seemed to infect those around him. By six o'clock Castillo, Garrido, and Ureña had somber expressions. At 6:37 the overweight sergeant returned his book and left. A minute later the short guy, beaming and looking extremely pleased, did the same. At 6:40, simultaneously, the men interested in mechanics and baseball departed.

"What a quartet," Leticia said as she carried the books to a small lift that would return them to their Orkin-fumigated bookcases.

. . .

Whenever the owner of the Roxy movie theater received a thriller or a mystery from his distributor, he walked two and a half blocks, knocked on Benigno Ureña's front door, and said—to the man's wife, usually—that it would be an honor to treat the sergeant to a private showing of that week's feature film. In addition, he left a flyer with the name of the picture, its top stars, and the rest of the cast. Out of fifteen or twenty such invitations a year, Ureña accepted two or three. The fuming projectionist doing unpaid overtime would begin running the film close to midnight, once the last public showing had finished.

The stratagem of isolating the policeman was the only clever way the owner had come up with to prevent incensed mystery buffs from asking for a refund. When the man known in the neighborhood as Cannonball went to a regular show to watch a thriller, other moviegoers had learned, he acted bizarrely. During the first suspenseful scene, the obese man would chuckle. As the movie went on and more riddles and puzzles were added, the cop frequently guffawed. If the solution was inductive or derived from a microscopic clue or several brilliant conjectures, he split his sides uproariously, then wiped away the tears streaming down his cheeks. No one in his right mind wanted to risk an evening in jail for shushing him.

The five-foot-seven man with sparse brown hair had the same age and waistline—46. After twenty-three years in the force and an eighteen-year childless marriage, Ureña's elementary school education had fallen back to third or fourth grade in mathematics and Spanish. Since he belonged to the tolerated but never accepted category of the pure professional, devoted considerable chunks of his free time to studying the behavioral patterns of Havana's best-known criminals, and didn't extort money from retailers, he only had made sergeant second-class.

Ureña had never cracked open a book on criminology and declined most lab results with thanks. Occasionally he slapped disrespectful young punks in the face, but he was against more brutal methods and had never tortured or killed a man. Despite such significant shortcomings, he got assigned to the most important cases because he had the best snitches in town, a prodigious memory, and the tenacity of a spider dwelling in a coop. Among his remarkable feats was Contreras's busting back in '45, which was why Grava assigned him the Château Miramar case. The hulking Benigno Ureña was a simple, honest man totally lacking in guile, the only one of his kind among all those involved in the Capri heist and the subsequent murders.

The election was getting close and the chief of the Bureau of Investigations was hard-pressed for men to take preemptive action against demonstrations, so Grava figured he could deemphasize the real reason for a minor personnel shuffling. He sent for Ureña on October 24, a Friday. Everybody knew that if the regular chain of command was bypassed, something illegal was brewing. The professionals who had chosen to ignore official criminality loathed Grava's summonses as much as the experts on third degree and the corrupt cops from the Department of Supplies loved them.

Grava was a dresser, and Ureña's cheap, outmoded, and crumpled black muslin suit made the colonel frown with displeasure.

"You're taking Gallego back to the library this afternoon," Grava affirmed.

"Yes, Colonel."

"Talavera and Brunet will go with you."

Immediately, Ureña realized that Mariano Contreras had been sentenced to death, but he swallowed his revulsion and faked the indifference of moral eunuchs.

"As you order. What shall I say to Garrido and Castillo?"

"Tell them to wait. I'm having both reassigned to the special Election Unit. You won't use radio cars, right?"

Ureña wondered whether the man was an absolute idiot. "Of course not, Colonel."

"Well, if you nail Ox, leave him with Talavera and Brunet and phone me from the Ministry of Communications."

"Yes, sir," the sergeant said as his imagination flashed forward. In the huge Plaza, facing the José Martí Memorial, Grava's cronies would retrace two steps, aim their guns at Contreras's back, and pull the trigger, one shot each. Prisoner trying to escape.

"Dismissed," the colonel ordered, then pressed an intercom key. Ureña sighed, rose, and left Grava's office.

That afternoon Evelina and Leticia, the librarians, witnessed a nearly identical replay of the previous Friday. There were two new bibliophiles and fewer bandages on the short bald man's fingertips, but when the four strange readers left, the heavy man with the sweet tooth appeared to be nearly as relieved as the victim of the strange accident. Before going back to the Bureau, from a pay phone on the ground floor of the Ministry of Communications, Ureña reported to Grava that Contreras hadn't shown up. Meanwhile, Talavera and Fermín waited in a '58 Austin Cambridge and Brunet impatiently tapped the wheel of a '56 Studebaker.

Over the next six days the sergeant slowed down considerably and developed a very bad temper. Scruples lurking in his conscience surfaced. For the first time ever, he found himself involved in a stakeout aimed at killing a fugitive in cold blood. Ethical considerations aside, the reason escaped him. Grava's lust for money was legendary, and shooting Contreras on the spot would make restitution impossible. Returning money to its legal owners almost always brought about a kickback that went to line the colonel's pocket. Like many other officers, Ureña had learned about Grava's tantrum after being told that Loredo had been shot dead before revealing where he'd stashed his cut. It dawned on the sergeant that something vital concerning the Capri robbery had escaped him. In fact, he lacked three essential facts jealously guarded by Grava: the total stolen, what had been given back, and Lansky's request that he question Contreras personally.

Filled with serious misgivings, he entered the colonel's waiting room at dusk on October 30, a Thursday. He spent the next two hours and ten minutes sitting on a hard mahogany bench. Anticipating good news, Grava smiled when he saw the sergeant waiting for him and waved him into his office.

"Get me a beer," Grava ordered to the aide on the graveyard shift. "Would you like one, Ureña?"

"No thank you, sir."

"Permission to leave," the aide said.

"Granted."

Grava freed his waist from a 9mm Browning automatic and shoved it into the right top drawer of his desk. He pointed at one of the two armchairs; Ureña made the cowhide creak horrendously when he sat. Grava eased himself into the swivel chair.

"Spill it out, Ureña. I see you're crammed."

"Me? Crammed?" the astounded Ureña said, pointing at his chest with his thumb.

"What were you doing out there? Waiting for a bus?"

"No, Colonel," the sergeant said, smiling blandly. "I just want your authorization to call off the library stakeout."

"Why?"

"It's a waste of time. Contreras is too experienced to walk into it. He probably knows his buddies are in the can and won't show up."

Grava nodded in apparent agreement. "I see. And what are you gonna do tomorrow? Scratch your ass?"

Ureña felt something, his pride possibly, rebelling inside him. "With all due respect, sir—"

"Answer me, you toad. Are you gonna scratch your fat ass all day long?!" Grava bellowed.

The sergeant bit his lower lip and glanced at the top of the desk.

"I'd keep investigating his whereabouts," he said at last.

"'Investigating his whereabouts,'" Grava mimicked. "For three weeks you've been 'investigating his whereabouts,' *cojones*!

Now, listen to me, Ureña. Tomorrow you take Gallego to the library. You nail Contreras, leave him with Brunet and Talavera, then give me a call. Is that clear, Sergeant?"

"Yes, Colonel. Permission to leave."

"Get going. And ask the moron out there if he sent the orderly to the North Pole to get my fucking beer."

"At your service. Good evening."

"Fuck off, Ureña."

Right then, the sergeant's deep resentment toward his commanding officer evolved into hate.

...

Fermín Rodríguez scraped the aluminum plate, swallowed the last mouthful, then placed both the plate and the spoon on the coarse cement floor. He guzzled the remaining water in a discarded ten-ounce can of peaches, tilted it, and watched a few drops fall to the floor. After sighing deeply, he rose from the wooden stool; the waistband of his pants fell to his groin. Fermín jerked it up and with two steps reached a thin mattress on the floor. He wiped away two big cockroaches before sitting down on it and resting his back against the wall.

Self-deprecation, finding himself in jail, the stench, and the lousy chow had made Fermín a very depressed man. He interrupted his arm-and-neck movement to learn the time of day. When he was taken to the showers, the guard's watch had read 11:15. Goaded by the jailer, he had taken less than ten minutes to shower and shave, perhaps two more to dry off and to wipe his shoes clean on a leg of his dirty jail pants, so it must have been around 11:30 when he was marched back to his cell. His corn-flour-and-sweet-potato lunch had been served a half hour later, so he still had to wait over three hours for his usual Friday-afternoon ride.

Sergeant Ureña would approach the cell, the hanger with the nicely washed and pressed clothes dangling from his thumb. He would greet him with something like "C'mon, Gallego, let's go read a little," then pass the garments through the iron bars. Getting dressed would make him feel momentarily like the man he used to be. Then, as soon as the tie was suitably knotted and he had slipped into the jacket, Cannonball would hand him a Bauzá cigar, the personal mark intended to fully restore his usual appearance and reward his collaboration. From their cells, Abo and Meringue would see him going out and wonder where he was being taken. They were kept in complete isolation, unable to meet even in the toilet, so probably neither of them knew he'd blown the trumpet on them. Or maybe Ureña had told them. But from the compassion shining in Abo's gaze, he didn't think so.

Bitterly, Fermín realized that his physical appearance could be restored, but that his manhood had dissolved in the shame of confession, in the cold sweat on his forehead whenever he recalled Talavera and the wide, high torture chair. The corporal had shown him in fifteen seconds how little he knew himself. He had been convinced he was tough and loyal, ready to die rather than double-cross his buddies. And today, his nails growing again, his money and prestige lost, he was getting ready for another act of treason, just to keep his nuts hanging down there. Feeling sure that he didn't fear death was no consolation; a lesser threat could obviously break him wide open.

Where was Wheel? Holed up, no doubt about it. But the dude loved his wife and kids too much. Any day now he'd risk a night visit to see them and the motherfuckers would collar him. What about Ox? No dame, no family, nothing. Nobody would find out his phone number; he'd jerk off if bedding a broad might jeopardize his freedom; to party he'd listen to music on the radio and swill a beer a night. Ox had always sneered at people who bragged about how tough or loyal they were. Ox had said once that human behavior couldn't be predicted. How right he was! No, Ox wouldn't go to the library this Friday or any other. Of course not. Then, how come he could not shake off this sense of doom?

...

At two o'clock sharp the alarm rang and Benigno Ureña opened his eyes. His wife had never grown used to his napping position—his interlaced fingers resting on his chest, like a corpse in a casket. Ureña placed his arms alongside his body and flexed both hands to restore his blood circulation as the clock's spring wound down and the ringing decreased, then ceased. After a few seconds he lumbered off the bed, marched to the bathroom, and like all big-bellied men took a leak trying to judge the accuracy of the spout by ear. The sergeant flushed the toilet and went back to the bedroom. He dressed, combed his hair, sipped from the demitasse of freshly brewed espresso presented by his wife, then kissed her good-bye and left the rented house where he had resided for the past eight years.

Behind the wheel of his already rare '47 Kaiser Custom, Ureña squinted at the north wind, low clouds, and cold drizzle which were launching a gray attack on the city. He enjoyed the uncharacteristic gloomy weather with the same delight shared by most people getting 340 sunny days a year. Driving up Forty-second Street, he took in the pedestrians hurrying under umbrellas, raincoats, or newspapers, the brilliance of neon signs against the day's opacity, his defective right windshield wiper. On Kohly Avenue his mind moved back to Contreras.

He knew that every week the odds of Ox stopping by the library got better. On the seventeenth he would have bet a year's wages against it; today he wouldn't risk a month's. The sergeant had seen many hardened, astute criminals flunk the isolation test. If the man hadn't had the foresight to hop aboard something and get the hell out of his turf, he would come back to find out how things were going. Ureña wanted very much to collar Contreras and charge him with murder and theft, but if Ox was killed on the spot he would be accountable.

Ureña had been a very mature twenty-one in 1933 when General Machado fell from power. Angry mobs had taken to the streets and avenged the countless murders committed by the dictator's henchmen. One cruel torturer in particular had been dragged to his death in the streets, leaving a trail of blood and flesh on the cobblestones. The obese sergeant knew about the burgeoning revolution, suspected that the present dictatorship was near its end, and feared a new settlement of accounts. Not a good time to sully his reputation, the sergeant thought. He had to wangle his way out of this.

At 2:36 P.M. Ureña pulled over to the curb at the corner of Twenty-fifth and Thirty-second Streets, and four minutes later he entered the Bureau's squad room on the third floor. He swapped a few jokes with colleagues, made sure that both unmarked cars were ready, then informed Talavera and

Brunet they would depart at four sharp. From his locker he picked up the prisoner's clothes and a fine cigar, and then went down to the basement. Arrested men were held incommunicado in individual cells, excluded from due process by virtue of the suspension of constitutional rights. The jailer accompanied Ureña to the cell and opened the gate as the sergeant eyed the prisoner knowingly. Fermín followed the rule of standing up at the rear.

"Here, Gallego, get dressed."

...

In his cabin, Contreras watched the drizzle through the wooden window shutters, cocking an ear to the soft murmur it made as it fell on the surrounding foliage. The smell of wet earth wafted into the room. He awaited his first outing with anticipation tempered by concern. To reassure himself, with his left elbow he brushed the butt of the gun on his waist.

After a last drag, he threw the stub out. He hadn't made plans beyond seeing Fermín. Later he'd make up his mind, decide if it was safe to spend the night with Teresa, send out for fried rice and shrimp-filled wontons from the Segunda Estrella de Oro, maybe even visit an optometrist tomorrow morning. He also had a fantasy: cruising by the Capri in a taxi. The phone rang and he approached the bedside table where it stood. It was 3:02 P.M.

"Hello."

"Your taxi is waiting, Señor Suárez."

"Be right over."

He followed the walkway, covering his head with a copy of that morning's *Diario de la Marina,* and with long strides headed straight for the clinic's entrance. With dyed hair, lacking a mustache, wearing a dark blue muslin suit over a white dress shirt, a sky-blue tie, and glittering black shoes, he looked in his mid-forties. The gardener, one of the *antibatistianos* who admired Contreras by virtue of Pedro's unbridled imagination, watched him openmouthed.

"Ain't you gonna use your car, Señor Suárez?"

"No, Felipe. The doctor prescribed me some pills and I'm not supposed to drive while on them."

"Ahh," the good man said, trying to figure out whether he had been told a joke or a coded message.

The '54 Plymouth had ample space in the backseat, partly by design and partly because the driver was a very short Spaniard close to sixty who had to pull the front seat all the way forward to reach the pedals.

Contreras asked to be taken to the corner of Galiano and San Rafael Streets, shot a backward glance, then reclined on the seat. The car left the neighborhood, took the right lane of 100th Street, and crept along twenty kilometers below the speed limit, which suited the passenger fine. As they turned onto Rancho Boyeros Avenue, Contreras relaxed and looked out the window, a rare pleasure for a man who nearly always drove. A traffic cop waited out the rain beneath the Mambo Club's porch, his Harley-Davidson leaning left and looking sad, probably because her rider was sweet-talking a hooker. Near the fountain popularly known as Paulina's bidet, after a president's mistress, Contreras noticed for the first time the bubblelike skylights atop a sports complex.

He recalled his amazement at the transformed Havana he'd found after nine years in the slammer. His line of business had demanded that he absorb all the changes before beginning operations. It took him a while to learn all he needed to know about modern locks, safes, and alarm systems; about the new generation of snitches, fences, dope dealers, freebooters, hoodlums, cops, motherfuckers, and cocksuckers. Leyland buses, painted white, had replaced trolley cars; there were new office buildings, stores, and cinemas. Self-service cafeterias were a novelty to him, as were cars with automatic transmission. Even bras were easier to unhook, for God's sake! A whole new world for the same old fools.

The Plymouth took Ayestarán Avenue. The suburban quietude became like a crazy symphony played by roaring buses and trucks, blaring radios and jukeboxes, a jet of steam escaping from a laundry's boiler, peddlers crying out their wares, gurgling sewers, bawling schoolchildren getting a kick out of returning home under the rain, the continuous squelching of tires on the wet asphalt.

He got out of the taxi in the heart of downtown Havana and entered Woolworth's to mix with the crowd. Fifteen minutes later he was back on the sidewalk, where he hailed another taxi, asked to be taken to the interprovincial bus terminal, then leaned back on the seat of the '55 Ford. For five blocks it stopped raining, but as the vehicle took a right on Reina Street, a real torrent began. The number of pedestrians flagging down occupied cabs increased with each passing minute.

The temperature had dropped a little by the time Contreras arrived at the bus terminal. He took a granite stairway to the second floor, crossed a long and wide waiting room, reached a wall parallel to 19 de Mayo Street. From an aluminum-and-glass window he peered at the National Library's main entrance, almost three hundred yards away. He would need to use binoculars to identify people coming in and out the place, something impossible to do in the presence of fifty or sixty waiting passengers. Contreras chose a nearby wooden bench and spread out his wet newspaper to hide behind it and read.

...

At 4:06 P.M. two cars cruising 20 de Mayo Avenue turned left on a side street, coasted past the General Accounting Office, and parked on the huge esplanade that was Plaza Cívica, facing the José Martí Memorial. The two men in the '58 Austin Cambridge debated something for half a minute, then the passenger got out. Wearing a raincoat over a rumpled suit, he crossed Rancho Boyeros Avenue to enter the National Library. Six minutes later the Austin's driver did the same, under a newspaper.

Inside a '56 Studebaker, Sergeant Ureña and Fermín Rodríguez remained deep in thought as raindrops drummed on the car's roof. The handcuffed Fermín had to use both hands to roll down the passenger's window a little. Ureña imitated him. A cigar protruded from the handkerchief pocket of the prisoner's jacket. The dashboard clock said 4:25 when Fermín asked a question.

"Has it been raining long?"

"Since one," Ureña said. They talked weather for two or three minutes and concluded what most people—except weather forecasters—felt certain of: Winters had been colder when they were kids.

Fermín also broke the next silence. "He won't come."

"We'll see. Here."

Ureña handed the bald man a matchbox. Fermín raised his hands, drew the cigar out, bit its end off, lit it, returned the matches. "Thanks."

He meant it. Cutting down from five or six cigars a day to one a week had been an ordeal. The only thing that made him look forward to Fridays was the damn cigar.

"Well . . . let's do it," the sergeant said as he pocketed the matches. "I'll take the cuffs off, you go in."

Fermín raised his eyes to the sky through the windshield. "I'll get soaked."

"Nah. It's a drizzle. Cover yourself with this newspaper. Walk fast, but don't run, 'cause if the notion crosses my mind that you're trying to get away, I'll go for your legs. But I'm a lousy shot and might get you in the head. Anyway, I'll get you—you can bet on it."

Under an umbrella lent to him by the desk sergeant, Ureña followed Fermín. With the cigar clenched between his teeth, the prisoner entered the library. Ureña slowed down, and at the building's portal paused to let the umbrella drip away.

"Look, Leticia, the bald midget," Evelina whispered as she saw Fermín approaching the subject-matter wooden cabinets.

"Something strange is going on," Leticia said in the low tone demanded of reading room attendants. "They always come on Fridays, at the same hour. Neither is interested in what they pretend to read. They size up everyone and leave just like they came in, one by one."

"But . . . they don't even glance at each other," Evelina observed.

"I know, I know. It's so bizarre!"

"It's like a Hitchcock movie."

"Oh, my God!"

"What?"

"Here comes the fat man."

. . .

Mariano Contreras glanced at his watch and returned to page 8, but in fact his eyes remained glued over a headline as he figured out his next move. He waited three more minutes, until a female voice boomed over the loudspeakers announcing an immediate departure. Then he rose to his feet and left the place. Nine cabs waited in line; he chose the next to last, a '54 green Chevy driven by a bespectacled man in his mid-forties.

"Where to, sir?"

"I'm meeting a lady. Let's circle the library back there for a while. Then we'll go to Hotel Presidente."

The man turned the ignition, a faint smile on his lips. Some dame playing the field, he figured. A headscarf would cover her head, big dark sunglasses her eyes, and she'd talk in whispers to her Don Juan. A perfect run with a nice fare and a juicy tip.

A stream from a terrace drainpipe fell on the Chevy's roof as it left the terminal's covered entrance. The dashboard clock said 5:22 when the cabdriver took a left on Bruzón Street. The drizzle and the overcast sky made him turn on his city lights. He circled the library twice clockwise, as his passenger eyed the sidewalks closely. At the beginning of the third lap, Don Juan changed his mind.

"Look, pardner. Take Independencia, go up the library's ramp, and pull over. I'll see if she's inside, waiting for the rain to let up."

"As you wish."

"Here, take this couple of coconuts and wait for me," Contreras said as he handed over two one-peso bills to the driver. "Sit tight, and your patience will be rewarded."

"Don't worry, pal. I've been there. But today, to be frank, the weather is against you."

A few moments later the taxi went up the driveway and parked by the left curb. The cabbie turned off the lights, cut the ignition, pulled the emergency brake, then turned on the radio. Contreras followed the sidewalk and reached the building's wide portal, where he shook and folded his newspaper. As though profoundly interested, he read the names of thirty-six continental patriots engraved on the deep red granite. Having read about Bolívar and Washington, he guessed the remaining names also belonged to illustrious founding fathers from North, Central, and South America. Pretending to be at a loss, he crossed the threshold and entered a huge circular lobby, where a thin, white-haired woman smiled encouragingly at him.

"Can I be of assistance, sir?"

Contreras shrugged his shoulders, smiled apologetically. "Well . . . no. The rain, you know? Just passing time."

"Have you visited us before?"

"No."

"Come in, come in. Take a look while you wait for it to clear up."

Contreras returned her smile. Gripping the newspaper behind his back with both hands, turning his head frequently, he paced along the polished marble floor. Beyond the lobby, to the right, two elevator doors, one closed, the other wide open; an old man in a gray uniform inside the cage. The attendant nodded politely. Contreras nodded back, then looked left to a wide pink-marble stairway, its majesty ruined by aluminum handrails.

He kept up his apparently distracted snail's pace through a long hallway, glancing at the glass cabinets in which sat rare editions, approaching the gray marble counters, the one to the right devoted to periodicals, the other to books. He greeted Evelina and Leticia with a smile and stepped up to the huge mahogany cabinets storing the library's collection by subject, author, and title. Craftsmen had done a remarkable job. There were 140 drawers on each side. He pulled one out; it slid smoothly. Several hundred cards, perforated at the bottom, were held in place by a bronze rod. Contreras raised his eyebrows, tilted his head, curved his lips in admiration, then closed the drawer. He edged his way forward to the left reading room, the spot Gallego had suggested.

"That guy, twenty years ago . . . ," Leticia intimated, a subtle, sultry nuance in her voice.

Evelina inclined her head in agreement. "Yeah, and you were five and I was seven then."

Contreras heard a gust of rain hitting the tightly shut horizontal panes of aluminum windows. Above them, through glass windows, a virtually black sky could be seen. Long fluorescent lamps were spaced out evenly along the ceiling's acoustical tile. He lowered his gaze to the reference section. Large shelves housing encyclopedias, dictionaries, yearbooks, and legislative summaries served as movable partitions that formed a rectangle where four unoccupied reading tables stood. With his next two steps Contreras reached the forty-by-fourteen-yard reading room. Fifteen tables formed three lines at its center; six writing desks lined each side. It was 5:40 P.M.

Fermín was reading something at a central-line table, a cigar stump between the fingers of his right hand. Contreras's peripheral vision registered and dismissed six or seven book-worms; he took a step forward to simulate a casual encounter. Out of the corner of his eye, he sensed movement to his right. At the end of the reading room a fat man jerked to his feet and stared at the newcomer. Contreras was taking a second step when his brain compared the rotund face with stored images and immediately flashed a warning to every organ, nerve, and muscle. His suprarenal glands began to operate in emergency mode.

Contreras's right hand flew to his waist; the newspaper fell to the floor. The last time he had seen Benigno Ureña lit up his mind's eye: two or three years earlier, as their cars waited out a red light. The sergeant hadn't seen him, perhaps lost in thought on how to collar somebody, or just dog-tired, but Contreras had committed his profile to memory. He was heavier now, had a receding hairline, an indifferent expression on his face. The sergeant stood motionless, staring at him wide-eyed, empty hands at his sides. Contreras was drawing the Colt to shoot him, hesitating if he ought to, when Fermín jumped from his seat, shouting and pointing.

"CUIDADO!"

Contreras turned left, raising his weapon. A smiling thin man was forcing back the slide of an automatic. Contreras pulled the trigger. The bullet ricocheted off an aluminum molding. Talavera lost a fraction of a second while instinctively dodging. The corporal lifted his gun again, and a frantic Contreras fired three more shots. The first two slugs ended up embedded in books on a shelf, but the third pierced the lower part of the torturer's windpipe, snapped the seventh cervical vertebra and the spinal cord, then exited through the upper back, making a hole the size of a lemon. Talavera's smile remained in place as he fell, staring vacantly, his legs feebly kicking.

Eduardo Brunet, from behind a table on the left at the back of the reading room, took aim and fired his Browning twice. One bullet buzzed an inch to the right of Contreras's right ear and splintered the closest card-catalog cabinet; the other broke the glass of a window and got stuck in a limestone wall. Hunkering down behind a writing desk, Contreras saw Fermín frantically crawling in the direction of Talavera and figured he was going for the automatic on the floor. Brunet reached the same conclusion, so he fired two more rounds, aiming at Fermín. The slugs were deflected by the legs of tables and chairs, changed course several times, disappeared into thick volumes.

Contreras watched Brunet aiming again at his buddy and fired his fifth shot. It was lost in the humid dusk after puncturing a window. The cop turned to the fugitive and fired twice. Contreras felt his left foot give under him and looked down. The heel of his shoe had been partially torn out by a stray bullet. Fermín seized Talavera's .45 Colt. Ureña turned his reading table sideways and ducked behind it.

Contreras registered movement to his left. A young man who had been industriously practicing his integral calculus six seconds earlier dived to the floor and rolled over to the wall. Even closer to Contreras, a Ministry of State orientalist, who'd been placidly studying Mikado Court sketches before the shooting started, sat tight, holding the book over his head and urinating profusely. Then Contreras heard a different gun report and a shout.

"You're gonna get it now, motherfuckers!"

Fermín had also turned over a writing desk, and now crouched behind it. Its inch-and-a-half thick mahogany top provided one square yard of dubious protection. Gripping Talavera's gun in his right hand, with his left shoulder Fermín pushed the piece of furniture between the tables arrayed at the center and the writing desks lined alongside the wall. Brunet lost what little cool he had left and fired twice over the creeping thing, but the bullets missed Gallego. As he feverishly changed clips, Brunet noticed that Ureña, ten yards to his right, was doing nothing except crouching. The cop was stunned into immobility for a full second.

"Ureña! Ureña! What's the matter with you! Shoot, goddammit, shoot!"

Astonished by Ureña's inexplicable behavior, shaken by Talavera's demise, and fearing Fermín's relentless progress, Brunet rose and opened fire at the improvised barrier. Contreras took careful aim. Brunet's third empty shell had just been ejected when a .38 slug drilled into his chest, broke the fifth rib, invaded the heart's left ventricle, pierced the left lung, and finally broke the scapula. The body collapsed as the echoes of the gunshots gradually faded away.

Not one step, word, shout, sob, or cough could be heard. From behind the writing desk, Fermín questioned Contreras by wrinkling his nose and shrugging. Contreras slid his forefinger over his throat, then pointed to his Colt and made a zero by joining his thumb and forefinger. Fermín puffed his cheeks out and spread his arms to inquire about the sergeant. Contreras was thinking of something to say when Ureña bellowed, his voice broken by tension.

"Ox, Gallego, don't move."

The seven slugs in his Parabellum deliberately finished their short journey inside walls and books, rekindling fear in attendants and readers. Fermín peered over the edge of the writing desk, aimed, next fired twice. The slugs drilled the tabletop and missed Ureña by inches.

"Gallego, Gallego!" Contreras bawled out.

Fermín glanced at his buddy and saw him shaking his head repeatedly. Nonplussed, openmouthed, he watched as Contreras rose to his full height, his empty gun pointing to the floor.

"Ureña." In a normal tone now.

From behind the parapet. "What?"

"Are you . . . okay?"

"Yeah."

Contreras bit his lower lip for a second. "We're leaving," he probed.

"Can't stop you; I fired my last shot," the sergeant shouted. He wanted all the witnesses he could find. "But you ought to turn yourselves in. I mean, I *order* you to turn yourselves in."

"C'mon, Gallego, c'mon," Contreras said. Crouching, without taking his eyes from Ureña's overturned reading table, Fermín joined his pal.

"Why?" he asked.

"He warned me."

"He what?"

"Gave me a break when he saw me coming in. Didn't shoot until now, and he did it for appearances. C'mon."

"Are you out of your fucking mind?"

"Goddammit! Move!"

Both men turned around and started for the main entrance, Contreras hobbling somewhat on account of the partially dislodged heel. Every few steps they looked over their shoulders; no one was to be seen. Fearing for their lives, readers and attendants remained under marble counters, behind doors or pieces of furniture, lying on the floor. Both elevator doors were closed, the stairway deserted, the lobby empty. In a firmly closed office, the courteous willowy woman who had welcomed Contreras was desperately flipping the pages of the telephone directory.

"Pocket the gun," Contreras said as he returned his revolver to its waist holster. Fermín looked back one last time to be sure he was doing the right thing and then, holding the hammer with his left hand, he pulled the trigger and stuffed the warm automatic under his belt.

"Now what?"

"Let's see if a green Chevy is still out there."

The cabbie hadn't heard the shooting because of the rain. He had been acoustically isolated in the closed car, the radio tuned to his favorite cha-cha-cha program. He spotted Don Juan coming out, a short bald peewee after him, both darting down the sidewalk. The drizzle, of course. But what about the dame? He noticed the taut expression of his fare, now looking rather unkempt. Both men jerked open the back doors and hopped in. The driver turned off the radio and started the engine.

"My chick couldn't make it, champ. The rain, I guess. But I bumped into this pal of mine and we're gonna have a coupla beers. Take us to the . . . Puerto de Jagua is okay, buddy?"

"Sure," Fermín said.

Ureña heaved a sigh of relief once he made sure that the other two cops were dead. The orientalist had collapsed on the reading table. Standing now, the math student conscientiously slapped clean his clothes, as though laundry bills were his most pressing concern. Ureña sashayed, solemn and pathetic, to the marble counter beneath which Evelina and Leticia sobbed and sniffed back mucus.

"Come out, please. I'm a police officer. Where's your phone?"

PART THREE

Eight

ariano Contreras turned his head in embarrassment and stared at the bathroom door. Fermín's attempt to fight back tears had failed and they were sliding down his cheeks like he hadn't wept from the time he was four. He probably hadn't, Contreras surmised. In their childhood, crying was a sign of weakness, the kind of thing *hombres* didn't do, and possibly Fermín had been, like himself, a sneering bully who would make tattletales whine and blubber. Well, now the man was catching up, head bowed, sniffling back mucus, trying to repress the sobs that made his shoulders shake. To spare his friend the humiliation, Contreras decided against yanking out some toilet paper from the holder to dry the floor.

He didn't doubt for a second the story's authenticity. Had Gallego spilled the beans the minute he was collared, his nails wouldn't have been plucked out. Had he thrown in the sponge after two or three nails, the undamaged fingers would have given him away. No, he had been subject to something a lot worse. In the macho culture they were raised in, what could be worse than threatening a man with castration? And then let him live, of course. Let the whole

Havana underworld learn that Gallego, the tough guy who everybody knew had won a hundred-peso bet by screwing six broads in one night in the presence of seventeen witnesses, was now a eunuch.

For an instant Contreras wondered what he would have done. He dismissed the thought immediately. Nobody ought to pass judgment, he told himself, because no one knew what his reaction would be. It was one thing to picture yourself under the circumstances, something altogether different to experience the ordeal. The best thing was to know nothing about the others: not their latest addresses, nor their phone numbers or hiding places. And to try to shoot your way out if you were cornered, then blow your fucking brains out if you couldn't—anything rather than fall into the hands of those beasts. Under Batista the rules of the game had changed. Before him you could expect to get pushed around, boxed on the ears, clubbed on your head—the kind of music most guys could face. Ureña had tongue-lashed him for fifteen minutes prior to slapping him twice when he was busted in '47. And that had been it.

Now he owed his life to the fat sergeant. It was there for all to see. The big question was why. He couldn't figure it out. Moral scruples? The guy wasn't a bleeding heart. Fear? He wasn't a coward, either. Siding with him? Cannonball wasn't corrupt. He hoped the other two cops were dead. If so, nobody could refute the sergeant's version. Of course, seething with rage, Grava would take it out on him, maybe slap him in the face, have him suspended, but the colonel wouldn't shoot or torture the sergeant. He was too respected and well known; besides, it would send the wrong message to the rest of the force.

"Gallego, get ahold of yourself."

Fermín rose from the chair and shuffled to the bathroom. They hadn't walked into the Puerto de Jagua. As soon as the unsuspecting cabbie had driven off, they'd flagged another taxi and asked to be taken to Mantilla. A third cab left them three blocks away from the clinic. Nothing had been said in the presence of the cabdrivers, but Contreras rightly guessed his buddy had blown the horn on him. No one else was present when Gallego had suggested the rendezvous, and his partially healed fingers confirmed Ox's suspicion. Once in the cabin, Fermín recounted his nightmare. Ox felt sure his friend had to get it off his chest, so he listened intently until Gallego broke down.

Sitting on the bed, his coat off, his forelock hanging down on his forehead, Contreras lit a La Corona and waited.

Fermín came out avoiding the eyes of his friend, plopped on the chair, kept his gaze on the floor.

"So, you . . . told everything."

Gallego nodded.

"And?"

"Next morning they took me to the bank."

"The bank?"

"I rented a safe-deposit box to store my share."

"Ah."

"Five days later, on the way to the infirmary for a change of dressings, I spotted Abo and Meringue in different cells."

"What?"

"They collared Abo and Meringue, too."

Anguish gripped Contreras. He couldn't care less about Meringue, but with Abo he had a very close bond. When they pulled jobs, he assigned the easiest task to the team's youngest, kept his eyes on him constantly, taught him all the tricks. One month before the heist he'd instructed Heller to invent himself a credible life story and arrange for a hiding place nobody should know of, to get lost from all his usual hangouts for a minimum of six months. The stupid fool.

"You know if they were tortured?"

"They didn't look it."

"What about Wheel?"

"I don't know."

"Go on."

Fermín breathed deeply. "Then they took me to the library for three consecutive Fridays. Ureña used to come to my cell around three-thirty and . . ."

Contreras didn't interrupt. Fermín was leaning forward on the chair, elbows resting on his knees, eyes on the floor, eyebrows raised. He talked in a low, apologetic tone and frequently turned the palms of his hands up, as though seeking absolution, body language that pointed at his inability to excuse his own behavior, Contreras thought. But this wasn't church and he wasn't a priest. He understood, but would never forget.

"Okay. You got it out of your system," with something approaching patience. "Now let's leave behind the whole thing, Gallego. What happened, happened. Stop blaming yourself. I would've done the same thing had I been in your place."

"No you wouldn't."

"You never know, Gallego. Never. How about a sausage sandwich and a beer? I'm starving. Then let's see if there's something we can do for Abo and Meringue."

A male nurse able to use an extra peso on a quiet night went for the snack, and then they started debating the best course of action. Both knew the smart thing to do would be to dig a thirty-foot-deep hole in the middle of nowhere and bury themselves alive for a year. But that remained on the back burner as the passive alternative. What could they do for Heller? Rancaño would be towed along behind the affection both men felt for their junior partner.

Even before the food arrived, it was plain as day that nothing violent was feasible; negotiation was the sensible way. They had one thing to trade, but it wasn't mentioned. The food was eaten in silence, Fermín torn between his consuming desire to repair the damage he had inflicted on others and the unfairness of asking his rescuer to sacrifice his future. Swilling his second beer, he made a suggestion.

"Listen, Ox. Maybe we contact Lansky, say if he manages to have Abo and Meringue released we'll tell him who organized the hit."

Contreras grunted and smiled bitterly before saying what he would have considered unthinkable eight hours earlier. "Gotta give my cut back."

Faking surprise. "What?"

"Oh, c'mon, Gallego, don't play dumb. You know the only thing that can make Lansky listen is my cut. He probably knows that the Moor recruited us. And if he doesn't, he ain't gonna ask Grava to let loose two thieves 'cause he wants to have a talk with me. But my cut might buy their freedom."

Fermín wanted to pump his pal's hand, pat him on the back, congratulate him on his placing loyalty and friendship above personal gain, but he thought it proper to look resigned and pretend to reluctantly go along with Contreras's proposition. "If that's what you think best . . ."

It took them nearly two hours to work out a rough draft; for another hour they made minor adjustments, and that clinched it. Five minutes after three in the morning they left the cabin and slowly followed the walkway, looking for Pedro and feeling a humid chill. They found the night watchman as he moved from one of his clock keys to the next. Contreras introduced Fermín under an assumed name and told Pedro that his *compañero* would rent the other cabin for a few days. Then he asked the pensioner to get beneath the light cone of an incandescent bulb protected by a dark green metal lamp shade.

"Take a look at his fingernails, Pedro."

"*Coño!*" Pedro whispered after casting a horrified glance at the tissue growing over the purplish skin.

"Fifth Police Station," Contreras explained. "Right now they must be giving the same treatment to some other revolutionaries."

"Sons of the Great Whore!" the night watchman mumbled, grinding his teeth.

"We need your help. No risk at all. You have my word."

. . .

Benjamin Ashkenazi was chief rabbi in the modern synagogue at the corner of I and Eleventh Streets in Vedado. The light-skinned clergyman was six feet tall, serious-looking, bald, and wore rimless bifocals. At 2:50 P.M. on Saturday, November 1, he was in his small book-lined office, sitting at his desk, sipping hot tea and studying the Talmud, when the doorbell rang. Ashkenazi sighed, got up, and marched to the door, wondering whether it was some Cuban who didn't know about the Sabbath's strict rules or a Jew confronting some serious problem. He was mildly surprised to find a well-clothed, well-fed white boy roughly twelve years old.

"Yes?" the rabbi said.

The boy extended a thick envelope to Ashkenazi. "That señor on the corner gave me two pesos to deliver this."

The rabbi looked to where the finger pointed. An old man in a black beret turned and walked away.

"Thank you, young man. That's very kind of you. Thank you," Ashkenazi said as he accepted the envelope.

"You're welcome," the boy said before turning and trotting down the steps to the sidewalk.

Ashkenazi closed the door and returned to his office, sat down, and inspected the envelope. It had been addressed to The Rabbi, Eleventh and I Synagogue, Vedado. From the central drawer of his desk, Ashkenazi produced a letter opener and slit the envelope. He found ten hundred-peso bills and a note, written in Spanish.

November 1
Jehovah has revealed to me that before 9 p.m. tonight you'll deliver the following message to Mr. Meyer Lansky at the Havana Riviera Hotel.

    "The tobacco grower wants to give it back. He will phone tonight at ten."

    The enclosed money should be assigned to helping Jews in distress.

Ashkenazi thought things over for nearly three minutes before storing everything in a side drawer. Then he resumed reading.

Three hours later, at sundown, he looked up the Riviera's switchboard number in the phone book, then dialed it. He had to fight off several intermediaries before Eddie Galuzzo patiently explained to him that Mr. Lansky was not available. Galuzzo feared that Ashkenazi simply wanted to put the screws on Lansky for the synagogue, so when he politely informed the rabbi that he had been authorized to take any messages, Ashkenazi translated the note for him in his serviceable English.

Eddie Galuzzo kept his gaze on the phone's rotary disk for a moment. He perfectly recalled the tobacco-grower-and-disabled-son act.

"Would you mind repeating that?" he said at last.

"The tobacco grower wants to give it back. He will phone tonight at ten."

"And how did this message reach you, Father Ashcondasi?"

"Mr. Galuzzo. I am not your father and my name is Ashkenazi. Please tell Mr. Lansky that if he wants to read this note and learn how it came into my possession, I will receive him at eight this evening. It has been a real pleasure to talk to you, sir. Thank you kindly. Good-bye."

Like most men leading organizations, Lansky was a shrewd politician. He entered the synagogue with Galuzzo one minute before eight, then dedicated no less than ten minutes to asking and learning about the Jewish community in Cuba; he also offered to help in whatever way he could. Lansky made it appear as though the note was a secondary matter when Ashkenazi handed it over to him at 8:14.

Lansky read and pocketed the piece of paper. A meaningful glance at Eddie Galuzzo made the Riviera manager produce a sheaf of bills that he passed to his boss. Lansky counted one thousand dollars and begged Ashkenazi to accept his modest contribution. Once Galuzzo and Lansky left, Ashkenazi entered the two thousand in the synagogue's records as anonymous offerings and forgot the whole thing.

Back at the Riviera, Lansky read the note respectfully. The night before, totally aware that he couldn't hide the National Library fiasco from the Commission's ambassador, Grava had given Lansky a grossly exaggerated version: Contreras and four gunmen had rescued Gallego; two police officers had been killed; the incompetent man in charge had been suspended. Lansky decided to exclude the Cuban colonel from the negotiations to avoid his frustrating interference. Next he sent for Bonifacio García, showed him the note, and, accompanied by Galuzzo, they waited for the call in Lansky's suite.

That same evening, a little before seven, Mariano Contreras pushed in the swinging doors of the Two Brothers, a bar with a bad reputation on Avenida del Puerto. Good-looking hookers and unadulterated liquor had made it the favorite watering hole for many sailors and stevedores, but the Two Brothers was also infamous for the deals cut at the left end of its long, solid-wood bar. Once shady waterfront transactions had been successfully completed, a lot of money changed hands as smugglers collected from their clients and Customs inspectors took their bribes. The owners of the place donated five hundred pesos monthly to the police station's captain to be left alone; two bouncers kicked out the uninitiated who once in a while started a fight. In fact, the Two Brothers was one of the safest bars in Havana. Pickpockets and con men left it alone, pimps waited for their women outside, cops never went in, despite the fact that, when a pleasant breeze blew, the marijuana smoke billowing out of the locale could be sniffed a block away.

When Contreras made his entrance and scanned the place, five men out of thirty-odd clients exchanged worried glances. One of the owners, two professional smugglers, and two dope wholesalers knew that if a snitch reported that Ox had entered the Two Brothers, ten squad cars would converge on the block and all bets would be off. No police captain in his right mind would turn a blind eye on one of the most wanted men in Havana, perhaps *the* most wanted man, excluding revolutionaries. What had happened at the National Library the previous evening had spread like a firestorm among those who had reason to know: cops and criminals. The smugglers and the dope wholesalers dropped bills on the bar, waved or winked at Contreras, then left. The owner smiled sheepishly at his new client.

It was common knowledge that Silvio Molledo always ended the day quietly sipping a double shot of Palma rum at the Two Brothers. One double shot, nothing more. Nobody interrupted him because people knew the best way to make Molledo mad was to try to cut a deal with him when he was having his drink. You could talk to him before or after, but never during. Contreras spotted him at the farthest end of the bar, perched on a high, four-legged wooden stool. He sashayed directly over to him.

"How're you doing, Molledo?" he said, his back to the bar, elbows on the bartop, eyes roving around the entrances. He wore the blue suit, a narrow-brimmed hat in vogue, and Ray-Bans.

The most knowledgeable man on the waterfront turned his head and stared at Contreras. "Fine. Hey, you screwing some young chick?"

"Why?"

"Dyed your sideburns."

Contreras just smiled.

"I heard you're in trouble."

"You heard right."

"Wanna talk to me?"

"Yeah."

"Shoot."

"Shouldn't I wait till you finish your drink?"

Molledo guffawed. "Nah. Maybe your day was rougher than mine. Go ahead."

Contreras lifted his eyes to the owner and nodded. The man half-filled a bucket glass with Palma rum, hurried to his latest client, and returned to his position by the cashier.

"I need to arrange whatever has to be arranged to get six men on board one of those fruit ships sailing to Honduras. There's one leaving on the eighth."

Molledo sipped some rum. Contreras didn't touch his drink.

"Including passports and visas?" Molledo needed to know.

"No, I'll take care of that."

For nearly half a minute Molledo considered something. "I guess it can be done."

"No guess, Molledo. It's either yes or no. I can't plan ahead on a guess."

Molledo turned to face Contreras. "Can I be sure I won't die tomorrow? Can I be sure one of my contacts won't die on me the day after? Can I be sure the fucking ship won't sink in a coupla days? No, right? So, I guess it can be done. Take it or leave it, Ox."

Contreras grinned and shook his head. He turned and sipped some rum. "I take it. Do your best, Molledo. I really need it."

"Tell me something I don't know."

Contreras turned again to face the bar's entrance. "How much?"

Molledo pulled down the corners of his mouth and tilted his head sideways twice. "Three thousand. If I need more I'll let you know. If it's less I'll give you the change."

From the inner breast pocket of his jacket Contreras produced a package wrapped in a newspaper page. He dropped it on the bartop, close to Molledo's right hand. "Here's five. No change; it's all yours. I'll call you here the day after tomorrow, around seven o'clock, to check how things are going. Okay?"

Molledo nodded. Contreras turned and took another sip.

"Gotta leave, friend."

"Good luck, Ox."

"You gonna pay for my drink?"

"Rich guy like you? You pay for your own rum."

It was Contreras's turn to guffaw. He dropped a one-peso bill on the bartop and left the Two Brothers.

At ten sharp, from a pay phone outside the Sierra night-club, on the other side of the city, Contreras dialed the Riviera number and asked for "Mr. Meyer Lansky." The three operators on duty had been warned, and the call was transferred immediately to the suite. Bonifacio García answered.

"Hello."

"Mr. Lansky, please."

"Who's calling?"

"The tobacco grower."

"Are you fluent in English?" García asked.

"No."

"Mr. Lansky doesn't speak Spanish. He wants me to interpret for him. He's right here, at my side."

There was a short silence at the other end. "Okay. Tell him I'll give back my cut for my freedom and for the release from jail of my men."

Being a lawyer, García was surprised to find out that so much could be said in so few words, but he translated faithfully. Lansky half-closed his eyes, tilted his head to the right, and said, "I'm interested." García concluded that this was verbal-economy day and said it in Spanish over the mouthpiece.

"That's what I figured," Contreras said. "Tomorrow evening, at seven, a car with your negotiator ought to wait by the curb at the corner of Paseo and Línea, on the right side of Paseo coming from the sea. One of my men will get in and bring him to me. Then we'll talk."

García prayed for a refusal while Lansky mulled it over. The lawyer didn't like to stick his neck out and felt sure he'd be asked to come along and interpret. He preferred low-risk shady deals that yielded good profits, and with each passing day he feared more and more his involvement in the aftermath of the heist. He saw himself on his way to some unknown place to meet with a guy who had killed four men in three weeks. Sweat appeared on his forehead.

Lansky nodded.

"Agreed," García said.

"Tell me the make, year, and color of the car."

After swift deliberation, Lansky chose Galuzzo's car, a '58 black Thunderbird with Dade County plates. García passed over the description.

"Okay. No cops. Some other car follows the Bird the deal's off."

García was midway through the translation when he heard a receiver being placed in its cradle.

"He hung up," the bewildered lawyer said.

Lansky shrugged his shoulders. "What else had to be said? Okay. Now, Eddie, I want you to cut a deal with this guy. García will go with you. We know what the man wants; let's discuss what we can deliver."

...

Sunday, November 2, 8:30 A.M. Wearing a bus driver's uniform purchased by Pedro, the night watchman, at El Zorro, a clothing store specializing in all sorts of uniforms, Fermín Rodríguez boarded a cab at the entrance to the clinic and asked to be taken to La Palma. Five minutes after reaching the busy crossroads, he flagged down a second taxi and ordered the cabbie to take him to the middle-class suburb of Mulgoba, very close to Havana's international airport. It took him forty minutes to get there; he could have made it in ten if he'd gone straight from the clinic, but he was following every rule in the book, including taking roundabout routes.

Fermín was smoking La Corona cigarettes—which tasted like shit to him—to change his usual cigar-chewing expression. The uniform was intended to further alter his appearance by hiding his attention-getting bald head beneath the cap, and to provide justification for the dark sunglasses many bus drivers wore. The gloves had been discussed extensively. Few Cuban drivers wore them, what with the predominantly humid, hot weather, but showing his bare hands would have been even worse, so Contreras ordered a pair of skin-colored thin cotton gloves from Pedro. The night watchman couldn't find the required color and bought a white pair. Fermín tried to keep his hands out of sight as much as possible, and had a story ready: He suffered a skin rash and the doctor had ordered him to protect his hands from the sun's rays.

Some bus drivers also carried a small handbag with their pack of cigarettes, matches, a little flask of espresso, eyeglasses, keys, driver's license, wallet, and other things that would make their pockets bulge. Fermín's handbag held only one article, with a full clip, a round in the chamber, and the safety off. This time they wouldn't get him alive, he'd told himself.

He dismissed the cab at the suburb's tree-lined, two-lane entrance and went in, looking at street signs and consulting the classifieds of *Información.* Twenty minutes later he pressed the doorbell affixed to the left post of a padlocked wooden gate. Set back maybe forty yards, surrounded by a barbed-wire fence enclosing a hundred-square-yard lot, stood an unpretentious three-bedroom house with a roof of red Spanish tile. Tire tracks with wild grass in between had made kind of a short dirt road from the gate to the porch. A yellow dog bolted out, barking ferociously. It was followed by a man in his sixties wearing khaki pants and a white undershirt who kept ordering the dog to pipe down. Fermín sighed patiently.

"What can I do for you, señor?"

"It says here this house is for rent," Fermín said, pointing to the newspaper.

"Yes, it is."

"I'm interested."

An hour later the deal was closed and Fermín pocketed the keys and a receipt stating that Señor Francisco Marrero had paid 160 pesos; half of it covered the rent for November, the other half was a one-month deposit. Fermín took his time trying to find out how everything worked, inspecting the closets, sitting on the living room couch, testing the mattresses for comfort. He wanted to give the impression that his family of four hoped to spend many months, if not the rest of their lives, at the furnished house. Before leaving, José, the man taking care of the place for the owner, wanted to know why Señor Marrero wore gloves. Fermín told him. "Ahh . . . ," said José before putting on his shirt. He lived in the nearby town of Santiago de las Vegas and left immediately, his dog happily wiggling its tail. Fermín closed up, walked back to the highway, and took a cab.

At 4:30 P.M. the bus driver went into the Trianon movie house, located on Línea between A Street and Paseo, to watch the double feature. In the foyer, the woman standing behind the wooden container accepted his ticket, tore it in two, then stared at the gloved hands. At 6:30, when the main feature had just begun, the short man left. The attendant stared some more as he paused to light a La Corona and put on his sunglasses before going outside.

Fermín crossed Línea and reached Paseo. The six-lane avenue had a wide, landscaped median divider. Its flowerbeds, ornamental trees, and cast-iron public benches with closely spaced boards on their seats and backs provided a nice shady place where people could sit and chat. The allure of the cool sea breeze from the nearby Malecón was a factor as well. In the afternoons, boys and girls rode bicycles and skated and threw balls and climbed trees and occasionally broke a leg as their parents, or the servants who cared for them, exchanged opinions on child-rearing. In the evenings, couples necked on the benches; after midnight some acrobatic lovemaking had been known to take place there.

The bus driver chose an empty bench on Paseo between Línea and Eleventh Street to keep an eye on the block where Galuzzo's Thunderbird would park. Fermín wiped his hands dry on the legs of his pants, gave a pull on his cigarette, and stepped on the butt. He had never been able to stand the taste of burnt paper. At 6:57 a car that fitted the description crept along the agreed-on block looking for a parking space, didn't find it, turned right on Línea. The same thing happened two minutes later. At 7:02 its driver finally managed to squeeze the big vehicle between a Chevy and a Nash, then killed the lights. Fermín kept his eyes glued to the vehicle for over a minute. Nobody left the car.

Night had fallen. The children and the adults had left for supper; it was too early for the young couples. Fermín unzipped his handbag and rose to his feet. He sauntered down Paseo, crossed Línea, and, gripping the butt of the automatic, approached the Bird's passenger door.

"I'm supposed to take you somewhere," he said to Eddie Galuzzo.

Galuzzo didn't understand a word of Spanish. He turned to Bonifacio García, sitting behind the wheel.

García ducked and addressed Fermín in Spanish. "Hop in."

Fermín opened the right rear door and got in.

"Where to?" García asked as he turned the ignition.

"The airport."

Nothing more was said for the next fifteen minutes.

...

Fermín Rodríguez released the padlock of the wooden gate, swung open both halves, and stood back to let García drive in. As he closed the gate and reinserted the padlock in the chain, the car's lights went off and the ignition was cut. The front door of the house was pulled open, but no one stood in the doorway. From their seats, Galuzzo and García peered at the softly illuminated interior. García lacked the training to figure out that the man inside didn't want to become an easy target by silhouetting himself against the light burning in the living room, but Galuzzo smiled knowingly. *The sonofabitch!* he thought.

This time Fermín approached the driver door. "You can get out now."

Galuzzo and García confronted Contreras in the dining room. There were nods and a laconic exchange of cool hellos; no hands were shaken. Contreras signaled to the chairs and they all sat. García had seen Contreras's mug shot, but stared at the man as if he were a Martian. After the Château Miramar murders and the National Library shoot-out, the lawyer had come to expect a pirate minus eye patch, someone tall and heavy with a bushy black mustache and a nasty scar on his left cheek. But he faced a plain-looking guy wearing a rumpled, dark jacket over a white open-necked shirt. He had the appearance of a tired, widowed accountant who'd just arrived home after a day of number-crunching. What took García out of his own thoughts was the smoke from Fermín's cigar. The bus driver was pampering himself, feeling he had earned it. García made a face.

"I have over two hundred grand of your money," Contreras said, looking Galuzzo right in the eye. García began interpreting. "As far as we know, police have nailed three of my men. This one here had 213,000 stashed away and 1,800 on him. The other two took a 120,000 cut and didn't have time to spend more than four or five thousand, so you've recovered at least 320, perhaps as much as 330. If I give you back two hundred thousand, you'd recover no less than 520, and we grabbed 627 and a half. So, you'd lose 108."

"Just a minute," García said as he produced his notebook and a fancy fountain pen from his pockets. "Let me jot down the numbers; I'm getting confused. Let's start from the top, okay?"

Contreras nodded. "I have over two hundred grand . . ."

When he got to the point at which he'd been interrupted a minute ago, Contreras paused. García finished translating as Galuzzo looked at the figures on the page. "Tell him to go on," Galuzzo said.

"A fifth man has his sixty-thousand cut, or what's left of it," Contreras carried on, "but I don't know where he is, and it seems the police haven't found him either. Anyway, he might refuse to give back his money; I can't force him."

Contreras paused again and García finished translating, a smile playing on his lips. Contreras had a bad feeling. Had anything happened to Wheel? Something these bastards knew about? García nodded at him to go on.

"We've had some expenses and will have some more before this is settled. So, from where I stand, I figure a 108 loss might be more . . . amenable to Mr. Lansky than a 308 loss. I'm willing to give back two hundred thousand if the Bureau frees Heller and Rancaño, and the fifth man too, if he is in jail. Aside from that, I need five Cuban passports with visas for México, Panamá, and Honduras, and I want Lansky himself to escort us to the plane or ship we'll board. One of you two will stay with us until we reach our destination safely. I'll hand over my money once we're inside the plane or ship. And that's it."

García finished translating. For some strange reason, Eddie Galuzzo liked the guy. He would've credited him with the winning combination—balls and brains—were it not for the idiocy of returning his money to save a couple of jerks. Like Cubans liked to say, this dude was a shit-eater.

"Show me the money," Galuzzo said.

The American hoped to win points with a quick solution. García didn't have to translate Contreras's reply. It was an unequivocal smile that made Galuzzo feel slightly uncomfortable.

"Listen, you," Galuzzo scowled, "the Bureau of Investigations is at our service. The manhunt covers the whole fucking island, and any minute you two can find yourselves surrounded here. You give me the money now and you got a good starting point: Mr. Lansky will call off the Bureau and you'll be free to go."

Contreras shook his head before brushing the warning aside. "If it's done, it'll be my way or none at all; take your pick. And pray for my safety, mister, 'cause if the Bureau gets to me you'll never recover those two hundred gees. Bet your life on it. Now, these two envelopes hold twelve passport-sized photos each of the two of us, just in case you guys wanna play ball. On their backs we've written the names we'll use. You'll have to take pictures of Heller and Rancaño after their release. Maybe the other man too, if he's found."

Galuzzo seized the small, cream-colored envelopes and stuffed them into a pocket before speaking. It was good to have recent pictures of the two toads. They would be given to Grava if Lansky didn't like their offer.

"As part of the deal, Mr. Lansky needs some information from you," Galuzzo said. "He might forgive and forget if you cooperate."

Contreras nodded in agreement.

"Who planned the Capri job?"

"A jeweler named Elias Naguib. You know who recommended *me* to *him*?"

García was the first one to knit his brow. When he finished the translation, Galuzzo appeared intrigued too.

"Who?"

"Colonel Orlando Grava, the chief of that Bureau of Investigations that's tracking us down."

García was too astonished to translate. Galuzzo prodded him in the arm. "This guy says Colonel Grava recommended him to Naguib."

García and Galuzzo locked gazes in full stupefaction. Then the American lowered his eyes to the tabletop, searching for a plausible reason for Contreras to have made up such a lie, but couldn't find any. Either the man had gone bonzo or he was telling the truth.

"Grava introduced you to Naguib?" Galuzzo asked in a low tone.

"No. Five months back Grava told Naguib how to contact me, public places where I used to hang around."

"Are you implying Grava knew that Naguib was planning a hit on us?"

"I don't know that for sure. But Naguib promised the police wouldn't chase us 'cause he'd talk to Grava after we pulled the job."

Galuzzo shook his head. "Your story can't be verified. Naguib's dead."

"I know. I was there when one of your dealers shot him. I believe I did you a small favor. For free."

The ensuing silence was becoming a little embarrassing as Fermín relit his cigar. García wrinkled his nose when the smoke reached his nostrils.

Galuzzo got up. "I'll tell Mr. Lansky your demands. When will we meet again?"

"We won't meet again before the last day, at the airport. But I can phone."

"Okay. Call 2-4500 at two sharp on Tuesday morning. If Mr. Lansky has made up his mind, he'll let you know."

...

At 10:50 P.M., in the Riviera suite, Galuzzo and García finished telling the story. Lansky stared at the photographs. He experienced the satisfaction of a crossword fan who's just filled in the last word.

"Our colonel is a bagful of tricks," Lansky mused.

"If the man told the truth," Galuzzo said.

"Oh, yes, it's true," Lansky stated. "My nose confirms it."

Galuzzo and García exchanged a glance.

"On the way back we went over the split again, 'cause something's wrong . . . ," Galuzzo began.

"We won't keep you any longer, García," Lansky interrupted, turning to the lawyer. "Thanks a lot. Would you mind handing over the notebook page with the amounts Contreras mentioned?"

Feeling excluded, the lawyer ripped the page out and handed it to Lansky.

"Thank you. I'd appreciate it if you'd come to my house tomorrow evening to interpret for me," Lansky said.

"Sure, Mr. Lansky."

"Okay, you may leave now."

After the lawyer departed, the boss lit a cigarette and asked Galuzzo for two sheets of hotel stationery. Lansky slid his backside to the edge of the armchair the better to reach the low coffee table, then produced and uncapped his gold-plated Parker. On one sheet he jotted down from memory the amounts returned by Grava. On the other he copied Contreras's version. Smoking placidly, he spent a few minutes moving his eyes from one set of numbers to the other and making calculations.

"According to Grava, the bald guy only had 58,000 on him. Contreras says 215,000. The difference is 157," he said distractedly.

"So?" Galuzzo prodded him.

"That's pretty close to what was found at Naguib's apartment."

Staring at the two papers, Galuzzo lifted an eyebrow. He was at a loss. "Excuse my stupidity, Mr. Lansky, but I can't understand what you're getting at."

"Let's suppose Contreras is feeding us bullshit to incriminate Grava—Grava never met Naguib; he's a white lily. Okay?"

"Okay."

"They found 162,500 at Naguib's," Lansky went on. "That's exactly twenty-five percent of 650,000. Now, let's further suppose that the morning after the heist Naguib heard from somebody, Willy Pi probably, that Contreras had taken 650 from the Capri. Let's also suppose that for some reason Naguib wasn't expecting to get his cut in the next few days and that Willy's cut was twenty-five percent of the take. If Willy was in a hurry to collect, Naguib might have secured Willy's share from his own dough, brought it to his apartment, and told Willy he could pick it up that same evening. Then Contreras suddenly knocks on Naguib's door with 313,500. You follow me?"

"So far, yes."

"Good. Something happens then—maybe there was an argument over the split, who knows? The thing is, Willy shoots Naguib, Contreras shoots Willy, and leaves with the money he brought in. Contreras didn't know there was 162,500 stuffed in a drawer. He splits Naguib's and Willy's money with the bald guy. Half of 313,500 is 156,750. The bald guy had 213,000 stashed away—the 60 he first got and this new bundle. You with me?"

"Yes, sir. But it doesn't add up. He should've had 216,750."

"He had 1,800 on him, according to Contreras. Police pocketed some money, or he gave his mistress a few hundred, that's not important."

"Probably."

"When White Lily grabs that money he starts doing what I just did and realizes there might be a surplus. How come? He's got the bald guy's statement. He knows what they took and how they split it. The only possible explanation is that the cash found at Naguib's had nothing to do with the heist. Since everybody assumed that that money belonged to us, he decides to keep us in the dark so he can pocket the 156,750 Contreras had given the bald guy."

Galuzzo stared at Lansky as parts clicked into place in his brain. "Sonofabitch," he hissed.

"Now, let's suppose Contreras told the truth and White Lily is in fact what you just said. Let's suppose he did recommend Contreras and knew Naguib was organizing a heist on us."

"No!"

"Just a supposition. In this scenario, the motherfucker has been buggering us since God knows when."

"We can bring a couple of boys from New York or Chicago and get rid of him," Galuzzo said.

"No. This is just business. Maybe he even got the driver's cut."

"The fucking sonofabitch!"

"Leave me alone now. I've got to figure out which of the big fish I ask to have a heart-to-heart talk with Grava, make him understand he has to return our money and let go the two creeps he's got in the clink. Wouldn't it be great if we make a profit on this?"

...

At dawn on Monday, November 3, as members of the Cuban Army, Navy, Air Force, intelligence services, paramilitary organizations, and the police got ready to implement an artificial normality for the day's general election, three black, brand-new Cadillac sedans came to a stop in front of the wide stairway that led to the Bureau of Investigations' main entrance.

From the one with official plate number 3 emerged Major General Francisco Lavernilla, chief of the General Staff and father of the Air Force's commander-in-chief. Second only to Batista, the man preserved a proud countenance despite a serious liver insufficiency and a lost war. Three drivers and three bodyguards remained in the vehicles.

Escorted by a captain and two lieutenants toting Uzis, he hurriedly climbed the stairway as his brown eyes absorbed details. Stress had reduced his lips to thin, wrinkled lines. Under the visor of his cap, his forehead showed deep lines from permanent concern. The two startled policemen standing guard at the huge doorway presented arms imperfectly. The duty officer came around the two-foot-high wooden platform on which his desk stood and guided the four men through an immaculate gray hallway as he stammered words of welcome. In Grava's office, the nonplussed cowardly aide managed to click his jaws shut after realizing Lavernilla didn't need to make an appointment. Without knocking, he turned the handle of the colonel's inner sanctum.

"Major General!" the astonished Bureau chief said as he quickly came to his feet and flashed his most appealing smile. He had showered and shaved at home and was overdressed in a splendid Prussian-blue gabardine suit. On the writing desk, an Esterbrook pen, documents, an evenly burning cigar in an ashtray, and a half-cup of espresso attested to his habit of beginning work early. Lavernilla closed the door in the faces of his aides-de-camp, took his cap off, placed it under his left armpit, and glared at the colonel.

"Please, sit down," Grava begged, his mind frantically searching for what he had done wrong.

"No," with an imperious tone.

"Let me take your cap."

"No."

Grava raised both eyebrows, his eyes seeping humility. His smile was quickly becoming a grimace. "A cup of espresso maybe?"

"No."

"And . . . uh . . . to what do I owe the honor of your visit, Major General?"

"I came here this morning," Lavernilla began in a soft voice as he lifted his eyes to the ceiling and rocked on his heels, "to take a crap on your mother's cunt, Gravita!"

The second part of the sentence had been shouted at the top of the general's lungs, flaming eyes drilling into Grava's. The three men standing in the waiting room had mixed reactions. The police lieutenant paled; the Army officers smiled.

The colonel's knees wobbled. Forgetting protocol, he collapsed on the high-backed Mexican chair.

"Major General, I can't imagine why—"

"You're a shit-eater, Gravita."

"But, Major General, what have I done?"

"Pick up all the money you siphoned out of Meyer Lansky and take it to his home right now."

Grava felt his hands sweating and trembling uncontrollably. "The money that I siphoned?" he asked feebly.

"Were you in cahoots with the Moor who planned the Capri heist?"

"Who? Me?"

"ON YOUR FEET!" Lavernilla bawled.

Looking sickly pale, Grava jumped to attention.

"Answer me, asshole," Lavernilla demanded, his flabby cheeks trembling with anger. "Did you participate in the planning stage?"

"No, Major General, sir!"

Lavernilla inhaled deeply and let his eyes roam around the room. "What's the stupidest animal on the face of the earth, Gravita?"

"I don't know, Major General, sir!"

"Of course you don't. How could you if you belong to the species? It's the donkey. You're a donkey in a business suit. Fucking the man who advises Fulgencio on a million things, from where to invest abroad to where we can buy weapons now that the fucking Yankees support the Party comrades. Give back everything, down to the last penny, you hear me? The percentage he paid you and the money you stole from him. Is that clear?"

"Major General, allow me to—"

"You wanna keep being boss of this stinking slaughterhouse?"

"Major General, I—"

"Yes or no?"

"Yes."

"You have until ten this morning—almost three hours," Lavernilla said after glancing at an impressive Patek Phillipe on his left wrist. "Also give him the two suspects you collared.

He wants to question them and . . . I don't care what he'll do to them when he's finished."

"As you order, Major General, sir."

"Go to hell, Gravita," Lavernilla said, putting on his cap before turning around, yanking open the office door, and stalking out.

...

Lansky humiliated Grava by refusing to see him personally and was sleeping soundly when a smiling Eddie Galuzzo faced the grim-looking colonel at the Fifth Avenue mansion a little before ten.

"My dear colonel, how nice to see you," said Galuzzo sarcastically.

"I no spik Inglish," Grava said.

"Well, I certainly don't speak your gobbledygook, motherfucker. To what do we owe the pleasure of your visit?"

"Mr. Lansky, plis."

"No Mr. Lansky, you dickhead. Mr. Lansky sleep," Galuzzo scoffed, joining the palms of his hands, resting his left cheek on top of them, and closing his eyes for a second.

Grava fought for control by emptying his lungs with ballooning cheeks. *The son of a whore is in the know,* he thought. "Mony here," the truly irked colonel said, slightly lifting the two embossed-leather Mexican briefcases he held.

"Good, good, money good." Galuzzo was having the time of his life. "Give me," he said, extending his hands.

Grava kept his arms at his sides. "García, plis."

"No García. García sleep too. 'Sleep,' you understand?" He repeated the mime act before closing the smile and deep-freezing his gaze. "Give me the fucking money."

Grava frantically searched in his mind for the translation of *recibo* into English and didn't find it. "*Recibo,*" he said.

"What?"

"*Re-ci-bo.* You take mony, you give *mi re-ci-bo.*"

"Oh, 'receipt,' you mean? Sure, I'll give you a receipt. Let's go to the library, we'll count the money, and I'll give you a signed receipt. This way, scum."

At half past ten Galuzzo signed a receipt for 209,000 pesos.

"Okay, motherfucker, here you are. Now, I was told you'd also hand over two scumbags. Where are they?"

"I don unnerstan."

"Prisoners. Cuban prisoners, from the Capri job?"

"Ah."

Grava stormed outside, waved to the escort vehicle in the driveway, boarded his own car, and slammed the door shut. From the second Cadillac two plainclothesmen stepped out and signaled Heller and Rancaño to do the same. Unable to understand what was going on, Abo and Meringue were guided to the mansion's doorway, where their handcuffs were removed. As the cops returned to the car, the prisoners took in the well-appointed living room, then exchanged wide-eyed expressions and curled their lips in total incomprehension.

Galuzzo wiggled his fingers at Grava's car. "Bye-bye, cocksucker. Don't you ever *think* of fucking us again. Hope somebody's arranging a hit on you."

The two cars burned rubber on their way out as Galuzzo turned and closed the door.

"Well, well, what have we got here."

The prisoners thought it proper to remain silent.

"García, come over here," Galuzzo yelled.

The Cuban lawyer had been waiting in the living room, out of sight.

"Yeah, Eddie."

"Take a look at the creeps," Galuzzo sneered as he pointed at the two prisoners. "Jesus, they stink! For your own sake, have them take a shower before you begin."

Armed with a tape recorder, the Cuban lawyer separately questioned the stupefied prisoners. By late afternoon he reunited them in a bedroom whose only window was protected by an ornate iron grille painted white. García told them to take a seat.

"Now, listen to me. You're in the safest place you can be. You manage to escape from here, you're dead. Understand? Dead. And it's not my people who will shoot you. It'll be the police. So, the best thing you can do is to take it easy for the next few days. When and if there's any news, I'll let you know."

That evening Silvio Molledo was having his usual double shot of Palma rum at the Two Brothers when the barman told him somebody wanted him on the phone. Molledo glanced at the pay phone on the opposite corner. No, not the pay phone, the barman explained; the man had dialed the private number in the small office at the back. Molledo pulled out the gold pocket watch he had used for twenty-three years. It read 7:19. The barman led him to the office and left.

"Hello," Molledo said into the mouthpiece.

"Hi, friend. I keep spoiling your drink every coupla days."

"Good tippers are allowed to."

"How are things going?"

"I've talked to a few people. They think it can be done, but I don't have anything firm, what with the holiday. The offices with all the rubber stamps were closed. The guys who sign the papers were casting their ballots. Maybe tomorrow I'll be able to get something done."

There was silence at the other end. "Then I suppose I'll have to call you again the day after tomorrow. Same time is okay with you?"

"Yeah."

"Sorry to bother you so much."

"No problem."

"Bye."

Observing the holiday, the casinos didn't open that evening. After a late dinner at the Fifth Avenue mansion, Bonifacio García translated the highlights of the taped interrogation for Lansky. Nothing new, the boss commented at the end, just corroborative statements. Learning that Abo had been collared at the dog races or that Rancaño was the guy who wanted to set up a gambling parlor didn't mean a thing to him.

Galuzzo joined them after midnight and the three men talked shop until 2:01 A.M., when the phone rang. García marched to the library and lifted the receiver.

"Hello."

"It's the tobacco grower."

"Would you prefer talking to Heller or to Rancaño?"
The caller took a split second to answer. "Heller."

Guarded by Galuzzo, the wide-eyed young man trotted into the library nearly a minute later. He had been sleeping soundly, but now fear made him feel very alert. García extended the handset to him.

Cautiously. "Yeah?"

"Abo?"

"Ox?"

"How're you doing, Sweet Dick?"

"*Coño*, brother, what's happening? Where are you?"

"There's no time for that. Do as these people tell you. I'm giving back my mazuma to buy off our freedom and leave Cuba, the five of us. You know anything about Wheel?"

"Not a word. Hey, listen, Gallego disappeared from—"

"I know, I know. He's okay, at a safe place. Remember this: Do what these people ask you to do. Say hello to Meringue for me. Put the man back on now."

Heller returned the phone to the lawyer. With a nod, Galuzzo signaled the way back to the bedroom. The prisoner turned and left, followed by the man from the Riviera.

"Are you satisfied?" García asked.

"Very much."

"Mr. Lansky needs to know when you plan to travel."

"When will the passports be ready?"

"It depends on how long I have to wait for the fifth man. Have you located him?"

"Not yet."

"Shall I go ahead with the other four?"

Silence.

"Well?"

"Yeah. Go ahead. How long will it take?"

"Two or three days."

"Then we'll leave next Saturday, the eighth."

"Where will we meet?"

"I'll let you know at noon that same day. Should I call this number?"

"Just a minute."

García went back to the living room and explained things to Lansky. Lansky heard him out, then pulled himself up from the armchair. He shuffled into the library, accompanied by the lawyer. "Translate," he ordered.

"Mr. Lansky says that yes, you can call this number at noon next Saturday. He wants you to know he doesn't bear any grudge against you and your men. You were hired to do a job, and did it well. But he wants to make three things very clear. The first is: He doesn't want any additional demands at the swap. Stick to the deal—two hundred thousand in exchange for your men and passports."

"Passports with visas to the three countries I mentioned," Contreras interrupted.

"Right; you made that clear when we met. Second thing is: He won't be there, but gives you his word that all your conditions will be met. And the last thing is that whatever you and your men do in the future, you shouldn't mess with us again. It'll be full-scale war with no prisoners taken if you pay no heed to this warning. You understand?"

"I do. Tell Mr. Lansky there'll be two substances in the money bag that burn fast when mixed. A sudden movement and the bills will go up in smoke in ten seconds. Good-bye."

...

On Tuesday, November 4, Silvio Molledo visited the Vaccaro Lines pier and the offices of Passengers and Luggage, Repression, and Smuggling and Legal Proceedings, all under the Port of Havana's Customs and Excise Department. He also marched into the Commerce Exchange Building, rode an elevator to the sixth floor, and gained entry to the Harry Smith Travel Agency.

Bonifacio García had a very busy day too. In the morning he visited the Ministry of State and talked to friends before greasing their palms. After lunch he headed out to a men's store, where, estimating heights and weights, he bought two suits off the rack, one maroon and one charcoal-gray, as well as two long-sleeved dress shirts and two ties. From the store he drove to a photo studio and with twenty pesos convinced the owner to close up shop for the day and accompany him to take the photographs of two clients. On his way to the Fifth Avenue residence García told the photographer that the passport-sized photos had to be ready the next morning. In the evening he got on the phone and before nine had talked to the consuls of Honduras and Panama, the Mexican consul absolutely refusing to take the call at his residence.

On Wednesday afternoon, Silvio Molledo repeated his tour, picking up the things he had asked for and surreptitiously handing over sheaves of bills of varying denominations. Two hours had gone by when he deposited everything in his safe and went to have a talk with the proprietor of a Diamond T truck that made a living hauling cargo from and to the port.

That same morning, García drove to the studio early, collected Heller and Rancaño's photos, and headed for the Ministry of State. An hour later he left the building with four new passports and drove to the Panamanian Consulate, then to the Honduran legation. By the time he got to the Mexican Consulate, it was closed for the day.

"Yeah, yeah, I know, the phone in the back," Molledo said to the barman in the evening. After two minutes spent giving instructions, he returned to the bar, finished his drink, and went home.

...

"Black guy, in his fifties or sixties, dairy-farm worker?" Contreras probed.

The middle-aged man with the ruddy complexion took his red baseball cap off and scratched his head as he glanced at the whitish soil. He also had on tennis shoes, old faded jeans, and an unbuttoned, short-sleeved checkered shirt that revealed a muscular chest and sixteen-inch biceps.

They were standing by what remained of a small hill, one kilometer away from the town of El Calvario. Not a single cloud could be seen in the beautiful blue sky. The hill had stayed uncut for several millennia until the owner discovered, forty years earlier, that beneath the barren, three-inch-thick layer of earth covering the hundred-yard-high elevation lay a million tons of hard rock. With limited capital he set up a stone mill and started selling different sizes of ground stone to concrete contractors, block manufacturers, and people in the home-building business. At present, half the hill had disappeared and blinding sunlight reflected off the ivory-colored, top-to-bottom vertical wall that faced the two-lane road between Mantilla and El Calvario.

The middle-aged man was known to everybody, except his wife and kids, as Dynamite. Using six-foot-long, thirty-five-pound bullpoint iron bars, he and his assistant drilled blasting holes. After the sticks were inserted, they lay a very heavy net, made from discarded steel towlines, over the area to prevent pieces of rock blown away by the explosion from harming anyone. Then the fuses were lit and the two men got out of the way. Once the dust settled, they retrieved the net. Both were in great physical shape; shaking hands with one was like gripping a two-by-four.

Dynamite and Contreras had known each other for over fifteen years. The man with the dyed hair held a bag with half a pound of black powder he had just bought, which was the reason for being there. But being so near El Calvario, he recalled that Wheel often mentioned that his father-in-law earned a living in a dairy farm close to the small town. Knowing that the stone miner also lived there, and wondering whether he should try to find the old man and sound him out about his son-in-law, he asked Dynamite if he knew anybody who fit the vague description he'd given him.

"You don't know his name?"

"Nope."

"Strange that you ask. Yes, there's an old black couple lives on the outskirts. Very poor people, you know. And, yes, I believe he milks cows at a dairy farm. I hadn't heard about them until a few weeks ago. Their son-in-law was gunned down by the police."

"WHAT?"

Dynamite was taken aback. Ox wasn't known as a short fuse.

"Well, it's what the town gossip says. Why do you ask? You don't even know his name."

Contreras forced himself back to normal. "Oh, I guess being here made him come to my mind. He's related to someone I know. His son-in-law was a revolutionary?"

"How should I know? They buried him at our cemetery, I hear. The word is this old man and his wife learned what had happened after the burial, when their daughter took her two kids to their hut."

Squinting, Contreras stared at the huge wall in front of him, then inhaled deeply. "Do me a favor, Dynamite, willya? I might have to stand on the highway for a half hour before an empty cab cruises by. Why don't you take me to La Palma in your heap."

"Sure. What happened to your Chevy?"

"Tune-up."

"And what happened to your hair?"

Contreras just smiled.

"C'mon, let's go," Dynamite said.

...

On Saturday, November 8, as gold-rimmed clouds enhanced the magic of a tropical sunset, three cars stopped by the curb at the entrance to the Vaccaro Lines pier.

Eddie Galuzzo and Bonifacio García emerged from a black '58 Thunderbird with Dade County plates. A dark blue '59 Buick released Fat Butch, Dino Cellini, Arturo

Heller, and Valentín Rancaño. Tom Brodsky, Tony Razoni, and Joe Silesi got out of a dark maroon '58 Cadillac sedan.

On the sidewalk, the six Americans clustered around the three Cubans and, led by Fat Butch, briskly approached the galvanized-pipe-and-wire-mesh gate. A strong westward breeze flapped their clothes; the straight hair of the hatless Cubans lost all semblance of order. At the gate, a Maritime Police corporal listened to García for a few seconds, palmed a twenty-peso bill, and let the group in. Nine wild gorillas would have blended better with the surroundings.

They marched along the pier following a railway track embedded in the pavement. Eighteen distrustful eyes gazed at the long warehouse to the right; the forklift operators and sinewy stevedores carrying out their chores blatantly stared back with no less mistrust. Two trucks were positioned at the end of the pier, facing the entrance. To their left, a moored merchant ship, the name *Fundador* on the bow, its smoke-stack spewing out burnt fuel oil, seemed capable of sailing away at a moment's notice.

Built in the Lubeck shipyards three years earlier, the *Fundador* displaced 1,600 tons fully loaded. It was 66 meters long and had a 10-meter-beam breadth. Two refrigerated holds could stow fruit between four and minus ten degrees Centigrade; it had half a dozen three-ton cranes and was manned by a crew of twenty-two men on its crossings from Puerto Cortés, Honduras, to Jacksonville, Florida. That morning the captain had vacated a cabin shared by the steward, the purser, an oiler, and a sailor by telling the four men they would stay in Havana with full pay and out-of-pocket expenses. A fifth sleeping space was provided by the third mate's recent appendectomy.

Two men left the cabin of a Diamond T truck at the end of the pier and sauntered toward the incoming group. Mariano Contreras, his freshly rinsed hair blown back by the wind, firmly gripped a leather overnight bag in his left hand; his right closed around the butt of the Colt inside the pocket of his dark blue muslin jacket. Fermín Rodríguez, wearing the same clothes he wore when he was collared, had Talavera's automatic in the small of his back, ready to fire. They were the first to reach the ladder hanging from starboard, and stopped alongside it.

The approaching group checked its progress ten steps away. Eddie Galuzzo and Bonifacio García drew nearer to Contreras and Fermín. Heller smiled faintly, beginning to believe in miracles; Rancaño had a grave expression on his face.

"You managed to get the Mexican visas?" Contreras asked of the lawyer.

"At the last minute, yes. They cost more than four visas to heaven. What do you need them for? This ship is going to Honduras."

"Give my friend the passports," Contreras said.

For nearly two minutes, Fermín inspected the five passports closely. Then he made the agreed-on sign: running his left hand over his bald head. From the warehouse shared by Customs and Immigration offices, Silvio Molledo emerged. He hurried toward Fermín, took the passports, trotted back to the building.

García was no longer comforted by the fifteen thousand dollars that had been transferred that morning to his New

York bank account and was chickening out fast, casting frightened glances in every direction. Three days in the same ship with a bunch of criminals wasn't his idea of a holiday cruise to Central America.

Galuzzo took a Philip Morris to his lips, cupped his hands around a very modern Ronson butane lighter, and tried to light it, but the breeze didn't let him and he ended up throwing away the cigarette. Fermín felt the sweat under his armpits and wished he hadn't left behind the cigar he'd been chomping on a few minutes earlier in the truck's cabin. Contreras spotted the gloomy expression on Rancaño's face and smiled encouragingly.

Less than three minutes later, in what was probably the fastest proceeding ever carried out on that particular pier, Molledo came back and returned the passports to Fermín. The bald man gave García his and stuffed the others in the left pocket of his jacket.

"Let's go up," Contreras said.

Nobody paid attention to the first mate's welcoming words. The captain left the bridge, from where he had observed everything, to guide the eleven men to the sailors' mess hall, then departed. Fat Butch closed the door. Contreras placed the leather bag on the table, opened it, carefully pulled out a flask containing white phosphorus in fresh water, and threw it into the pier's murky waters through an open porthole. Then he returned to the table and removed twenty wads of fifty-peso bills and ten of one-hundred-peso notes.

Joe Silesi sat, and within eleven minutes had deftly flipped over the corners of three thousand bills. Nobody said a word. The only sounds were the droning engines, coughs, sighs, shuffling feet, the clicking of lighters, and the rasping sound made by Contreras's hands as they swept black powder out of the bag and threw it into the sea.

"Okay," Silesi said, lifting his eyes to Galuzzo. Contreras handed over the bag to the man from the Riviera and Tony Razoni put the money back inside it. He was closing the lid when Contreras addressed Heller and Rancaño.

"Step over here."

The swap completed, Galuzzo signaled in García's direction with his thumb. "We want this man back in perfect health."

The lawyer interpreted in a firm, almost menacing tone.

"For everybody's sake, his and ours," Contreras began, and paused. He was getting to like using a translator; it gave him more time to figure out what he should say to the enemy. "It would be best if police don't board this piece of junk when you go ashore, and if no PT boat intercepts us in territorial waters. We'll stand watch, twenty-four hours a day, for the first two days. We value our health too."

García hadn't thought about that, and translated with supplicating eyes, believing his employer unscrupulous enough to plan some revenge after recovering the money. To compound his fear, a pilot's tug was approaching the *Fundador* for the castoff. The chugging of its engine might have been mistaken for a Maritime Police launch getting ready to storm the ship.

"You keep worrying so much, your blood pressure will go sky-high," was Galuzzo's comment. Then he shook hands with García and turned around. Fat Butch opened the door for him.

The ladder was lifted as soon as the Americans went ashore. Two men released mooring lines and the pilot's tug began its work. In the ship's mess hall, the exultant Heller and the ecstatic Rancaño could barely suppress their urge to congratulate and thank Ox and Gallego, but the presence of García made them restrict themselves to smiles and handshakes.

At 8:09 P.M., when the *Fundador* left behind Morro Castle and veered west full steam ahead, Contreras felt safe enough to grant García's request to retire to his cabin. Once there, the lawyer swallowed a strong sedative, hoping to sleep all the way to Puerto Cortés.

On deck, elbows resting on the railing, the four survivors stared at the countless city lights and hundreds of multicolored neon signs blinking along the Malecón as they took swigs from a bottle of rum presented by the captain. Contreras was releasing pent-up frustration; the others repressed excitement. With brief nods, Ox accepted praise for his generosity, then informed Abo and Meringue of Wheel's possible fate. Meringue wasn't overwhelmed by grief, but Abo looked deeply shaken, and began searching for a way to discredit the story. It was some other guy, some other family, it was just a coincidence, Wheel was okay somewhere, maybe in Santiago de Cuba. No, his pal was too clever for Grava's goons.

"How did they get to you?" Contreras asked.

Abo told the truth; then it was Rancaño's turn. Contreras was nauseated by Meringue's galling stupidity, and sorely disappointed in Heller for his devil-may-care behavior, but he kept his opinions to himself and waved away their belated regrets. For several minutes, as they were getting a glow from the rum, nothing was said. The engines' humming, the swooshing of the breeze, and the bow's plaintive rumble were the only sounds heard. Then, Contreras took a deep breath and addressed the rocky coastline.

"Good-bye, Cuba. You'll be a better place to live in with four shit-eaters less."

. . .

In the living room of his Havana Riviera suite, Meyer Lansky smiled faintly as he peeked inside the travel bag on the coffee table. In an armchair, facing the boss, Eddie Galuzzo stubbed out a butt on a green-spotted marble ashtray. Through the plate-glass window, the lights from a small merchant ship en route to Central America could be seen on a strip of dark calm sea.

"If somebody had told me on October tenth that we'd turn a 41,500-peso profit on the Capri heist, I would've thought the man was loony. We've got to find a way to let Joe Bananas know the final outcome of his little scheme," Meyer Lansky said.

He lifted his eyes to the ceiling and heaved a sigh of relief. His prestige had been restored; he was a happy man.

"It was a great World Series, don't you think?"

. . .

At that precise moment, in a ramshackle old hut illuminated by a smoky kerosene lamp, a beautiful Negro woman, her father, and her mother were rendered speechless after opening one of the two pressure cookers they had dug up twenty minutes before.